Devil's Brew

Felicity Pulman

First published by CreateSpace in 2011
This edition published in 2015 by Momentum
Pan Macmillan Australia Pty Ltd
1 Market Street, Sydney 2000

A CIP record for this book is available at the National Library of Australia

Devil's Brew: The Janna Chronicles 5

EPUB format: 9781760300258
Mobi format: 9781760300265
Print on Demand format: 9781760300555

Cover design by Raewyn Brack
Edited by Kylie Mason
Proofread by Laurie Ormond

Macmillan Digital Australia: www.macmillandigital.com.au

To report a typographical error, please visit momentumbooks.com.au/contact/

Visit www.momentumbooks.com.au to read more about all our books and to buy books online. You will also find features, author interviews and news of any author events.

Felicity Pulman is the award-winning author of numerous novels for children and teenagers, including *A Ring Through Time*, the Shalott trilogy, and *Ghost Boy*, which is now in pre-production for a movie. *I, Morgana* was her first novel for adults, inspired by her early research into Arthurian legend and her journey to the UK and France to "walk in the footsteps of her characters" before writing the Shalott trilogy – something she loves to do. Her interest in crime and history inspired her medieval crime series, The Janna Mysteries, now repackaged as The Janna Chronicles.

Recently awarded the inaugural Di Yerbury writer's fellowship, Felicity will spend several months in the UK in 2015 researching and writing the sequel to *I, Morgana*. She has many years experience talking about researching and writing her novels both in schools and to adults, as well as conducting creative writing workshops in a wide variety of genres. Felicity is married, with two children and six grandchildren, all of whom help to keep her young and technosavvy – sort of! You can find out more about Felicity on her website and blog: www.felicitypulman.com.au or on Facebook.

Also by Felicity Pulman

Chapter 1

It was late summer of the year of our Lord 1141, and Winchestre was abuzz with rumors of a possible confrontation between Henry, Bishop of Winchestre and brother of King Stephen, and Empress Matilda, rightful heir to the throne of England. No-one doubted that the matter must be settled, given the empress's determination to seize the crown from her cousin Stephen, but everyone hoped that it could be settled amicably – everyone, that is, except Janna and the empress's own entourage. Although they, too, prayed for a peaceful end to the matter, the discovery that all along the bishop had been in league with the queen to further the interests of his brother, the king, led them to fear the worst. Uncovering the bishop's treachery had resulted in the death of several men, with such tragic and horrifying consequences for Janna that she was finding it almost impossible to put the past behind her.

A shaft of misery pierced her heart at the memory of Ralph. His death had left her with an aching sense of loss and betrayal; of desolation, grief and anger. She thrust aside her memories of Ralph and focused instead on the ordeal ahead, for once again she was making the journey to the estate belonging to her father, John fitz Henry. Although she'd already visited the estate on several occasions, she was sick with nervous anticipation. She swiped her sweating hands down the fabric of her gown to dry them, and checked the contents of the purse hanging from her girdle once more. Usually she wore the purse inside her gown, close to her skin to keep it safe, for therein was the proof that must surely persuade her father that she really was his daughter. Her fingers touched and pressed, feeling for the roll of parchment, a letter written by her father to Eadgyth, her mother, explaining his prolonged absence and assuring her of his love. Her mother had never read the letter because, Janna had discovered to her dismay, she didn't know how to read. And now she was dead. It was because of her mother's death, and the manner of her dying, that Janna had sworn to find her father and bring the man responsible for Eadgyth's murder to justice.

It had been a long journey, and hard, but the end was close now, so close. Warin, her father's steward, had told her that Sire John spent most of his time with his wife and children in Normandy, so Janna had written him a letter. Loving Eadgyth as he had, surely the news that he had a daughter would hasten his return to Winchestre? Unless, of course, he was content with his new life and his new family, and had laid the ghosts of the past to rest. In which case he might never come at all.

She pushed the unwelcome thought from her mind, and turned to her companion. He rather resembled a goblin: a man in his late middle age with wispy gray hair and a nose too large for his face. She had met him along the road while in the company of a band of pilgrims, and had come to like and trust him. "Do you think he's here yet, Ulf," she asked, "or is this just another wasted journey?"

The relic seller paused for a moment and stretched, easing his muscles under the weight of the heavy pack he carried. "There's been more than enough time for your message to have reached Lord John, and time enough too for him to board a ship from Normandy, lass."

A smile lightened his face. "Happen he's waiting for you right now. And if not..." He gestured to the huge dog that trotted at his side. "Happen it's time to set Brutus onto that shifty old bag-o-bones, just to find out if your message was ever sent!"

"Warin wouldn't have dared withhold it!" But the same thought had gnawed at the back of Janna's mind ever since she'd penned the letter to her unknown father and handed it over to the reluctant steward.

"If your father hasn't arrived yet, I'll see if Brutus can frighten the truth out of that whoreson," Ulf promised.

Janna reached down to fondle the dog's ears, and Brutus paused long enough to lick her fingers. They hadn't always been friends; it had taken a long time to win the dog's trust. And until she succeeded, Janna had been frightened of him, just as she was sure that Warin, her father's steward, was afraid of him now, for the hound was large and ferocious, an alaunt bred specially for hunting. On previous visits to the estate, they'd accepted the steward's glib reassurance that the message had been sent and it would be only a matter of time before her father appeared. Perhaps Ulf was right; perhaps it was time now to scare Warin into telling the truth.

But what if her father was waiting for her even now? Janna's stomach gave an uneasy quiver, even though she'd been too nervous to eat any dinner at all. Instead, she had sipped a mug of ale while Ulf wolfed down a hearty meal of blood pudding. She had met him at the Bell and Bush, a tavern just off the high street close to the East Gate and St Mary's Abbey, the Nunnaminster, where she had taken up residence in the guest quarters until such time as her father appeared. She and Ulf always met there before their pilgrimage to her father's manor. He told her little of how he occupied his time otherwise. Janna knew that he had taken cheap lodgings in Tanner Street, where the water course needed by the tanners and dyers ran, and which consequently bore the stink of their trades, and that he eked out a living as a purveyor of the precious relics of saints. She knew better than to ask him where he found the wonders that he peddled, for she had her suspicions but didn't want them confirmed. He was a rogue, she felt sure, but she trusted him in everything that mattered. Besides, he had been good to her in the past, and she valued his friendship and support. Especially at a time like this.

"Have you seen anything of Master Thomas and his players?" she asked, curious for news of the jongleurs who had accompanied them part of the way to Winchestre.

"Nay, not yet." Ulf chuckled. "They must have found a safe haven somewhere else, but I'm sure they'll be here in time for St Giles's fair."

"Everyone will be here for that!" Janna exclaimed, clapping her hands together in excitement at the very thought of it. Although she hadn't been long in Winchestre, she'd already sensed the buzz of excitement as craftsmen worked all day and by the light of rushes and candles at night in anticipation of increased sales of their goods. She looked along the high street, noting the chapmen with their bulging packs, and the wealthy merchants who were already in town and anxious to secure the most advantageous positions in one of the rows of stalls now being constructed or refurbished on St Giles Hill. "You should do well at the fair, Ulf," she said.

"I intend to!"

Janna was tempted to ask what relics he had to trade. She smiled as she thought of the white feather he'd given her, now nestled among the treasures in her purse. She was fairly sure it had come from one of the swans that cruised up and down the River Itchen, although Ulf had told her it had once belonged to the Archangel Gabriel. Wherever it had come from, the present had cheered her at a time of great loss and anguish, and she treasured it.

The section of the high street known as Chepe Street was becoming ever more crowded, as people finished their dinners and came out of the alehouses to barter and buy goods from the shops

4

and pentices spread along the length of the wall of the old palace. Bolts of fabric, cords and ribbons, slippers and boots, candles, soap, and spices were traded, as well as gold and silver adornments, candlesticks, and fine plate and pottery dishes for those wealthy enough to afford extra luxuries.

A line of carts trundled past, heaped with supplies, bound for the old palace in the center of the town. Janna frowned. It seemed an odd place to store goods when the palace was so obviously unused. Her attention was diverted by the beggars among the throng, hands held out for alms. Some were blind, some crippled, and some, Janna suspected, were merely chancers, preferring handouts to a hard day's work. Touched by the sight of a young girl balancing an infant on her hip, she reached into her purse for a coin, certain the pair must be orphans, for the girl looked little older than six or seven summers. She was concerned, knowing they would be living a hand-to-mouth existence if there was no adult to care for them. She held out the coin, which was quickly snatched by a grubby hand. "God bless you," she said, and received an incomprehensible mutter in reply.

Janna wondered what had happened to the children's mother. Perhaps she had died in childbirth, which was often the case, but surely there must be a father or aunt or grandparents to look after them? She looked about for someone, and saw a flicker of movement as a man ducked out of sight. Janna was left with the impression of whiskers and a stained tunic. Had he been watching out for the pair? Was this how he supported his family? She moved on, hoping that her coin would be put to good use and not wasted in one of the alehouses.

Her nose twitched. The stench from the open drain that collected water and refuse from the streets that fed into the high street was bad enough, but they were also passing a fishmonger. Janna held her breath; some of the fish were not altogether fresh. When forced to breathe once more, she drew in the reek of the butchers' shops. Carcasses of hares and plump birds dangled from hooks; livers, lights, and the body parts of larger animals were spread out on a stained counter. A pack of dogs had gathered to stare hopefully at the prizes just out of their reach.

Janna smiled then as she caught sight of a young boy hurtling down the street in pursuit of a hoop that he bowled merrily before him. She realized that he was heading straight for her and hurriedly stepped out of his way, only to have him swerve at the last moment and crash into her. With a gasp, Janna went down, taking an elbow in the face as the boy tried to stop himself from falling. Brutus started to bark and circle around the fallen pair. Janna cautiously levered herself up into a sitting position. The child shrank against her, staring at Brutus with wide, frightened eyes.

Ulf darted forward. "Now then, lass, have you hurt yourself?"

"No, I'm unharmed." Janna waved at him to take Brutus away and turned to the boy. "Are you all right?" Silly question, she thought, as she noticed blood trickling from a gash on his leg.

He nodded and tried to stand, but got caught up in the hoop and fell on top of her. Janna's breath was knocked out of her body; she gave a strangled whoop as she struggled to suck air into her lungs. She doubled over, breathing quickly, while the child untangled himself.

By now they had attracted quite a crowd; everyone pressed in close to see what the fuss was about and to offer solicitous advice. Someone reached out a hand and hauled the boy to his feet. Probably his mother, Janna thought, for she began to scold him for running off, all the time patting him down and fussing over him with gestures that spoke louder than her words of her concern over the runaway child.

"I 'pologize if he has caused you harm, mistress," she said, turning to Janna with an anxious expression. "But 'twas an accident, no more 'n that."

Janna stood up and, still breathless, began to brush the mud and muck from her gown, for she had fallen close to the gutter that ran down the center of the street. She thought of the meeting with her father and her spirits sank. Her fine gown had become increasingly shabby since she'd received it as a gift from the abbey and now it had picked up a trace of excrement from a passing horse that she hadn't managed to avoid when she fell. She almost found it in her heart to wish that her father was still absent, for she did not want to meet him looking so disheveled and dirty.

"Do not trouble yourself, mistress," she said, recognizing that her efforts to spruce herself up were futile. Annoyed, she couldn't resist bending down so that her head was level with the child's. "And you, young scoundrel, just watch where you're going in future!"

Shamefaced, he buried his head in his mother's skirts. Janna forced a smile and turned away, searching her heart to forgive him his high spirits. Still feeling somewhat breathless and shaky, she pushed her way through the crowd that had gathered, and went in search of Ulf. He was holding on to Brutus with some difficulty, for the dog was excited and still barking furiously, straining against Ulf's tight hold of his ear. When the relic seller saw Janna, he let go and the dog bounded over and jumped up, almost knocking Janna down again as he gave her face an enthusiastic lick.

"Brutus! Ugh!" Janna pushed him away and wiped her face on her sleeve.

"That's one way to clean yourself up," Ulf said with a grin. His nose wrinkled as he observed Janna more carefully. "Would you like him to lick your gown too?"

Janna grimaced. "I'm just wondering if I should throw myself into the river before going to see my father."

Ulf's smile contracted into a concerned frown. "I'm sure he'll love you no matter how you look – or smell!"

"Don't!" Janna began a reluctant inspection of her gown to see just how bad the damage was – and caught her breath in a gasp of alarm.

"What?" Ulf grabbed hold of her arm. "What's wrong?"

Janna didn't answer. She couldn't. She held up the cut cord that once had secured her purse to her girdle. The purse was gone, along with her father's letter and the gifts he had given to her mother: the ring bearing his crest and the brooch with a loving message inscribed on it. She'd lost all the proof that she was who she said she was. How could she hope to convince him now?

"Christ's bones!" Ulf's shocked exclamation echoed Janna's despair. Knowing that it was probably hopeless, she scanned the crowd just in case she recognized anyone from the group that had gathered around her and the boy when they fell. That was when it must have happened: some cutpurse taking advantage of the accident, and her inattention. But people were going about their business as usual, no-one showing any interest in her at all.

"Did you see anything? Notice anything?" Ulf asked.

Janna shook her head. She was still speechless with shock. Not only had she lost her father's gifts, but all the coins she had saved were also gone – the coins that were meant to keep her in comfort at the abbey until her father's arrival.

Everything was gone. Janna closed her eyes, trying to come to terms with the full magnitude of her loss.

Ulf was already scanning the crowded street with narrowed eyes, looking for anything untoward, anyone skulking about and trying to hide, or hastening away lest guilt be detected. Janna remembered how casually she had opened her purse to find a coin for the orphans. Had their guardian been watching, deciding even then to help himself to more? Or had someone else been tempted by the bulging purse, thinking there were riches for the picking inside? If so, they would be sadly disappointed, for in truth Janna had already spent much of what she'd been given, both by a grateful Emma for saving her lover's life, and by Robert, Earl of Gloucestre, as a reward for her part in unmasking the bishop's treachery. The treasures left in her purse were, for the most part, of value only to her.

And now they were gone! A shroud of misery enveloped Janna. Too stunned even to cry, she wrapped her arms around her body and hugged herself for comfort, to keep herself from flying apart. She had nothing left; nothing to live on or to live for. Nothing to give meaning to her life. The thief had taken less than he thought, but far more than he knew.

Ulf touched her arm. "What can I do to help?"

Dumbly, Janna shook her head.

His mouth tightened into a thin line. "I'll keep my eyes open and spread the word," he promised. "Sooner or later that whoreson will be tempted to sell your father's ring, or the brooch." He smacked his hands together, a sound so loud that Janna jumped. "Then we'll have him!"

Janna sighed. It was a slim chance, but a chance nevertheless. But there were far more pressing problems to deal with now. Somehow she must find a way through, find the strength to carry on.

"Don't mind how you look, lass," Ulf said bracingly, understanding something of her dilemma. "Let's be getting on to your father's manor and pray that he's arrived at last." He eyed Janna thoughtfully. "Even if he hasn't, you must ask that steward to prepare a room for you, for I doubt the good sisters of St Mary's will house and feed you if you can't pay your way."

"No!" Janna shuddered at the thought of Warin. "I'm not staying with that dreadful old man if my father's not there. I won't!" Perhaps she could persuade the sisters at St Mary's to let her stay in return for her help in the infirmary. She shook her head, knowing it was unlikely. While she'd lived at Wiltune Abbey she had come under the guidance of the infirmarian there, putting into practice the ancient healing skills she had learned from her mother, as well as the knowledge of medicine that Sister Anne had taught her. These skills she had offered to the infirmarian at St Mary's Abbey when she'd first arrived, but her help had been rejected. The infirmarian and her assistant were protective of their demesne and guarded it jealously from outsiders. There was no room for her in the abbey's infirmary, just as there'd be no room in the guest house either if she had not the coin to pay for it. She closed her eyes, fighting tears.

"Don't worry, lass. We can make a plan, but it might not come to that if your father's here." In spite of his reassuring words, Ulf's expression was troubled as they turned into Alwarene Street.

"Perhaps we should call in to St Peter's and ask for help?" Janna suggested, as they passed a small church.

"You could pray to St Anthony or St Jude."

Janna lifted an enquiring eyebrow.

"Patron saint of lost things. Or lost causes. Take your pick."

"Lost things, yes, but not lost causes, thank you!" Janna considered for a moment. "I'd rather pray for a pox to take the villain who stole my purse!"

"In that case, I don't know who you should ask." Ulf's troubled frown smoothed into a grin as he cupped her elbow with his hand and hurried her on. "The church says nowt about vengeance – not for the likes of us, any road."

But vengeance was what Janna wanted. Her blood surged hot at the thought of her stolen possessions and, as she reflected on why she needed her father's help, her rage intensified. Her mother had been poisoned, and by a man who was so far above them in status that Janna had been unable to name him. Instead, she had seen her mother buried in unhallowed ground, denigrated and scorned by the villagers and their priest, while the murderer walked free. But she would bring him to justice. She would! She would shame him before everyone. Somehow she must convince her father that she was his unknown daughter, and persuade him to act on her behalf.

They were nearing the imposing door of her father's house. Janna's hands trembled as she tried to smooth her hair and dust herself down, while Ulf tugged the bell pull.

"Yes?" The same portly personage with the fringe of gray hair opened the door to them. "Oh, it's you again," he said, and gave an incredulous sniff as he caught a whiff of Janna's gown. "Sire John has not yet arrived from Normandy," he continued, repeating what he'd told them in the past. He was already closing the door when Janna cleared her throat.

"We wish to see Master Warin," she said, her voice trembling.

The doorkeeper looked them up and down.

"Now!" Ulf insisted. Beside him, Brutus growled.

Reluctantly, the doorkeeper stepped aside, and once more escorted them through the hall to a room at the back, the scriptorium where the steward carried out his work on her father's behalf. Janna wondered how long they'd be kept waiting this time. Warin seemed to have any number of hiding places, including the orchard where they'd once found him half asleep. He'd been thoroughly disgruntled at being disturbed, even after being told that his lord's daughter wished to make her father's acquaintance. Janna wondered how he managed to conduct any business at all when his manner was so surly and disobliging, and when he seemed to spend so little time on his legitimate duties.

She began to prowl around the scriptorium, searching for anything that looked like a letter, just in case one had come from her father, John. A thought struck her. She'd been given his name: Johanna. Would that be proof enough?

Janna shook her head, knowing it was unlikely. She continued to search through the pages of parchment piled upon the table, picking through the numerous accounts and receipts among them. She scanned the pages, taking note of the huge quantities of wool and other goods listed there. They must come from some great estate out in the country somewhere, for this manor here in Winchestre was not nearly large enough to be other than a residence and collection point. It seemed that the steward conducted a thriving business on her father's behalf – when he could be bothered.

"What do you think you are doing?" Warin hobbled forward, disapproval carved in every line on his face as he snatched the sheets of parchment from Janna's hands. "Your father's affairs are not your concern. Only I am privy to this information." He glared at her, his expression turning even more sour as his gaze swept down her gown and he smelled its pungent aroma.

"My father is still not here, then?" Janna kept her voice steady with an effort, unwilling to show the steward how needy and despairing she felt.

"No." Warin shot a nervous glance at Brutus. "I told you before to keep your dog on a lead," he told Ulf, in a show of bravado.

Ulf ignored him. "We're tired of waiting," he said sternly. "In fact, we're wondering if Mistress Johanna's message was ever sent to Normandy at all."

"Of course it was!" The steward puffed out his skinny chest, indignant at having his word questioned. "Indeed it was. I sent one of my men straightaway to Southampton with it."

"Which ship did he travel on?"

"The..." Warin gulped. "The...er...the *Marie Louise*."

"Has the messenger returned?"

"Yes. Yes, he has. Just a few days ago."

"But your master didn't come with him?"

"No." Warin eyed Brutus, and looked quickly away. "The message did go, I swear it. Roger took it, and he handed it over on his arrival at your father's demesne. He told me so, and I have no reason to doubt his word. It is not my fault if your father does not wish to answer your summons." A spiteful smile curved his mouth. "Perhaps he does not believe your claim?"

"Send for the messenger," Ulf said quickly, noting Janna's stricken expression. "We would like a few words with him, if you please."

Warin heaved a martyred sigh and hobbled to the door. He was gone some time, but finally reappeared with a young man in tow. He was hardly older than Janna, being some nineteen or twenty summers all told. His bright brown eyes brimmed with a friendly curiosity as he inspected her. He took a couple of disbelieving sniffs.

"This is Roger," Warin said curtly.

"You took my message to Normandy, Roger?" Janna asked.

He bobbed his head in acknowledgment.

"You took it to my father's manor?"

"Yes, my lady."

"And you saw my father?" Janna couldn't hide her eagerness – or her disappointment when Roger shook his head.

"No, my lady."

"But you were told to take the message to my father!" Janna looked angrily from Roger to Warin. "Didn't you tell him that?"

"Yes! Yes, of course I did," the steward said.

The youth's bright demeanor had vanished, replaced now with a wary sullenness as he realized he was in trouble. "I asked to speak to Sire John, but the dame, his wife, said that he was absent on business. So I gave the message to her instead."

"Blanche?" Janna was horrified. "You gave the message to Dame Blanche?"

The youth nodded.

"And what did she say?"

"I understood none of it, for the dame spoke in the language of the Normans. She talked to her steward, and he told me to wait. So I did, in case there was a message to bring back to you. But after a time, the steward told me there was no reply and I could leave."

No reply? Had the message ever reached her father? Or did "no reply" mean he might come to England and see for himself the young woman who claimed to be his daughter? This thought cheered Janna slightly, as did the one that followed: Her father might well have to settle affairs on his estate in Normandy before he could make the crossing to England. But what was she to do in the meantime, while she waited for him to come?

"Thank you, Roger." Janna wished she had a coin to reward the young man for his trouble. Even more, she wished that the message had fallen into her father's hands instead of going to Dame Blanche. Had she read Janna's message? Would she have passed it on to her husband if she understood Janna's claim?

The youth bobbed his head again and scuttled quickly away, his beaming smile betraying his relief that he wasn't in trouble after all. Janna shot a glance at Warin. She could not, would not, cast herself on the steward's mercy.

"We'll return in a few days," she said curtly, and gestured to Ulf that it was time to leave.

"I shall look forward to your visit," Warin replied softly. Janna sensed the malicious satisfaction that lurked beneath his words.

Ulf whistled to Brutus, and together they left the scriptorium and passed through the door into the street outside.

"Toad!"

Ulf gave Janna a sympathetic grin. "If you won't seek shelter here, where will you go instead?"

Janna had no answer. The future seemed unbelievably bleak. She had no choice but to wait for her father, and hope that he would come to England. But for now, her most important task must be to work out how she might survive until her father's arrival.

Chapter 2

"What will you do, where will you go, until your father arrives?" Ulf asked again. They had gone back to the Bell and Bush to discuss Janna's future, and had managed to find a couple of stools in a corner where they could sit and talk in comfort. Ulf had ordered a pitcher of ale, and now he poured some into their mugs.

Janna took a disconsolate sip. "I don't know," she confessed. She should make the most of the ale, and the most of Ulf's company, for after this she would be on her own and forced to beg for bread and shelter. Anxiety churned her stomach; she felt ill with it. Seeking distraction, she looked about.

The Bell and Bush was far more modest in size than the taverns at the West Gate, which were strategically placed for visitors to Winchestre, but Sybil Taverner kept a respectable house that was well regarded for the quality of the food, wine and ale served there. Being close to the East Gate, and to the fairground atop the hill of St Giles, the tavern was particularly busy at this time of year. Packmen, merchants and traders alike had crowded in with eager expressions on their faces, for the taverner had rung the bell that signified there was a new brew on tap and gave the establishment the first part of its name. The second part of the name came from the sign that helped all travelers identify a place that served ale: a green bush affixed to a pole outside the door.

Janna had been in Winchestre long enough to know that the tavern was greatly resented by other alewives, who believed Sybil Taverner was taking away their customers. The most prosperous alehouses, owned by those who complained loudest, were Heaven, Hell and Paradise. These were situated on the high street close to the cathedral and were especially handy for customers on the way to and from their devotions or their shopping. But Janna preferred to meet Ulf at the Bell and Bush, for it was slightly more salubrious than the alehouses up the high street and the ale was of better quality. Or so Ulf said.

Trying to take her mind off her troubles by identifying its flavoring, Janna took a sip of ale. She swilled the liquid around her mouth, identifying the various herbs the taverner had put in the gruit, for it was different from the brew she and her mother used to make. Rosemary, alecost and sweet gale. She could recognize those, all right, for sometimes she'd used them herself, perhaps with elderflowers or wormwood. She wondered why the taverner didn't add wild hops to the mix. True, they gave a slightly bitter flavor, but the ale was more thirst-quenching in hot weather. More importantly, the hops helped to preserve the brew and keep it fit for drinking.

Janna took another sip. This was a pleasant combination, but when brewing their own ale, Janna, on her mother's instruction, had always added a particular herb to the barley mash, one with a distinctive flavor and a special purpose.

"The ancients believed that sage was a sacred and holy herb, while our own people knew it to be a cure for all complaints. Better yet, it's thought to bring long life and prosperity to all," Eadgyth had told her. Janna had kept silent, not wanting to question why they were still so poor when they had such a quantity of sage growing in their small garden.

It hadn't helped her mother live a long life either, Janna thought now, and felt the familiar heaviness of unshed tears behind her eyes. Hastily, she forced her thoughts onward. What else had gone into the ale they'd brewed? Always an extra dash of honey to help with fermentation and counter the bitterness of the hops, for Eadgyth liked the ale she drank to have a touch of sweetness to it. Janna took another sip, rolling the liquid over her tongue to taste it. Since leaving their home she'd never again come across the distinctive brew she and her mother used to make. As with everything her mother had taught her, their ale was made from Eadgyth's own recipe, to suit her taste, or else to suit the need to which it would be put, for it would taste quite different if used for medicinal purposes. Extra herbs would be added: bishopwort and wild mint for fever; horehound for a lung complaint; or *herba benedicta* to ward off evil and disease and to act as a tonic for the body.

Memories of Eadgyth flooded Janna's mind, along with the knowledge that every link she'd had with the past was now gone. She could not hold back her distress, and hastily swiped her sleeve across her brimming eyes. She and her mother had parted after a quarrel, and Janna had never had the chance to make peace. The guilt of her furious outburst haunted her still. What would her mother say if she could see her now? Would she approve of the path Janna had chosen, her quest to find her father?

Probably not, for Eadgyth had believed her lover unfaithful. Being unable to read his letter, she had died not knowing the truth: that John had loved her with all his heart, but had been delayed because he had gone to Normandy to seek permission from his father to break his betrothal in order to marry her. Believing him faithless, and with a child growing inside her, Eadgyth had run away. She had sought shelter, and been refused, and thereafter had kept Janna close to her, teaching her all she knew of the art of healing, but never telling her the truth about herself or her lover, Janna's father. She would not have approved of what Janna was doing because she wouldn't have understood it.

"Janna? Try not to fret, lass. Let us rather talk about how you're going to manage until your father arrives." Ulf's anxious voice brought the difficulties of her new situation rushing back. Her spirits dropped even lower, crushed under the burden of memory. She'd lost everything.

Janna straightened her shoulders and took a deep breath. Yes, she'd lost everything – except her courage. Her hands clenched into fists, her nails cutting into the soft flesh of her palms. The pain helped her to come back to herself, and shift her focus to the tavern and her present predicament. She took another deep breath and quietly exhaled, trying to calm her fear. It was easier to dream of the past than confront the future, but confront it she must.

"Any ideas?" Ulf prompted.

"No. I don't know what I'm going to do."

"I wish I could offer you shelter but that wouldn't be seemly. Maybe I could find you a room close by, so I can watch out for your safety?"

"I have no coin to pay for a room," Janna said tiredly. "And I will not live on your charity either," she added.

"But you can't live too close to me," Ulf rumbled on, clearly not paying attention. "'Tis the poorest, meanest, *smelliest* part of town!"

Janna patted his hand. "I'll have to look for work somewhere, find something I can do that will also provide shelter." She thought for a moment. "Perhaps I could offer myself as a scullion in a kitchen, or as a lady's maid?"

"Nay, lass!" Ulf's horrified exclamation drew several curious glances their way. "You're the granddaughter of a king!"

"Without the means to prove it," Janna said dryly. "Besides, I know what it is to be poor and needy, and to work hard just to survive. When my mother was alive, we lived in a small cot at the edge of a forest. We had a few hens and two goats, and a little plot of ground to grow our vegetables and the herbs for my mother's potions. But there were many times we went hungry."

"Herbs and potions? There are several apothecaries in town who might be glad of an able assistant. But whether they'd employ a young woman…" Ulf's enthusiasm, which had so quickly caught fire, now seemed in danger of snuffing out. Then his expression brightened again. "What about Robert of Gloucestre, now he's back at the castle? You're known to him. You should ask him for help." He took a long swallow of ale, and wiped his mouth dry on the back of his hand. "After all, he's your…What? Uncle?"

"And the Empress Matilda's my aunt!" Janna said flippantly, recognizing suddenly that this was true. The thought rendered her speechless for a moment. "But how can I go to them, dressed in this filthy gown, and with nothing to prove I am who I say I am?"

"You can clean yourself up a bit. Any road, no matter how you look – or smell – they owe you for what you did, delivering that letter of warning about the bishop!"

"Shh!" Alarmed, Janna looked around at the crowd gathered in the tavern. Only Ossie, the simple giant whose role was keeper of the peace, caught her eye. He was vigilant as usual, but there seemed no need for it, since conversation was muted. News and opinions were being exchanged in low undertones, for everyone was worried about the presence of the empress's army, and the apparent lack of rapprochement between her and the bishop. There were rumbles from the merchants, who were torn between wanting to stay for the great fair and the money they stood to make, set against their concern that trouble might erupt and then they'd be caught up in it and their goods put at risk. There was also disquiet among the townsfolk, who knew they stood to lose everything if a peace could not be patched up.

The mention of the empress's name attracted Janna's attention, and she leaned closer to listen to the muttered conversation taking place at a table nearby.

"...and when the Empress Matilda summoned him, Bishop Henry told the messenger that he'd get himself ready. But it seems that he's fled from the city instead. And the earl is at the castle, waiting – although I know not how long his patience will last." The speaker was a tall, well-set man with a shock of brown hair and a florid complexion. Janna thought he must be a merchant, for he was better dressed than his companions and seemed to be paying for the ale they drank.

"But the bishop's brother, the king, is still imprisoned, and the bishop has now sworn allegiance to the empress. Why, then, has he fled?" asked a young lad.

The merchant shrugged. "The bishop was ever a devious man. Could be he's with the garrison at his palace at Wolvesey, preparing for war in case it comes to that."

"I heard he was holed up in the keep of the old palace, awaiting orders from the pope," said one of the merchant's companions.

"He may be waiting for the queen's troops to arrive. I heard she's recruited as many as a thousand strong under the command of that Fleming, William of Ypres!" said someone else.

"Murdering bastard!" The merchant gave a chesty cough, cleared his throat and spat into the rushes. "I'm told they're already on the march. The empress needs to get the bishop on side before they arrive, or this could get right out of hand." He looked around the crowded table. "Winchestre may have spoken for Matilda, but Stephen's queen won't let it rest, not while her husband is kept in prison. And neither will the Londoners. They can't abide the empress, with her high-handed ways. They want King Stephen back on the throne."

"But if they go to battle now, what of the fair?"

"Never mind the fair. What about us?"

The merchant's mouth tightened. "Best to pray for peace, for we'll all be ruined if there's trouble now. Whatever happens between the king and the empress, we're the ones who'll pay the price."

He glanced around the crowded tavern. Janna immediately bent her head and pretended she was taking no notice of what was being said. The man seemed to know what he was talking about, and she was keen to hear more.

"Look what's happened up north!" he continued. "Barons changing sides according to who can promise them the most. They're so desperate for land and wealth they care not that towns and villages are being burned and crops and animals destroyed as a result of their greed. There's nothing but ruin and devastation, and the people are starving. And it'll happen here too, unless someone puts an end to this madness!" The merchant took a long swallow of ale. "Pray that the Fleming doesn't come, nor his troops with him," he continued angrily. "They'll burn your homes and rape and kill your wives and daughters. If they think you have some worth, they'll take you hostage – for a fee. Otherwise they'll kill you too." He surveyed his companions with a somber expression. "The question is, should we take our chances here, or flee Winchestre now, before it's too late?"

"You worry too much, Master Alan!" A young woman paused beside them to top up their mugs of ale. She had a pert and pretty face framed by a cascade of golden locks, which her veil did little to conceal or contain. Janna had noticed her on other visits to the tavern; her task was to serve ale to the patrons, although she seemed to spend most of her time flirting with them. "With all them soldiers around, I ain't going nowhere!" She wound a sinuous arm around the merchant's shoulders and gave him a squeeze. "But I'd save myself for you, darlin', if you but said the word."

His black mood seemingly forgotten, Alan laughed and pulled her down onto his knee. "And what word would that be?"

"Ah, you know what I mean!" And she dipped a playful hand down to stroke his crotch.

With a broad grin, Alan tipped up her face and gave her a smacking kiss. The serving girl giggled and nuzzled his ear.

"Ebba! I'm paying you to serve the customers, not entertain them!" The taverner's sharp voice sent the young woman springing to her feet once more.

"Jealous, Sybil?" Alan took hold of the girl's hand, preventing her from moving away. The taverner scowled at him. Janna watched, curious to see the outcome of this contest of wills.

"I've told you before, Alan. If you want to see Ebba, you can do it in your own time – not mine!" Sybil's face had flushed red with temper.

Alan stood up and faced her. Then he cleared his throat and spat onto the rushes once more, the gob of spit narrowly missing the hem of the taverner's gown. "I bring you good custom, Sybil," he said curtly. "But I can find ale as good, if not better, at Heaven up the street. Or Hell. Or even Paradise. Do you want me to leave, and take my friends with me?"

The two glared at each other. Ossie stepped forward, ready to use his muscle in Sybil's cause, but she acted first. She grabbed the serving girl's arm and dragged her away from Alan. He shook his fist after them, seeming undecided whether or not to carry out his threat. Ossie stepped closer. One of the merchant's companions tugged on Alan's tunic, forcing him onto his stool once more.

Janna wondered how he came to be so well informed. Another of Bishop Henry's spies? Or was he in the empress's camp? Noticing that Ulf had opened his mouth to speak, she put her finger to his lips to silence him. She was keen to hear what else the merchant had to say.

Having herself brought word of the bishop's treachery to the Earl of Gloucestre, Janna had not been surprised when he had returned – with his half-sister, the empress, and a large body of troops – to face the bishop and demand allegiance. The wonder was why they hadn't immediately declared war on the bishop, but perhaps the earl was having one last try at diplomacy. But if the rumors were to be believed, the bishop and Stephen's queen were now calling in all *their* supporters to oppose the empress. A confrontation seemed inevitable. The only question was how long the standoff would last, and who would be the victor once battle was joined.

"I thought the bishop had turned his back on his brother. I thought he was on side with the empress now," the young lad tried again.

Janna leaned closer to hear the merchant's reply. "The bishop is also the Pope's legate here in England. And Stephen is the pope's anointed sovereign, not Matilda. Small wonder if the bishop is waiting for advice from the pope, and delaying his attendance on the empress until it comes."

A sudden exclamation, followed by an angry shout, spun her around. The noise had attracted everyone's attention, and the hum of conversation died. Ebba had dropped a laden trencher. Mashed pastry and gobbets of meat in brown gravy spread out over the floor rushes.

"You clumsy girl!" Sybil shouted.

"It's not my fault." The drudge eyed the taverner sullenly. "I tripped over the rushes." She kicked at the loose rushes covering the floor to illustrate her point. And also perhaps to cover over the worst of the mess she had made.

"Clean it up at once!"

The taverner turned to walk away. The girl scowled after her, and stuck out her tongue. A ripple of laughter circled the room. Encouraged, the girl put her thumbs to her ears and waggled her fingers. The laughter grew louder, and Sybil swung around to see its cause, in time to catch Ebba still mocking her.

Her lips tightened and she strode back to the girl. "Get out," she said curtly. "The good Lord knows I've warned you often enough about your behavior here. I've given you more than a few chances to mend your ways."

Ebba retracted her tongue, and slowly put her hands to her sides. A mocking smile curved her mouth as she sashayed over to the merchant. "I don't need to work in this poxy hovel." She flung the words over her shoulder. "I have better things to do with my time." She leaned over, giving Alan a good eyeful of the curve of her breasts. "You'll look after me, won't you, darlin'?" she breathed.

The room was silent, waiting for the merchant's response. He smiled slightly, and pulled the young woman onto his lap once more. Sybil put her hands on her hips and glared at them both. Alan picked up his mug of ale and held it to the girl's lips. She drank greedily, then set it down with a sigh and wiped her mouth with the back of her hand. She grinned at Sybil, then leaned over to rub her soft cheek against Alan's whiskers.

Sybil watched, saying nothing. Then, with an impatient exclamation, she turned on her heel and walked through the back of the tavern and out the door.

Silence followed her exit. Janna eyed Ebba, wondering if she regretted what she'd done. It seemed a chancy business, throwing away employment to live as a merchant's leman, especially when the arrangement had been thrust upon him and was not of his own making. For herself, Janna preferred to be independent, no matter what tasks fell her way. And, as the thought came into her mind, so did the solution to her problem.

"Wait here for me," she said, pressing Ulf's arm lightly as she rose from her stool. Before he had a chance to ask where she was going, she set off, following in Sybil's footsteps. Here, it seemed, was the answer to her dilemma. True, she had no experience to speak of, but if what Sybil had said was true, neither had the hapless Ebba when she'd been taken on as a serving maid. And Janna knew she had several advantages over Ebba; these she would stress once she'd tracked down the taverner. With luck, Sybil would look kindly on her and offer her a position here. Janna looked around the crowded tavern, smelling the enticing scent of hot pies and fresh-baked bread. Here she would find shelter *and* food. Two of her problems, and those the most pressing, would thus be solved.

There were several buildings in the fenced yard, including a latrine. Janna could smell it from where she stood. There was a tethering post to one side for the patrons' mounts. They stood in a line, snorting and stamping restlessly, and adding their steaming piles to the generally noxious odor. A faint glow shone through the windows of the largest building. Janna thought it might be the kitchen and started toward it, picking up the seductive aroma of a rich stew as she came closer.

She found Sybil within, a wet rag in her hands, chivvying the potboy for not scouring a pan to her satisfaction. The cook stood by, watching them as he slowly stirred the pot of stew that dangled from a hook above the fire in the great hearth. Janna's nose twitched in appreciation; saliva seeped into her mouth. She remembered then that she'd had no dinner and realized, suddenly, that she was ravenous. But now was not the time to think about her stomach; now was the time to save it.

"If you give me that cloth, mistress, I will clean up the mess on the rushes," she said quietly.

The taverner swung around to face Janna. Her eyebrows lifted as she noticed the luxurious cloth of Janna's blue gown, and lifted further as she caught the stink of it. Her eyes moved up to Janna's face and she studied her, looking thoughtful.

"Now why would you do that?" she said at last.

"I need work in order to live, mistress, and it seems that you need a new serving maid."

Sybil's eyes narrowed as she gave Janna a more careful inspection. "The work here is hard, and the hours are long. You are too highborn for my tavern. Better suited as a customer than a worker, in fact."

"I cannot be a customer, for I have no coins left to pay for either food or ale." Janna held up the cut cord of her girdle for the taverner's inspection. "A thief has taken all I own, and I have nowhere to go and no-one to support me." The truth of her words suddenly hit her with the force of a body blow. "Please, mistress. I will work hard for you, I promise you that." In spite of her good intentions, her voice quavered on the last words.

"Have you ever worked for your living before?" Sybil's gaze dropped to Janna's fine woollen gown, inspecting more carefully now the signs of wear and the splashes of filth where she had fallen into the mud and muck on the street.

"I have worked hard all my life." Janna hesitated, wondering what to say to convince her that she was in earnest, and how much of her past she should reveal. "My mother and I lived in a cot at the edge of the forest of Gravelinges for many years," she ventured. "It was a hard life, and we often went hungry, for we had little land to support ourselves. But my mother was a *wortwyf*, a healer, and traded her services for the goods we needed. That was how we managed to survive. I helped her brew her potions – and I also brewed our ale," she added quickly, hoping it might help convince Sybil to hire her.

"Why did you leave your mother, and your home?" It was clear from Sybil's expression that she suspected Janna might be another Ebba. It was also clear that, in the taverner's eyes, it meant she was more trouble than she was worth.

"My mother died." Better not mention she was only looking for employment until such time as her father returned to Winchestre. It would count against her, and besides, she had no idea how long it might take her father to come – if, in fact, he'd ever received her letter at all. And if he believed what she'd told him.

"The cot we lived in was burned to the ground," she went on, hoping to soften the taverner's stern expression into sympathy for her plight without revealing the fact that it had been the villagers who'd turned on her and set the cot alight. "I couldn't stay there, and have been on the road since, traveling about in search of...of employment. Please, mistress, I need to work and I'm willing to do anything you ask. Please give me a chance?"

Sybil eyed her, still suspicious. But the tavern was full and Janna knew she needed help. She thrust the damp cloth into Janna's hands.

"Clean up the mess, then, and take orders for food and drink from the customers. Be sure you remember what is said to you, for it is a waste and costs me good silver to provide them with what they haven't ordered, don't want, and won't have."

Janna wondered if that was something else about Ebba that had annoyed the taverner. "I'll do my best, mistress," she promised, and hurried out before Sybil could change her mind. Her future was safe, at least for tonight.

She pushed past a couple of drunken patrons who had come out to use the latrine at the end of the yard, and re-entered the tavern. Inside, patrons were bawling for service while Ebba giggled and preened at Alan's table. She went at once to Ulf and whispered her news to him. He jerked upright, aghast as he came to understand what she was telling him.

"But you can't! You're a – mpphh!" he spluttered, as Janna clamped her hand over his mouth to stop his words.

"Yes, I can. And I will." Wasting no more time, Janna strode over to the mess. She carefully scraped the worst of it onto a wooden trencher, using the last clean portion of the wet rag in a vain attempt to wipe the gravy off the rushes spread over the floor. They should be changed on the morrow, she thought. In fact, judging from the scraps of food and stains of splashed ale, they were well overdue for a change. She straightened and looked around.

Her actions had told the patrons of her function, and now she was deluged with demands for ale, wine and food. She had no way of remembering everything; instead, she focused only on the most demanding patrons, carefully repeating what they wanted. Then she turned to the others who clamored for her attention. "I'll return to take your orders in a moment," she promised, and rushed outside to the kitchen before she could forget what she'd been told.

She rattled off a list of dishes to the cook, while Sybil nodded and looked pleased. She thrust two large jugs of ale into Janna's hands then, and bade her return and refill the mugs of the customers.

"What about those who want wine?" Janna had little knowledge of wine, for she and her mother had neither the means to make it nor the spare coin to buy it.

"I'll see to them myself."

"How will I know who has paid and who hasn't?"

Sybil frowned at Janna's naivety. "They pay before you give them a refill. Here, you can wear this." She rummaged through a pile of linen until she found a clean apron. She thrust it at Janna. "Put the money in the pocket." She showed Janna the patch sewed on the side, with its drawstring tie. "I shall be keeping an eye on you, so don't think to cheat me, miss," she warned, and picked up a couple of trenchers to take through to the tavern. Janna wondered if that had been yet another of Ebba's sins. It would be easy enough to sneak a coin or two, and probably very tempting to do so. But she wouldn't fall into that trap. She needed the work and would do nothing to jeopardize it.

Thereafter, Janna was kept busy refilling mugs, taking orders, and serving food. It was hard work, and she was tired – and hungry. She managed to snatch a gravy-soaked crust from one of the trenchers and stuffed it into her mouth, chewing it with relish. The fare at the abbey had been plain and wholesome, but plentiful. Now she was reduced to stealing leftovers! She smiled wryly to herself, and continued to keep an eye out for any extra tidbits.

Her feet ached by the time Ossie pushed out the last customers and Sybil declared the tavern closed. Ulf had departed long since, after a brief word assuring Janna that he would continue to visit her father's manor in case there was news. "Keep your heart up. It can't be long now until he comes," he said, hoping to lift Janna's spirits, and going on to assure her that he would ask around about her stolen possessions, and also drop into the tavern regularly in case Janna had news for him.

"Do you have somewhere to sleep?" Sybil asked.

Janna thought longingly of her comfortable pallet at the convent, and resolutely shook her head. "No, mistress."

The taverner eyed her thoughtfully. "I have my own room above the tavern, and some extra space, which I sometimes let out to customers," she said.

Janna wondered if she was being offered free accommodation. "I have no coins to pay for a bed."

Sybil nodded briskly. "In that case, Ebba slept in the kitchen beside the fire. With Wat, the potboy."

"May I take her place?" Janna had come across the potboy through the evening, and had taken a dislike to him. His job, when not turning the spit, was to wash the cooking pots, and to clear and wash the dirty mugs and dishes. All these tasks he did with a sullen air, and not carefully enough unless Sybil was standing over him. Janna had seen several trenchers and mugs still spotted and stained after his ministrations. The boy was young enough not to pose any physical threat to her, but he was surly and rude, and she didn't relish sharing a sleeping space with him. Still, it seemed she had no choice. Another thought sent a shiver of alarm through her body.

"Where does the cook sleep? And…and Ossie? I can't stay in the kitchen if they bed down there." They were both grown men, and Janna had no intention of spending her nights fighting for her virtue.

Sybil smiled in understanding, apparently pleased at this manifestation of Janna's modesty. "Elfric sleeps at his own cot – with his wife and children. And Osbert – Ossie – sleeps downstairs in the tavern to guard the premises. Ebba has had no trouble with him and I doubt you will either. Come with me." She led Janna out to the kitchen and pointed to a small nook beside the great hearth. "Ebba used to make her bed over there. When she couldn't find someone else's bed to share!" Her lips tightened momentarily. "I will wake you at cockcrow, for there is much to do tomorrow. 'Tis lucky the spill happened this night, for I've already asked Ossie to go to the river and cut fresh rushes in the morn. But the old must be swept up and burned in the yard before the new rushes can be laid."

Janna nodded. That would be her and the potboy's task, she felt sure. Dirty, smelly, messy. And hard. Her spirits sank. Having observed Wat in action, she felt sure he'd be less than helpful come the morning. "What herbs will you have me strew on the new rushes, mistress?" she asked.

"Herbs?" Sybil peered more closely at her in the dim light from the banked-down fire as if suspecting some sort of trickery.

"I learned something of herbs and healing from my mother," Janna said, deciding it best not to mention how much more she'd learned from Sister Anne at the abbey at Wiltune, for it would sound like boasting and perhaps blight her prospects. "We always spread tansy or fleabane among the rushes in our own cot – to keep down the fleas and other biting creatures."

"Yes?" Sybil nodded impatiently.

"But we also used to strew meadowsweet or violets, or even wild rose petals, to sweeten the air, for those other herbs have a strong scent. It's quite unpleasant."

The taverner thought for a moment. Then she shrugged. "I only have the herbs we need for brewing and cooking in my kitchen garden."

"I can pick tansy and fleabane out in the water meadows, along with flowers with just as sweet a perfume as those cultivated in a garden. If you give me leave, I will pick some and prepare them for you."

Mistress Sybil kept silent. Janna wondered if she was thinking it was a ploy to get out of cleaning the tavern in the morning. "I can go at a time when it's not so busy," she pleaded, thinking how pleasant it would be to roam outside the walled town, in the fresh air. After an afternoon and evening spent in the stuffy, smoky atmosphere of the tavern, her soul ached for it. "There won't be time to pluck the herbs and flowers before Wat and I get rid of the old rushes and spread the new, but I can go any time after that, whenever you can spare me."

She cast a quick glance at the potboy, to make sure he knew she was including him in this chore, and that the taverner had heard her. Wat scowled at her, and continued shaking down his pallet, spreading it out and making himself comfortable for the night. Janna was pleased to see that he'd taken the Ingle-nook on the other side of the fireplace; she would not have to lie in close proximity to him.

The taverner looked at Janna's gown once more. "Take that off and sponge it down; it might clean up all right. But I can see that it was once a costly garment. It's not suitable for serving customers, for they'll spill ale on you, and worse, if they've taken too much to drink and haven't time to reach the yard. I have an old tunic of russet you can wear while you're here, and I'll keep your gown safe for you once you've tidied it up. I'll bring the tunic for you now, and a more useful veil to keep your hair out of the customers' drink and food." Without waiting for a reply, she hurried out of the kitchen.

"Thank you, mistress," Janna called after her. She felt warmed by the taverner's offer. She hadn't received permission to go out looking for herbs, but it seemed she was still to be rewarded for showing initiative and a willingness to work. While she waited for Sybil's return, she shook down Ebba's pallet and spread it out. It was warm beside the banked-down fire; too warm, but she knew she'd be glad of the warmth as winter closed in.

If she was still here by then. A black despair engulfed her as she recalled the events of the day. She'd set out so full of optimism, hoping that her father would be here in Winchestre and that he would receive his daughter with loving arms. Instead? Janna shook her head. Everything had gone wrong. Everything.

Chapter 3

Janna woke, stiff and cramped, and with the smell of stale food and smoke in her nose. She caught sight of her rough homespun tunic and frowned, thinking for a moment she was back in the cot at the edge of the forest. She looked about the room for her mother. And then realization hit her, and she squeezed her eyes shut and groaned as memories of the previous day flooded her mind. Her spirits plummeted; she wanted to curl up into a little ball on her pallet and make the world go away. With a huge effort, she roused herself instead. There was the taste of ash and grit in her mouth, and she licked her lips and swallowed a few times to get rid of it. Her empty stomach growled, reminding her that she hadn't eaten properly for quite some time. She would have to talk to the taverner about meals; surely she would be fed while she worked here?

She looked about at the signs of the cook's trade. The hock of ham, flitch of bacon, and strings of sausages hanging from the rafters set her mouth watering. Piled close to the bread oven were baskets of onions, parsnips and cabbages, and sacks of grain. Above them, bunches of dried herbs hung from hooks fixed to the wall. She stood up and inspected them carefully, in case there was something she could use to sweeten the new rushes once they were down. There was garlic, rosemary, mint, thyme and sage, all of them aromatic, but Janna would rather pick fresh plants if she could find what she wanted in the water meadows. A small cabinet caught her eye. Curious, she turned the key and found inside a row of small, stoppered pots and a box of salt.

"You're not allowed to touch those!" Wat shouted.

Janna ignored him. Clearly this was Sybil's precious store of spices. Presumably the cupboard was usually locked, but perhaps Sybil had been so upset by Ebba's behavior she'd forgotten to take out the key. She hesitated, but curiosity got the better of her. She began to pull out the stoppers and smell the contents. Her keen nose identified caraway, nutmeg, cloves, ginger, grains of paradise, coriander and anise.

"You'll be out on yer arse if Sybil catches you." Wat's eyes gleamed with malicious glee.

Janna gave him a withering glare and locked the cupboard. She left the key in place. Saliva flooded her mouth as she noted a large crock of honey. She licked her lips, tasting its sweetness in her imagination. Several large pots had been unhooked from the long chains over the fire and left to one side. She lifted a lid and stared dubiously at a mix of tripe and onions congealed in a bed of white sauce at the bottom of the pot. She shuddered. Tripe was one of the cheapest cuts and she had often eaten it, but the tasteless dish was by no means her favorite. The next pot revealed a rich stew of marrowbones. Her stomach gave a loud gurgle and she looked about for a ladle.

"That's not for us." Wat picked up a loaf of old bread. He sawed off a generous slice, and then poured himself a mug of ale from a cask nearby. "You can take some too," he said, and sat down on his pallet to break his fast.

Wasting no time, Janna picked up the knife and hacked off a chunk of bread for herself. Bread and ale; it was her usual morning meal, but she couldn't help hoping that there might be something extra, some cheese or meat to put on the bread, when it came to their dinnertime.

Ossie ambled in, still yawning and rubbing sleep from his eyes. As he began to help himself to bread and ale, the cook also arrived. "You," he said, when he noticed Janna. "You can get chopping up onions and parsnips for the pot."

Janna eyed him thoughtfully. "Mistress Sybil told Wat and me to sweep up and burn the rushes this morning," she said through a mouthful of bread. She swallowed some ale to wash it down, and took another bite. She didn't know what her duties would entail, but was sure that the taverner's instructions were more important than the cook's. She was happy to help him, if there was time to do so, but she wouldn't neglect her duties to do it. A thought made her pause. "Where is your kitchen garden?" she asked, still chewing. "What herbs do you grow?"

Elfric stared at her for a moment, and then grunted, "See for yourself. It's back there." He jerked his thumb behind him.

"Thank you." Janna walked out quickly, before he could think of any more tasks to give her. In the cool freshness of the day, she looked for any signs of a garden. The door of one of the smaller buildings was open now. Inside, she could see the taverner up on a ladder bending over a mash tun, busily stirring its contents. Steam rose in a cloud; Sybil's face was damp with it, and with the sweat of her exertions. Janna sniffed, recognizing the malted barley smell of a new brew. She kept on, hurrying past the latrine, which was easily identified because of the strong odors wafting from it, and the random puddles nearby, which told of the tavern's patrons who were either caught short or couldn't be bothered to use the premises provided. She wrinkled her nose and headed on toward a fenced-off area within the yard, guessing it must lead to the kitchen garden, for there were no obvious signs of any greenery among the buildings.

A makeshift gate led into a small garden plot. To her disappointment, it was largely taken up with rows of vegetables: peas, beans, leeks, onions and cabbages. Only a few herbs grew in a corner: the rosemary, alecost and sweet gale she'd identified in the ale, but also garlic and white mustard, plus the mint, thyme and sage she'd found drying in the kitchen. She picked several sprigs of the last three for want of anything better to add fragrance to the rushes. They would do for the time being.

Dreading what lay ahead of her, she walked back to the brew house to ask the taverner where she might find a broom or a rake. Sybil was now busy adding the gruit to the strained wort in a separate container, and Janna breathed in the fragrance of the herbs

Absorbed in her task, Sybil barked instructions and sent Janna on her way. "Get Wat to help you, and keep an eye on him," she advised. "He's a lazy runt of a lad, as bad as his sister."

Easier said than done, Janna thought resentfully later, as she raked up the filthy, reeking rushes from the tavern floor, and shouted for Wat to bring back the barrow so she could pile on another load. He was getting slower and slower, and she wondered how he was managing to waste so much time out in the yard.

"I'll take a turn with the barrow, and you can do some raking for a change," she told him when he finally put in an appearance. He shrugged, looking surly. Janna gladly surrendered the rake to him and picked up the handles of the heavy barrow. Once outside in the fresh, sunlit air, she felt a little more kindly toward Wat. It was indeed a temptation to linger. Resolutely she wheeled the barrow over to the dirty rushes already smoldering on the fire and added its contents to the pile. She pulled a face as a nest of small black beetles scuttled to safety. Her skin was already itchy from the fleas and lice she'd disturbed, and she bent to scratch her ankles where the worst of the bites were centered.

The change was long overdue, she thought, as the bright sunshine revealed trapped bones and bits of meat and other decaying substances among the rushes. She knew them to be a haven for any creature in search of a meal, including rats and mice, for there'd been the swift scurrying of a small furry body when she'd started to disturb the floor covering.

Recollecting her irritation with Wat, she hastily wheeled the barrow back for a fresh load, to find the young lad aimlessly prodding about with the rake.

"Not like that!" she said sharply, feeling irritated all over again. "Gather it up into a pile so you can fork it onto the barrow."

"You do it, then."

Heaving a resentful sigh, Janna took the rake from him and bent to her task once more. Wat stood stolidly beside her, making no effort to help as she began to fork the fouled rushes onto the barrow.

"Enjoying the entertainment?" she asked.

Wat glowered at her.

"Make sure you don't strain anything!" she said sarcastically, conscious of her aching arms and a sharp pain in her back from all the bending and stretching she was doing.

"Am I like to hurt meself?" He sounded genuinely concerned. Janna gave an annoyed snort and continued to fill the barrow. "Lazy runt of a lad" about summed it up. She comforted herself with the thought of a walk in the water meadows later, if only she could persuade Sybil to let her go. If she and Wat could finish this task quickly, there might be time to go before a rush of customers came in for their dinner.

"Hurry up," she told Wat, once the barrow was full. "Come back here as soon as you've emptied it."

He scowled at her, but didn't reply. Janna watched him stump off with the barrow, then bent wearily to her task once more.

After Ossie had laid the fresh rushes, Janna sprinkled over them the aromatic herbs she'd picked in the kitchen garden. They would dry and add fragrance to the green, sweet rushes, and she would strew other flowers and herbs too, if given permission to gather them.

As soon as she'd finished her task, she hurried to find the taverner to ask leave to go. "I'll pick tansy and fleabane to keep away the lice and beetles," she promised. "I found whole nests of them in the straw as I raked it up."

Sybil tilted her head and looked her over as she considered her request. "You can't go now. It's almost dinnertime and the tavern will soon be busy. But you may leave as soon as the rush is over. Ask Elfric to give you a hempen bag to carry what you pick. I want you back as soon as you hear the bell for Vespers. Customers will start coming in again, and I'll need your help to serve them. And Janna, before you come into the tavern, ask Elfric to give you something to eat. I don't want you picking food from the customers' trenchers again. At least, not while they can still see you!"

Janna blushed scarlet. She'd thought no-one was looking, but it seemed Sybil didn't miss much. That fact alone was worth remembering. Her observation was reinforced when the taverner rounded on Wat. "I haven't seen you putting yourself out to do very much as yet," she said, and set him to removing all traces of the burnt rushes from the yard.

As Sybil had predicted, Janna was kept busy over the next few hours, but as soon as she was allowed, she collected a bag and a sharp knife from Elfric and hurried from the tavern, feeling her spirits lift as she went out through the East Gate and turned right toward the high turrets of the bishop's Wolvesey Palace and the water meadows beyond. On her left was the hill of St Giles. The air rang with the sounds of hammering and sawing, but Janna could see little beyond the palisade that had been constructed to enclose the site and prevent anyone sneaking in without paying a toll. She found it hard to imagine the scene within, although Ulf had told her that merchants and craftsmen who carried out the same trades always set up together at the fair to sell their wares. *"It's possible to walk along a row and find all the wool merchants in a line, or shield or candle makers, or* gold- and silversmiths," he'd said. "*Even the foreign merchants keep together in their own rows to sell expensive goods such as wines, spices, silks, glass, fine pottery and ivory. But it's not only fancy stuff for sale up there,*" he'd added. "*There's corn and hay, firewood and charcoal, and also beasts, fish and birds, including some you've never seen the likes of before. Weird and wonderful they are, just you wait and see!*"

Janna gave a little skip of excitement as she thought of the treat to come.

Ahead of her was another green hill named for St Catherine, and she could see also the stone spires of the Hospital of St Cross. She had walked this way several times with Ulf, who'd told her that the hospital had been founded some years before by Henry, Bishop of Winchestre, "to house thirteen indigent men and feed another hundred," he'd said, adding that he'd gone to the hospital several times in the past to ask for the dole when he'd been starving and had no coin to pay for a meal.

"Dole?" Janna had queried.

"Ale and bread, and a dish of some sort."

Perhaps she should have begged for the bishop's dole rather than take the job at the tavern! But Ulf had said it was to feed hungry men; he hadn't mentioned women at all. Yet she could get just as hungry as any man, though she would rather have employment than have to beg for her bread.

She passed several weeping willows growing beside the River Itchen, and quickened her pace, for they brought a heavy, aching grief and reminded her of what she had lost. The same stately swans she'd seen before still paddled against the rushing water that swept down to the mill, although their cygnets were now almost fully grown. Janna envied the swans their serenity as they ducked their heads into green weedy growth looking for food. Winchestre might be on the brink of war, yet they cared nothing for that, nor did they care that she had lost her purse and all her treasures, and might well have lost her father too.

Janna swallowed hard, her mouth suddenly dry. She shook off her morbid thoughts and tried instead to recapture the pleasure of her walk in the water meadows. They were looking their best in the bright sunshine. Narrow runnels of water threaded through the grass, glinting in the sunlight. Yellow, pink, scarlet and blue flowers studded the lush field and reeds growing beside the rushing river, while ducks and moorhens splashed and squawked at her as she passed by. Janna paused frequently to sniff the fragrant air, and to pick what she wanted. Out of habit, she also picked whatever healing herbs came her way, for there was no telling when they might come in useful. If the plant was small enough, she plucked it out by the roots, for she had a mind to take over a corner of the kitchen garden. There would be room enough for some new plants, and she could certainly persuade Sybil of their usefulness.

It occurred to Janna that Sybil might be willing to try a new recipe for the ale she served, to give her customers the choice of something different. Wild hops, thyme, meadowsweet and sage were added to the bag, along with wormwood, betony and woundwort. On spying a small copse of trees she walked over to investigate, hoping to find among them just what she wanted. Pulling out the sharp knife, she cut herself a stout stirring stick from a young ash tree. She searched hopefully for the long brown wings of the fruits, but it was still too early. She made a mental note to keep looking out for ash keys, for they too had their uses in a brew.

She walked back into the water meadows, now picking stinking fleabane and the aromatic yellow buttons of tansy. She wrinkled her nose against the smell, for she'd gathered them in sufficient quantity to repel even the most determined biting creatures. She was sure Sybil's customers would appreciate being able to enjoy their ale and wine without the maddening itches of lice and fleas.

A lark soared skyward, filling the air with its glorious song. Listening, Janna felt her spirits rise with the small bird, all care forgotten as she watched its joyous flight. She remembered her mother's pleasure in nature: "God's great cathedral," Eadgyth had called the forest where they lived, and the garden they had tended beside their small cot. Truly, on a day such as this, Janna felt close to Him and marveled at what He had created in such abundance. She walked on, so rapt in her meadow ramble that she quite forgot about time passing, and the duties awaiting her at the tavern. It was with a great start of alarm that she heard the bells of St Mary's peal out the hour of Vespers. Other bells chimed in, sending a great shout of sound across the water meadows.

Answering their urgent summons, Janna turned on her heel and sped back toward the East Gate. Sweat trickled down her back as she ran. She felt a cramp of pain in her side, and stopped to take a few quick breaths. *Aelfshot*, the old ones called it, believing that this sort of discomfort was caused by pricking darts shot by small elves. Her mother had taught Janna several charms to recite to remove the unseen dart and protect herself, but from her own observation Janna knew that a short rest worked more quickly than anything else to relieve the pain.

Fear gripped her. What if Sybil scolded her for being late? What if she was having second thoughts about employing her? Janna ran on, ignoring the pain in her side as she fought to catch her breath.

Once through the East Gate she was about to turn toward the tavern when a young boy attracted her attention. Unable to believe what she was seeing, she stopped so abruptly that people coming from behind crashed into her and grumbled when she didn't move.

Hamo! Could that really be Hamo skipping ahead of her down the street toward the shops and shambles of Chepe Street? No! Common sense told Janna this couldn't be the small lad she'd once rescued, for she had left him many moons ago in the care of his cousin Hugh at the manor farm not far from Wiltune. Yet she was almost sure...

Intrigued, she began to walk once more, eager to see for herself if it really was Hamo, and if his cousin Hugh accompanied him. Filled with impatience, she pushed past a plump merchant and his wife, and saw that indeed it was Hamo. Beside him...? Janna's spirits leaped high as a grasshopper in spring. Hugh! She hadn't been dreaming after all. They were both here, in front of her, Hamo now tugging on Hugh's sleeve to gain his attention while Hugh dawdled, his eyes on an attractive young woman who, with her mother, was coming toward them. Janna smiled wryly as she noted the direction of his gaze; noted too that the young woman was entirely aware of his regard. Judging from her flushed cheeks and the glint in her eye, his interest was not unwelcome. Hardly surprising, Janna thought, remembering her own reaction on first meeting the handsome young lord. Truly, he could melt the hardest of hearts!

He and Hamo hadn't seen her yet, for they were walking in the same direction and their backs were turned to her. Janna could see only the sides of their faces, but knew that she wasn't mistaken. She quickened her steps to catch up with them.

What marvel had brought them to Winchestre? Automatically, her hands went to her hair to smooth and tidy it, for there was a time when she'd thought Hugh might be falling in love with her, even though he was highborn and she was merely the daughter of a *wortwyf*. She was sure she hadn't imagined the attraction growing between them during the time she'd spent at the abbey, when she had nursed him back to health. Dressed as a nun, and a protégée of the infirmarian there, she had enjoyed her new status, and had seen in his eyes that Hugh had registered the change in her, and that he appreciated it. More, that he found her attractive and desirable.

And now he was here, walking away from her but still within calling distance. Delighted, Janna opened her mouth. Abruptly, she closed it again, as her fingers touched the coarse homespun veil concealing her hair. She looked down at her russet tunic and reconsidered her approach. Perhaps she should wait a while, at least until her father came to Winchestre. True, she was the illegitimate granddaughter of a king, and close kin to the woman who would be queen. If she could prove her identity, her new status would put her far above Hugh, for although he was a lord, he was landless and dependent on his aunt for a living. In fact, he had told her himself that he must marry – and marry well – to secure his future. Janna gave an excited skip. Once she'd seen her father, once she'd persuaded him that she really was his daughter, she could reveal all to Hugh. Surely he would ask her to marry him, for she would be an impressive match for him then. And they would be happy together.

Without conscious thought, she scanned the crowd for Hugh's right-hand man. Her heart thudded as she spied Godric walking slightly ahead of his overlord. But it almost stopped beating when she saw who was with him: Hamo's nurse, Cecily. The two of them had their heads close together in conversation. Cecily would do better to pay attention to her young charge, Janna thought sourly, before scolding herself for her lack of charity. It was plain that Hamo had grown beyond the need for a nurse and was enjoying his cousin's company. Her gaze returned to Godric. Even though his back was turned to her; even though he too had changed since last she saw him, for he was now grown into manhood, still she would have known him anywhere. She wished he would turn around so she could see his face when he recognized her. He must know that she'd left the abbey; he must believe that she was gone away from him forever.

But – and the realization humbled her big opinion of herself – perhaps with her gone from his life, he no longer thought of her at all? He'd twice offered her marriage, but she'd turned him down. Now, here he was with Cecily, and looking well content in her company. Janna recalled how, so long ago, she'd mistaken them for man and wife when she'd seen them together in the market square. Once more she berated herself for not rejoicing that her oldest friend had found love elsewhere, yet still she felt a keen sense of loss. Were he and Cecily now wed? The thought pricked her mind like a nasty, scratching burr. And yet, in truth, it was a good match. Cecily was Dame Alice's attendant, while Godric seemed to have risen to a status that now matched Cecily's own, given the way he was attired.

Agitation had quickened her footsteps; she was gaining ground on Hugh and his party. She stopped abruptly, earning a round curse from a passerby who cannoned into her. If she caught up to them, they would see to what depths she had sunk once more. She might be well connected, but until she could produce her father she would rather not meet them at all.

Recalling her purpose, and its urgency, she reluctantly turned to the tavern. The bells had stopped ringing the hour; she was more than overdue and would have to face the wrath of the taverner. She began to run. Aware of her rumbling stomach, and thinking she might as well eat her fill before she was dismissed, she hastened through the tavern and out to the kitchen, pausing briefly to wash her muddy hands at the pump as she passed.

"There you are, then," Elfric greeted her. "Mistress Sybil is looking for you, and I warn you, she's not happy."

"I lost track of the time!" Janna dumped her bag onto the kitchen table. She put a protective hand on it as Elfric wandered over to inspect the contents. "These are for strewing among the rushes," she said swiftly, not wanting him to see what else she'd been picking. "They won't serve your purpose at all. Except for this, maybe." She pulled out some sprigs of water mint, hoping to blunt his curiosity. "I'll see to the rest of the herbs later, if I may keep the bag a while longer?"

Elfric nodded and turned back to his cooking fire. "Here," he said, handing Janna a fat sausage and a heel of bread. "You can go and find Sybil after you've eaten. Tell her I kept you helping me out here, and that's why you're late." He poured Janna a mug of ale as she took an appreciative bite of the mince-stuffed intestine.

"Mmm. Delicious," she said, savoring the mouthful.

Elfric smiled. "You could do worse than work in this tavern," he commented, "though you should have come back when Sybil told you. She doesn't like to be disobeyed. But if you work hard, as I saw you work this morning, you'll find she'll do right by you."

Remembering the gift of the rough tunic she wore, Janna nodded. She hastily scoffed the rest of her treat, washed it down with ale, and headed to the door.

"Wait." Elfric handed her a couple of wooden trenchers laden with food.

"Who are these for?"

"Don't ask me. I just do the cooking." Elfric turned back to the stew pot hanging low over the fire. With trenchers balanced carefully, one in each hand, Janna cautiously sidled out the door and into the tavern.

"Here!" Sybil caught sight of her and hurried across, directing Janna to put the food down in front of the two men who had ordered it. "Where have you been?" she hissed crossly.

"I'm sorry, mistress." Janna was about to repeat the cook's lie, but met Sybil's bright gaze and thought the better of it. "I lost track of the time," she admitted.

Sybil drew back, hands on her hips as she studied Janna closely. "Have you been reporting on me to one of those alehouses in the high street?"

"No, of course not!"

"It wouldn't be the first time my rivals have sent someone here to spy on me."

"Well, I'm certainly not one of their spies, and I have a bagfull of plants to prove it!" Janna wondered if the taverner had any grounds for her suspicion. She remembered the merchant's threat to take his custom elsewhere. The other alehouses were further up the high street, and did a roaring trade, being situated so close to the great cathedral and shops. Surely they didn't need to poach Sybil's trade as well?

The taverner eyed her, still suspicious. "I'll be watching you," she promised, and thrust two empty pitchers into Janna's hands. "Go and refill these from the new barrel in the brew house and hurry back. I can't serve this crowd on my own, you know."

Grateful for the second chance she'd been given, Janna hurried to do as she was bid. As she neared the door at the back of the tavern, she noticed Alan, the merchant. He was with a new companion this time, a bright peacock of a man. A flagon of wine stood on the table in front of them, along with two goblets. They were huddled together, conversing in such low tones that even though Janna passed as close as she dared, she could not hear what they were saying. There was no sign of Ebba. Janna hoped, for the girl's sake, that she had not already been cast aside by the merchant. Even as she was thinking it, the merchant looked up and saw her.

"What are you staring at?" he demanded.

"I..." Janna paused and nervously licked her lips. "May I fetch some more wine for you?"

"No." The merchant bent his head to his friend once more. Janna hurried on her way, mulling over the sight she'd seen. Ale one day, and wine the next. Evidently the merchant was out to impress his brightly dressed friend. While Sybil served the wine herself, Janna had seen enough the night before to know that it didn't come cheap, imported as it was from across the sea.

Janna's mind was full of questions as she filled the pitchers from the barrel containing the latest brew. Was it the merchant who'd ordered the wine? Or was this Sybil's gift, as a way of making sure that he stayed loyal to her tavern? And who was the peacock?

Someone with whom the merchant hoped to do business, perhaps even someone in the bishop's or empress's employ? Perhaps he was the source of the merchant's information about the stand-off between the two. She made sure, as she brought the filled pitchers back into the tavern, that she walked slowly enough to have a good look at the merchant's acquaintance. In uncertain times such as these it was as well to watch and be careful.

Her curiosity grew as, not long afterward, the merchant's companion pushed back his stool and strode out of the tavern. With narrowed eyes and pinched lips, the merchant watched him go. Janna wondered if he was angry because the wine was still to be paid for, or because he'd argued with his companion. One of her questions was answered when Sybil hastened across and thrust out her hand, palm up. No making up with the customers, then. It was all business with Sybil.

The merchant's expression darkened as he reluctantly opened his purse and drew out a silver coin. Their two heads came together, and Janna drifted closer.

"...shamed me in my own tavern!" Sybil hissed, as she thrust the coin into her pocket. "I won't have it, do you hear me? You may visit the tavern if you wish, but don't you dare bring your leman in here!"

The merchant sat back, seeming undisturbed by her fury. "What we once had between us is finished," he said coldly. "You made it quite clear at the time that you weren't interested in my offer. So what is it to you if I take someone younger, and prettier, to my bed?" He cleared his throat and spat into the rushes.

The taverner snatched up a goblet. For a moment, Janna thought she was going to throw its contents into the merchant's face. Evidently she decided against it, for she banged it down and stepped away. "Get out," she said tightly. "You are no longer welcome in my tavern." As she hurried off, Ossie strode across and stood over the merchant to make sure he'd leave as he'd been told. Janna quickly turned aside, not wanting anyone to know she'd been listening to their altercation. She was ashamed of her curiosity, but she also felt sorry for the taverner. Sybil was an attractive woman, but she was past the first bloom of youth. The hard work and cares of her life had left their mark in the lines on her face, although her body was still slim and lithe. But it seemed that, in the merchant's eyes, she was no match for the fresh-faced Ebba. Whether Sybil had any feelings left for the merchant or not, it must hurt to be so humiliated, in public, and in her own tavern.

As she continued to serve the customers, fend off those who were too forward with her, and steer in the right direction those who were too drunk to find their own way out to the latrine, Janna's thoughts moved on to the unexpected presence of Hugh and his young companion and cousin, Hamo, and their entourage. She kept busy pouring ale into mugs and serving trenchers of food while she listened to the latest news circulating in the tavern to see if she could find out why they were in Winchestre.

The merchant had said that the empress was here with a large army. Janna remembered past reports that had put Hugh in the company of Robert of Gloucestre, the empress's half-brother. If he had come to Winchestre to support his liege lord, it could mean that Hugh's uncle by marriage, Robert of Babestoche, might also have answered the call to arms.

Janna's nerves jumped with alarm at the thought. She knew that Robert of Babestoche wanted her dead; wanted it so badly he'd already sent an assassin after her to ensure her silence. Janna had managed to fight off the villain, but might not be so lucky next time. If Robert was here, it was almost certain that he would have his manservant, Mus, with him. Only one thought quietened her fears: Robert of Babestoche had no idea where she was, certainly not that she was in Winchestre. No-one from her past life knew that. It seemed she'd had a lucky escape when she'd stopped herself from hailing Hugh. She must take care to stay out of his way, and keep them all in ignorance of her presence here.

Janna shivered. If Hugh had come in answer to the empress's summons, Matilda must expect the worst. The thought of Hugh going into battle made Janna's stomach knot in fear. Only one thing puzzled her: If Hugh was here for such a dangerous cause, why on earth had he brought Hamo with him?

Chapter 4

Janna soon settled into the routine of the tavern. The days were long and hard, but she told herself she was lucky to have found bed and board. True to his promise, Ulf visited often, although his news was never welcome: no, there was still no sight of her father, nor had the steward had any word from him. And no, there was no sign of the stolen brooch or ring either.

"Perhaps the fair will bring your father here," Ulf said optimistically, as Janna brought a mug of ale to his table.

She puffed out a sigh, hardly daring to believe him.

"Don't lose heart," Ulf urged. "Write him another letter. I can take it to the steward, and this time I'll tell Roger it must go to your father, no-one else."

"I have no parchment or anything to write with."

"I'll get them for you."

Janna forced a smile at Ulf's efforts to cheer her. It was true she'd begun to lose hope that her father might ever come to Winchestre, but she couldn't make up her mind whether it was because he'd never received her letter, he didn't believe her claim, or he didn't want to acknowledge her. She reminded herself that all the misfortunes of her early life had only come about because Eadgyth hadn't trusted him enough. Perhaps she should learn from that and give him the benefit of the doubt?

"Thank you, Ulf," she said, more warmly. "I will write again if he doesn't come soon. But I hope you may be right – he may be timing his visit to coincide with the fair. If he doesn't come for that, then yes, let's make another plan."

Ulf drained his mug. "I'll come again soon," he said, and stood up to leave.

Janna continued to busy herself with the customers. She was coming to know the regulars now: those who spelled trouble, and those who smiled and paid her compliments when she waited on them. The merchant no longer came to the tavern, but she recognized some of his hangers-on. Janna usually served them, for she sensed that the taverner wanted nothing to do with them either. She wondered why the relationship between the pair had ended. While not wanting to be accused of prying into matters that were no concern of hers, she gave in to temptation and asked Elfric what he knew.

The cook grinned as he spooned savory stew into bowls. "They used to be lovers," he said cheerfully. "But I suspect he was after a share in the tavern as well as the share of her bed. At any rate, Sybil broke off their relationship. She likes her independence, that one. She won't have any man telling her what to do and taking over her property and profits."

"The merchant doesn't seem to lack money," Janna ventured. "Why would he want a share of the tavern as well?"

"He might look like he's wealthy, but as to how he earns a living?" Elfric tapped the side of his nose. "A bit fast and loose with the law, if you ask me. But he has friends in high places and a reputation to maintain. None of those things comes free." Elfric reflected for a moment. "But perhaps it's just that he resented Sybil's free spirit and thought to curb it by taking a share of her business."

Janna was silent as she digested his words. Money – or power? Maybe both. Or was Elfric too cynical, and was it something else that had caused the rift?

"Whatever the reason, she put an end to their liaison," Elfric continued.

"He'll not gain much from Ebba."

"That's not why he's taken her in." There was a twinkle in Elfric's eyes as he waved her on her way. Janna carried out the bowls of stew, feeling foolish. Of course a man like Alan was attracted to Ebba's obvious charms. But it wouldn't last. How could it?

*

The sound of shouting was the first indication that something was amiss. The tavern fell silent as customers pricked their ears to listen to the tumult outside. It seemed to Janna that all within suspected its cause but had suspended belief, just for a few moments, in the desperate hope that they were wrong and that all might yet be well. She looked for Sybil, and noticed the taverner was pale with fear and had backed against the wall for support. Everyone froze, listening fiercely, and then, without further ado, the customers surged to their feet and rushed into the high street to find out what was going on. Janna followed them.

There seemed to be some sort of riot taking place in the center of the town, for the street was full of people scurrying to and fro, while a sonorous clanging sounded above the shouts and curses, each booming thud spurring the onlookers to even more frenzied activity. Curious as to the cause, Janna hurried up the high street toward the old palace at its center.

At the heart of the tumbling knot of people was a troop of soldiers bearing swords and shields, grim determination on their faces. Sunlight glinted on their conical helmets and the metal rings of their hauberks. Those in front had a battering ram and were pounding against the heavy iron gates barring the palace. It seemed that the empress had indeed run out of patience with the bishop's prevarication. But Janna suspected that the bishop and his troops were well supplied with arms and armaments, as well as provisions, for the carts traveling to the palace gates had grown in number and brazenness over the past few days. Rumor had it that the bishop had fortified the great tower within when taking over the old palace some years ago, and it was apparent now that it had become his headquarters for the coming siege.

A blaze of light flashed across the sky, and Janna tilted her head to watch its path, only understanding what it was when it fell short of the royal castle. She looked for the source of the fireball and realized it had been hurled from siege engines mounted within the bishop's stronghold. The day of reckoning had finally come.

That had not been the first fireball, she realized, as she sniffed the smoky air. And then another fiery missile arced through the sky, followed by another, and yet another. All were aimed at the castle but most fell short, setting alight shops and houses. The acrid stench of burning grew stronger.

"That devil's firing on his own town!" The speaker next to Janna had a bundle on his back and a baby in his arms. His wife beside him clutched a little girl's hand. White-faced and numb with despair, they were a still, small center among the terrified crowd heaving around them, who now were giving full voice to their rage.

Janna noticed a flag bearer. She recognized his pennant: red, with three clarions in orange, their shape similar to the small portable organ played by troubadours. She'd seen the insignia before, when she'd gone to the royal palace to demand a meeting with the earl. These must be Robert's men, come to besiege the palace and put an end to the storm of deadly fireballs. She pressed closer, looking for Hugh, but their helmets and the collars of their hauberks obscured their faces and she was unable to recognize anyone. However, she understood their purpose well enough. The soldiers were ready to charge in just as soon as the gates were breached. Curious, she moved even closer, believing herself still far enough away to escape to safety should the need arise.

Surrounding the armored knights were their vassals, all carrying an assortment of weapons. Most of them were without the protection of full armor. Some wore a hauberk, or a helmet, but some wore only padded gambesons reaching to their knees. Fearful for Hugh's and Godric's safety, Janna squinted her eyes for a better view of the earl's troops. A great roar went up as the iron gate buckled. The clanging of the battering ram ended with a loud bang as the gate fell. At once the earl's men surged through, only to be met by fierce opposition from the bishop's troops, determined to protect the palace and its siege engines at all costs. Locked in close combat, the two opposing sides shoved and pushed and finally erupted back into the street. Suddenly, Janna found herself caught up in the melee and unable to escape.

Blocking her path to safety were the shopkeepers whose homes and property were under threat. Shutters were being hastily closed and doors locked. Hapless citizens, carts and arms piled high with all they could salvage, were trying to forge a path to safety, earning savage blows, curses and kicks as they got in the way of the soldiers. The cries of the dying and injured and the deadly crackle of greedy flames added to the general cacophony. Flying embers created new hazards. A man screamed and flung himself sideways as molten lead from a blazing rooftop dripped onto his head. Where the fires had caught, they blazed so brightly that Janna knew those owners and shopkeepers would have been unable to save anything, perhaps not even their lives.

The crowd pushed and shoved its way through the town, trying to reach whatever parish church was closest. Some of the townsfolk were smudged with soot after braving the firestorm to salvage what they might. Others had taken fright and fled without thought, carrying only those too small or infirm to look after themselves. But many of the wooden churches had begun to burn, forcing the desperate citizens back out into the street to try for the safety of the cathedral itself. Alarmed screams added to the din, for the earl's men were still intent on battering their way through into the palace to put an end to the stream of burning fireballs, and seemed determined to run over anything or anyone in their way.

Aware of how close she was to the fighting, Janna tried in vain to escape. Her heart pounded in terror as she found herself carried inexorably closer to the entrance of the palace.

"Hoy! Out of my way!" The sudden shout sent her reeling backward. She burrowed into the throng in an effort to reach safety, but still she was pushed on, for the crowd was now too panic-stricken to know where safety lay or how to find it.

A new danger became apparent as a small contingent of the bishop's troops, mounted on fine destriers, erupted from the old palace. At the sound of the clarion call, the earl's men hastily regrouped. In close formation, and with swords and battleaxes held high, they prepared to face this new threat. The destriers aimed straight for the crowd. The citizens scattered in panic. There was a clash of weapons, savage yells and grunts of pain. Men were unhorsed and wounded. They screamed in agony as they fell. Riderless warhorses ran wild, aiming lethal kicks at any who crossed their path. And all the while, new fires ignited and Winchestre burned.

With desperation in her heart and a prayer on her lips, Janna dodged to one side and looked about her, peering through the haze of smoke in an effort to find a way past, somewhere safe to hide, for men were fighting in close combat all around her, and woe betide anyone who got caught in their midst.

Suddenly, and right in front of Janna's horrified gaze, one of the bishop's men was unhorsed and a foot soldier closed on him with a vicious curse. At once the soldier sprang to his feet and, with drawn swords, the two men stalked each other, cutting and thrusting, each trying to take the advantage. Shaking with fear, Janna tried to shrink out of their way. The bishop's man lunged, his sword slicing into his opponent's padded gambeson. Janna felt her own flesh tense in sympathy as she imagined the steel blade penetrating through soft skin, muscle and entrails. The soldier howled in agony and blood flowed freely from the wound. With a choking whimper, he fell and lay writhing on the ground.

Janna had to force her shaking legs to move. She tried to reach him, hoping she might be able to staunch the bleeding, or help him in some way. But before she could take even a couple of steps, the bishop's man ended his victim's life with a chopping blow across the throat, almost taking the man's head from his body. Blood spurted. The soldier's body convulsed before collapsing into the stillness of death. With one enemy dispatched, the bishop's man swung around to face another behind him. Kill, or be killed. A moment's inattention made all the difference between life and death. Janna found herself saying a fervent prayer that Hugh and Godric would stay safe, and that Hamo and Ulf had not been caught up in this madness at all.

She tried to break free but was hemmed in by the crowd, and jostled and kicked without mercy. Soldiers swarmed everywhere, cursing the frightened citizens who got in their way, for their blood was up and they were fighting for their lives. The noise was terrifying – battle cries and the screams of the dying, both human and animal. Grunts and curses, the clash and clang of weapons. A haze of smoke made it hard to breathe, and Janna cupped her hand over her nose.

"Out of my way, God damn you!" The shout brought her wheeling around in time to see a destrier and its rider charging toward her. Fright kept her stationary for long moments. She saw the fierce expression of horse and soldier alike, the deadly hooves flying through the air, coming closer, closer. The horse reared –

Panic-stricken, she leaped aside and felt a hoof strike her shoulder like an iron club, then they were past and she was on the ground, desperately trying to roll out of the way of crushing hooves and spurred boots. She fetched up against a pentice, one of the many stalls that hung off the palace walls. She dived inside, seeking shelter. The shopkeeper and his wife were hastily shoving their goods into sacks, while outside a small donkey shifted restlessly under the burden of the laden baskets tied to its back, its ears pricked to the sounds and smells of the street.

"Out!" The trader jerked a thumb at Janna, his meaning plain. His wife looked apologetic, but did not contradict her husband, reaching around him to gather a fistful of leather gloves to thrust into the bag she held open.

Shakily, Janna rose to her feet. She wrapped an arm across her chest and felt her shoulder, gently probing for signs of a break. She could feel no grating bone as she gingerly rolled her shoulder around, and was thankful. She knew she would bear the bruise for a long time to come.

"Your pardon," she whispered, and slipped out again, with a hand on her elbow to help support her arm and keep it close to her chest.

The crush of soldiers was centered around the palace gates, but beyond, toward the East Gate, Janna thought the crowds seemed thinner. Desperate to reach the sanctuary of the tavern, she sidled some way along the palace walls, and as soon as a gap opened she forced her way to the opposite side of the street and up a narrow laneway. Once safely there, she sank down to recover her breath and check her injured shoulder more carefully.

Her probing fingers felt nothing out of the ordinary, and she breathed a quick sigh of gratitude. Just a bruise, then, and she knew what to do to soothe it, even had the herbs at hand to make up the necessary salve. Keeping to the back lanes, away from the madness in the high street, Janna found her way through the maze to the safety of the tavern. The gate leading into the yard at the back was barred tight against marauders. She stood for a moment, considering her options. Then, with a quick look around to make sure no-one was paying attention, she hitched up her tunic, knotted it out of the way, and climbed up and over the gate.

It seemed strange to be doing something she hadn't done since childhood, since going out into the forest in company with her mother, and shinning up trees to pick tender leaves, new flowering buds, or fruits, or whatever else Eadgyth needed for a concoction. But the skill was familiar, and Janna didn't hesitate as she found foot and toe holds, wincing at the pain of her bruised shoulder as she climbed.

The yard was empty of horses and patrons, but there was still some movement between tavern, kitchen, and brew house. The bustling figures stood still as they saw the intruder come over the gate. Sybil stepped forward, with Ossie behind her, as Janna dropped to the ground and hastily unknotted her tunic.

"Have you taken leave of your senses?" Sybil demanded, as soon as she recognized Janna. "Where have you been?" A hard hand closed around her arm and she was dragged into the tavern. Once inside, Sybil let Janna go and glared at her. Her white face and grim expression told Janna how frightened she was, but her words proved that, first and foremost, she was a businesswoman. "I am pleased to see you safe, but I need your help to get everything down into the cellar. Quickly! We have no time to lose." She flapped a hand in the direction of the yard.

The tavern was empty of customers, and Sybil had pressed Wat and Ossie into service. Wat led the way, hefting a heavy sack of grain. This he pushed through a small hatch at the rear of the tavern, which Janna knew led to a ladder down into a cellar where Sybil stored the imported barrels of wine. The hatch was usually well hidden behind a screen, but the screen had been pushed aside, and she watched the potboy climb down, his head getting lower and lower until it disappeared altogether, while Ossie awaited his turn.

"Hurry up!" Sybil gave her a push, and Janna raced to do as she was told. Once outside, and knowing that she was safe for the moment, she looked around and began to understand Sybil's fear. The smoky haze in the air was growing thicker as more and more properties were ignited by the flying fireballs. They were coming from both directions, for the empress's troops were now hurling missiles at the old palace in the center of the town in retaliation for the bishop trying to burn down their own stronghold. The Bell and Bush, being close to the East Gate, was beyond their target, but the fireballs were flying so wildly that Janna knew they certainly couldn't count on surviving the bombardment unscathed. A dark spire silhouetted against a reddish glow across the street told her that at least one firebrand had left its mark on St Mary's Nunnaminster. She quickly crossed herself, praying that the nuns would find a safe shelter.

"Janna!"

Coming to herself with a start as she heard Sybil's shout, Janna ran into the kitchen, seized the biggest basket she could find, and began to fill it with pots and pans, using her left hand for the task. She picked up the basket, wincing as its weight dragged on her sore shoulder. After a moment's thought, she set the basket down and found the hempen bag she took on her occasional rambles into the meadows and where she kept those herbs she hadn't already used or planted. She added the dry bunches of herbs hanging from the walls. Last, she tried the cabinet housing the precious pots of imported herbs and spices, but it was locked.

She slung the bag across her shoulders, picked up the heavy basket, and staggered out and into the tavern. Every step was a torment; it felt as if hot needles were piercing her bruises. Sybil entered just ahead of her, carrying a large pot from the brew house stuffed full with her brewing herbs and implements. Janna recognized a wooden mash stick and strainer poking out the top. She smiled to herself. In spite of fearing the worst, the taverner was making sure that, once this was over, she would be able to resume her trade.

"Don't forget to bring the spice cabinet," she reminded Sybil, as she passed the goods into the cellar, and the taverner nodded. Janna's eyes widened as she peered down and noticed the numerous barrels of wine stored there, and the heaped sacks of grain and barley malt already shifted by Ossie and Wat. She straightened and gently rubbed her shoulder, wincing at the pain.

"What's the matter with you?" Sybil asked.

"I hurt my shoulder." Janna didn't want to explain the terror of what had just happened, but Sybil was too preoccupied to show sympathy. She'd begun to unpack what had been brought in, and was busy stacking the goods out of the way. "Get down here and give me a hand with this," she snapped. "And you two – " she waved a hand at Ossie and Wat, " – fill the barrels and roll them over from the brew house. Once you've done that, bring the spice cabinet and everything else you can carry from the kitchen. Things will be safe enough down here – and so will we, God willing."

"Where's Elfric?" Janna hoped no harm had come to the affable cook.

"Gone to his family, to keep them safe if he can. May God spare us all this day." Sybil crossed herself, and Janna hastily copied her action. She still wasn't sure whether or not she liked Sybil, but she certainly respected her. Although it was in her own interest to keep the tavern open for business, Janna wished she could leave, so that she could keep a look out for Hugh and Godric, and also for Ulf, for she feared greatly for their safety. Besides, she felt guilty hiding in the cellar when, with her knowledge of herbs and healing, she could seek shelter in the cathedral with other townsfolk and help with the wounded and the dying. She tried to ease her conscience with the thought that nuns fleeing from the burning Nunnaminster, including the infirmarian and her assistant, would surely have taken refuge at the cathedral. But doubts nagged her: even if the sisters had managed to escape the burning building, would they have been able to reach the safety of the cathedral? Her sense of duty pricked at her until she could stand it no longer.

"Mistress Sybil, may I leave the tavern? I want to – "

"Leave?" the taverner interrupted. "Where could you go that is safer than here, pray?"

"I want to go to the cathedral. To – "

But Janna was given no chance to explain her intentions, for the taverner gave an impatient hiss. "Get upstairs and help me bring down the bedding, and everything else we can carry." She gave Janna a push toward the ladder. As Janna opened her mouth to argue, Sybil continued, "If you want to keep working for me, you'll do as you're told. I expect your first loyalty to be to me."

"But – "

"And be sure I'm watching you. If you leave now, don't bother to come back here. There'll be no job for you, no food or shelter either." She thrust a basket into Janna's hands, and followed her up the stairs.

Side by side, the four labored until the cellar was crammed with assorted bits of furniture, along with bags and baskets of produce and the means to cook and serve them, plus the barrels of ale and wine that would assuage their thirst if the siege continued. Eventually, a reluctant Sybil acknowledged there wasn't room for another thing. In fact, there was barely enough room for themselves. With everything stored and safe, Janna managed at last to persuade the taverner to let her go outside for a look around. In truth, Sybil seemed pleased to have one less body cramped into the stuffy confines of the cellar.

"I'll bolt the door from inside. You'll have to knock when you come back, and hope that we'll hear you ," she instructed. Janna nodded, and hooked the hempen bag over her shoulder. She'd partly unpacked it, but had kept back those healing herbs she thought might prove useful. Now she was pleased that her last ramble had been recent enough that some of the leaves were still quite fresh.

Once out in the street, Janna was relieved to note that the buildings behind the tavern seemed still untouched by fire. She hoped their good fortune would continue, for they would need the use of both kitchen and brew house to cater to their customers once the fighting was over.

All seemed quiet now, but that didn't mean it was safe, given that the town was full of soldiers with anything from murder to ravishment in mind. Keeping to the shadows, Janna turned into the high street, nervous about what she might find but knowing she had a duty to help the wounded and the dying if she could.

Chapter 5

The long gloom of twilight had finally given way to night, but smoldering fires illuminated the darkness. Appalled, Janna looked about her at the devastation wrought by the ill-aimed missiles from both palace and castle. The flimsy shops and pentices that had once lined the palace walls were gone. The walls themselves were breached in parts. Through the gaps, she could see that the palace was largely in ruins. A thick cloud of choking smoke hung like a pall over everything. Some soldiers still lay where they had fallen, either caught by the fireballs or slaughtered in battle. Now it mattered not which side they had supported, for death had favored them equally. Janna gave each an anxious inspection, but recognized no-one. The pity of their untimely deaths stayed with her as she hurried down the high street, keeping to the shadows. She wondered if either side had scored a decisive victory, or if they had to do it all again on the morrow.

A group of soldiers stumbled out of Hell, drunk and high-spirited on stolen ale. Their clothes reeked of it. Janna pressed into the ruins of a shop to hide from them, praying there was enough cover to mask her presence. Heart-stricken and afraid, she held her breath and stayed still, for she knew her fate if she should be seen. But the soldiers reeled on down the street, looking for pickings elsewhere, snatches of song marking their progress.

At last, when she judged it safe enough, Janna came out of hiding. Moving more cautiously now, she retraced her steps along the high street and turned into the lane that threaded between the Nunnaminster and the cemetery and led to the cathedral itself. The nunnery, where she'd so recently taken shelter, was now a smoking ruin. Janna caught her breath as she pondered the fate of the nuns who had lived there. Unconcerned with the battle for power between empress and king, and innocent of everything but their wish to serve God and live in peace, they too had been swept up and destroyed in this madness. Had they managed to escape with their lives?

She scurried on, starting at every sound and furtive movement in the shadows. Scavenging rats – or humans? Either seemed likely. While Janna knew she could hold her own against any four-legged creatures she might encounter, the thought of pitting her strength and wits against stray soldiers sent quivers of fear through her body. She should have brought a knife with her, along with the hempen bag. It was foolish – dangerous – to be out in the night alone in the aftermath of a battle, she knew that, but still she forced her steps onward. Her mother had taught her the art of healing, and during her time at the abbey, Sister Anne had taught her even more. She could not let that knowledge go to waste when it was possible that her presence might help to save even one life. Hugh's, perhaps. Or Godric's. And what of Ulf and Hamo? Janna quickly crossed herself. Pray God that the youngster hadn't been caught up in the turmoil this day.

Another thought came to her: Robert of Babestoche! If Hugh had taken part in the melee, so must Robert have been pressed into service. Janna smiled to herself in the darkness at the idea of her old enemy lying dead. It would give her great peace of mind to know he could not harm her ever again. And if he'd died horribly, so much the better!

She passed through the cemetery. All was dark and quiet for the dead were long gone, marked only by their gravestones. She wondered if their spirits were watching; if, like her, they mourned and regretted what had taken place. The hairs pricked on the back of her neck as the sound of soft footfalls came to her ear. Frightened, she quickened her steps, and heard the soft thudding of boots come closer. Her heart pounded as her imagination conjured up ghastly images of those dead who could not lie quiet in their graves. What if it was Robert, come back to haunt her for her vengeful thoughts? Even worse: what if it was the living, with looting and raping on their minds? She began to run, stumbling in the dark, but was stopped mid-flight as her wrist was caught and held.

"Janna?"

"Ulf!" She could hardly see him but recognized his voice. "Christ Jesu, Ulf, you scared me half to death!"

"I'm sorry, lass." He loosened his grasp. "I thought it was you, but I couldn't be sure. I didn't want to shout out, in case there were soldiers nearby, but I didn't want to lose you in the dark either. That's why I ran after you. I own I'm greatly pleased to see you safe. I went to the tavern but it's all closed up. I hoped you'd found somewhere to hide. You certainly shouldn't be wandering around out here on your own."

"I'm going to the cathedral to see if I can help tend the wounded. Will you escort me?"

"Of course. I was on my way to seek shelter there myself." Ulf hefted his pack more securely onto his shoulder.

"And you've managed to save your relics as well as yourself?" Janna was overjoyed that Ulf had escaped unscathed.

Ulf nodded. "That bishop's made a right mess of the town, and there's talk of more fighting to come." He patted his pack. "There'll be plenty of people praying to the saints to save their lives, as well as their property. I'm going to be busy tonight."

Janna grinned. It was an ill wind, she thought, knowing that Ulf was bound to profit from the terror of the townsfolk.

Utter chaos met their eyes when they ventured through the cathedral's great doors and into the nave. It looked like a marketplace, crammed with the belongings of those seeking sanctuary within. Some had also brought their livestock, the assorted smells and anxious cries of birds and animals adding to the general cacophony. People stood about in knots, commiserating with their neighbors and calling down a pox on both bishop and empress alike. Standing in front of the altar was a priest, intoning prayers in a loud voice designed to quieten all and command their attention. Instead, it had the opposite effect, for all those within raised their voices ever louder to continue their conversations, contributing further to the uproar. Children shouted and chased each other, babies howled, and mothers, wives and sweethearts wept and prayed over their dying and their dead. Janna felt a great relief as she noted several black-robed nuns, refugees from the Nunnaminster, bringing water and comfort, tying bandages, and ministering potions to ease pain and discomfort.

Recognizing the infirmarian and her assistant among them, Janna left Ulf's side and hurried to offer her services.

The infirmarian frowned as she watched the lowly serving maid approach. Her expression transformed into a look of shocked recognition. "Is it really you, Mistress Johanna?" Her disbelieving glance swept from Janna's face down to her rough homespun tunic and back again.

"Yes." Janna didn't want to waste time on unnecessary explanations. "I offered you my help once before, and I hope you'll accept it now," she said, going on to remind the nun of her tuition under Sister Anne, the infirmarian at Wiltune Abbey.

Sister Benedicta nodded, her relief evident as she steered Janna toward a group of soldiers and townsfolk lying close to the huge arches at one side of the nave. "I've managed to rescue some salves and bandages from our abbey," she told Janna. "But everything else of value is gone – our precious vestments, our relics, our books – all burned." Her face contracted with pain and fury. "Our bishop and the empress have much to answer for regarding their deeds this day."

"But you all escaped with your lives?"

"Yes, in the mercy of Christ." The infirmarian indicated the trestle table on which stood all the supplies Janna would need to treat the wounded. "Brother Edgar has also given us medicaments from St Swithun's Priory and is here, helping us."

"I've brought you some healing herbs." Janna handed them to the nun, confident that either Sister Benedicta or Brother Edgar would know their use, and would have more chance to brew potions and mix salves than Janna herself.

The infirmarian opened the bag, looked inside, and took a suspicious sniff.

"Soapwort and sanicle for cleansing the wounds, and selfheal, comfrey and marsh mallow to soothe and heal. There's burdock leaves for burns, and better still if you can combine them with egg whites. There's wood lettuce for pain. And if you have something ready-made for a bruise, sister – " Janna touched her sore shoulder, " – I'd be much obliged."

"There's a salve of comfrey root and bishop's weed, you may use some of that." The nun pointed to it. As Janna unscrewed the pot and dipped a finger into the cool unguent, the nun plunged her hand into the bag and brought up a fistful of the contents to see their worth for herself. Her expression cleared. "Well done," she said. "I'll give them to Brother Edgar. He'll make them up as necessary." She paused, watching Janna's awkward attempts to massage the salve into her shoulder.

"Give that to me." She took the pot and drew Janna further into the shadows. "Show me," she commanded, and breathed in a soft whistle as Janna pulled the tunic off her shoulder. "'Tis the color of a ripened plum!"

"I got kicked by a horse," Janna explained, wincing as the infirmarian's fingers touched her tender flesh.

"Lucky it wasn't your head," Sister Benedicta commented, as she smoothed on the ointment with gentle fingers. "That's all I can do for you at the moment," she added, "but this should ease the pain and fade the bruising."

"Thank you. My shoulder feels better already."

The nun nodded and bustled off in search of Brother Edgar, the bag of herbs hooked over her arm. Left to her own devices at last, Janna immediately began a search among the injured and dying. Taking care to shade her face within the folds of her veil in case she should encounter Robert of Babestoche, she walked slowly along the line of bodies ranged down the nave. She felt sick with apprehension. But there was no sign of Hugh or Godric, or even Hamo. Or Robert, or Mus either. She scanned the long line of petitioners waiting for admittance to the sanctuary behind the altar and the monk's quire, but recognized no-one. Ulf had told her all about the shrine of St Swithun when he'd shown her the badge he'd purchased on his first and only visit there.

"It's right good business for the cathedral, all those pilgrims," he'd said cheerfully. "We all had to come through the same door to pay our dues and buy our badges and that. Then we went into a small chapel on the side to give thanks to Saint Christopher – 'cause he's the patron saint of travelers, you see. After that we went on to the Chapel of the Holy Sepulchre. That's where the saint's relics rest in the feretory. It's beautiful, Janna! Like a cave hollowed out of stone, with gold and silver on the altar, all a-sparkle in the candlelight. And behind it, painted on the walls, is the story of Christ's Passion. It was worth the admission fee, for certain! All that color and splendor – I never seen anything like it in my life before. You must go and see it for yourself, lass."

Janna had promised that she would. She no longer had the coins to pay for a visit, but she hoped the petitioners would find comfort from their communion with the saint. The queue was growing longer even as she watched. People were desperate for St Swithun's intervention in the danger in which they now found themselves.

She began a closer inspection of the wounded soldiers, targeting those most in need of attention. She felt a great relief that Robert of Gloucestre, Bishop Henry and even the empress herself were not among the crowd. Was it God's will that they'd been spared, or did it just mean there'd be another siege on the morrow, and another after that, until such time as a decisive victory was won?

With her second inspection completed, she went off to find a bowl, clean water, a handful of rags and a sharp knife. She began to remove the hauberk of an injured knight. The man groaned, half fainting with the pain, but he was conscious enough to know that she was trying to help him and did his best to cooperate with her whispered instructions.

Next, she cut away the bloody fabric of his padded tunic, and then the torn linen shirt he wore underneath, gently pulling the material away from where it had stuck to his skin, and taking care that no cloth or metal was left to poison his blood. The soldier groaned again. His face was yellow and beaded with sweat. From his badge, Janna could tell he was one of the bishop's men. She pushed the thought to the back of her mind, knowing that she would treat him just as well as she would any of the empress's supporters.

She drew in her breath as the wound was exposed. A savage thrust from an enemy sword had pierced the soldier's armor and found his side – but not his heart, God be thanked, or he would have been dead by now. Nevertheless, the damage was terrible and he was in great pain. Janna soaked a cloth in the basin of water and soapwort leaves, and did her best to cleanse the gash. It might be possible, she thought, to stitch the sides of the wound together for it was long and deep. But she had little experience with such a thing. Did Sister Benedicta? She inspected the wound more carefully. It was deep, but the cut itself was not wide. If tightly bound, the flesh should knit together – if the soldier survived the injury.

With a sigh, she went in search of a healing salve of woundwort, and selected also a long linen strip from a bundle that had been torn from a sheet. As she administered the salve, the soldier lay senseless for the pain had become too great for him to bear. Janna was glad he'd found relief from his suffering, but hoped that this was not a sleep that would lead him down into death. Once her task was completed, she went in search of Sister Benedicta, thoroughly unnerved by the soldier's distress.

"Do you have any syrup of poppies?" she asked, knowing a concoction brewed from the white flowers of the poppy was the best of all remedies to dull pain.

Sister Benedicta nodded. "Only a little," she said, producing a small flask. "Use it sparingly, and only on those who most need it. For the others..." She showed Janna a large flask of dark liquid. "A decoction of willow bark," she explained. "It eases pain."

"Thank you." Janna wished she'd thought to ask for it earlier. She picked up the two flasks and hurried back to look after the next wounded soldier. In the past, with her mother and at the abbey, she had learned to treat diseases, sprains and broken limbs, but never before had she attempted to treat injuries as terrible as these. It worried her that her knowledge was so inadequate. Despite her best intentions, she knew that some of these men would die in her care, and she muttered the prayers and charms she had learned from her mother as she cleaned them up and tried to make them comfortable.

A few soldiers tried to make light of their terrible injuries. Silently saluting their courage, Janna soothed them and gave them sips of the poppy syrup. Others, not so badly wounded and seeking distraction, teased her with flirtatious banter. Janna smiled and replied in kind, glad to do whatever she could to cheer them up. Overhearing one of these exchanges, Sister Benedicta looked scandalized and Janna wondered if she would be forbidden any further contact with the wounded men. But the nun reined in her disapproval and, instead, complimented her on her labors.

"I want you to watch something," she said, and drew Janna over to a man who looked decidedly uncomfortable yet bore no obvious sign of any wound.

"Fell off his horse," Sister Benedicta explained.

The soldier reared up in indignation. "I took a buffeting and was unhorsed," he said, furious that his misfortune should be so misconstrued. Sister Benedicta ignored his protest. She produced a round ball covered in wool and lodged it under the man's armpit. Then she took hold of his shoulder, which seemed to hang loose and disjointed.

"Hold him tight and watch carefully," she instructed. Without allowing the knight time to react, she gave his shoulder a quick wrench, using all her strength to force it back into place. He gave a howl of pain, quickly muffled as embarrassment set in.

"You'll see a lot of dislocated shoulders," the infirmarian told Janna, ignoring the soldier's discomfort. "Also broken limbs." She turned to the knight. "That's the penalty for falling off a horse."

"I didn't fall – "

But Sister Benedicta had already moved on. Janna gave the man a sympathetic grin and followed after her, interested to find out what else the infirmarian might be able to teach her.

"And here's a broken leg," Sister Benedicta said, ignoring the man's groans as she peeled away his leather greave to examine the source of his pain. "Do you have any experience with this?"

"I helped Sister Anne set a broken arm at Wiltune." Janna's lips twitched as she recalled the young girl who had daringly climbed a tree, only to fall out of it the moment she was discovered and ordered to come down.

"Same thing." Sister Benedicta, it seemed, wasn't one to waste words. She bustled over to their small supply of medicaments and bandages, and Janna noticed a bundle of stout sticks of varying lengths. "You can help me by holding one of these and keeping his leg straight," she instructed, as she selected two of the longer sticks and a handful of bandages before going back to the wounded soldier.

His face was gray; sweat stood out on his forehead in great globules. With infinite care, the infirmarian straightened his leg to lie beside one of the sticks. "Hold them steady together," she said, and began to bind the stick to the soldier's leg with the bandages. The soldier uttered little mewing sounds of distress as Sister Benedicta worked. Janna sought to distract him by asking his name and questioning him about his home. But he was in too much pain to answer, so she sought to find some other topic that might hold his interest and remembered what else Ulf had told her about the patron saint of Winchestre.

"Being a stranger to these parts, you won't know about St Swithun," she said brightly. "He's our patron saint, and his bones are right here in the cathedral. You can pray to St Swithun while you're here, for he's known to answer prayers and even work miracles. You can also visit his shrine if you like, when you are able to walk once more."

Finding no response to this invitation, Janna hurried on. "The bishop's first miracle happened on the day he met an old woman in great distress. She'd dropped a basketful of eggs and every one of them was smashed. No-one's sure if the bishop actually bumped into her, causing her to drop the eggs, or if the eggs were maliciously smashed by the workmen he'd set to building a new bridge to the east of the town. But by the saint's blessing, the eggs were miraculously restored whole to the old woman!"

Still no response. The soldier's face was screwed up tight with pain; his breathing came in little hiccupping sobs. It was hard to keep cheerful in the face of his evident distress, but Janna did her best. "There's a rhyme about the bishop that's said in these parts," she told him.

> *St Swithun's day, if thou dost rain*
> *For forty days it must remain.*
> *St Swithun's day, if thou be fair*
> *For forty days 'twill rain na mair.*

No reaction. Janna wasn't sure if the soldier was even listening to her. "Do you know why they say that?" she asked, continuing before the soldier could answer: "It seems that the saint told everyone that he wanted a poor and humble burial outdoors, so that passersby might tread on his grave and the sweet rain of heaven would fall on his final resting place. That's what he said, and that's what they did. But when the minster was built, it was decided to move his body inside the cathedral and bury it along with the old English kings and other dignitaries. But there was such a thunderstorm on the day he was reburied, and the rain fell in such torrents, that people believe it was his curse on those who had ignored his instructions and disturbed his rest."

"Johanna!" There was a stern note of warning in Sister Benedicta's voice.

"But he's still here, and very popular with the sick and with pilgrims," Janna concluded in a hurry. "There have been many more miracles since he was placed here in the new cathedral. Perhaps you could pray to him too?"

The soldier stirred, and looked at Janna with a painful smile that was more of a grimace. Janna smiled in return and patted his hand. "With God's grace, your leg will come out good as new if only you have patience," she told him.

"Don't walk on that leg for two full moons," Sister Benedicta added more practically. She handed to him the other stick she had selected. "Use this to support your weight." And she left even as the soldier tried to thank her.

If that was hard, the next lesson was even more difficult as Sister Benedicta paused beside a soldier who sat half-propped against a stone pillar, an arrow embedded in his back. She tut-tutted to herself, then turned to Janna. "I fear it will do more harm than good, but we can't leave him like this," she said, and crouched down beside the wounded man. Janna held her breath as the nun gently tried to withdraw the barbed arrow, stopping almost immediately as the man screamed in pain.

"There's nothing else for it." Sister Benedicta's voice was grim with foreboding. She held the flask of poppy syrup to his lips, encouraging him to take a large swallow, and then another. It was this liberal use of the precious syrup that told Janna just how bad the man's injury was and how much worse its treatment would be. The infirmarian seized a knife and cut off the arrow's flight, before slicing away the man's gambeson and shirt to expose the full extent of the wound. She took a deep breath, grasped hold of the shaft and, using both hands and with all the force she could muster, shoved it right through the soldier's body. His cry was cut off as he slumped into unconsciousness. With a quick, businesslike gesture, the nun cut off the sharp arrowhead and pulled the long shaft back and out. She bowed her head then and quickly crossed herself. "*Dei gratia*," she whispered, while Janna swallowed hard, her mouth suddenly dry.

"Well done," the nun said briskly as she rose to her feet. "I was afraid you might also take leave of your senses when faced with that." She gestured to the still figure now slumped on the floor. "Patch him up as best you may. I've watched how you've been treating the injured and I know you can do it as well as any one of us here."

"I'll do my best." Janna bowed her head, feeling her face flush at the unexpected compliment.

"I suspect there's too much damage done for him to survive. It's in God's hands now, but do what you can for him." Sister Benedicta bustled off, leaving Janna struggling to find a reply.

She squatted down beside the unconscious figure. At least she couldn't hurt him any more than he'd already been hurt, she thought, as she began to bathe and dress his terrible wound.

*

The night wore on, exhausting and seemingly endless, punctuated by the groans, prayers, and screams of the wounded and the dying. The air was heavy with the stench of vomit and blood, urine and the voided bowels of the dead, mixed with the odor of sweating, unwashed bodies and the ordure of animals. But bedlam gradually turned to order as merchants, townsfolk, lords and villeins were sorted into those in need of treatment as opposed to those merely seeking sanctuary. United by war and leveled by the circumstances in which they found themselves, some engaged in a joking camaraderie while others managed to fall asleep.

Janna gave what comfort she could, but medicaments were scarce and some wounds so terrible as to be beyond the help even of prayers. She and the nuns labored without pause to make the soldiers and those civilians caught in the melee as comfortable as possible, but several died, including the soldier with the arrow wound. He hadn't regained his senses, and Janna was grateful for that, for the wound had been as severe as the infirmarian had predicted. Nevertheless, she regretted that she hadn't had the skill to save him after all, and couldn't help wondering if someone else might have had more success.

The first light of early dawn was slanting through the high windows as Janna at last bade farewell to Sister Benedicta.

"You've done well tonight and I am grateful for your help," the infirmarian said, cocking her head sideways as she noticed Janna's downcast face. "We can't save them all," she said gently. "Their lives – and their deaths – are in God's hands."

And in ours, Janna thought.

"Why did you leave us so abruptly?" Sister Benedicta asked, prepared to show friendship and kindness now that Janna had proved her worth.

"My purse was stolen. I lost the means to pay for my bed and board at the abbey."

"And we can't offer you shelter at all now, though your skill is most welcome here if you can stay a while longer with us," the nun said tiredly.

Janna hesitated. "I'm sorry, I can't. I've found employment at a tavern nearby, and I'll lose my position if I don't go back there."

Sister Benedicta looked scandalized.

"It's honest work! And I need employment." Janna was sorry to refuse the nun's request. In spite of feeling upset over the soldier's death, she took pride in her knowledge and ability to heal and bring comfort to those in need. But she knew the nuns would not be able to stay at the cathedral once the siege was over. They would have to find other convents in which to serve, and although they might even suggest she go with them, she couldn't do that. She had to remain in Winchestre to wait for her father, and for that, she needed to keep working at the tavern.

The nun gave a rueful smile. "God bless you for coming to our aid. You have my prayers for your soul," she said, clearly unhappy with Janna's choice.

Janna was about to defend herself further, but realized it was probably a waste of breath. "I'll come back and help you when I can," she promised instead.

The nun nodded in gratitude, and sketched the sign of the cross over her head. "Go with God," she said, and turned back to start the weary round once more.

Janna looked for Ulf. She found him, bag open and in earnest conversation with a prosperous merchant and his family. She had no doubt they were in the throes of buying protection from him, so she waved farewell once she'd caught Ulf's eye, and stepped out into the gray dawn.

The air hung heavy, thick with choking smoke from the fires around the town. Janna tried to smother a fit of coughing, not wanting to make any sound in case someone was lurking about. Casting fearful glances over her shoulder and jumping at shadows, she scuttled swiftly down the high street and turned toward the tavern. She found the door still barred against her; she gave a gentle knock, hoping someone would hear.

There was no response. Janna wondered if they were all still down in the cellar. It seemed she had no choice but to go around into the lane and climb over the gate into the yard once more. Her shoulder gave a painful throb at the very thought of it. She knocked again, louder this time, hoping that she would be heard by those inside, but not by any marauders with looting on their mind. She glanced around nervously while she waited, but all was quiet. Finally, she slipped off her boot and gave the door several almighty thumps and called Sybil's name.

It seemed like an age before she heard a cautious response: "Who is it?" Janna recognized Sybil's voice.

"Me. Janna," she replied, and listened to a metallic grating as the bolt slid back. As soon as the door was opened, she slipped inside and looked about. Now that there was some light to see by, she noticed that the tavern had been stripped of almost everything it was possible to remove. "Have the looters been in here?" she asked anxiously.

Sybil jerked her head in the direction of the cellar. "There's nothing left worth stealing," she said, with a grim smile. "What news from outside?"

"Devastation. Much of the town has been burned. The old palace has been badly damaged, but the castle still stands." Janna wondered whether to pass on the rest of the information she'd gleaned from listening to conversations between the soldiers in the cathedral, and decided it was in Sybil's interests to know the worst. "They say the empress is safe within the castle, but that her uncle, King David of Scotland, and the Earl of Gloucestre command her troops from inside the town's walls, and that fighting will continue until one or other side gains victory."

Sybil gave a loud snort of disgust. "God save us from ambitious men," she spat. "They'll be the ruin of us all." Janna wondered if she included her ex-lover among them, but didn't like to ask. Nor did she have the chance, for Sybil continued, "It seems quiet enough outside. Does the fighting continue even now?"

"No." Janna shook her head. "All's peaceful for the moment."

"Then you're back just in time to help me set things to rights before we open up for customers."

"You're opening the tavern today, mistress?" Remembering their terror, and their labors to get everything out of harm's way, Janna was incredulous that Sybil expected them to go through it all again.

Sybil shrugged. "Just to serve ale, for I have no cook. I suspect Elfric will stay to protect his wife and child through this unrest. But the brew house and the kitchen are untouched, and there's wine and ale for any who seek it. Men are known to want to drown their sorrows in troubled times. Especially soldiers."

Sybil's eyes narrowed in calculation. "This is my chance to entice patrons away from my rivals at the West Gate, and also from the alehouses nearby. I aim to make my tavern the most popular in Winchestre! And you and Wat and Ossie will have to help me. But..." She paused, and her brow furrowed into a frown. "I can't risk looters coming in and causing havoc here. What's the chance of that, do you think?"

"I saw no sign of anything like that on my way back here. Most people seem to be taking refuge in the churches or the cathedral.

But they may venture out if it stays quiet." Janna thought about the grain they'd saved, and all the food. "I don't know if any cookshops will open today, but we can probably find something for our customers to eat if they're hungry as well as thirsty."

"And I suppose I can call on some of my regular patrons to help keep law and order in here if Ossie can't cope." The taverner was sounding more enthusiastic by the moment. "Wat!" she bawled, giving Janna no chance to reply. "Get your lazy bones up here. You too, Ossie. There's work to do."

Janna groaned inwardly. After her hard and wakeful night, all she wanted was to curl up on her pallet and go to sleep. But it seemed that Sybil had other plans and this day would be as long and hard as the night she'd just spent. Cursing silently, Janna plodded wearily to the cellar. Sybil, she noted with amusement, had managed to save the green bush from the pole outside, and this was Janna's first task: to fix it to the pole once more so that everyone would know the Bell and Bush was open for business. She ventured a little further to glance up and down the high street. She couldn't see if any of the alehouses were open, but there were a few people wandering about. Hopefully, they were thirsty.

"Janna! Give me a hand setting out stools and tables!" Sybil's irate shout sent her scurrying inside once more. At the forefront of her mind was the thought of those she knew and loved – and those whom she hated and feared. There was no way of knowing where any of them were or if harm had befallen them. But if they were safe, there was a strong possibility they might choose to visit the Bell and Bush, especially if this was the only tavern open. And if they did so, what could she do about it other than stay alert and on guard against possible danger?

Chapter 6

The next few days passed by in a haze of exhaustion for Janna. She went to help tend the wounded at the cathedral when she could get away, for skirmishes continued intermittently and there were always new patients to take the place of those who died. But Sybil kept her busy for much of the time. As well as serving ale and wine to those customers who braved the streets to visit the tavern, Janna also baked griddle cakes to top with a slice of ham or bacon, the easiest fare to serve until Elfric came out of hiding and returned. All the while she kept an anxious lookout for her friends, ever hopeful that they had survived and had not been wounded. And she was always conscious that, at any moment, her arch-enemy, Robert of Babestoche, and his murderous henchman, Mus, might also walk in. The knowledge kept her tense and watchful.

There was no joy in the gatherings at the tavern. Those travelers who had come for the annual fair had now fled the town, for it was clear there would be no fair this year. Those who were left, townsfolk and merchants alike, walked around in a daze of misery, trying to come to terms with the fact that the goods and produce they'd accumulated for sale had either been destroyed in the fires or were too damaged to sell. Their livelihood had gone, and sometimes their homes and all their supplies as well. Some who could still afford it rented pallets from Sybil and took shelter above the tavern. When they came down for ale and something to eat, they mostly sat in sullen silence and misery. If they spoke, it was to complain of the continuing unrest and the scarcity of everything from food to those goods essential to daily living. It was reported that the dole was still available from the hospital at St Cross for those in need, and that some food was also being handed out at the castle. But supplies were dwindling and nothing was coming in to replace them.

Often there were strangers present in the tavern. While Janna thought some might be merchants or chapmen trapped by circumstances, she suspected that most of them were soldiers. Although they took care not to identify themselves as such, or indicate whose side they were on, still they were the target of evil looks and muttered curses – and sometimes even raised fists. On those occasions, Ossie stood by to eject the troublemakers, offering free ale to those who helped him keep the peace. Everyone wished heartily that the empress and the bishop and all their troops would leave Winchestre and take their argument elsewhere.

But the siege continued, made more urgent by the news that Stephen's queen had mustered an army in support of the bishop. Under the command of William of Ypres, the soldiers had now encircled the town to prevent any aid or supplies from getting through to the empress and her army, or the townsfolk. The castle had suffered some damage, but the old palace in the center was so badly destroyed that the bishop had removed his troops to his palace at Wolvesey, in the south-east quarter of the town. The townsfolk took some small comfort from the fact that, although hostilities between the two sides continued, no encounter proved as ferocious and devastating as that first terrible firestorm.

An alarming story began to make the rounds. Janna listened as it was repeated in the tavern one afternoon by a traveler who claimed to have seen, with his own eyes, what had actually happened.

"They're running out of water and food in the castle, that's what the soldiers told me," the traveler said breathlessly. "I met a large party of the empress's supporters on the old Roman road, sent by the Earl of Gloucester to Wherwell to establish a safe base in the west from which to bring in supplies. I caught up with 'em and talked to 'em. And I thank the good Lord that I did not try to keep up with 'em because, when they got to Wherwell, they found the queen's troops waiting for 'em." The traveler passed a shaking hand through his hair, still sweating at the memory of his close escape.

"I arrived later, but hid myself when I saw the terrible slaughter going on. There was no mercy shown by the Flemish mercenaries or that devil's spawn, William of Ypres, not even when the empress's party sought sanctuary in the abbey. The queen's troops set fire to the abbey, and then massacred the empress's soldiers as soon as they surrendered. I know not what happened to the good sisters of Wherwell Abbey, for the abbey was burned to the ground and the town with it. Everywhere has been sacked. Rather than risk my life going through their lines, I decided to come back to Winchestre and try to leave by another route."

"That won't be easy," a customer chimed in. "The queen's troops already control all the roads to Winchestre from London and the east, and now the west and north are barred if what you're saying is true. And the Londoners themselves are also on the march, I hear. We're surrounded by the enemy."

The traveler nodded wearily. "I overheard one of the queen's soldiers say they plan to starve the empress and her followers into submission, and now I know how they mean to do it. But we're trapped here too – unless we can find a way to slip their noose!" He gave a loud sniff to signify his disgust with the situation.

There was a collective drawing in of breath as his audience absorbed what they'd been told. They were forced now to face the unthinkable: that the empress might lose Winchestre, and might even be taken captive herself. And if that happened, they would be left at the mercy of the queen's mercenaries and the Londoners. A shudder ran through the room. Everyone knew now what that meant.

To add to the prevailing gloom, reports had been circulating of an outbreak of disease in the town. Some said it was the sweating sickness, and others the Great Death, all of which caused panic among the customers of the Bell and Bush. Janna had wondered if it might be enough to persuade Sybil to close the tavern, but the taverner was reveling in being one of the few establishments still open for business, and was keen to make as much profit out of the troubles as possible. "For the tavern might burn down tomorrow," she told Janna, "and then where would I be?"

And where would I be, Janna wondered in turn. But she didn't voice her concerns. After hearing the traveler's tale, she was beginning to question if it might not be safer to try to find a way out of Winchestre, and flee the troubles, at least for the time being. But if the rumors were true, there was nowhere to go other than into the arms of Stephen's queen and her troops.

She heard the question endlessly debated in the tavern. Those who had relatives with whom they could shelter had already fled; others who now tried to leave returned with terrifying confirmation that the roads leading out of Winchestre were blocked, and no quarter would be given to the empress's supporters if caught.

Meanwhile, the siege of Winchestre continued. In a concerted effort to knock out the empress's troops when they tried coming through the North Gate, the bishop rained fireballs over the northern part of the town, burning Hyde Abbey to the ground in his zeal. More refugees flocked to the churches, but most came to the cathedral for shelter, for many of the churches had fallen in the path of the bishop's firebrands. The number of dead and wounded grew apace. Janna went to the cathedral when she could, every time dreading who she might find there. As the days went by, and there was no sign of Hugh, Godric or Hamo, she began to hope that perhaps they had fled before the siege began. She couldn't bear to think of them in danger.

But there was little opportunity to brood, for most of her time and energy went into her work at the tavern. Every time the alarm went out, Sybil set them all to carrying everything movable from the tavern down to the cellar for safekeeping. On one occasion, their luck ran out. The kitchen caught alight, and the blaze threatened to spread to the brew house and to the tavern itself. At once Sybil promised free ale to any who stayed to take part in a bucket brigade, and a number of willing helpers lined up to carry water from the canal that ran nearby. They didn't manage to save the kitchen, but they did prevent the fire from spreading. And as a result of the celebrations that night, the tavern ran out of ale.

Because the brew house had escaped the blaze, thereafter it also served as a kitchen, with Sybil and Elfric getting in each other's way as they went about their various tasks, becoming more and more short-tempered with each other in the process. This day Elfric had gone out to scrounge whatever he could find in the way of food, using coins from Sybil's horde to sweeten the trade, for there was a great shortage of just about everything, including barley malt for brewing. Meanwhile, there was a new wort ready and waiting to be flavored.

Knowing how short-handed Sybil was, and thinking to make the most of the situation, Janna found some of the herbs she'd collected and set aside when first she'd thought of experimenting with the brew. She made a selection and put them in a bag before offering to help the taverner. She wasn't ready to commit to her idea just yet, but this was the first step along her path.

The taverner accepted her offer with relief, giving the liquid a final stir before wiping her sweating face on the corner of her apron. "This one's been strained and I've added the gruit. You need to keep it boiling for a little while longer." She handed the mash stick to Janna and pointed a finger at a second large container. "This one's ready to be strained into barrels for serving."

Once the taverner had left the brew house, Janna quickly threw a handful of wild hops into the steaming wort. She looked at the size of the container and then added several more handfuls, hoping she wasn't overdoing it. She'd never prepared ale in such quantities before. She felt a little shaky as she realized she'd set her path and was committed to it. She took an exploratory sniff. As she'd suspected, the taverner had stuck to her same tried-and-true recipe: rosemary, alecost and sweet gale. It was a good base for what she had in mind. Janna smiled as she selected several other herbs to throw into the mix, then looked about for the crock of honey among the supplies that had been rescued. The pot stood in pride of place, and she scooped up a large dollop and added it to the hot liquid. It would make the ale more potent, while the taste would off-set the bitterness of the hops.

Next, she turned her attention to the ale that Sybil had said was ready for straining and serving. Janna knew that what she put in now might make no difference at all, but it was worth a try. She carefully added a mix of herbs and ash keys, and gave the liquid a vigorous stir. It was too late to add hops, but the ash keys would help to preserve the ale, while the sage would give the brew the distinctive taste that Janna remembered from her childhood.

After leaving the liquid some minutes to settle, she tasted it again. More sage, she thought, and added an extra portion, followed by a generous spoonful of honey. She laid the mash stick aside and found the stick she'd cut from the ash tree while out in the water meadows, which she'd hidden in the brew house hoping for just this sort of opportunity.

Eadgyth had always insisted that their brew be stirred with wood from an ash tree. "*The ancients called ash the tree of knowledge and wisdom,*" she'd said. "*The bark of the ash flavors the ale in a special way. But ash trees also have great healing powers – magical powers, Janna. When we drink ale stirred with a wand of ash, not only are we refreshing our spirits and our souls, we are also giving ourselves protection, health and prosperity.*"

Eadgyth's words rang clear in Janna's mind as she stirred, tasted, added a little more sage, and tasted once more. Thinking about it now, she could understand the value that her mother had placed on all these properties, although given the hard life they'd had, it seemed they'd needed more than sage and an ash stick to help them.

Finally satisfied with her new brew, she left it to settle a while longer. Let Sybil say what she would, the patrons of the tavern would have a stronger, sweeter brew to taste this night, a taste that would remind Janna of her home and her childhood.

She was still in the brew house and had just finished straining the ale into barrels, when Ulf came to find her. "The taverner told me you were out here," he said. Janna looked at his grave face, and instantly feared the worst.

"My – my father has come? He's been hurt in the fighting?" she stammered.

"No."

"He's dead?" Janna felt suddenly giddy. She stretched out blindly and Ulf caught her hand.

"No, Janna! Nowt so bad as that. But bad enough. The bishop's fireballs have razed much of the northern side of the town. The street of the Jews has been all but destroyed, along with many properties in adjoining streets." There was great compassion in Ulf's eyes as he continued. "Your father's property is one of them. It's gone, Janna. It's burned to the ground. There's nowt left."

Janna felt faint. She clutched Ulf, needing his support.

"The steward has fled, and everyone else living there with him," Ulf continued. "I asked around, but no-one has seen them since Winchestre began to burn."

"Are they – could they have died in the fire?"

"I don't think so. I looked around the ruins in case there was anything to salvage, anything to tell the whereabouts of your father in Normandy. But there was nowt like that at all. No bodies neither. I also asked at the chapel of St Michael nearby. It's a miracle it still stands. Some of the townsfolk have taken refuge there – but not Warin, or the gatekeeper. Nor even Roger."

"So they ran at the first sign of trouble," Janna said bitterly.

"It looks that way. One of the merchants said he didn't think anyone was in residence even afore the troubles started."

Janna was silenced, both by the cowardice of her father's steward and also by the inescapable fact that her final – her only – link to her father had gone. Yes, he was somewhere in Normandy. But where? And how was she ever going to find him now?

"I'm right sorry, lass."

Ulf's voice broke through Janna's misery. She found she was still clutching him, and reluctantly let him go. This was her problem, not Ulf's.

She shook her head, trying to clear her thoughts and see a way through this new calamity. "Whatever shall I do now?"

"You could go to Normandy, seek him out there," Ulf ventured.

"Where? How?" Janna's voice was flat with despair.

"You're right, lass. It's probably best if you stay here and wait. I suspect he never got the message you sent him. Either that, or this blessed trouble between his kin has kept him away. But once he hears what's happened to his property, someone must surely come to oversee the new building and manage your father's affairs. You just need to keep looking out for him."

"Do you think my father might come himself?" Sudden hope brought new light to Janna's eyes.

"Aye, 'tis possible. Why not stay here a while longer and see what happens? Besides, it's more than your life's worth to try to leave Winchestre right now. I'll stay on a bit myself. There's a lot of people who are in need of comfort and are willing to pay for it." Ulf patted his bag. It seemed to Janna that it was less bulky than usual, bearing out the truth of his words. "But I'll have to move on eventually. There'll be nowt left for me here once the troubles die down. I might go on to London. I need to find somewhere safe and with enough trade to keep me going through the winter."

He looked so apologetic, Janna hastened to reassure him. "I understand. Don't worry about me, Ulf. I'll manage on my own. I'll do as you say. I'll wait until spring next year, and if no-one's arrived by then I'll go to Normandy myself." Her spirits quailed at the thought, but she kept a bright smile on her face. She didn't want Ulf to feel sorry for her.

"At least you have employment and shelter here." In spite of his comforting words, Ulf didn't look too happy about it.

"And I've been promoted! See, today I'm in charge of the brew!" Sudden doubt assailed Janna. "Wait a moment. Taste this, and tell me what you think." She poured some of the new ale into two mugs and held one out to Ulf. "It's my own special recipe. I just hope it meets with Sybil's approval – not to mention the ale taster!"

"I shouldn't worry about him," Ulf advised, as he took the mug from her. "The people of Winchestre have more important things on their minds than waiting for an official to say whether they can drink a new brew or not." He sniffed the brew and then took a cautious sip.

Janna took a mouthful from her own mug, and was instantly transported into the past as she savored the contents. She swallowed the ale in a long series of gulps. "What do you think? Do you like it?" she asked anxiously.

Ulf sipped again. "Hmm," he said doubtfully. "I'm not too sure about this one, lass."

"Ulf!" Janna felt devastated, until she noticed the bright twinkle in his eyes. He grinned at her and drained his mug.

"Delicious!" He smacked his lips. "This is a right good brew. I've never tasted anything quite like it." He tipped up the mug to lick the last few drops. "It's a bit sweeter than usual, and there's summat in it I can't quite tell. What is it?"

"It's..." Janna began, but decided instead to keep the recipe a secret. If Sybil liked the new brew, she would also want to know what Janna had put in it. But if Janna kept the ingredients to herself – well, she would be guaranteed employment for as long as Sybil wanted her brew. "It's something that will bring you long life and prosperity," she said.

"I like the sound of that – especially the last bit!"

"Me, too!" Janna picked up an empty pitcher, ready to fill it to the brim. Now that Ulf had given his seal of approval she would try her new brew on the customers.

"I pay you to work for me, not entertain your friends." Sybil's voice signaled her coming, and Ulf shot Janna a guilty glance. She grimaced in return, remembering how the taverner had scolded her predecessor. But she was no Ebba, and the taverner knew it. Janna felt secure enough to defend herself.

"Ulf had some urgent news to give me." A wave of misery washed over her as she faced again the full extent of her loss. But she struggled on. "He's not interrupting my work. See, I've already strained the wort. It's ready." She quickly removed the bung from the barrel and filled the jug.

"Hmm." The taverner wasn't prepared to back down quite so easily. "You'd better get back to the tavern and start serving it, then." She sniffed the air and shot Janna a suspicious glance. "You haven't been tampering with the ale, have you?" As Janna wondered how to reply, Sybil continued, "I'll finish off here. You get outside and tie the bush to the pole. And take your friend with you." She flapped her hands at them like a farmwife harrying hens.

Relieved to be pardoned, Janna beckoned Ulf to follow and quickly led the way to the tavern. Once over the threshold, she stopped to let her eyes adjust to the dim light within. Automatically she looked about at all the customers, wondering who was first in line, who the most impatient, and who the most important. Who should she serve first? With a sudden gasp, she lowered her head and skipped behind Ulf.

"Hide me," she whispered, as she tried to sidle backward through the door.

"What's the matter?" he asked, so bewildered by her actions that he stepped aside, leaving her once more exposed to the eyes of all the patrons. It was too late; Janna had seen the sudden flash of recognition in Godric's eyes even as she'd tried to duck out of his sight.

"I have to go!" She thrust the jug into Ulf's hands and took to her heels. She was almost at the brew house when she heard Godric's voice.

"Janna?"

For a moment she thought to dash into the brew house and hide, but common sense told her that he had followed her outside and would continue to follow her until he'd seen for himself whether or not he was mistaken. Reluctantly, she swung around to face him.

"Janna," he said again, more softly this time. His hand trembled as he reached for her arm, as if to make sure she was real. His touch ran through Janna's body with the force of a lightning bolt. Dazed, she stared up at him, slowly becoming aware of the changes that time had wrought. Godric was a man now, tall and with shoulders broad and strong enough to bear whatever troubles might come his way. Janna had the impression that hardship and disappointment had molded the angular planes of his face, even though his expression showed only his delight in seeing her again. His clothes reflected his new status while emphasizing his manly physique: the knee-length wool tunic stretched wide across his shoulders and was belted around his narrow waist. It was worn with long breeches and fine leather shoes, as befitted the companion of a lord.

Conscious of her own lowly status, Janna freed herself from his grasp and backed away, fighting an overwhelming sense of loss as she did so.

"What are you doing here? Christ Jesu, Janna, what has brought you to this?" Godric's voice carried no condemnation, only concern as he surveyed her homespun tunic and stained apron, so different from the sober garb of a lay sister. "I'd heard you'd left the abbey, but hoped you'd found safety and happiness elsewhere."

Although numb with despair, Janna tried to summon up a smile. She would have given anything to avoid this meeting, yet it seemed that, after all she had endured, there was still a final humiliation she must undergo.

"Janna?" Ulf asked anxiously.

"It's all right, Ulf. I know this man. He's my…friend."

Ulf nodded. Godric watched until the relic seller had disappeared through the door of the tavern before turning back to Janna. "I thought I'd never see you again! I can't believe my good fortune in finding you here!" He reached out to caress her cheek. At his gentle touch, a host of memories tumbled through Janna's mind. Their meeting in the forest when he'd rescued her from a wild boar. His help and support during their desperate search for a missing boy, a search that had almost ended with their own deaths. Now, when it was too late, she realized that Godric had always been there when she needed him; always ready with wise counsel; always safe, dependable and strong.

She crossed her arms over her chest, trying to contain the emotions that surged through her like a tidal wave. Seeing him here, standing in front of her, had made her realize she was mistaken in her belief that what she felt for Godric was friendship. Stricken, she stared at him as another memory came into her mind: her curt dismissal when he'd told her he loved her, when he'd asked her to be his wife. How could he forgive her for that? And why should she think he would wait for her, when she had left the abbey without telling him that she was going or if she'd ever return. Meanwhile Cecily was close at hand and available, and Janna was sure their overlord would be more than happy to give his permission for them to be wed.

Now that it was too late, Janna could finally understand her devastation when she'd seen him with Cecily in the marketplace, and mistaken them for man and wife. Not friendship. Love. She closed her eyes so that he could not read her pain.

"Janna," he said quietly. She felt his arms fold around her, and draw her close. Shutting her mind to her fears, she moved into his embrace. His kiss melted her heart, her bones, her body. This, then, was how it felt to be held, to be loved, to be wanted and valued. She clung to him as his kiss, gentle at first, became more urgent, more demanding, and her body responded to his touch. She was on fire with wanting and understood, from the way Godric held her, that his need was just as great. All thought stopped as she gave herself up to the dizzying sweetness of being held by a lover who would make her his own. She had no sense of time passing until a stern voice brought her back to her surroundings.

"Janna! You forget yourself! There are customers about!"

Mortified, Janna realized that Sybil must have been watching them until her patience ran out. She reluctantly freed herself from Godric's embrace, becoming aware once more of the odoriferous yard, stained with puddles of spit, vomit and piss, and the patrons hurrying to and from the latrine.

"I must get back to work," she told him, shame staining her face at how low she had fallen.

Godric nodded in understanding. But his voice was heavy with warning as he said, "We are well met for another reason, Janna. Sire Hugh is inside and you should speak to him. I'll keep him in the tavern until you have a free moment to hear his news."

"Don't you go back in there empty-handed. You've neglected our customers for long enough!" Sybil beckoned to Janna from the doorway of the brew house. Janna squirmed with embarrassment.

"I'm sorry, mistress," she said, hoping the taverner didn't think she carried on like that with other patrons of the tavern. "Godric is an old friend and – "

"And a dear one, by the look of things." A small smile quirked the taverner's lips, giving Janna comfort that she hadn't been misunderstood after all.

"Very dear," she confirmed, thinking Sybil not quite so hard-headed and hard-hearted as she liked to pretend. Anxious to prove that she still had her mind on her work, Janna quickly filled two large pitchers with the new brew and took them across the yard to the tavern.

"And get that bush tied up outside!" Sybil shouted after her.

A swift glance around established the fact that Godric was seated at a table with Hugh. They were waiting to be served, like any other customers. She noted that Hamo wasn't with them, and felt a surge of relief that the boy must be safely home again at Hugh's manor.

Trying to conceal her agitation, Janna set down the pitchers and looked about for the bush. It was brown now, and wilting at the edges, but still recognizable for what it was. Once she'd tied it to the pole, she rang the bell to attract the attention of any who might not already know about the new brew. That done, she hurried back inside and began to serve the ale, all the while conscious of Godric's and Hugh's close watch on her. She felt deeply ashamed of her straitened circumstances; she couldn't imagine what Hugh must think of her.

But Godric's kiss had buoyed her spirits, and she told herself that his opinion was the only one that mattered.

"It is well that Godric has found you, for we need to talk," Hugh said, as she paused momentarily at a table close by to set down a trencher of griddle cakes and a stew that she suspected had more hedgerow weeds and herbs than meat and vegetables in it.

"As soon as I have a free moment," Janna promised.

Her opportunity came during a quiet lull after everyone's mug had been filled and food had been served. Hugh beckoned her over. "If the taverner complains, tell her we're ordering a meal," he said, with a glance over Janna's shoulder at Sybil. Janna looked down at the empty trenchers in front of the pair, and raised an eyebrow.

"That dish of pottage wasn't very filling."

Janna felt indignant on Sybil's behalf. "Supplies have become scarce in Winchestre. You should know that many people are starving, my lord, with not even our poor fare to fill their bellies!"

"I know that. It's an excuse to talk to you, that's all." Hugh lowered his voice. "I didn't believe my uncle when he told me he'd seen you."

"Lord Robert knows I am here?" Janna drew herself erect, sweating with sudden fright as she absorbed the news of this new threat.

Hugh nodded soberly. "I'm afraid he does. That is – " He checked himself. "He said he thought he'd seen you in the cathedral, helping to tend the sick. He himself had a *slight* wound, which he said needed attention." Hugh's emphasis on the word "slight" told Janna what he thought of his uncle's courage – or the lack of it. "I told him he must have been mistaken, and I think he agreed with me, but I've been looking for you ever since, just in case. I must say, I never expected to find you in here. We only stopped at this tavern because we were hungry. And thirsty."

Janna looked at Godric. "I'm so glad you did," she said.

"But why are you here? Why are you working as a...a..." Hugh flapped his hands in the air, unwilling to put into words how far Janna had fallen.

"I'm..." Janna was about to tell them of her search for her father and how near she was to finding him, but realized that there was nothing left to tell. Despair filled her as she recalled Ulf's news of the ruined manor house. "Now that I've left the abbey I have to work for my living," she said instead.

Hugh bent closer, his voice so low that Janna had to lean down to hear him more clearly. "Do not fear Robert," he whispered. "I shall tell him I have looked everywhere for you and that he was definitely mistaken. But you must take care to stay out of his way, for he hasn't forgiven you and will do all he can to bring you down."

"I shall look out for him, I promise you. And if he wants an alehouse to slake his thirst, tell him to go to Hell!" Hugh might know of the alehouse or he might not. Janna didn't care; he could make of her comment what he liked. She was about to leave, but he caught her arm and drew her close once more.

"You must not say anything to anyone of my warning, but I can tell you that Robert won't be a threat to you for much longer." Hugh's voice was so quiet Janna could hardly hear him. "You must leave Winchestre, Johanna, at once, while there's still time. Keep to the fields, don't take any of the roads. And stay out of sight. Don't trust anyone." Without warning, he pulled her close and his lips brushed her cheek in a fleeting kiss. "Please – keep yourself safe." He let her go and leaned back on his stool.

"But I don't understand. Why won't the lord Robert be a threat to me for much longer?" Confused, Janna turned to Godric, hoping that he might explain something of Hugh's meaning. But his face was a shuttered mask, his eyes without warmth.

"Shh! You must not speak of it. All that I've said, I've told you in confidence." Hugh scanned the room, checking that no-one was paying them any attention. But the customers were more intent on filling their bellies with ale and food; none looked their way. Hugh turned back to Janna. "Why did you leave the abbey? I know you talked about going in search of your father, but you surely won't find him here." He waved a hand, indicating the tavern.

Janna looked around, seeing it through Hugh's eyes. He didn't have to elaborate on how far she'd fallen since she last saw him. She willed Godric to say that she was still the same young woman they both knew, that her circumstances made no difference to the person she was inside. But to her disappointment, he kept silent.

"You don't need to stay here, you know," Hugh continued earnestly. "I once offered you a home at my manor farm, and I would still welcome you any time you wish to return."

"That is kind of you, my lord." Although Janna was tempted, she wasn't sure it would be in her best interests to accept Hugh's offer, should she fail in her search for her father. Godric would be there, of course, and what she most wanted was to be close to Godric. But Hugh was his overlord and Godric would be forced to abide by Hugh's plans for her – whatever they might be. Janna cast a sideways glance at Godric as she remembered that Hugh had just kissed her. Had Godric already jumped to the wrong conclusion? Was that why he wouldn't look at her now? It was true that she'd been greatly attracted to Hugh when first they'd met. And that bond had seemed mutual, had grown deeper while she'd nursed him back to health at the abbey. But so much had happened since then, including her reunion with Godric.

"Have you abandoned your search for your father? Is that why you're here in Winchestre?" Hugh persisted.

"I'm still looking, but I haven't found him yet." *But I do know who he is. It seems I'm the illegitimate granddaughter of the old king. What do you think about that, my lord?* She longed to tell Hugh and Godric everything, but could not, for she had nothing in her purse to prove her claim, nor even her father's manor house, or his steward, to show them. To forestall any further questions, Janna asked one of her own.

"What brings you to Winchestre, my lord? Was it the earl's call to arms?" She wouldn't admit that she'd already seen him even before the siege began.

Hugh gave a rueful laugh, looking suddenly self-conscious. Intrigued, Janna looked to Godric for an explanation, but he was sitting with arms folded and head bowed, studying the wet-slopped table as if it bore the secrets of the universe.

"Although my aunt is a tenant of the king, her sympathies have long been with the empress. Especially at this time," Hugh said into the silence. "Yes, I came in answer to Robert of Gloucestre's call for support, as I have before. But in fact I was already near Winchestre when the call came." A smile twitched the sides of his mouth as he looked down at Janna. "As I recall, I was on my way home from another such skirmish when we first met."

"You were riding your destrier through Wiltune, my lord. You looked as if you owned the world!" Janna remembered the occasion only too well.

Hugh's face shadowed. "Unfortunately I don't own the world, or anything like it! Even my armor and weapons belonged to my father. They came to me after his death. As for the destrier, I won him in battle. But he is mine now, and we have grown close over the months we have served together. He is, indeed, a fine mount, fierce and spirited, quick to bite and kick when necessary, and fleet of foot. I credit him with saving my life on more than one occasion."

Janna was surprised that a noble lord like Hugh should have so little to call his own. But then she remembered that he was entirely dependent on his aunt for everything, including the manor farm he managed in her name until such time as his cousin was old enough to take it on for himself.

"Service to the earl in battle is one way I can win riches and land for myself," Hugh continued. "It's the dream of every landless knight, but it's not a dream to be proud of. You snatch the spoils of battle, those horses that have been abandoned, and the armor of dead men. You loot villages wherever you may, and burn what's left so the enemy can find no succor. Most important of all, you hope to capture a baron and hold him to ransom, knowing that the silver paid for his release will buy you land and wealth of your own in the future."

Janna gazed at Hugh, amazed that he would admit so much to her, yet with a knot of sickness in her stomach that told her he spoke the truth. This was the reality of war and its aftermath.

"Most young knights go willingly to battle, but some who do not need the spoils of war live in dread of a call to arms. Like my uncle. Unfortunately for him, every last man was pressed into service before the siege of Winchestre. And it's become a battle we're unlikely to win."

"Of course, the earl knew he'd be unable to forge a new alliance with the Bishop of Winchestre. That's why he brought you all here, to decide the matter once and for all." Janna stopped abruptly, realizing she was giving Hugh secret information.

"You're remarkably well informed." *For a drudge in a tavern.* The words hung between them, even though Hugh did not utter them.

"You hear all sorts of things in a place like this, my lord," she said hastily. She wished she knew what had prompted Hugh's warning and why he seemed so down-hearted and uncomfortable – he hadn't seemed so when she'd spied him in the high street with Hamo. She wanted to ask what had brought them all here, but to ask him outright would be to admit she'd known he was in Winchestre before his appearance at the tavern. "And how is your family, my lord? How fares the young lord?" she asked instead.

"Hamo is well." Hugh hesitated. "In fact, he's here too, but in the circumstances, I wish he wasn't!"

"He's here in Winchestre!" Janna was horrified.

"He's not here in the heart of things, he's on a manor farm near Tuiforde with his nurse, Cecily." Hugh stopped, looking even more uncomfortable. His gaze switched from Janna to a point across the room. "They're staying with Geoffrey fitz William and his wife."

"And did you bring your cousin to visit them, my lord?"

Hugh nodded. "My aunt decided that it would be good for Hamo to meet Sire Geoffrey, for as soon as Hamo is old enough he will join the lord's household to learn about a knight's duties and responsibilities, just as all young squires must do, and just as I did too."

"You spent some of your boyhood with Sire Geoffrey?" Janna was fascinated to hear of Hugh's early life, for she'd always supposed he'd lived at Babestoche with his aunt until moving to her manor near Wicheford. Yet she'd learned that it was common practice for the sons of nobility to be brought up in the households of other family members, or friends, although Hamo still seemed far too young for such a doting mother to let her only child out of her sight.

Still avoiding Janna's gaze, Hugh said, "Our families have known each other for a long time."

"And you came to keep your cousin company?" Janna hinted, with a questioning glance at Godric. Why was he here too?

"My aunt suggested that I bring Hamo to meet Sire Geoffrey. She told me to accompany him, said it was in my best interests to do so. Of course, there was no hint of this trouble brewing, not then."

"And?" Janna prompted, knowing there was more to this tale than Hugh had confessed so far. She knew she was taking a liberty in pushing him, but plagued as she was by curiosity, she was determined to find out why he seemed so uncomfortable.

"And Sire Geoffrey has a daughter. Eleanor."

"Ah." Janna was beginning to understand what Hugh wasn't telling her. "And is Sire Geoffrey's daughter betrothed – or wed?" she asked innocently.

"No."

Janna waited for Hugh to elaborate on his answer. When he stayed silent, she decided she would have to push him further. "And is she of an age to wed? Is she beautiful, my lord?" She looked quickly at Godric, and found him staring at Hugh with an unreadable expression.

Hugh hesitated. "Yes, she is old enough to wed," he said finally. And then added in a more definite tone, "And yes, she looks well enough."

"She is a comely woman, you said so yourself, sire," Godric exclaimed hotly.

"True." But Hugh didn't sound particularly enthusiastic, and in that one word Janna read his reluctance to commit to a marriage that he needed but didn't want. Perhaps seeking to avoid further questions, Hugh rushed into an explanation. "Fortunately, Sire Geoffrey's property is some miles south of Winchestre. Once the battle started and the queen's troops began to encircle the town, we felt that Hamo would be safer there than attempting the journey home. It will give him a chance to become acquainted with Sire Geoffrey's household."

"And I am here to speak to Eleanor's father about the property his daughter will bring to her marriage, for it will come under Lord Hugh's care and my management when it is done," Godric explained, finally losing patience with Hugh's prevarication.

Hugh's lips tightened. "And Cecily is here, not to look after Hamo, but because she would not be parted from you," he retaliated.

Godric cast him a resentful glance, but kept silent.

So that was the truth of their relationship. Janna tasted the bitter ashes of defeat. It was as she'd thought: Godric and Cecily had made a match, perhaps even at Hugh's instigation. For Godric had said nothing of love, she realized now, even though she'd imagined it in his delight and in the way he'd held her in such a close embrace. Whatever their kiss might have meant to him, there was no future for her and Godric, for his future was already decided elsewhere.

Janna had thought, when she heard Ulf's news about her father's manor house, that things could not get worse, that she had finally reached the end. Now she realized that despair was infinite and deep. She had the sensation of being caught in a vortex, spiraling ever downward, no longer in control of her destiny. She tried to marshal her thoughts, knowing she could not turn her back on everything she'd achieved thus far. She must keep the solemn vow she'd made to her mother to avenge her murder, and that meant she must keep on until she found her father – even if she died in the attempt. She drew in a deep breath and made a desperate effort to steady herself.

Until now, she'd suspected she might never see Godric – or Hugh – again. Fate had brought them to her, and even if Godric and Cecily had made a match, Hugh had not – at least, not yet. In saving him from an unwanted marriage, could she at the same time save herself? Was that the best, even the only way forward?

All she had in her favor was the possibility of one day finding her father, of finding her true place in the world. But could she jeopardize Hugh's future on something so chancy? Perhaps she could, if he was willing to take the risk with her. She could only ask questions, and find out.

"Is it your wish to wed Mistress Eleanor, my lord?" she asked.

Hugh looked miserable. "It is my aunt's hope that we will. Eleanor was betrothed to the son of a baron as a child. But – but he died in battle, before they could be wed."

"And now she's looking for a new husband?"

"Her father is on her behalf." Hugh hesitated for a moment. "He would look further for someone higher than me, for she will bring a large dowry to the marriage, and will inherit everything on her father's death." Perhaps misreading Janna's compassion as judgment, he rushed to defend himself. "I have never made any secret of the fact that I have nothing in my own right, and that I must marry well! And it seems that Eleanor looks upon me with love, even if not with her father's favor. In fact, without her family's friendship with my aunt, I doubt things would have progressed even as far as they have. But her father knows me from my time in his household, and so does Eleanor, and she is forever at her father now to make this match." He kicked viciously at a wooden stool standing close, the movement expressing his frustration with the situation as he said bitterly, "I haven't spoken to her yet, but it seems that I must. But I tell you, Johanna, I would far rather follow my heart in this."

At last he looked her full in the face, his meaning written plain upon his features. Janna stared back at him, wondering what to do for the best. Should she tell him about her expectations in the hope of a marriage proposal? But, if her high hopes came to naught, the marriage would be blighted and their relationship soured beyond repair. She didn't want that for him. And she certainly didn't want that for herself.

"Then may I wish you good fortune with your wooing, my lord," she said instead. It took all her determination not to look at Godric, lest she betray her utter devastation that he was lost to her. "I must go about my duties," she muttered, and whisked away.

But she could not stop her thoughts from churning as she continued to serve ale and food to the customers. She'd believed, after Ralph, that she would never love or trust anyone again. Indeed, her heart shriveled small at the memory of how badly hurt she had been. This meeting with Godric had shaken her more than she'd thought was possible. Now that she'd come to a true understanding of her love for him it was all too late. His loyalty lay with his overlord – and with Cecily. And he knew it. That must be why he'd turned away from her after the passionate kiss they'd shared. Perhaps he and Cecily were already wed, and that was why Cecily would not be parted from him. Whatever Godric's circumstances, it seemed Janna could stake no claim on his heart or his life. So she must look to her own future, whatever that might be.

She dragged her mind from Godric back to Hugh and his intended bride, Eleanor. She wished them both well, but couldn't help wondering what might have happened if she'd spoken of her own promising fortune. She remembered Hugh's many acts of kindness, the admiration in his eyes when she'd nursed him back to health at the abbey, and the attraction growing between them. She knew she hadn't imagined it. It seemed certain, from the look he had just given her, that he would be willing to join his future with hers – if only she could bring something to the marriage.

She couldn't bring love, but she might be able to bring him a connection to the crown. In return, she might find comfort for her own aching heart. She was sure Hugh would make a loving companion and in return she thought she could make him happy, happier than he might be if he married Eleanor. But with Eleanor, he was assured of a promising future. With Janna, he had no guarantee of anything at all. It seemed that Hugh had his eye on a wealthy wife, but now that they'd met up again, perhaps he might find the courage to choose a different path? If so, Janna was determined that it was his choice to make, and only then would she decide if she could go through with it. And that decision would have to wait until after she had found her father and fulfilled the oath she had sworn to her mother. That must come before everything.

"And it'll serve you right if you die a destitute and lonely old maid," she told herself, feeling hot tears of self-pity sting her eyes. As she went to the brew house to refill the pitchers with ale, she tried to cheer herself with the thought that she was not alone. Her father might come to Winchestre and, while Ulf was here, she had at least one friend on her side. Two, if she counted Godric. Three, if she counted Hugh. Godric might be with Cecily, and Hugh have expectations of Eleanor, but there was no reason why she couldn't count them as her friends.

She looked down at her russet tunic and apron, now blurred through her tears but no less real. They were the flag for how far she had fallen. Friends? She shook her head at the folly of her thoughts. Godric and Hugh were far above her now. They would not introduce a lowborn skivvy into their circle of society. She was a fool even to think of it.

*

"...the new brew." The words penetrated Janna's misery. Suddenly recollecting her earlier experiments with the ale, she stopped filling up the customers' mugs and paused to listen.

"New brew?" Sybil sounded puzzled. "It's the same as usual."

"No, it's not," the speaker said. He took another swallow and smacked his lips. "I don't know what you've put into it this time, mistress, but it's good."

"Yair, it's different." The man's companion drained his mug and set it down with a bang on the table. "I'll have another."

There was a general murmuring as several customers quaffed the contents of their own mugs and passed their opinions on the brew. Noticing Janna standing nearby clutching a jug, they beckoned her across to them.

"Do you know anything about this?" Sybil shot Janna a sharp look as she approached the table.

"No. Well, yes, I – " Janna hastened to fill the proffered mugs.

"Brew house. Now." Sybil jerked her head toward the door and walked away.

"Be kind to her, mistress!" one of the men called out. "She makes a better brew than you do!"

From Sybil's grim expression Janna knew she was in trouble, so she was pleased that the taverner had at least heard the compliments before she walked out.

"I don't like to be made a fool of by anyone, least of all you!" Sybil rebuked Janna as she entered the brew house.

"It was not my intention to make a fool of you, mistress," Janna pleaded. "It's just that – that I used to make ale under my mother's instruction and – and suddenly I felt heartsick that she was dead and that…and that…" She tried to blink back the tears she'd been holding in check ever since she'd faced the destruction of her prospects and the truth about her own hungry, lonely heart.

Sybil frowned. "You went behind my back, without asking permission. You might have ruined the brew!" Her eyes narrowed in suspicion. "Or has someone put you up to this? Are you trying to sabotage my business?"

"Of course not!" Janna wondered why Sybil was so mistrustful, and what more she could do to allay the taverner's suspicions. "You heard what the customers said. They *like* the new ale!"

"It's as well for you that they do," Sybil snapped. "What did you put in it?"

Janna hesitated. She wanted to keep the recipe a secret, in the hope that her knowledge would secure her employment. On the other hand, Sybil was steaming like a pot on the boil, furious that Janna had shown her up in front of her own customers.

"Some new herbs and a dollop of honey," she admitted grudgingly. "And I stirred the brew with a stick of ash."

"Ash?"

"My mother always told me that the ash was a tree of knowledge and wisdom, and if we stirred our brew with it, it would bring us health, protection and prosperity. And the bark adds flavor to the ale." Janna wondered if that admission would be enough to satisfy Sybil. But it wasn't. Without commenting further, the taverner drew a full mug of ale from the barrel and took a cautious sip.

In spite of her anger, her grim expression softened a little as she rolled the liquid around her tongue before swallowing it. "Sage?" she guessed, and Janna nodded. She wondered if the taverner could also taste the ash keys. But Sybil didn't mention them, saying only, "The brew tastes a little sweeter than usual, but it's quite refreshing." She took another sip. "Why sage? And honey?"

"For the taste." *And to make the brew more potent and last longer.* But this, Janna kept to herself. "I hoped that a different brew, or even a choice of brews, might keep our customers loyal once the other alehouses open," she said. She swallowed hard, summoning up the courage to continue, "I've also added some extra herbs to the gruit in the new brew."

"You've *what*?" Sybil's face flushed dark with rage. For a moment Janna feared the taverner was going to hit her.

"Just for a change," she said hurriedly. "It'll taste even better than this new brew, I swear it."

Sybil gave an angry sigh and pursed her lips. "We'll be running out of supplies soon enough, even sooner if you've spoiled the new brew. I might have to close the tavern, and then where will you be?"

Janna's small show of confidence instantly evaporated in the face of this new threat. "How long can we hold out, do you think?" she asked quickly.

Sybil shrugged. "I won't be able to keep you on if I close."

So this was Sybil's way of paying her back for not asking permission to change the brew. Indeed, it was probably no more than she should have expected under the circumstances. Janna tilted her chin, determined not to let Sybil see how her words had stung.

"I can always take my recipe elsewhere," she said quietly.

Sybil glared at her. Janna held her gaze. It was the taverner who looked away first. "Get on and serve the customers," she said, and turned her back to snatch up a pitcher and open the bung on the new barrel of ale.

Janna took the filled pitcher from her and hurried off, conscious that in the battle of wills with her employer she had won the first round. But her brief feeling of elation died abruptly once she re-entered the tavern. Automatically she looked about for Godric and

Hugh, and saw that they were leaving. But they were not alone – two men had joined them. Hugh had an arm around each stranger and appeared to be urging them out the door. Janna studied his new companions, curious to identify them if she could.

It was a great mistake, for even as she thought they seemed familiar, one of them turned to look over his shoulder and she recognized the red face and piggy eyes of Hugh's uncle by marriage, Robert of Babestoche. Just as she'd seen him, so had he seen her. With a gasp of alarm, she ducked her head to avoid his scrutiny. But she was too late. She saw him stop and wheel around; saw Hugh's hand tighten on Robert's shoulder as he tried to turn him away; saw Godric step into his path to prevent him coming after her. Robert stayed still. But his companion did not. With only a fleeting glance, Janna recognized the man who'd once tried to silence her for ever – Mus. She didn't wait to see anything further. She turned and fled into the yard, through the gate and down the lane. She didn't pause to see if she was being followed, but made for the only place she knew where she might find shelter. She ran as if the devil himself was after her, for indeed, that was how she thought of Mus. With one fearful glance over her shoulder, she shot down the lane leading to the cathedral.

She heard shouts and pounding footsteps, coming closer, sounding louder. She didn't dare look again. She ran on, feeling pain cut like a knife into her side. She gulped in ragged gasps of air, but felt as if she was suffocating. And still she ran, until at last the great doors of the cathedral loomed before her. Without pausing, she burst through them and collapsed onto the floor.

She crouched low and closed her eyes as she felt herself spinning down into darkness. Panic gripped her, but she couldn't move, couldn't speak or cry for help. All she could hear was the thunder of her heartbeat and the ragged whooping of her breath as she tried to drag air into her tortured lungs. Bright lights flashed behind her eyelids; sound ebbed and crashed in waves, and she knew that she was about to faint. Hours – or perhaps only moments – later, she felt something cold and wet on her neck, and a voice came to her through the darkness. "Keep your head down, Johanna." She recognized the speaker: Sister Benedicta. She relaxed then, and let herself float off into the void. She was safe.

Chapter 7

Once the waves of dizziness had passed, Janna felt ashamed of her weakness and was embarrassed that she'd drawn attention to herself in this way. She tried to stand up and was pushed down again by Sister Benedicta.

"I'm feeling all right now," she reassured the nun, and proved it by rising to her feet, although she took care to anchor herself against a stone pillar. "I thank you for your care but truly, the faintness has passed." She glanced fearfully around the cathedral, but there was no sign of Mus. The space was less crowded with townsfolk seeking shelter now that the danger had eased, but there were still many wounded soldiers needing treatment, and also some civilians, women and children among them. Janna felt a surge of anger that the innocent should also be caught in this fight for the crown.

"Now that I am here, let me help you," she offered. She knew Sybil would not take kindly to her running away, and that staying here in the cathedral would only compound her transgression, but not for anything would she risk another encounter with Mus. Sister Benedicta looked as if she was about to protest, but Janna didn't give her the chance. Instead, she walked over to the children and crouched down to see if she could cheer them with a story.

Once everyone was bedded down for the night, Janna also tried to sleep. But her rest was troubled by nightmares: Mus crept up on her with a wire snare in his hands while she stood frozen with fear, unable to get away. Robert stood by and smiled, and Godric turned his back and walked off. She opened her eyes, feeling a great wave of relief to find herself surrounded by the safe stone walls of the cathedral. She forced herself to stay awake until the full horror of her nightmare had subsided, only to fall asleep again and dream of Godric once more. This time he was with Cecily. They were walking hand in hand through the water meadows, picking flowers and herbs just as Janna herself had done. She asked Godric to give her some sprigs of sage, but he gave them to Cecily instead. They walked away, their figures dwindling until they disappeared altogether.

Janna woke with tears on her cheeks and black misery in her heart. It was safer, after that, to stay awake. And so she spent the rest of the night flitting among the patients, bringing a mug of ale to a thirsty soldier, a draft of horehound to quieten the hacking cough of a small child, holding patients' hands and soothing them with reassuring words. She massaged bruises with a salve of woundwort and goose grease, and renewed a bloody and suppurating bandage, cleansing the wound before binding it with new cloth and tying it with care, taking pride in her handiwork and pleasure in being able to use her healing skills once more.

But the new day brought a new terror. Janna had spent part of the morning helping the nuns tend the wounded until she deemed the tavern would be crowded enough for her to return to her work in safety. Just as she was about to leave, the great doors were flung open, revealing a solid phalanx of men, some in armor and with swords drawn.

"No!" Sister Benedicta hurried to the entrance to ward them off. Janna marveled at her courage: one small, stout sister facing a group of men intent on forcing an entry. They had checked and were eyeing her dubiously, seemingly pondering the wisdom of cutting her down if it meant putting their immortal souls at risk. But the infirmarian was not alone for long – almost immediately her sisters streamed to the entrance to join her. A bell clanged, warning of the trouble, and within moments the sisters were joined by the priest, his acolytes and, shortly afterward, the prior and all the monks from the priory attached to the cathedral. They made a formidable wall as they assembled in front of the soldiers.

"What is your purpose in coming here?" the priest challenged.

A man wearing some semblance of armor stepped forward. Janna pressed closer in an effort to identify him. Was this Earl Robert at the head of the empress's troops, seeking sanctuary? But she didn't recognize the man, or his insignia, nor was there any sign of the empress. She surveyed the soldier and the grim-faced militia behind him. She remembered Hugh's whispered advice that she should flee while there was still time. If not the empress's army, was this instead the infamous William of Ypres, feared and detested by all who had the misfortune to cross his path? A frisson of terror ran through her. What had happened to bring these men to the very door of the cathedral?

"The empress has fled, and her army with her." The man smiled, but there was no warmth in his eyes. He reminded Janna of a snake eyeing its prey. The resemblance intensified as his tongue darted out to lick his lips. Clearly, he was relishing the situation.

A whisper of distress echoed around the cathedral as the occupants began to realize the consequences of the man's words.

"They have escaped your clutches, then." There was satisfaction in the priest's voice.

"The empress managed to evade the queen's troops, but her half-brother, Robert of Gloucestre, has been taken, along with most of his men."

Godric and Hugh! Stricken, Janna put her hand to her breast. Neither had the money to pay a ransom. Had they managed to escape, or were they even now – ? Janna couldn't bear to complete her thought.

"The empress's army fled like rabbits before a fox, abandoning those mounts they did not need and dropping their possessions as they went: weapons, armor, shields, cloaks and precious vessels, so anxious were they to save their own skins. But we captured them anyway!" The man chuckled at the memory, a mocking laugh that boded ill for the unhappy captives. "After such a rout, they will not lightly take up arms again. The empress's war is finished, and the citizens of Winchestre with it! And a pox on all of you for supporting her cause at the expense of the king!"

He stepped forward, but the men and women of the church closed ranks behind the priest and held fast.

"Get out of our way!"

Janna knew then that they had come to loot the church: to take the gold and silver, the precious cross and chalices, the relics and fittings. What they did not destroy they would sell to the highest bidder. And, to keep their actions hidden, they would probably slaughter all witnesses. Her heart juddered with fear; she began to mutter a prayer to save her soul.

A sudden realization penetrated her terror. The leader of this rabble spoke in the Saxon tongue. Not Flemish, nor even Norman French. This couldn't be William of Ypres and his mercenaries then, so who were these people? Londoners? Would they be likely to show more mercy than the Flemish? She remembered hearing how the citizens of London had risen against the empress, forcing her to flee to Oxeneford. They had shown no mercy then. Her hands were clammy with sweat as she waited for the rabble to invade the cathedral.

"You will not enter! You will not sack and pillage God's house, or you will have to answer to the Bishop of Winchestre for your actions," the priest said coldly.

The soldier checked, perhaps deciding he needed to rethink his strategy.

"And on your death you will have to answer to a higher power even than our bishop," the priest continued, making the most of the advantage he had won. "God is watching, as are his saints and all the angels. Beware, lest you imperil your immortal soul."

Still the soldier stood his ground, but behind him Janna could see his men shuffling and fidgeting, and whispering to each other. The solid block of his support began to unravel as, one by one, they peeled off and hastened away, keen perhaps to find easier pickings elsewhere. The soldier and the priest faced each other down while behind them, in the cathedral, those taking refuge held their breath in terror.

At last the soldier turned away. "Keep your flock inside, priest, if you value their lives," he said curtly, and strode off.

"And so it has begun." The priest closed the great doors behind him, and turned to face them all. He looked exhausted, and ill with worry. "The Londoners have come to ransack Winchestre, and it's only a matter of time before the Flemings join them," he said. "You must pray for your families and friends, and all who are not in here with us."

He did not have to say any more, for Janna could imagine exactly what was going to happen outside the cathedral, might even be happening already. The empress and her army had scattered, run for their lives. This, then, was the meaning of Hugh's warning. She could only hope that he'd heeded his own advice and that he and Godric had found somewhere safe to shelter. She knew that the king's supporters, under the leadership of the cruelest villain of them all, William of Ypres, would not hesitate to burn, to rape, to kill and pillage, to lay waste to Winchestre and all who lived within its walls.

112

She found herself praying in earnest now, not only for herself but for Godric and Hugh, and also for Hamo. Hugh had said that Sire Geoffrey's manor was some way out of Winchestre; Janna hoped it was far enough to keep the boy safe. And Ulf. Where was he? Any looters would be glad to seize his bag of relics, but would they leave Ulf alive during the taking of it? Janna shook her head, knowing the answer.

She found herself praying also for Sybil, and for Wat and Ossie and Elfric. Would they have had time to take shelter in the cellar? Would the soldiers even think to look for a hidden storehouse? Or would they be content to lay waste only to what was on display, not knowing there was more to find?

Janna's hands clenched; she was shaking with rage even as she continued to pray. Hugh's warning meant that this retreat had been planned in advance. She could not forgive the empress's troops for running away and leaving the citizens to face alone the depredations of the Londoners, along with William of Ypres and his troops.

She was distracted from her prayers by a growing tumult outside: screams and shouts, the thudding of horses' hooves and their frightened whinnying. The priest stayed by the door, ready to open it to anyone seeking sanctuary. But few came; Janna imagined that the townsfolk were probably being cut down before ever they could reach safety. She sank to her knees and blocked her ears, willing her imagination to stop casting pictures of what was happening outside the cathedral. But the sounds penetrated, terrifying in their implication. Smoke drifted through the windows and some, the young and the elderly in particular, began to cough as it swirled and thickened around them. Janna rose wearily and went to help those who most needed relief.

The bells had ceased to ring. The thick smoke made it impossible to see how the day was passing, or tell when night fell. From his post by the door, the priest said prayers and told stories of the miracles of Jesus in a vain attempt to lift their spirits. As his voice failed, the prior from St Swithuns adjacent to the cathedral took his place, and continued to do what he could to take their minds off what was happening outside.

*

Janna had no way of knowing how long they were incarcerated in the cathedral. Minutes passed as slowly as days. She spent the time in a state of terrified anticipation, which she tried to blunt by filling her hours with caring for the wounded and entertaining the children. What little food was left was kept under the watchful eye of Sister Benedicta. She began to dole it out only to the children and later, only to those children who were older and strong enough to survive. Sickened, Janna tried to turn deaf ears to the pleas of the mothers with toddlers, those too old to be suckled but too young to thrive alone, should there be no release soon from their prison. And her rage grew at the senseless waste of war. She had supported the empress's cause from the start, but felt her sympathy waning fast as she contemplated the consequences of the lady's ambition. And the king's. And she wondered what would happen next, with the king and the empress's half-brother both held captive by their enemies. Would they call a truce? Would one side yield to the other? Or would the fighting continue until either the king or the empress was dead?

Gradually the tumult outside subsided, but it was a long time before the priest deemed it safe to open the great doors. The captives streamed out and stood blinking in the pale sunshine, appalled at what lay before them: bodies of the dead and dying, and the smoking ruins of the town. It was a scene of utter devastation and destruction.

Yet not everyone had died in the onslaught, nor had everything been destroyed. As the group slowly began to disperse, so other survivors began to trickle out from their various hiding places, reassured by the priest's presence that it was safe to show themselves at last. Families were reunited with joyful cries, but there were also loud lamentations as the dead were identified and mourned.

Janna began her search, praying that Hugh and Godric, and also Ulf, had got away in time. She felt sick with fear as she traversed the lane and came into the high street, keeping always in the shadows and starting at any unexpected sound. She looked along the street, noticing that all the shops had been destroyed. A sudden yowling sent her heart ricocheting into her throat, and she froze in terror until she noticed the source of the unearthly yell. The cat had lost one eye and its tabby fur was badly burned along one flank. Janna held out her hand to it, and called softly, but it flattened its ears at her and hissed, then sprang away and ran for its life. Janna crept on, expecting the worst, yet still with the hope that the tavern and its occupants might have escaped unscathed.

The wall surrounding the bishop's palace was partly demolished; the palace itself was a smoking ruin, as were the shops and pentices that had hung from the wall like ticks on a dog. A dead beast lay in the market square. Janna wondered if its carcass would be salvaged for food to feed the starving survivors, and saw several townsfolk with knives out and baskets at the ready, bearing down on it. She shuddered and moved onward, but recognized no-one among the ruins. Hopeful that those she loved might have escaped the murderous onslaught, she retraced her steps toward the East Gate and the tavern. This part of town seemed to have escaped the worst of the firebrands, although smashed doors spoke eloquently of the depredations of the marauders. Janna wondered nervously if any of them were still roaming about now, hungry for pickings.

She was too afraid to go directly to the tavern, and so cut down through the laneways and into the yard instead. The gate had been wrested from its mooring post and lay buckled and useless to one side. To Janna's relief, the tavern itself seemed intact, although the brew house bore the charcoal scars of a passing fire. She pushed open the door and ventured inside. Barrels of ale stood against the wall, but when she bent down to unstopper the bung, suddenly desperate to slake her thirst, she realized the barrel had been drained dry. As had the other two, she noted, when she saw the discarded bungs lying on the ground. The mash tun and containers had also been emptied. Some of the brewing utensils were gone, perhaps looted or taken to the cellar for safekeeping. Everything else had been trampled underfoot and was damaged beyond repair. It was utter, senseless vandalism, and Janna shook her head over the waste of it.

"What are you doing in here? Get out!" The voice was shrill, but Janna knew it all the same. She whirled around, and saw the terror leach from Sybil's face as she recognized her. "And just what do you think you're doing in here?" the taverner demanded, as she sheathed the sharp knife she'd wielded in readiness to protect herself and her property.

"I came to see if you were all right, mistress, if you had survived the terror." Janna was surprised at the surge of relief she felt on seeing Sybil. Sudden tears pricked her eyes and she blinked them back, feeling foolish. But the taverner had noticed, and her expression softened.

"Yes," she said shortly. "Wat, Ossie and I took refuge in the cellar, but Elfric left to protect his family and we haven't seen him since. Those whoresons ransacked my tavern – and the brew house too, as you see. But thanks be to God, they got too drunk to find the hatch leading to the cellar, and that saved our lives." Sybil shuddered at the memory.

"I was very angry with you for changing the recipe of my ale," she continued. "And I was furious when you ran out without my permission. I was resolved not to take you back, not under any circumstances. Later, I feared for your safety, for I know what happens to women when soldiers get hold of them! But it seems that in spite of everything you have survived, and I own that I am pleased to see you. I know, now, that in the midst of all this carnage there's no room for petty grievances." She paused for a moment, considering. "I cannot pay you for your services, Janna, at least not for the moment. Most of my stores have gone, and it may be some while before I can open my doors to customers again. But you may take shelter here, and share what little food we have, if you'll help me put the place to rights. Do you agree?"

"Oh, I do! Thank you, mistress." Janna restrained herself from throwing her arms around Sybil in gratitude. "I will do all I can to help you," she promised, as she followed her into the tavern. It was a chaotic jumble of smashed stools, benches and tables inside. Looking around at the damage, Janna realized that much had gone missing; Sybil would have to start her business all over again. She glanced at the taverner, thinking to commiserate with her loss, and saw her nod with satisfaction.

"They destroyed what they couldn't take," she confirmed, adding with a twinkle, "but they missed out on just about everything of value." And she beckoned Janna to follow her to the hatch in the darkened corner, so that Janna could see for herself what had been saved, and what needed to be done to set the place to rights again.

Chapter 8

The glorious colors of autumn gave way to the cold winds of winter as the people of Winchestre salvaged what little they could in order to put food in their mouths and rebuild shelter for their families. The townsfolk's earlier enthusiastic support for the empress's cause had waned, although they still spoke of the king, his mercenaries and the London militia with disgust and virulent curses – but quietly, for the bishop openly supported his brother now and no-one wanted to risk being branded a traitor. But the townsfolk could neither forget nor forgive what had happened in the aftermath of the siege. All of them had either suffered personally or knew someone whose house or shop had been looted and destroyed. Family members had been tortured or put to death. Those who had managed to survive lived on the borderline of starvation, for crops had been destroyed and animals butchered to feed the marauding armies. They scavenged fields, rivers, hedgerows and woodland for anything edible, be it weeds, birds, squirrels, coneys or even fish, if they were lucky enough to catch one. But many, in the extremes of hunger, resorted to eating vermin, including rats and mice. There was no money to spend in any of the alehouses or taverns, although Sybil did her best to ensure that there was always ale on tap and at least one dish available for those few travelers who came their way.

Not even the parish churches had been safe from the ravages of the London militia and the Flemish mercenaries. Some reported twenty, others said that as many as forty churches had been either burned to the ground or looted and destroyed. It seemed a miracle that the priest had managed to keep the cathedral and all its occupants safe.

As Janna had suspected, the situation between king and empress was still not resolved, and the ebb and flow of their fortunes was discussed nightly among their few patrons. In a shocked whisper, one traveler reported the news that, in her panic to get away from Winchestre, the empress had galloped twenty miles to Litlegarsele in the company of Brian fitz Count and Reginald of Cornwall.

"But she didn't feel safe even there, so she insisted on riding another eighteen miles to the castle at Devizes." The packman paused, with a glint in his eye, to take a refreshing gulp of ale. "For the sake of speed, and safety, she rode astride her mount like a man," he confided. "That's what one of the servants at Devizes told me, and he had it as an eyewitness report from the empress's own party. But it seems even Devizes wasn't considered safe enough, and so the empress decided to press on to Gloucestre. But by then she was so saddle sore and exhausted they had to strap her onto a litter between two horses. That was how she entered Gloucestre, and by then she was more dead than alive, so the servant said!" The packman looked about, well pleased with the effect of his news on the assembled customers, especially when one of them offered to buy him another ale.

"And now? What will the empress do now?" the customer asked, beckoning Janna over to give their mugs a refill.

The speaker shrugged. "Earl Robert has been captured. What can she do but give up?"

"What of her uncle, the King of Scotland? I heard he'd been taken too."

The speaker chuckled. "He was taken, all right, not once but three times – and he managed to buy his way out of captivity each time. The earl was not so lucky. He's too valuable to trade."

The earl's fortunes were the subject of great debate and discussion. He was given much credit for fighting a rearguard action at the ford at Stoche and delaying pursuit so that the empress might escape, although in so doing he had been captured, along with several other knights, and was being held prisoner at Roucestre in Kent. Janna wondered if Hugh was among those captured with the earl, and listened avidly whenever the talk turned to that fateful night, hoping for news of him and, by association, also of Godric. She longed to know that they were safe.

New rumors began to circulate. First it was suggested that there be a prisoner exchange, the earl for the king. But the earl would not agree to it, on the grounds that an earl's life was not worth that of a king. If the king was to be let free, he said, then it should be in return for the freedom of his followers as well as himself. But that was unacceptable, and so a new tactic was tried. This time, on behalf of the king, Bishop Henry offered the earl lordship of the whole land and promised that he'd be second to the king if only he would abandon the empress. But the earl refused all bribes and blandishments and stayed steadfastly loyal to his half-sister.

Opinion was greatly divided on the wisdom of this, with some believing he should change sides like all the other barons had done, while others praised him for his loyalty and courage. Another rumor began to circle in the tavern: that Stephen's queen, on realizing that the earl was not open to bribes, had threatened to send him to imprisonment in Normandy. But in return, Robert had told her that her husband, the king, would spend the rest of his days in captivity in the wilds of Ireland.

It seemed they'd reached a stalemate. As the weeks passed, the people of Winchestre waited to see what would happen next.

Now that everything had settled down, travelers began to pass through Winchestre in greater numbers, bringing more news from outside. Janna kept her ears continually stretched for any news of Hugh, Godric or Ulf. She'd continued to comb the city, hoping to catch sight of them, but they seemed to have disappeared. She alternated between hope that they'd managed to escape, and despair that they had not.

Meanwhile, there were new developments in the fight for the crown, news that set everyone aflutter, for it meant that royalty might come again to Winchestre. There were mixed feelings about it: excitement at seeing the royal family set against a deep and abiding resentment for the damage their armies had done. But the feelings of the townsfolk weren't taken into account, for once it had become clear to the bishop that the earl's loyalty could not be bought with promises, and that threats wouldn't work either, new and elaborate negotiations for a prisoner exchange began, this time with the earl's blessing.

At last, and according to the agreed arrangements, the king was released from the castle keep at Bristou. From there he traveled to Winchestre, where the earl awaited him, leaving his wife and family as sureties for the earl's release. Once the king arrived safely in Winchestre, the earl was freed. Leaving his son as surety for the return of the queen, the earl then set out for Bristou. And finally, when the queen and her companions were safely returned to Winchestre, the earl's son was released to join his father.

And so everyone went free at last, and it was as if the empress's rise in fortune had never happened. The king's barons once more swore their allegiance to him, and he celebrated the Christ Mass at Canterberie in fine style and with a crown on his head. Meanwhile, the empress and her entourage had set up their headquarters at Oxeneford Castle, and everyone wondered who would strike the next blow in the bid for the crown.

All this was common conjecture in the tavern. Thanks to Sybil's hoard of coins, and careful trading with traveling merchants and property owners far enough away to have escaped the worst of the siege, the tavern had come back into the business of serving ale and wine long before the alehouses in the high street, attracting customers who showed no signs of changing their allegiance once Hell, and later Paradise and Heaven, opened their doors for business. Janna took partial credit for the tavern's continuing success. Before winter set in and it was too late to gather herbs, one of her tasks had been to walk out into the water meadows to cut herself another stout stirring stick of ash, and to gather a quantity of ash keys, sage, wild hops and other herbs for the gruit so that she could continue to make the ale to her mother's old recipe.

This she did with Sybil's consent, persuaded as the taverner was by customers clamoring for the "new ale" they had tasted before the troubles began. Janna noticed the taverner kept an eagle eye on her preparations, obviously keen to find out the recipe so she could use it herself. But after Sybil's kindness to her, Janna did not begrudge showing her how the gruit was made, explaining how adding honey would make the brew stronger, and wild hops and ash keys would help it stay fresh for longer.

Once the danger was over, Elfric had returned, and he and Janna and Sybil continued to get in each other's way in the brew house as they fought for use of the fire burning there. Meanwhile Sybil used her connections, as well as some of the coins she'd saved, to order a supply of wine from Normandy, and also to rebuild the kitchen along with a new bake house. She supervised the workmen and harried at their heels until it was done.

As soon as the kitchen was in working order once more, Elfric lit the fire in the new hearth and set to creating pottages and stews, using whatever supplies Sybil had managed to save, buy or scrounge. The fare was not nearly as bountiful as before, and Janna suspected that as well as bartering, there was much gleaning in the wild going on, for food as well as for firewood. Some dishes had a distinctly unusual taste – dog, perhaps, or horse meat – disguised by a liberal seasoning of herbs and mustard, imported spices no longer being available. But so long as sufficient quantities of ale and wine were quaffed, the fare was also wolfed down with apparent relish. In these hard times, people were delighted to find food and drink to fill their bellies, even if they struggled to pay for it.

It was a cruel winter, bitterly cold and with a constant driving rain, and Ossie nailed pieces of hide over the windows to keep out the drafts and the wet. The cresset lights that burned continually cast a glow around the tap room, creating a cosy snugness, although the air was tainted by their vapor and the smoke from the fire. Janna continued to keep a lookout for Godric and Hugh, and also for Ulf, but there was no sign of them. Not even the merchant or his companions came in. She was surprised, for the Bell and Bush was one of only a few places still serving wine, and she'd thought that might be enough to tempt the merchant to make peace with Sybil. She wondered if the taverner minded his absence, and if she still harbored a soft spot for him in spite of everything. The thought came to her that the merchant might have died during the siege, as so many townsfolk had done. Or he might have lost everything and no longer had the coin to pay for his ale, or wine, or even his leman. Many people were starving, scavenging for food, shelter and something to keep them warm in the bitter winter weather. Only those with a pressing need to travel took to the road; most stayed thankfully indoors, conserving their energy and what little goods they had.

After the siege, and perhaps in atonement for the damage his firebrands had done to the city, the bishop had summoned a synod with the purpose of trying to alleviate the misery of his people. It was decreed that a plow should have the same privilege of sanctuary as churches, and that anyone attacking those engaged in agricultural labor would be excommunicated. But it was too late; the marauders had not left even the wherewithal to plow the land and sow seed for the coming year. While men could queue for the dole at the Hospital of St Cross and receive at least one meal a day sufficient to feed themselves and their families, many others went hungry. It was some comfort to Janna to know that Sybil did what she could, doling out leftover scraps and sometimes even good food, if there was any to spare, to those desperate women and children who came begging for help.

Numbers visiting the tavern dwindled, as did Sybil's hoard of coins. But the fire continued to burn bright, offering warmth and shelter and the illusion of peace and comfort. At Janna's suggestion, but only after a long argument, Sybil lowered the price of a mug of ale to persuade customers away from the alehouses and into the tavern. While this swelled the number of their patrons, it did nothing to increase Sybil's popularity along the high street.

Janna worried continually about Godric and Hugh. Had they got away to safety, or had they been captured along with the Earl of Gloucestre and his party? She knew well that neither was wealthy enough to be worth a ransom, especially not Godric. But Hugh's aunt might be prepared to pay the price for them. Or Hugh's betrothed? But Eleanor's father disapproved of the match; he would be in no hurry to hand over good silver for an unwanted son-in-law and his companion. Janna was haunted by the thought that Godric and Hugh, and also Ulf, had been slaughtered along the road, like so many others who'd been caught in the trap.

Occasionally, when she had some free time, she visited the ruins where once her father's house had stood, hoping that she might find him there, but she always returned discouraged and disheartened by his seeming indifference to the state of his property. Common sense said that her father wouldn't let his estate stand in ruins indefinitely, that either he would come himself or appoint someone to come in his place. But how long would it take? And what if no-one ever came? She greatly missed Ulf's cheerful presence, and wished he was there to give her some advice, for he knew well the ways of the world and its people and she was sure he would know what to do for the best.

*

As the iron-hard earth of winter at last yielded to soft spring rain and new growth, the hides were taken down from the windows to let in pale sunlight, and Sybil declared that the tavern needed a good spring cleaning. Janna soon discovered that this was hard work, for it meant a fresh whitewash for the walls and a change of rushes for the floor, but at last the doors of the tavern were opened wide and welcoming. With a new brew of ale ready for serving, Janna fixed a green bush outside and rang the bell. She paused a few moments on the doorstep, savoring the sunlight, fancying she could feel its slight warmth through the fabric of her tunic. She tipped her face up and closed her eyes, feeling the touch of the sun on her face like a blessing. On a day like today, all things seemed possible.

She ventured further to look up and down the high street. All around the city now were signs of rejuvenation. A few people were out and about for, with the gradual rebuilding of the town, traders and townsfolk alike had begun to visit once more the shops and pentices that were springing up along the street, and the markets that were again finding goods to trade. With coins in their purses, they visited the tavern as well. Although a ready source of credit and money supply had dried up when the Jews had fled their burning homes, some had now begun to trickle back and had started to build up their businesses. Their presence gave confidence to a town badly in need of a belief in itself. Everywhere Janna looked, she could see signs that people were ready to put the past behind them and get on with their lives. Even nature was in tune with the town's regeneration, she thought, as she noticed the daffodils that had thrust their golden heads through a small patch of straggly grass. She felt a lifting of her spirits and smiled at them, taking courage from their shining faces. She went inside, through the tavern, and out to the brew house in the yard to fill pitchers and get everything ready for the day's trading.

It seemed to Janna that even the tavern's customers were happier, thanks to the change of season. Instead of complaining about the empress and the king, lamenting what had passed and fearing what might happen in the future, they spoke of what had been accomplished since the siege, and what more they hoped to achieve. There was laughter and good-humored bantering, and Janna found herself smiling as she served them all in turn.

But she was lonely, so lonely. In spite of her belief that she would never see him again, thoughts of Godric haunted her. Janna prayed that they'd followed Hugh's advice to her and had made it safely home, even if it meant that Godric and Cecily would now be wed, and possibly Hugh as well. But what most exercised her mind were thoughts of her father. She'd begun to despair that he would ever come to Winchestre, yet every time her thoughts turned to Normandy, her courage failed her. First she would have to journey south to a port, and find a ship to take her across the sea. How would she pay for such a thing? And once she arrived there, what then? She had only the vaguest notion of where Normandy was, or how big an area she would have to search. She knew only that her father lived there, but not where his home might be.

Sybil was waiting for her in the brew house. "You've worked hard over the past months, Janna." The taverner dipped in the pocket sewn into her apron and pulled out two silver pennies. "I told you I couldn't pay you a wage when you came back, but you deserve a reward now. It's partly thanks to you that the tavern is as popular as it is." A gleam of satisfaction brightened Sybil's face as she continued, "We've gained quite a few customers from Hell, Heaven and

Paradise!" She held the coins out to Janna. "Keep them safe and trust no-one."

Janna thanked her and pocketed them in her own apron. She hid a wry smile as she remembered the wealth she had once possessed, yet she had earned these coins by her own endeavors and they were doubly precious because of it. And as she pocketed them, the idea that had been lurking at the back of her mind suddenly became a distinct possibility: she could make and sell some of the creams and medicaments her mother taught her for now she had the means to purchase the extra ingredients she would need. Her work at the tavern had only ever been to keep her alive while she searched for her father, and the sale of her potions would help provide her with the means to travel to Normandy, if that was necessary.

*

As a first step, she took an inventory of the small patch of garden she now used as her own. She'd already planted a number of healing herbs, but she was determined to add to her collection so that she could also concoct the scented creams and lotions she'd once made for sale in the market place at Wiltune. Janna resolved to walk the lanes and water meadows once more, to take cuttings or else uproot and bring back some sweetly scented flowering plants. Roses and meadowsweet, violets and lavender too, if she could find some. It occurred to her that some of the plants in her father's garden might have survived the ravages of the firestorm. She would investigate the garden next time she went to inspect the site, and would salvage what she could.

As spring rolled on, and the days grew longer and warmer, Janna's small garden became ripe for plunder; it was time to start putting her plan into practice. To this end, she visited the apothecary to spend the coins Sybil had given her on beeswax, olive oil, and other items necessary for her preparations. She knew that once she set out on this course, she was committing herself to staying on in Winchestre, but if her venture succeeded, it would bring in coins enough to travel in comfort and safety at a later date – if her father had still not come. Meanwhile, she listened to the talk in the tavern. According to the travelers who passed through, the empress and her supporters were now holed up in Oxeneford and promising the earth, sky, sun and stars to any who would turn to their cause. It was enough to set the barons squabbling as each fought to gain more while protecting what he already had. Janna was particularly pleased when one traveler reported that the empress's fortunes had taken an upward turn – it seemed that the king had traveled north to subdue several disturbances and been taken ill at Northampton. Subsequent rumors said that he was near death.

There was also talk that, with the king out of the way, the Earl of Gloucestre had gone over to Anjou to ask Matilda's husband, Count Geoffrey, for his support in a final siege against the king's army. News came that he'd been delayed there, fighting alongside Geoffrey to help him secure Normandy. Rather than risk the barons' wrath by once again promoting herself to the throne, the empress was now promising that, if they would only support her, she would rule in the name of her eldest son, Henry, until he came of age. The next rumors to circulate said the king had recovered and was raising a large army to prevent the earl's return.

Janna listened to the rumors and continued to worry about her father's absence, visiting his estate whenever she could take leave from the tavern, in the hope of finding him or his steward there. She also kept a keen eye on the new shoots growing in his garden. Those she knew would be of use were harvested and carefully replanted in the tavern's kitchen garden. But the house itself was still a ruined heap, although the pile of rubble was fast growing smaller as anything of use was stolen to rebuild properties elsewhere. All over Winchestre, buildings were rising from the ashes. The old palace in the center of the town was one site that had seen no reconstruction. The bishop's men were reputed to be scavenging there, and using that material to fortify and enlarge the bishop's palace at Wolvesey, with the excuse that the palace had been cramped too tight and close to the cathedral, and therefore was not worth rebuilding.

A greater scandal centered around the burning of Hyde Abbey, for which the bishop was also held to blame. A fabulous gold cross covered in precious jewels, donated to the abbey by King Cnut himself, had collapsed and melted among the burning ruins. On the bishop's order, it had been salvaged and stripped. It was said that more than five hundred marks of silver had been recovered and thirty of gold, which were used to pay off those who had fought on the bishop's behalf during the siege, although the more cynical claimed that most of the proceeds had probably found their way into the bishop's own bulging coffers.

But at least part of his wealth was being put to good use, for both Hyde Abbey and St Mary's Nunnaminster were being rebuilt. Apparently the bishop was anxious to make amends for the damage done to these holy places by his firebrands. The London militia and the queen's mercenaries took the blame for everything else, for they had swept through Winchestre like a plague of rats, leaving terror and destruction in their wake. Horrifying tales of torture and death were still being whispered in taverns and alehouses, the stories accompanied by curses and tears. Buildings might be renewed, but shattered lives and broken hearts took much, much longer.

Janna took note of the changes as she hurried through the streets of Winchestre, passing masons, sawyers, carpenters, joiners, plasterers, smiths, coopers, carriers, thatchers, painters, craftsmen, and laborers alike, all of them busy about the task of rebuilding a once great town. The market close to the cathedral cemetery was trading again, as was a smaller market close to the north wall.

Her father's estate was one of only a few sites that still lay idle. She wondered if her father had been caught up in the troubles in Normandy. She wondered if he'd decided to abandon his estate in England for all time. She wondered if he was already dead.

*

Janna's usual welcoming smile, as she noticed a new customer, turned into a broad grin and a shout of delight when she recognized Ulf. The relic seller had come into the tavern, sat down, and deposited his heavy pack beside his stool before she noticed him, and his cry of delight echoed her own.

"Janna! I thought I'd never see you again!" He jumped up to embrace her, and they exchanged delighted hugs. He pushed her away then, and studied her closely.

"I looked for you everywhere on that last terrible day," he said. "Mistress Sybil said you'd run away, that you'd left the night before. She thought you were being chased, although she wasn't sure why. I feared the worst when I couldn't find you afterward. What happened to you?"

"I ran to the cathedral and found sanctuary there." Janna held up her hand as his lips framed a question. "It's a long story," she said quickly, "and I'll tell you about it some other time. I stayed in the cathedral until it was safe to come out, but when we heard what was happening outside I feared the worst for *you*!" She shivered at the memory. "However did you manage to escape?"

"With difficulty." Ulf grimaced. "As soon as I realized that the earl's army was in full flight, I hid in that small copse by the water meadows until nightfall. After I'd given up searching for you, I went south by way of hedgerows and fields, putting as much distance as I could between me and those murderous whoresons. Seeing it was the London militia causing the destruction here, I decided that London was probably the safest place for me to be through the winter. So I went there by roundabout ways, and that's where I've been until now. I called in to the tavern in the hope of hearing news of you, lass." He beamed at Janna. "I tell you, I felt sick at heart when I couldn't find you. I'm right pleased to see you safe."

"And I to see you," Janna assured him. She looked about in sudden concern. "Where's Brutus?"

"Outside." Ulf grinned at her. "There's such a maddle in here, I thought he'd have all the tables and stools knocked over if I brought him in. I've left him tied up with the horses."

"Poor Brutus. I'll give you some bread and gravy to take out to him to make up for it." Janna gestured at a stool. "Sit down, and I'll pour you some ale. No charge! And I'll come back for a few words as soon as I have a moment to spare."

Smiling broadly, she filled a mug and brought it to him, then set about serving the other customers who were flocking in, attracted by the sight of the green bush and the sound of the ringing bell. There were more customers than usual this day, for summer was at its height and the days were hot and long. It took her and Sybil some time to get to everyone, fill their mugs, take their orders, and bring trenchers of food to their tables. Janna looked around, content. The tavern was busy, the customers were happy, and now Ulf had come back. All it needed to make everything perfect was for her father to walk in!

Automatically, Janna's gaze flicked to the door. But if her father came, how would she know him? Would she feel some unconscious affinity to this man, her closest kin? She studied the crowd, testing her reaction to every man of middle age, anyone who might fit her father's description. But no-one caught her eye, nor did she feel any frisson of connection.

She glanced at Ulf, and felt a surge of hope. She had another pair of eyes to help her keep watch now. If her father, or his steward, came to rebuild the estate, they would be waiting for him.

*

It seemed that good fortune continued to smile on Janna. As she looked up from serving a customer a few days later, she saw Hugh coming through the door of the tavern. Light-headed with relief, she hurried to meet him. "What a pleasure to see you, my lord!" she said, and then noticed the boy following behind Hugh. "And your cousin with you!" She cast an anxious glance around for Godric.

"Janna!" Hamo had grown taller since Janna had last seen him, but he was still young enough to throw his arms around her in uninhibited delight. She hugged him in return, all the while conscious of her ale-splashed apron and homespun tunic. But Hamo seemed unconcerned, his face beaming with joy at the sight of her.

"I am pleased to see you too, Johanna," Hugh said, his own face relaxing into a relieved smile. "I've been worried about you since the last time we met. Please believe me, I tried to prevent...but I couldn't...er..." He shot a concerned glance at Hamo, and Janna at once understood.

"I managed to evade them and reach sanctuary in the cathedral, my lord. I stayed there throughout the...trouble. But what happened to you? And to Godric? Is he safe too?"

"Quite safe, yes. He chased after...er...and I found out later that he'd tackled him and knocked him out, so we knew you'd got away. Godric told me later that he'd lost sight of you once he'd brought...er...down, but he stayed on in Winchestre for several days, avoiding the king's troops while he searched for you. It was only after he found no sign of you that he finally came to join us at Tuiforde. We supposed you'd realized from my warning what was about to happen and that you'd managed to flee Winchestre in time. For my part, I knew the earl's retreat would turn into a hopeless rout. Being concerned for Hamo's safety should the fighting spread, I left under cover of darkness and travelled across fields and roundabout ways to Sire Geoffrey's estate." Hugh's air of bravado couldn't quite hide the shame lurking underneath, although Janna understood perfectly why he'd acted as he did. She wondered also how things stood now between Hugh and his betrothed.

"Have you been staying there ever since?" she asked.

"No." Hugh shook his head. "As soon as it was safe to do so, we took Hamo home to his mother. And delighted she was to see him too! I thought I'd never hear the end of her scolding, taking him into danger as I had."

"Mama worries too much," Hamo piped up.

Hugh ruffled his hair affectionately. "Yes, she does," he agreed. "But with good reason, on this occasion."

"I thought it was Dame Alice's own suggestion that you go courting and that Hamo accompany you."

"So it was. But I got the blame for not bringing him home as soon as the troubles started."

"And I was only allowed to come back here with Hugh because I gave Mama no peace until she agreed to give me leave." Hamo grinned broadly at Janna, looking mightily pleased with himself. "Even then, Hugh had to promise Mama that Winchestre was safe again before I was allowed to come."

"Is that true, my lord? What news is there of the empress and the king?" Janna had assumed things were quiet because there was nothing to tell. Curious, she looked to Hugh for an answer.

"The empress and her supporters are safely holed up in the castle at Oxeneford awaiting the earl's return from Normandy and Anjou, but the king has recovered his health and is busy securing all ports against Robert of Gloucestre. It seems that no-one will be going anywhere for quite some time. God willing, the people of Winchestre may have their fair in peace this year."

Janna was surprised by the joy Hugh's words brought her. Peace, however fragile it might be, was something they all coveted.

"I thought you'd know all this. I thought you heard everything in here," Hugh teased.

Janna smiled openly. "Good news is always welcome," she said. But there was a more pressing question she needed to ask. "Is Godric here with you?"

"No. I decided, in view of his good service to me, that I would appoint him my steward. As such, it's his responsibility to see to the harvesting while I'm here. He wanted to come back with me, but he understands where his duty lies."

"Godric's your steward?" Janna was delighted that he'd risen so high in Hugh's esteem. She wondered if Godric and Cecily were wed by now, but found she didn't have the courage to ask the question.

"Indeed. Godric might be lowborn, but I've never had any reason to regret his appointment. He's strict but fair, and everyone likes him. And he keeps a careful watch over everything. Above all, I trust him to tell me the truth. I know he'll serve me well once I...once we..."

It was the opening for which Janna had been waiting. "Are you betrothed to Sire Geoffrey's daughter now, my lord? Are you wed yet?"

"No, not yet!" Hamo answered for his cousin. "She's keen but you're not, are you, Hugh?"

Janna closed her eyes and wished she could disappear. She'd never have asked the question if she'd realized that Hamo would embarrass Hugh like this.

There was a short silence. She risked opening one eye, and became aware that Hugh was subjecting her to a keen scrutiny. She flushed uncomfortably under his gaze and looked away. Was that regret she could read in his expression? Was he still having second thoughts about his future plans?

"I'm afraid Hamo has the truth of it," Hugh confessed. "We are not yet wed, but Eleanor and I have come to an agreement at last, and her father has consented to the match. She is a good woman, and she loves me and will make me a good wife."

And she'll bring you a fortune. Janna felt rather sorry for Hugh. "So it is decided, then. My congratulations, sire," she said. "May I wish you every happiness for the future."

Hugh dipped his head in acknowledgment. "And you, Johanna?" he asked, seeming eager to change the subject. "Are you any closer to finding your father?"

"Not yet, my lord." Janna suddenly resolved to tell him of her search, and what she hoped to prove at the end of it. Now that Hugh's future with Eleanor was settled, her news could make no difference to his prospects, and he might even be in a position to help her.

"Why then do you stay in Winchestre if he is not here?"

Janna took a deep breath. "I have heard he lives in Normandy, but he has property here, and I hope that he may return to it. The estate was burned to the ground during the siege. His steward and servants fled, so there is no-one to ask what his intentions are. But – But I hope that he will return, for the estate appears to be of a good size, and there may be more than one." Janna remembered the sheaf of accounts she'd seen. "I believe his steward collected and traded a large amount of wool and other produce on his behalf before the troubles began."

Hugh's lips pursed in a silent whistle. "How do you know all this?"

"I visited the estate and spoke to his steward. I saw the correspondence and the records of his accounts." Janna paused for a moment. "And I sent him a letter," she added.

Hugh's eyes widened in surprise. "You can read and write?"

Janna nodded. "I learned how to do so at the abbey. Sister Ursel taught me."

Hugh looked impressed. "So you've found out who your father is? Who is he, Johanna?"

Janna hesitated. "My father is John fitz Henry. He's one of the old king's bastards," she said quietly.

There was an absolute silence. Janna only realized that they were both holding their breath when the silence was broken by the sudden whoosh of air as Hugh exhaled.

"How do you know that?"

Janna thought sadly of Ralph, who had found out the truth, although it was Ulf who'd interpreted it for her. "I had my father's letter to my mother, with his signature. And also his ring, which shows his initial, J for John, with a lion and a crown. I also had a brooch with an inscription."

"Had? Where are they now?"

"They were stolen." Janna looked into Hugh's face, searching for any sign of mockery. But there was none. Only the shock of her announcement was reflected there; shock and a growing puzzlement.

"But how do you know these came from the son of the old king? True, Henry had many illegitimate children. At least twenty, I believe. How do you know your father was one of them?"

Janna couldn't blame Hugh for doubting her, nor could she think of any way to convince him she was speaking the truth. "I didn't know what the ring and the letter meant, not at first. But I met someone who knew of my father and who told me where to find him." If only Ralph had lived, perhaps her message would have reached her father much sooner. But it was too late for if only, and for regrets. "I also spoke to the sisters at the convent at Ambresberie," she said steadily. "My mother lived there for a time. The sisters told me that my mother nursed my father back to health after he was taken ill with a fever while out hunting, and that they fell in love."

"Just as you looked after me when I was stabbed at the fair at Wiltune?" There was such warmth and regard in Hugh's voice and expression that Janna had to look away.

"Even so, my lord."

Hugh was silent for a few moments. Sneaking a sideways glance, Janna saw his hands clenched tight and knew his memories of that time were as unsettling as her own.

He swallowed hard. "So, was your mother a nun at Ambresberie Abbey?"

"Not a nun, no. Not really. But she was the infirmarian there." Janna could understand Hugh's shock and disbelief. Now that she'd put the situation into words, it was hard even for her to believe the truth of it. "And so I'm waiting here for word of my father. I'm waiting for him to come and see to the rebuilding of his estate so that I can introduce myself to him, for he may never have received my letter or know that he has a daughter. I can only hope, without his ring or the letter to prove my case, that he will believe me."

"Why didn't you tell me any of this before?"

"I held my peace simply because I can no longer prove my claim. I have no way of knowing whether or not my father will accept me for who I am." Looking at Hugh's desolate expression as he struggled to come to terms with her news, and an understanding of his loss, Janna wondered if she'd been a fool not to tell him earlier. Yet she'd given Hugh a chance to speak, to say he would take her out of love, that he would forsake everything just to be with her. And he had not. If she had spoken up before, and won him, she would always have wondered if he valued her only for her prospects. Hugh had chosen – but so had she, for Godric would always come first with her no matter what the future might hold.

There was no sense in dwelling on what might have been. "And what are your plans, my lord? Do you stay now with Sire Geoffrey until you are wed?"

Hugh nodded. He still seemed to be in a daze. Janna thought he believed her, and knew well that he was having second thoughts about his betrothed. To take his mind off his dilemma, and because she knew she'd have no peace of mind until she knew the answer to the question that nagged her day and night, she summoned up the courage to ask, "What news of Godric, my lord? And...and Cecily?"

"They're both well." Hugh attempted a shaky smile. "Now that Hamo has come to Sire Geoffrey to live in his household, he no longer requires a nurse, but Cecily begged my aunt to let her stay on at my manor. She's very much in love with Godric and I know she'll make a good match for him."

"Hugh wants them to wed." Hamo cast a mischievous glance at Janna. "I heard him tell Godric so."

"He asked me if that was a request or an order," Hugh grumbled. "I've told him that the marriage will please my aunt, and please me too. I value his stewardship of my land, and once Eleanor and I are married, she will need a companion. Cecily would be perfect for that position. I'm sure he realizes that the marriage is in his and Cecily's best interests."

It was the way of the world, Janna thought bleakly, that marriages should be made for reasons other than love. Just as Hugh's future had been decided for him, so had Godric's. She tried to console herself with the thought that Cecily would make a good wife for Godric. Unbidden, the memory of the passionate kiss she'd shared with him came into her mind. She trembled with suppressed emotion. "May I bring you ale and something to eat, my lord?" she offered. "Or wine?" she added hastily.

Hugh shook his head and sighed heavily. Janna was tempted to put her arm around him and comfort him as once he had comforted her, yet what she most wanted was to run away and not show her face again until they'd both left the tavern.

"Can I have some ale too, Janna?" Hamo asked.

Janna turned to the boy with some relief. "Of course you may," she said, and hurried away to fetch a pitcher and a couple of mugs.

But the shocks and surprises weren't over, she discovered, when she returned later with the wooden bowls of stew they had ordered. Hugh cast a quick glance at Hamo. The boy had picked up the spoon and fallen on the food with enthusiasm; he was paying no attention to them, and Hugh took the opportunity to beckon Janna closer.

"I came in the hope that you'd managed to escape the troubles," he said in a low voice. "I came to see if you were still here, because I need to give you a warning, Johanna."

"A warning?"

"Mus," he said, his voice dropping to a whisper. "I believe my uncle has sent him to look for you. And I'm afraid, so far as Mus is concerned, that his vendetta has now become personal. He blames you for his incarceration at Sarisberie, you see."

"Yes." Mus had been sent to work the abbey's farmland while she was staying there. He had come to kill her, but had made the mistake of trying to ravish her before he did so. She had managed to get the better of him, and he had been taken captive and put in prison, his actions judged according to both his crime and his intention. His overlord, Robert of Babestoche, had bought Mus's freedom, and now it seemed that he'd sent the man to finish what he'd started. After what had happened, Janna felt quite sure that Mus had a personal interest in carrying out his master's orders.

"Thank you for the warning, my lord," she said in a low voice.

"Mus knows you had employment here and I am sure he'll return. I had no trouble finding you, and neither will he, although I shall tell him that I've made enquiries and you haven't been seen since the siege began." Hugh couldn't keep the concern out of his voice, a concern that Janna shared.

"Thank you, my lord. I will take care," she promised. She should be safe enough in the crowded tavern if Mus came in, she thought, at the same time making a mental note not to venture out into the yard without either Ossie or Wat as an escort.

"My family has brought you nothing but grief." Hugh took Janna's hand, his thumb caressing her fingers. "I wish..." He fell silent, but continued to stroke her hand.

Janna wondered what to say. Was Hugh making up to her now that she'd told him about her father? She dismissed the thought as unworthy. There'd been an attraction between them right from the beginning. This show of affection was no more than what had already occurred between them in the past. Nevertheless, she should not encourage it, especially now that he was betrothed. Unaccountably, she felt a rush of concern for Eleanor and paused to examine the cause. It lay in the fact that, even while he was pursuing his intended bride, he was making overtures to her. Janna remembered the first time she'd seen Hugh in Winchestre with Hamo. Even then he'd been eyeing an attractive young woman as she passed him by. Was that how he was with every comely young woman he encountered? If so, Eleanor's path to happiness might be rocky indeed – while Janna herself might have had a narrow escape!

"I thank you for your concern, my lord." Janna withdrew her hand from his, and busied herself pouring more ale into their mugs.

"This search for your father," Hugh continued, looking somewhat hurt by Janna's action, "would you like me to make some enquiries on your behalf?"

"Would you?" Janna clutched the jug to her chest, excited by the possibilities. "I would appreciate it, my lord. Your..." She was about to say "father-in-law" but thought the reminder too raw in the circumstances. "Perhaps Sire Geoffrey may know of him and where I might find him?" And perhaps Sire Geoffrey might be appalled that a lowly drudge in a tavern was daring to claim kinship with a son of the old king!

"I'll ask him. I'll ask around," Hugh said, apparently not sharing Janna's qualms. "I'm sure someone will know how to make contact with your father."

"Thank you." Janna felt a rush of gratitude and relief. "Thank you so much, my lord." She became aware of raised voices trying to catch her attention, and raised hands snapping fingers and beckoning for service. "I must attend to the other customers. Please excuse me," she said hurriedly, and turned away before Hugh could say anything further.

Chapter 9

Janna had prepared a new brew and had rung the bell to summon customers to the tavern. The first sign that there was something wrong came when the patrons began to complain about the taste of the ale. They coughed and choked and spat it out, and emptied their mugs onto the rushes. Alarmed, Janna tried a mouthful, and realized they had good grounds for complaint. The ale tasted foul. Quickly she tasted the brew in the other barrels, but that too was contaminated. When the customers demanded a different brew, there was none to give them. Some had supped the ale in quantity, quaffing a long draft before realizing there was something wrong with it. They reeled outside to be sick, but some didn't get there in time. The air stank of vomit and Janna was hard put to keep her own stomach in check as she took a bucket of water and a wet rag to the puddles. Sybil also tasted the brew from all the barrels, and ordered that they should all be emptied.

Grumbling loudly on being told there was no other ale for them to sup, the customers streamed out of the tavern in search of comfort elsewhere. Even when Sybil belatedly offered them a cup of free wine to replace the spoiled ale, they stayed only long enough to drink it, not to buy more. The tavern closed early that night. Breathing fire and fury, not least over the inroads made into her stock of wine, Sybil interrogated Janna.

"I brewed it as I always do," Janna protested, quite unable to shed light on the mystery. "There was nothing different about the malt, or the gruit, I swear it." She thought for a moment. "Could it be that the water was tainted?"

"No!" Sybil snapped. "Ossie knows to go outside the East Gate to fetch it upriver."

Janna wasn't convinced. It was some distance to travel before the water ran clear and sweet enough to make a good brew, and there might be a strong temptation to take water from a canal within the town walls instead, water that might well have been contaminated by run-off from the tanners and dyers to the north. She wouldn't put it past Ossie to cart water from a nearer source if he thought it looked clean enough to chance it. But she didn't say anything, for the damage was done now. Nevertheless, she resolved to always taste the water before anything was added to it, and also taste the ale before it was served to the customers.

But Sybil wasn't finished grumbling yet. "If there's a complaint made about the ale to the ale taster, you're for a ducking in the river – or worse," she warned Janna. "Don't think I'll be taking the blame for this, miss."

"It's not my fault!"

Hands on hips, Sybil surveyed her. "I'll be watching you closely in the future."

Feeling resentful that she wasn't believed, Janna made up a new wort, meticulously tasting the barley malt, the wild hops and also the water before combining them in the mash tun. Every step was closely observed by Sybil. It would take several days before the brew was ready, and Janna knew the tavern would continue to lose business unless customers were prepared to pay the price for wine.

Nevertheless, the process couldn't be hurried, and besides, she was determined to do everything right. She tasted all the herbs that made up the gruit, pulling a face at some of the more pungent among them. As a final test, she asked Sybil to taste the ale once it was ready for serving to the customers.

"Perfect." Sybil smacked her lips, looking pleased for the first time in days.

Satisfied, Janna fixed the bush to the pole and rang the bell. Then she filled the jugs and took them out. But few customers came, and those only travelers who had not been told of the tavern's sullied reputation. The word had gone around; it seemed that previously loyal customers now preferred to try their luck elsewhere. But at least the tainted ale hadn't been reported, for they hadn't been asked to give an explanation nor make reparation in any way. Janna took some comfort from having escaped the ducking stool.

But she could not be easy in her mind. On occasion, a potential customer would come to the door, look around the empty tavern and back hastily away, preferring to go in search of livelier surroundings. One such, she was almost sure, was Mus. The moment she noticed him, she turned and walked quickly out of the tavern. She didn't dare go back for quite some time, in spite of Sybil's scolding. She didn't think Mus had seen her, but couldn't be sure. After that, she redoubled her efforts to make sure she was never alone in the yard, especially at night, but his face haunted her dreams, and several times she woke gasping for air, certain his hands had been around her throat.

In an effort to attract customers back to the tavern, Sybil offered ale at half price during the hour after Vespers. And Elfric put the new bake house to good use and invented a pie, with chunks of beef, onions and mushrooms simmered in a rich gravy to which ale had been added. The smell of it made Janna's mouth water as she took one of the pies out to a party of customers. They were strangers to the town and Janna hoped they would spread the word as they traveled about, so that more customers might be encouraged to return.

She set a knife, spoons and bowls on the table, and saw eager hands stretching out to cut and sample the appetizing fare. She turned to take another order, only to jerk around in alarm as a shout of outrage filled the room.

"What do you call this?" The traveler had jabbed his knife into a large chunk of meat and now he held it up for Janna's inspection. Peering closer, Janna realized there was a long tail attached to the morsel.

Her insides contracted in disgust. "I-I'm sorry, so sorry," she stuttered, and snatched up the trencher. She wanted to grab the mouse as well, but the man was still holding it on the point of his knife, his eyes glassy with disbelief as he swung it in front of the fascinated gaze of the others at his table.

"Please..." Janna pointed at it, willing him to put it down before the few other customers in the tavern realized what was wrong.

He stared at her. Then, with a muttered curse, he dropped mouse and knife onto the table, pushed back his stool and strode out, followed by his companions. Janna was instantly aware of how quiet the room had become. She looked up, and met accusing stares. Once again, the good name of the tavern would suffer.

Her mind was full of questions as she took the offensive evidence out to show Elfric. Tainted ale? Yes, it was just possible that there'd been something wrong with the water – because Janna was not prepared to accept that anything she'd put into the brew was at fault. But a mouse in a pie? Could it have gone in search of something to eat and been cooked in the filling by accident? It seemed unlikely.

That possibility was vehemently denied by Elfric when Janna set the pie before him. He was highly indignant at having his expertise questioned. "How do I know you're not responsible?" he muttered darkly. "First the ale, and now this."

Alerted by the uproar in the tavern, Sybil had come out to join in the interrogation. "You took the trencher through," she pointed out to Janna.

"The mouse didn't just drop into the pie! There was a layer of pastry on top of it!"

"Well, it was certainly there and in full view of the customers! If it didn't crawl into the pie filling by accident, then it must have been put there on purpose. Why? Can you tell me that?" Sybil's glance swiveled from Janna to Elfric and back again. They both shook their heads.

But Sybil's question remained with Janna for the rest of the night. She couldn't get the mouse out of her mind. Mouse – Mus! Was this a message from Mus that he knew where she was, and was watching her? Trying to discredit her? Last time he'd lain in wait and attacked her outright – and been caught. Was he playing a more devious game this time – cat and mouse, perhaps?

Or were the problems at the tavern actually directed at Sybil, to drive her customers away? Janna remembered the rival alehouses: Heaven, Hell and Paradise. No doubt they would be busier than ever as patrons of the Bell and Bush took their custom elsewhere. And there was certainly some bad feeling against Sybil for poaching their customers by lowering the price of her ale. Professional jealousy seemed a far more likely explanation than Mus's revenge, but Janna decided to investigate further before she voiced her suspicions. And she knew just the right person to help her.

*

"I want you to go to Hell," she said.

"Pardon?" Ulf blinked at her.

"And Heaven. And Paradise," Janna added quickly.

"That sounds more tempting. How do you propose I get there? Die? Or just fly straight up into the sky?"

"You walk down the high street."

"And why would I want to do that?"

Janna looked around the almost empty tavern. Ulf was one of only a few customers who had stayed loyal to the Bell and Bush following the fiasco of the ruined ale and the mouse pie. "Because I want you to spy for me."

A gleam of interest lit Ulf's eyes. "And what am I looking for, exactly?"

"I'm not sure," Janna confessed. Ulf had already heard about the recent upsets; now she explained to him what she was thinking. "I can't believe it happened by chance," she concluded. "I think it was done deliberately by someone trying to take custom away from the Bell and Bush. So, can you find out who owns the alehouses for a start?" Was she right in her summing-up of the situation? She was suddenly assailed by doubt. "Could you also..." She was about to mention Mus, but thought better of it. Ulf had never met him, and wouldn't know what he looked like.

"Also?"

"Also look out for Ebba?" Janna improvised. When she thought about it, the notion was actually quite credible. "You remember – the serving maid whose place I took? She parted on bad terms with Sybil, and there's no way of knowing what happened to her after that. If that merchant has thrown her out, she may have fallen on hard times. So, if it's not one or other of the alehouses wanting to pick up custom from the tavern, then maybe it's Ebba seeking revenge?"

Ulf rubbed his large nose, looking thoughtful. "Has she been back to the tavern? Have you seen her?"

"No. But that's not to say she didn't sneak in when no-one was watching."

"It's possible," Ulf granted.

"So, can you visit the alehouses and see who's there and what information you can pick up?"

Ulf grinned at her. "I could offer relics for sale, guaranteed to take care of a guilty conscience. What do you think about that?"

"If you can profit from it, Ulf, and flush out the culprit at the same time, so much the better," Janna assured him as she returned his grin.

*

The tavern was very quiet that night, and Janna soon got bored with so few customers to serve. Ossie put in an appearance periodically, but Janna knew he was spending most of his time in the kitchen, cadging food from Elfric, while Wat was barely to be seen at all. She caught Sybil eyeing her once or twice and wondered if the taverner held her responsible, and whether she was thinking of letting her go rather than risk anything else going wrong. There were certainly not enough customers to warrant her hire.

The thought frightened Janna. In the kitchen, at night after the tavern closed, she'd begun to concoct the lotions, salves and creams she'd learned under the tuition of her mother and Sister Anne. She'd been afraid she might have forgotten the recipes, and it was a joy to remember and use her old skills. She knew, from past experience, that her preparations would prove popular when she came to sell them, thus earning her a profit and, eventually, the means either to establish a small business of her own or finance her visit to Normandy. It would be a calamity if she had to leave the tavern now; it would put an end to all her plans. The thought fired her determination to get to the bottom of the mishaps.

She was quick to pounce on Ulf when he returned later in the evening, just as Sybil was about to bolt the door against the night. On seeing a customer, the taverner pushed it wide once more, but quickly stepped into his path when she saw Brutus trying to slink in behind Ulf.

"The dog's harmless," Janna reassured her. "And it's so quiet tonight, he won't get in anyone's way."

"I'm not having that animal in here." Sybil didn't budge. She put her fists on her hips and glared at Brutus. "You can tie him up out in the yard. That's where he belongs."

Janna pulled an apologetic face at Ulf, who merely grinned at her as he pulled a length of rope out of his pocket. "I'll be back," he said.

"Have you seen or heard anything interesting?" Janna asked, as soon as he returned. She sat him down, set up his mug and poured ale into it.

"I'll have a bowl of stew to go with this, mistress, if you please," Ulf shouted over her shoulder at Sybil, who was hovering close by. He gave Janna a wink as the taverner hastened out to fetch the food.

"I went to all the alehouses." He gave a loud hiccup to prove the truth of his words, and took a long swallow from the mug in front of him. "They're all doing a great trade, as busy as the Bell and Bush used to be." He wiped his mouth on his sleeve and burped gently.

"And?" Janna prompted impatiently.

"I spoke to the alewives. They seem decent enough. Keen for business, of course, but I doubt they'd play these sorts of tricks to steal custom from a rival – even supposing they were able to come into the tavern unobserved, which seems unlikely. They knew what had happened here, of course, and are delighted that Sybil has got her 'come-uppance,' as one of them called it. But I find it hard to believe that any of them is responsible for what's been happening here."

"And I suppose they couldn't count on our customers coming in to their own alehouses even if they did succeed in taking them away from the tavern," Janna said thoughtfully.

"But I did discover something of interest." Ulf leaned back on his stool and beamed at Janna, looking proud of himself. "That girl whose place you took. She's working in Hell now."

"Best place for Ebba, if you ask me."

"You'd think so if you heard her talking."

"Why? What's she saying?"

"Nothing good about Sybil, or the Bell and Bush. Says she's not surprised bad things have been happening here, given the way Sybil runs the tavern and the people she employs. It's 'the worst in the whole world,' according to Ebba. She seems to have done right well for herself, all dressed up and with airs and graces to match. But she's full of spite against Sybil, says the taverner was against her from the start and never gave her a fair trial. She hates you too."

"Me? Why?"

"Says you were after her job and that it's your fault that Sybil got rid of her."

"But that's ridiculous! You saw what happened. From what I can gather, the girl was useless. It was only a matter of time before Sybil let her go," Janna protested.

"That's not the way she's talking. She says it's because of your carelessness that the ale was tainted and the mouse got in the pie. And there's plenty who agree with her, after the bellyache you gave them with that ale."

"It wasn't my fault!" Janna punched his arm hard, not even trying to be playful.

"Ow!" Ulf rubbed his arm, looking rueful. "I know that," he said. "I'm only repeating what's being said elsewhere."

"I hope Sybil doesn't come to hear any of this." Janna knew she was likely to lose her job if she did. She prided herself on the brews she made, and was desperate to clear her name. "What's happening in Heaven and in Paradise?"

"They're both busy, a lot busier than here." Ulf looked around the deserted tavern. "I spoke to some of the customers, told them how delicious the new ale is at the Bell and Bush, and the food. But the word's got around there too. Still, it might do some good."

Janna wished she could share Ulf's optimism. "Thank you for trying," she said quietly.

"Another interesting thing." Ulf picked up his mug and drank deep, taking his time. "That merchant," he said at last. "The one who used to come in here a lot. The one that Ebba took up with." He fell into silence as Sybil came toward them, bearing a heaped bowl of stew. Janna stared at the huge portion, and wondered if Sybil was hoping to tempt customers back by giving them an extra helping. Judging by Ulf's wolfish grin, she thought the tactic might well prove very successful. Without further ado, he picked up the spoon and tucked in.

"Enjoy your meal." Sybil frowned at Janna. "Haven't you anything better to do than stand around tattling with the customers?"

Janna surveyed the empty tavern and raised her eyebrows. Sybil heaved an angry sigh and walked off.

"The merchant?" Janna prompted.

Ulf's response was to spoon up another portion of stew and chew contentedly. Janna knew he enjoyed teasing her, and had to restrain herself from grabbing hold and shaking him into speech. She tapped her foot impatiently.

"He was in Paradise."

"Not in Hell, with Ebba?"

"Nay." Ulf shook his head. "But, like Ebba, he seems keen to spread rumors and lies. I heard him telling one customer that the ale in Paradise is the best he's ever tasted. Which isn't true, as it happens. It tastes like rat shit. Well." He stopped to consider his words. "It's maybe not quite that bad, but it's nothing to brag about either."

"So why would he talk it up – unless it's to talk down the Bell and Bush?"

Ulf nodded. "My thoughts exactly," he said.

"Sounds like Ebba's got him wound around her little finger if they're saying the same things."

"If he's wound around her little finger, why isn't he drinking in Hell with her?"

"And who's been buying her new clothes and encouraging her to fancy herself, if not the merchant?"

"But he looks like he's fallen on hard times," Ulf said thoughtfully. "He's not nearly as full of himself as he used to be."

They looked at each other, mulling over the questions. "Can you keep on drinking there, try to win their confidence, see what else you can find out?" Janna asked, when no answers seemed to be forthcoming.

"If I do, you'll lose your best customer. Your only customer," Ulf added, as he glanced around the empty tavern.

"All in a good cause." Janna just hoped that, in the circumstances, she might keep her job long enough to solve the mystery and clear her good name. That alone was worth fighting for. Her hands clenched in rage as she thought of the lies being told about her. "You could start by finding out who's protecting that little viper now," she suggested.

"Ebba?"

"The same." Janna pulled a disgusted face. "If the merchant's had the good sense to throw her out, perhaps her new protector might appreciate a few words in his ear about what really happened around here!"

"I'll talk up your ale – and your reputation," Ulf promised, with a grin. He drained his mug, then ate the last of the stew, smacking his lips in appreciation. "And I'll see you tomorrow," he promised.

Janna was so preoccupied with what Ulf had told her, she forgot the threat to her own safety and so neglected to take her usual precautions. After the relic seller left, with Brutus bounding beside him, Sybil barred the front door, blew out the candles, and let Janna out into the yard. Janna heard the bolt of the back door scrape behind her as she set out for the kitchen, and realized too late that she should have asked Ossie to walk with her, as he usually did. She looked about the dark yard. Her imagination sprang to life, and with it the knowledge of her own danger. Every shadow posed a threat; every sly movement became an assassin. But in spite of her vigilance, the attack, when it came, took her entirely by surprise.

She felt her arms being seized and held from behind. A large hand clamped over her mouth. Without thinking, she bit hard, nipping the soft flesh of the man's fingers so that he yelled out in sudden pain. Janna stamped down, aiming for the man's instep, and was rewarded by a vicious curse. A faint light came from the kitchen as the door opened.

"Janna? Is that you? Are you all right?" Wat stood in the doorway, peering out into the night.

Janna wrenched her head sideways in a supreme effort to dislodge the man's hand. Even though she couldn't see him, she knew the identity of her attacker, for she recognized the sour-sweat smell of him from before. Mus. Fear almost paralyzed her, but she fought to stay strong as she gulped a quick breath. "Haaa – !" She managed no more than a short squawk before his hand clamped tight over her mouth once more.

Wat disappeared from the doorway. Janna blinked in disbelief. Surely the wretched boy must have realized something was wrong; surely he could have come to her aid. She kicked and struggled in Mus's arms, wild with terror. But he was stronger by far, his purpose fueled by resentment and a desire for revenge. His grip tightened, cruel and bruising.

"Shut your mouth!" he snarled, and dragged her toward the gate. It should have been locked for the night, but instead it stood half open. Janna's stomach lurched in dread; she knew that once Mus got her outside into the dark, lonely lane, she would die. Her struggles increased. Mus held her fast, his arm crushing her chest so tight she could hardly breathe. Remembering how she'd got the better of him before, she forced herself to stop fighting him and sagged against his hold, slack and unresisting.

He gave a grunting laugh. "I won't fall for that trick again," he said. His pace increased as he made the most of her lack of resistance.

Janna began to fight once more, desperate to gain time, just a few precious seconds before death claimed her forever.

She heard Mus give a grunt of surprise. His grip suddenly eased and she sucked a grateful breath into her aching lungs. Hardly daring to believe her luck, she broke free and started to run, expecting every moment that he would come after her. But he didn't. Instead, she heard a loud groan, followed by the thump of something hitting the ground. A wild whooping cry split the silent night.

In spite of her terror, Janna risked a glance over her shoulder, just in time to see Ossie burst out of the tavern door brandishing a piece of wood. He came galloping toward her, then came to an abrupt stop. Still unable to believe that she was safe, Janna's gaze moved on to the source of the triumphant shouting.

Wat was thrusting his fist in the air in a delighted salute to his own bravery. In his other hand he clutched a thin iron bar, which he waved at her.

"I got him!" he crowed. Janna smiled as his voice cracked into a high falsetto on the last word. "You're safe now," he shouted, consciously aiming for a deeper tone as he carelessly stepped over a dark lump on the ground. "He ain't goin' nowhere in a hurry."

"Well done, Wat!" Hardly able to believe her narrow escape, Janna looked at the crumpled figure. Just to make sure, she walked over and prodded him with her boot, in case he was pretending to have lost his senses. But he stayed where he'd fallen, silent and still.

"We can't just leave him here," she said uncertainly.

"Why not? Who cares if he's dead! He was after you, Janna. He would've killed you if I hadn'a got to him first." Wat airily hefted his weapon onto one shoulder. Janna peered at it in the dark and identified the iron poker that Elfric used to prod his fire into life. She winced as she imagined the damage it must have done to Mus's skull. She looked to Ossie for guidance, but the big man shrugged and kept silent.

"Let's just leave him here," Wat advised. "We'll ask Sybil what to do with him come mornin'."

"Good idea," Ossie mumbled, clearly not willing to take responsibility for anything.

Janna was about to argue, but then decided to keep her thoughts to herself. She didn't like to leave an injured man lying on the ground, but she certainly didn't want to bring him inside to tend his wounds. Nor did she want Ossie to summon help either, not if it meant lots of questions she didn't want to answer. "Why didn't you lock the yard gate, Ossie?" she asked instead.

"I did." The big man looked confused. "I did!" he said again, and swung around to prove his point. His eyes widened as he saw the half-open gate. At once he stalked over to examine it more carefully. "See! That bastard cut his way in!"

It was true; even in the dim light, Janna could see the damage to the gate. "Can you fix it, Ossie?" she asked. Even if Mus was out of his senses, they were still vulnerable to other troublemakers while the gate stayed open.

"It'll have to wait until the morrow. You make sure you bolt that kitchen door behind you tonight," he advised, and waited for them both to enter the kitchen before walking back to the tavern.

Janna didn't need to be told. As soon as she and Wat were inside, she barred the door behind them. After what had just happened, she regretted her uncharitable thoughts about the young potboy.

"I owe you my life," she said, "and I thank you." As reaction set in, her legs felt too weak to take her weight and she sank heavily onto a stool near the hearth. She was shivering with cold and fright. Now that she could see him properly in the glow from the damped-down fire, Wat looked very young and rather awkward.

"I saw you strugglin' with that man," he said. "I reckoned I needed a weapon so I ran to find one. Lucky he had his back to me. If he'd seen me comin', it could've been both of us a-layin' out there."

Janna didn't doubt his words. "It was very brave of you," she said quietly.

Wat grinned, regaining some of his cockiness at her praise. "Who is he, then? Why's he after you?"

It was a long story, and behind it was more than Janna was prepared to tell anyone. "He hates me, that's why." It was a compromise, but no less than the truth. Still, she could read the curiosity in Wat's gaze as he pulled out the straw-stuffed sleeping pallets and handed one over.

"Just call on me for help if ever you need it," he said grandly, and settled himself down for the night.

Wat slept the night in sweet contentment, perhaps dreaming of his bravery, but Janna had nightmares whenever she managed to slide into sleep. She awoke with a feeling of dread, wondering what the new day would bring. As soon as a rosy pink glow shone through the high windows, she jumped up from her pallet. She picked up the poker, just in case, and went outside, not knowing what to expect or how she should handle whatever might arise. But the yard was empty.

Janna blinked, and looked again. In part she was relieved that they didn't have a dead body to explain. But her greatest emotion was fear. Mus had gone. And when he returned, his anger would be greater than ever, and his desire for revenge even more urgent.

She went back to the kitchen, to find Wat stirring on his pallet. As he heard Janna come in, he sat bolt upright. "What have you done with him?" he asked breathlessly.

"Nothing. He's gone." Janna poured herself a cup of ale and sipped it thoughtfully.

"Do you think he'll come back?" Wat clenched his fist in the air, doing his best to bunch up the muscles of his arm inside his tunic sleeve.

Janna tried to look impressed by the sight. "I don't know, but I do thank you for being so brave last night." She looked up as Ossie shambled into the kitchen.

"'E's gone."

"But he may try again!" Wat breathed. Janna's two rescuers looked at each other and then at her. Janna wondered what she should tell them.

"I hope he won't return," she said, wishing she could believe it. "But can you both keep a look out for him, and let me know if you see anything suspicious?"

"You was expectin' him, wasn't you? That's why you always asked us to keep you company in the yard."

Janna nodded in answer to Wat's question. "And I hope you'll continue to keep me company, just in case?"

"Course!" he said stoutly. Ossie smiled in agreement. Janna felt slightly reassured. With Ossie's huge bulk on the one hand, and Wat's passionate need to prove himself on the other, she should be safe enough from Mus, or anyone else who sought to silence her on behalf of his liege lord. "No need to tell Sybil about any of this," she added, thinking that the taverner had enough on her mind to deal with.

Ossie sketched a cross over his mouth as a promise of his silence, while Wat again raised a clenched fist in the air. "Thank you," Janna said gratefully, and poured them both an ale.

*

The tavern was as quiet as ever that night. To Janna's relief, there was no sign of Mus, but Ulf came in early, smuggling Brutus in beside him while Sybil's back was turned. But all he had to report was that there was nothing further to report. Yet it seemed that his words had reached receptive ears, for along with Ulf, and in dribs and drabs, several other customers began to trickle in. Some were strangers to Janna and might well have strayed in from the street, but others had been loyal customers in the past and now looked a little shamefaced at their betrayal. But Sybil gave them all a fulsome welcome to show that she bore no grudges, and a free ale to make up for the ale they'd found too foul to drink and that had made them sick. Those few who also ordered food looked on with pleased amazement as heaped trenchers were placed in front of them.

Observing the customers' contentment, Janna thought it a shrewd move on the taverner's part. She knew her brew was sweet, one of her best; they couldn't help but enjoy it. Particularly if, as Ulf whispered to her in passing, they'd just come from Paradise!

A man in his middle age swept into the tavern, followed by a boy and an older man. Conversation came to a standstill as all eyes swiveled to observe the well-dressed newcomer. He carried himself with a lordly air, surveying the room in silence before selecting a table and drawing up a stool. Janna noted that his companion waited for his lord to be seated before sitting down himself. The man beckoned Sybil to him. Intrigued, Janna stopped what she was doing to watch.

"I'll have a pitcher of your best ale, mistress," he ordered. Sybil hastened away to fetch the ale herself, while Janna edged closer, unashamedly eavesdropping as the man began to question his underling. From what she could overhear of their conversation, it seemed that the underling was reporting on a property he was rebuilding. It also seemed that his lord was not at all satisfied with the progress he was making, for his tone was sharp and the underling kept shifting uncomfortably on his stool. The boy looked merely bored with the whole affair and stared boldly around the room. Janna was careful not to meet his glance, lest he accuse her of spying on them. Yet she was conscious of a nervous flutter of anticipation, for the man looked somehow familiar, while talk of rebuilding lent credence to a small and desperate hope that she was not mistaken.

Sybil placed the pitcher of ale and mugs in front of the lord with an ingratiating smile. After hesitating a moment to see if he would serve himself, she carefully poured ale into the mugs and stepped back, waiting for him to taste it.

He took a cautious sip, smacked his lips, and raised the mug for a long draft. "Your tavern was recommended to me," he told Sybil, as he put the mug down and waited for a refill. "I can see my informant was right about the quality of the ale you serve here." Janna stifled a smile. It seemed that Ulf had excelled himself when it came to spreading the word. Her ears pricked up as the man continued talking.

"I don't normally drink ale unless there's nothing else available." He grimaced, perhaps in memory of inferior ale tasted elsewhere. He lifted the replenished mug to his mouth for another hearty swallow. "But this," he said, as he lowered the mug once more, "this is how it ought to taste. This is how I remember it. Where did you learn to make ale like this, mistress?"

Janna stood stock-still, waiting for Sybil to reply, and perhaps to beckon her forward so she could take full credit for the brew. As she mulled over the significance of what she'd just heard, the flutter of hope, delicate as butterfly wings, grew into a whirlwind so strong she had to clutch onto the nearest table for support. She peered more closely at the lord.

His dark hair was lightly sprinkled with gray. He wore it long, and brushed into a fringe over his forehead in Norman fashion. As well, he sported both a beard and a mustache. He wore a long, pale blue tunic, elaborately embroidered at the neck and sleeves. Obviously a man of quality and style. Janna knew she had never seen him before, yet she was almost sure she knew who he was. She wished he would look at her, just for a few moments. What would she see if she looked into his eyes? But he was watching Sybil, leaning forward in anticipation of her answer.

The taverner clasped her hands and gave a saucy giggle. "'Tis an old family recipe, sire," she said, and fluttered her eyelashes at him. Reading his thoughts through his reaction to Sybil's news, Janna understood that the taverner might as well have saved herself the trouble of flirting with him. He blinked a couple of times, then slumped back onto his stool. He nudged the boy next to him. "Drink up, son," he said, and drained the rest of his ale in one mighty swallow.

Janna snatched up a full jug of ale. She was about to offer him a refill, but one of their regular customers grabbed hold of her. He thumped down his empty mug and waited until she'd filled it to the brim before launching into a long and complicated story about his missing wife. "Always devoted to me and the children," he rumbled, holding fast onto her sleeve lest she try to escape. "I can't understand it. I just can't." And he went on then to tell Janna that his wife had last been seen visiting the blacksmith's forge, "the one by the West Gate," he said. He shook his head, downed the contents of his mug in one gulp, and held out the empty mug once more. "I can't think why she'd go there when we don't even own a horse!" he grumbled. "It's not as though she needs a knife sharpened, or anything like that. I take care of that side of things. I keep everything in good repair. She's never wanted for nothing, my wife. I've always taken good care of her too."

Janna fretted impatiently, but he'd been a good customer in the past, albeit given to long monologues about everything from the weather, to his grievances over the troubles between the king and the empress, to the latest achievements of his young children. She knew she couldn't shake him off now that they were so desperate for customers, not without risking a rebuke from Sybil, so she listened with half an ear while she watched the man and his son, and tried to learn what she could from her observation.

"But you're a woman, so what do you think? Have they gone off together?"

"Eh?" Janna became aware that the customer was looking earnestly at her, waiting for her answer. Mentally, she kicked herself for not listening more closely, for she could see, now that she was attending to him, that he was in some distress and probably seeking comfort and reassurance from her.

"Because she didn't take the children, and that's not like her."

Janna wondered what on earth he was talking about.

"The blacksmith!" he said impatiently. "And my wife?"

Janna gave herself a mental shake while she carefully considered her answer. "Where does your wife's family live?" she ventured. "Could it be that she's gone to visit them, and been delayed for some reason?"

An expression of great relief spread over the customer's face. "That must be it!" he said, and banged the heel of his hand on his forehead as if to recall whether or not his wife had actually told him of her intentions. At last he let go of Janna, and shoved his empty mug in front of her again. "I need a drink," he said.

Janna suppressed a sigh. As soon as she'd poured his ale, she stepped toward the strangers' table, only to be brought up short when she saw that the stools were now unoccupied. At once she went to Ulf. "Did you notice two men and a boy sitting over there?" She waved a hand to indicate their position.

Ulf shrugged and shook his head. Janna tutted in annoyance. She hardly dared voice her hopes lest they come to nothing, but she couldn't ignore what she'd just seen and heard either. Surely that was her father reminiscing over the taste of her mother's ale! Or was she putting altogether too much importance on a recipe that her mother had taught her, which might well have been standard fare where her mother was born, and from where the traveler might also have originated? Quickly, she described the two men and the boy to Ulf. "Could you go after them, see if you can find them, see where their lodgings are?" she begged.

"Why on earth do you want me to follow three strangers?"

"I can't tell you now, but it's important. Hurry!" she urged. "Please," she added as an afterthought, but Ulf was on his way out by then and didn't hear her. Janna felt feverish with impatience and scolded herself for letting the party escape. What if Ulf couldn't find them? The only comfort left to her was the knowledge that if the man had enjoyed the ale as much as he said he had, there was a good chance he would come back for another taste of it.

As she'd feared, Ulf eventually returned without news and full of apologies. "I'm sorry, lass. I looked everywhere for the men you described, but I didn't see anyone like that. They might have gone into another tavern, or mebbe their lodgings, for I searched the streets up and down and there was nowt to see." In spite of his failure, Ulf's eyes sparkled with pleasure. Janna wondered what he'd found instead. She waited, half hoping, half dreading what she might hear.

"But?" she prompted at last.

Ulf could hardly contain his excitement. "But I told myself there must be a good reason you wanted me to follow them," he said, and tapped the side of his nose. "So I went as far as your father's estate. There's summat different about it. A pile of stone, a new pile. I think someone's about to start rebuilding."

"A new pile of stone?" Janna's heart gave a leap. "Will you go back tomorrow, see what you can find out?" she pleaded. "I'll go myself as soon as Sybil gives me leave, but it's hard for me to get away without a good excuse."

"I will." With an impish grin, Ulf swept her a sketchy bow. "Always glad to act as go-between for the son of a king and his daughter!"

Janna grinned back at him, feeling suddenly light-hearted. Mus, the troubles of the tavern – none of it seemed important now that she knew her father might be in Winchestre at last.

Her observation didn't seem so fanciful now that she'd heard Ulf's report. "You're right about the man I sent you after. I'm almost sure he's my father." As she went on to explain her reasoning, Janna remembered Hugh's promise. He'd said he'd make enquiries on her behalf, but he hadn't been back to the tavern since she'd told him her news. Grateful that at least Ulf was looking out for her best interests, she made a final plea: "Will you continue to keep watch on the site for me, Ulf? And pray that I'm not mistaken."

"I will." Ulf beamed at her, reflecting her joy. "You've every reason to feel hopeful, Janna. I'll certainly do all that I can to help you."

"Thank you!" To show her gratitude, Janna refilled his mug with ale and also poured some into a pan for Brutus to slurp. She refused to take any coin in payment. Sybil could take it out of her wages if she wasn't happy about it. But if she did, Janna would point out to the taverner that she owed thanks to Ulf for the customers who'd returned on the strength of his words of praise. That should be enough to guarantee Ulf free ale for at least a week.

Thereafter, Janna kept a closer eye on the customers than ever, and subjected Ulf to a desperate interrogation whenever she saw him. She tried to tell herself not to get her hopes too high, but inside she was coiled tight as twining bindweed, so desperate was she to see again the man who might be her father. The more she thought about it, the more convinced she was that she'd guessed right. And she made a solemn vow that, if he returned, he would not leave the tavern without first meeting his daughter. Whatever it cost in terms of her pride and his disbelief, she would tell him about her mother and herself. On that, Janna was entirely and utterly determined.

One thought bothered her. Her father had a wife and a family in Normandy, the steward had told her so. And in the tavern he'd called the boy accompanying him "son." What would her half-brother think when she introduced herself to them? His father might not have told any of them about Eadgyth. It seemed certain that none knew of her own birth. She was a stranger to all of them. Would the boy see her as a usurper of his father's affection, an older sister who might well become a threat to his own inheritance?

She must not expect to be welcomed with open arms. It saddened Janna to think that, in truth, she should allow for the fact that she might never be welcomed into her father's family at all.

Chapter 10

Janna woke to bright sunshine streaming through the kitchen window, and roused herself from her pallet. She stood and stretched, blinking sleepily against the shaft of light. Wat was still fast asleep, curled up like a squirrel. She walked over and gently shook him awake, prodding him with her foot when he grumpily turned over and relapsed into sleep. She wondered where Sybil could be. Normally the taverner woke them early, for there was always much to do before the doors opened to customers.

Janna hurried out into the yard to use the latrine. After washing her hands and face at the pump, she went to the tavern. Ossie was stretched out on his straw pallet, snoring, and Janna hastened up the stairs to fetch Sybil without disturbing him. But Sybil's bed was empty.

Puzzled, Janna went downstairs again and out to the brew house, the only other place where Sybil might be. She gave the door a push, but it caught and wouldn't open fully. Feeling the first stirring of unease, Janna pushed harder. When it still didn't budge, she peered around the door to see what was blocking it.

"Mistress!" She clutched at her heart, breathless with shock. Not wasting any more time, she edged through and fell on her knees beside the taverner. Sybil lay face down. Her veil was stained red from the bloody wound on the back of her head. Fearing the worst, Janna snatched up her wrist and felt for a pulse, as Sister Anne had shown her how to do at the abbey. She found nothing, and her panic grew until, suddenly, her questing fingertips sensed something. She pressed harder and felt the faint palpitation that told her Sybil's heart was still beating.

"Mistress Taverner!" she said urgently, and gently patted Sybil's cheek, hoping to rouse her. But the woman stayed limp and still, locked in the dark night of the unconscious. Janna reassured herself that at least she was alive. She gently removed the blood-stained veil to reveal the wound on the back of Sybil's head. Blood matted her hair, but when Janna parted the strands to examine the full extent of the damage, Sybil moaned pitifully and began to thrash about and try to turn over.

"Shh," Janna soothed her. "You're safe now, you're safe. I'll look after you." Not daring to try to move the taverner on her own, she patted her back to reassure and comfort her. After a few moments Sybil lapsed back into a swoon.

Janna didn't dare examine the wound again, for fear that Sybil might harm herself if she felt that she was threatened. She'd seen no fragments of bone mixed in with the blood, which led her to believe that the skull hadn't been crushed and therefore the wound was not mortal. She sat, stunned by what had happened, and overcome with remorse.

This was all her fault. She should have known Mus would come back to finish what he'd started. She should have warned Sybil to be on her guard, lest she be mistaken for Janna. Their clothing was similar, dressed as they were in homespun tunics and aprons, and with their hair covered by a veil. True, she was slightly taller than Sybil, but someone coming from behind could easily have mistaken the one for the other. Someone like Mus. But reproaches and blame would have to wait; it was more important now to attend to Sybil. She rose to her feet and went to summon Ossie and Wat.

To her relief, she found Elfric also in the kitchen, and quickly explained to the horrified trio what had happened, and what she needed. "Two long poles with a bed sheet tied between," she told them. "Sybil can't walk, so you need to fashion a litter and carry her up to her bedchamber. I'll gather together some medicaments to treat her wound." A lotion of water betony and sanicle for cleansing, she thought, and a healing paste. Plus something to ease the pain and help Sybil sleep, for sleep was the best remedy of all.

While she kept watch over Sybil and waited for Ossie and Elfric to bring the litter, she looked about the brew house for the weapon. There were several possibilities, but nothing bore any of the signs she was looking for: blood and hair. Not a thief taking a chance on what he could find, then, but a premeditated attack. Whoever was responsible had come prepared, and had taken the weapon away with him afterward.

Mus, she thought. It all came back to him. But how to prove it? She prowled around the brew house, this time looking for anything that could tie Sybil's injury to Mus. But all was neat and in place; there'd been no pot or pan throwing, nor were there any signs of a fight.

Janna knelt and checked Sybil's hands and under her fingernails for traces of skin or hair, anything that might point to the identity of her attacker. She even inspected Sybil's boots, but finally came to the conclusion that Mus must have escaped unmarked for it was obvious that Sybil had been taken completely by surprise. She'd had no chance to scratch or kick or bite him. He must have crept up behind her, mistaking her for Janna, and felled her with a single blow. She walked outside the brew house to look about, to see if the villain had left any trace of his visit.

Her search seemed hopeless. Customers regularly passed by on their way to the latrine. There were wet patches everywhere, puddles of piss, and spits and spats of vomit. She inspected the midden where scraps from the kitchen were deposited: rotting vegetables, skin, fur, feathers and offal all added to the stink, but yielded nothing of interest. Janna looked, and grimaced with distaste, and went back into the brew house.

As she tried to fathom the reasoning behind the attack, she felt increasingly uncomfortable. She didn't like where her thoughts were taking her at all: that the would-be assassin might well return to make sure he'd succeeded. It was a great relief when Ossie and Elfric finally appeared with the litter, accompanied by an anxious Wat. With Janna's help, they bore Sybil carefully upstairs, and eased her off the litter and onto the bed.

With Sybil resting safely, Janna hurried off to fetch what was already made up and to prepare what else she needed. How fortunate that she'd already put her plan into action and so had some medicaments to hand. Her first task was to persuade the half-conscious woman to sit up and sip some poppy syrup to dull the pain, after which she cleansed and medicated the wound, and bound it with a strip of clean linen.

"Don't worry about anything, mistress," Janna reassured her, as she helped Sybil lie down once more. "We'll take care of the tavern and the customers. You just rest here and get well." She hesitated; she was anxious to question Sybil, but didn't want to upset her. But her fears for all their safety needed to be addressed.

"Did you see who did this to you?" she asked.

Sybil lay quietly with her eyes closed. Janna wondered if she was out of her senses once more, or merely asleep. She was about to creep out of the room when she heard a faint sigh, an exhalation that might even have been a word.

"No?" Janna queried quickly. "Did you say no?"

Sybil licked her lips and tried to push herself up on the bed.

"Lie still!" Janna commanded. She waited a moment or two, and then questioned her again. "Do you have any idea who might have attacked you?"

"No." This time the answer was quite definite. "He must have come...from behind...and quietly...because I didn't see anything." Sybil's face screwed up in painful thought. She shook her head, and winced. "Nothing," she said faintly.

"Do you know anyone with a grudge against you who might have done this?" She held her breath, hoping against reason that Sybil might have been the intended target after all.

Sybil's breath escaped in a puff of bitter amusement. "There's plenty would like to see me go down."

"Can you give me a name?"

Sybil shook her head once more, grimaced with the pain, and closed her eyes.

Ebba? One of the alewives? Or the merchant, Alan? Janna couldn't rule any of them out.

"You must rest now," she advised. "And you mustn't worry. I'll take care of everything for you."

As Janna went about the business of the tavern, questions looped through her mind. The memory of the tainted ale and the mouse pie gave her some hope that she'd read the situation wrongly; that the attack on Sybil might have been motivated by a rival after all. But a deep disquiet soon overrode that faint thread of comfort. Mus was burning for revenge. Twice he'd fumbled an attempt on her life. What was he thinking now? That he had finally succeeded? Fear churned her guts to water.

Soon enough, he'd find out he'd picked the wrong target. And then he'd come back for another try – and this time he would take the greatest care not to fail. Briefly, passionately, Janna wished that Wat had killed Mus when he'd had the chance. She vowed to finish him off if given the opportunity. Meanwhile, she cautioned herself not to go anywhere on her own, not even out to the water meadows or to her father's estate.

She wasted no time in drawing Wat and Ossie to one side as soon as she re-entered the tavern. "Say nothing of what's happened to Sybil to anyone," she ordered. "We don't want customers to think this tavern is hexed."

The two nodded in agreement. Janna felt ashamed that her instruction was more for her own protection than Sybil's safety, although her reasoning was sound enough. She knew, from past experience, how quickly people would take fright if there was any question of the devil's hand in anything. "Back to work," she said briskly, and moved off to put her words into action. "I'll also warn Elfric to guard his tongue. Meanwhile, we'll be busy enough without Mistress Sybil here to help us."

With no taverner to keep an eagle eye on her, Janna felt free to sit briefly with Ulf when the relic seller swung into the tavern just after dinnertime.

"You're earlier than usual," Janna greeted him, thinking he looked exceedingly pleased with himself as he sank down onto a stool and settled Brutus beside him. "Do you have news?" She could do with something to cheer her spirits.

"Better than that!" Ulf beamed at her. Slowly, he unhitched his pack from his shoulder, opened it and delved inside.

Janna watched him on tenterhooks, hating how he teased her when he knew she was on fire with curiosity. "What have you got in there?" she demanded.

With maddening slowness, he withdrew something from his pack. He held it up in front of her, but she couldn't see what it was because the object was hidden inside his closed fist. She thought she was going to burst with impatience.

"Show me!" She jabbed her knuckles into his arm, only half in jest.

One by one, his fingers uncurled to reveal a silver brooch studded with multicolored gemstones. Janna recognized it immediately. She didn't need to look because she already knew what was there, but couldn't resist snatching it up and turning it over to read the inscription on the back. *Amor vincit omnia.* Love conquers all.

"Where did you find this?" she breathed. She turned it over once more and stroked it gently, just to reassure herself that her father's gift to her mother had really come back to her.

"One of the merchants in the high street had it out on display and I recognized it." Ulf's high good humor momentarily deserted him. "I don't know if he took it from you in the first place, but I turned over the rest of his goods in case he also had your father's ring and letter. But there was nowt else. I questioned him, but he told me only that he'd bought it from a chapman at a good price. He said the chapman told him he was selling his wares off cheap because he needed a cash sum in a hurry to pay off a debt. It may be true, but it's more likely the chapman was keen to offload stolen goods. I questioned the merchant about the chapman and his wares, and described your father's ring with the royal crest. He said he knew nowt about it, but I'm not sure I believe him. 'Tis certain he did well out of the deal, however it came about. And at least I've found this for you, lass."

"And I do thank you, Ulf!" Janna threw her arms around the relic seller, and gave him a smacking kiss on the cheek. "But..." Her delight rapidly faded. She wished that she'd kept the coins Sybil had given her, instead of now having just the few farthings she had saved from her wage. She slipped her fingers into the small pocket in her apron and brought them out. "I only have these to pay you for the cost of buying the brooch back for me. But I'll save my wages to repay you, I promise."

"Put them away," Ulf said, while a mischievous grin tweaked his mouth.

"I can't let you pay good money on my behalf," Janna protested, still holding out the small cut coins.

"I didn't." Ulf's grin widened.

"So, how did you – "

"I showed him my collection of relics," Ulf interrupted. "I swapped the brooch for the finger bone of Saint Giles himself!"

"But..." Janna didn't know what to say. She was well aware that Ulf purchased some of his relics in good faith, and probably paid good coin for them. She hated the idea of being so much in his debt for something so valuable.

"Don't worry your head about paying me back, Janna. I found a dead squirrel in the woods some while ago, and I kept some of its bones for emergencies." Ulf twinkled at her as he continued. "I also suggested to the merchant that he pray to St Giles not to lead him into temptation in the future. I think he's taken my warning seriously."

Janna shook her head in reproof, but with a broad smile on her face. "I don't want to know any more about it," she told him, "but I am truly grateful to you, Ulf." She slipped both the brooch and the coins into her pocket.

"You must keep it safer than that." Ulf fished into his pack once more and brought out a small leather purse, somewhat battered looking but still quite sound. "Tie this under your tunic," he advised, as he held it out to Janna. "Keep your treasures safe."

Janna hesitated.

"This is a gift," Ulf told her sternly. "Just thank me and do as I say."

"Thank you, Ulf." Janna pocketed the purse until such time as she had the privacy to stash away her reclaimed treasure.

"I still wouldn't risk putting the brooch in your pocket," Ulf advised. "Any sneak thief can pick a pocket in a crowded tavern, Janna. Pin it to your tunic for the while. It'll be safer out in the open."

Understanding the truth of Ulf's words, Janna did as she was bid. She knew it would look strange having such a fine object pinned to a drab tunic, but she took pride in her possession and touched it lovingly, feeling comforted and closer to her mother than she had since her purse had been stolen.

The tavern was busier than ever; it seemed that business was picking up at last. Janna made a point of greeting customers as they came in, and darted between the tables to serve them all, enlisting Ossie's help from time to time when she couldn't cope.

"You are welcome, sire." Janna's smile froze on her face as she looked more closely at the newcomer blocking the doorway. The man inclined his head and walked inside, accompanied by the smaller figure of the boy.

"Some ale, my lord?" she offered breathlessly, as she indicated an empty table. "I know you like my brew." As she noticed his stunned expression, she realized that she'd addressed him in Norman French, as befitted his rank, even though he'd spoken in the language of the Saxons to Sybil on his previous visit. Perhaps he was amazed that a humble drudge would be so forward – or so lettered – as to understand and speak his own language.

Janna returned his stare, hardly aware of how rude he must think her. She was too busy assessing his features. His dark brown eyes were just like her own. His hair was dark whereas hers was fair, for in that she resembled her mother. The scattering of gray told her he was a man in his middle years and of an age to have fathered a daughter of almost twenty summers. Her searching gaze moved on to his eyebrows, his nose, his mouth, looking for similarities and differences. All the while, her heart was hammering so hard it was difficult to think rationally at all. But at the center of her whirling thoughts was the certainty that this must, indeed, be her father.

His eyes narrowed as he caught sight of the brooch pinned to her tunic. The color blanched from his face. "Where did you get that?" he asked fiercely. He grabbed her arm and shook her hard. "Answer me, wench! From whom did you steal that brooch?"

"I didn't steal it!" Shocked, Janna stared at him. "It's mine, my lord. It belonged to my mother."

"That's impossible!" He turned to beckon Ossie, who was already hurrying toward him, alarmed by his raised and angry voice and the scene he was creating in the tavern. "I want her arrested," he said. "She's a liar and a thief."

"My lord, wait!" Janna pleaded. She turned to Ossie. "It's a misunderstanding. Please don't call the guards. I can explain everything, I promise you."

Ossie stared at her, unsure what he was supposed to do: obey an important customer or support someone whom he knew and trusted? Finally he shook his head and moved a short distance away.

"Give it to me." The man held out his hand. "Give me that brooch at once."

Slowly, knowing she had no choice, Janna unpinned it and handed it to him. It felt like losing her mother all over again. She blinked hard against the tears that flooded her eyes. As she had known he would, he turned it over. His lips moved as he silently read the inscription.

"Please, my lord, please give me the chance to explain." Janna fought to appear calm, to muster the words she needed, for it was vital that she give a good account of herself. She knew she wouldn't be given another chance to speak; indeed, might well be dragged away and cast into the castle prison if she couldn't convince her father of her identity. "Just a few moments of your time, my lord, I pray." It was an effort to keep her voice steady. She was angry and hurt, and very, very afraid.

He glowered at her, yet Janna saw a flicker of surprise cross his face as he studied her more closely.

"Do I know you?" he asked. "You seem familiar somehow. Were you employed on my estate before it was burned down?"

"No, my lord, we've never met." Janna wished Sybil was around to put in a good word for her. She cast a glance of appeal at Ulf, who was watching the scene with a worried expression. He jumped up and hurried over. He noticed the brooch in the lord's hands and understood the situation at once.

"That brooch belongs to Janna, my lord," he said steadily. "She's owned it all the time I've known her."

John glowered at him. "And who are you?"

"Ulf, the relic seller, sire, at your service." Ulf swept him a low bow. Janna groaned inwardly, knowing her father was unlikely to be impressed by Ulf's calling nor was he likely to believe anything Ulf might say. But Ulf was the only friend she had to speak up for her, and speak up he did.

"Your dau – " Janna closed her eyes, but Ulf caught his mistake and quickly corrected himself. "I've known Johanna for more than a year, sire. She's courageous and honest…and I'm quite sure that the Earl of Gloucestre himself would vouch for her good character if you were to ask him." He cast a triumphant glance in Janna's direction. She felt a sudden lift in her spirits, and nodded her thanks to him.

"Robert of Gloucestre?" John gave a contemptuous snort, clearly not believing a word of it. But now that Ulf had given her the key, Janna found the courage to speak up in her own defense.

"I visited the earl at the castle last year," she said steadily. "I had important news for him concerning an intercepted letter from the Bishop of Winchestre to King Stephen."

John's hand closed around Janna's arm in a vice-like grip. "Do not speak of that in here! Do not speak of it at all." It was clear from his warning that her father knew all about the letter. Janna hoped she'd said enough to capture his interest so that he would now hear her out. She waited for his permission to speak.

But it seemed that he wasn't sure, now, what to do. He released her, and drummed his fingers on the table while he thought about it. Then he jerked his head in Ulf's direction. "What we have to discuss is nothing that concerns you."

Ulf bowed. "With your permission, sire, I shall withdraw," he said formally, and returned to his seat. Understanding that he was no longer needed, Ossie hurried off. Janna remained standing in front of her father.

He sat down. His son, wide eyed with excitement, sat beside him. Janna waited for an invitation to sit down with them, but it didn't come.

"Explain to me how you came by this brooch," John ordered.

Janna's throat went dry; her thoughts flew away. Where to start? How to convince him? To give herself time to think, she looked at the boy. Her half-brother? He was slight, with a heart-shaped face and a rather sulky expression. She could see no likeness at all to his father. He must take after his mother instead – Blanche. The thought of her father's wife felt like a fist clenching hard around Janna's heart.

She blinked. Now that the time was here, she had absolutely no idea how to break the news to her father that he had a daughter. To her relief, Ossie came back with a brimming jug of ale and two mugs, which he set down on the table. "Some ale, my lord. On the house. For your trouble." He waited a moment, obviously hoping to hear what Janna had to say for herself, but John dismissed him with an irritated flick of his hand.

"I'm waiting."

To give herself a little more time to muster her thoughts, Janna filled the mugs, splashing the ale in her nervousness. All the while she was conscious of the man's close scrutiny.

"The brooch came from my mother, lord, as I told you," she said at last, and put the pitcher down, glad to be rid of it, for her hands were shaking so badly she was afraid she was going to drop it. "Her name was Eadgyth. But you knew her as Sister Emanuelle."

"What?" John surged up and grabbed hold of Janna's arm once more. "Is she alive, then? Where is she now?"

Janna drew in a breath. She had raised her father's hopes and now, somehow, she must find the words to tell him that her mother was dead. Knowing she couldn't trust him with the whole truth, not yet, she broke the news to him as gently as she could, saying only that her mother had drunk some tainted wine and died from it.

"No!" The man sank back onto his stool and bowed his head. Then he jerked up and faced Janna with blazing eyes. "I don't believe you!" he said fiercely. "My Emanuelle was a healer! She was the infirmarian at Ambresberie Abbey. Even if the wine was tainted, she knew how to cure the ills of the body, any diseases at all. Unless...Was it an accident?"

"You could say that, my lord. She died many seasons ago." Janna took a breath. "I am her daughter, and I buried her."

The man was silent. Janna could have wept for the grief she read on his face. All this time he hadn't taken his eyes off her. "So Emanuelle married again," he said softly, and with some bitterness. "You say you are her daughter. Who, then, is your father?"

The moment she'd longed for had come. Janna felt such fear she wondered if she was going to be sick, and swallowed hard against the nausea rising in her throat. She was acutely conscious of her surroundings, of her stained clothes and lowly status. She wished with all her heart that she'd kept the brooch hidden until she'd had time to fetch the precious gown from the chest in Sybil's bedroom; until she'd had time to dress herself to meet her father. He was far more likely to have believed her story if she looked the part. But it was too late now for regrets.

The thought came to Janna: She and Eadgyth had always been poor, had lived as paupers. This was who she really was, whether her father liked it or not. She straightened up and faced him bravely.

"You are my father, lord," she said softly.

Her statement was followed by utter silence. Janna did not dare to look at him now, nor his son. Feeling acutely self-conscious and miserable, she stared down at her feet and the rushes on the floor. They needed changing again. She blinked, and risked another glance at him.

John was still staring at her, thunderstruck. "By God, you do presume," he said at last.

A flash of anger stiffened Janna's resolve; it gave her the courage to defend herself. But her knees were shaking still, so she sank down onto a stool and gripped the table edge to give her strength. The boy swiped his hand through the air as if to wipe her presence away as she collapsed beside him.

"My mother told me nothing of you while she was alive, my lord," Janna said, trying to order her thoughts into the most convincing argument she could find. "It was only after she died that I found out that you left her to go to Normandy, to see your father the king. When you didn't return she thought you had deserted her. And so she went back to the abbey at Ambresberie to beg for shelter. By then, you see, she was carrying a child. Me."

"She was with child when I left her? But I…" John struggled to speak. "I had no idea."

"You wrote her a letter," Janna continued. "I know. But I only saw it after my mother died." She hesitated a moment, recollecting the words she had read so often they were engraved on her memory. "*Mon amour, ma cherie,*" she quoted, thinking this the best way to convince her father that she had seen the letter he wrote, even if she couldn't produce it now. She reverted then to the language of the Saxons, just as her father had done when he wrote to her mother.

"*I had hoped to return to you long before this time, but I find that my father has gone to Normandy and so I must follow him there. I cannot send a message to him for he will not understand why I need to break my betrothal to Blanche, nor will he forgive me unless I meet him face to face to explain why I am utterly unable to wed anyone but you.*"

Janna stole a quick glance at the boy – her half-brother. His face had paled; he was round-eyed with amazement.

"*He will be wroth, but I feel sure I will be able to persuade him that, in this, I know best,*" Janna continued her recital. "*While he has made a worthy match for me, I know that once he meets you and witnesses our happiness together, he will fall under your spell just as I have done, and will welcome you into our family and bless you as a daughter. For certes, no-one could be more worthy than you to be my wife, or bring such grace to our family.*

"*You have my ring, and now I send also this ring brooch to you to pledge my love. 'Amor vincit omnia.' It means 'love conquers all' – and so it shall.*

"*I will return as soon as possible, for I miss you more than life itself.*

"*Je t'embrasse de tout mon coeur, de tout mon corps, ma cherie. John.*"

There was a long silence after Janna stopped speaking. She waited for her father to say something, but he seemed incapable of speech. It was hard to read his expression. Knowing what a shock her words must have been, Janna felt some sympathy for him.

"I only realized after my mother died that she did not know how to read and write," she said, knowing this would be a bitter grief to her father. "Nor did she ask anyone to read your letter to her. So she didn't know you planned to return. She thought you had gone back to wed the woman to whom you were betrothed."

"But...how could she think that?" It was a cry from the heart. "How could she think I would marry someone – anyone – other than her?"

"But you married someone else," Janna reminded him. "You married Dame Blanche."

"Only because I thought your mother was dead! On my return from Normandy I searched everywhere, but I found no trace of her, not anywhere. Even the sisters at Ambresberie claimed to know nothing of her whereabouts."

"They were speaking the truth," said Janna. "When the abbess refused to shelter my mother, she set off for Wiltune and the abbey there. By then she was heavy with child, and she called herself Eadgyth, *wortwyf* and healer."

"And I was looking for a single woman, not a mother and child. And I was asking for Sister Emanuelle. Your mother never told me her real name. And now it's too late and she really is dead!" Grief convulsed John's features. He snatched up the mug of ale and drank deeply to disguise his distress.

"She died with your name on her lips. She never spoke of you to me, but she loved you all her life. And she never wed anyone else either." Janna wasn't sure whether it was a comfort or a curse for John to know that. "My real name is Johanna," she said, hoping to ease his pain. "She named me after you."

"Johanna?"

Janna inclined her head in agreement.

"And did your mother enter the convent at Wiltune? Is that why I couldn't find her? Is that where you were reared?"

"No." Janna couldn't help bitterness creeping into her voice as she began to describe their life to her father. "The abbess granted my mother a cot and a small piece of land close to the forest of Gravelinges. We eked out a living brewing potions and healing the sick."

"When all this time we could have been together," John whispered. "All this time wasted."

"What about my mother? What about us?" The boy's sharp voice interrupted John's reverie, drawing him back to the present with a start. Janna understood both the boy's anger and his father's predicament. She wondered if she would have done better to hold her tongue until she could speak to her father alone.

John sighed, and at last turned his attention to his son. "Your mother and I were betrothed at an early age," he said. "Even though I was not the king's legitimate son, my father wanted a good match for me and so it was arranged. But then I came to England, and joined a hunting party and fell ill. Your mother – " he turned to Janna " – nursed me back to health and we fell in love."

Janna nodded. This she already knew from the nuns at Ambresberie.

"After that, I knew I could marry no other than Emanuelle, and so we were wed."

"Wed?" Janna sat up straight, hardly believing what she was hearing. "You and my mother were wed?"

"Yes," John said grimly. "We were wed. And then I was faced with the task of telling my father what I had done, so I went in search of him. But he had gone to Normandy, and I was forced to follow him there. I had to do the honorable thing, you see, and explain to him, and to my betrothed, that I was already wed and that I intended to live in England. And I wrote to your mother to explain my continuing absence." His face crumpled. "I knew she could speak my language, but I wasn't sure she could read it. That's why I wrote the letter in the language of the Saxons. She never told me she was unable to read at all!"

"She was a proud woman." Too proud, Janna thought, remembering Eadgyth's refusal ever to speak of the past, of her perceived misfortune at the hand of her lover – her husband. She'd never dreamed that her mother had been legally wed. This was something to think about later, when all was quiet and she had time to mull it over.

"She taught you to speak Norman French?" John asked.

"Yes."

"But not how to read, presumably, since you say she could not. And you say also that she never spoke of me. How, then, did you find the letter? How did *you* come to read it?"

It was as though her father was trying to catch her out in a lie. "I found the letter after my mother died," Janna said steadily. "She'd hidden it away, along with your ring and the brooch. I knew how to write my name, Johanna. She'd taught me that much. And I recognized the letters in your signature: J-O-H-N. I wondered if the letter might have come from my father, so I went to Wiltune Abbey and begged sanctuary there. Sister Ursel taught me how to read. I wanted to learn so that I could read your letter, so I could find out who my father was. So I could find *you*."

"And where is my letter now?" In spite of his skepticism, John seemed somewhat impressed by her achievement.

Janna threw her hands in the air in a gesture of loss. "It was stolen. It was in my purse, along with your ring and the brooch, but my purse was cut. The brooch was returned to me today." She cast a quick glance over her shoulder at Ulf. He was watching her, and as he caught her eye, he winked and raised his thumb. Encouraged by the friendly gesture, Janna turned back to her father.

"But what about me? What about us?" The boy's petulant whine was as annoying as a gnat on a hot summer's night. Janna reproached herself for being so uncharitable. It was clear that this news of her father's had changed everything, both for his family and for herself. If her father believed what she'd told him.

With a sigh, John turned to face his son. "I searched a long time for Emanuelle, and eventually came to the conclusion she must have died." He shifted uncomfortably on his stool, perhaps wondering how to portray his subsequent actions in the best light. "I thought I was free to marry again. Believe me, Giles, I married your mother in good faith. I thought that, if I'd lost my only love, at the very least I could please the king, my father, by honoring the betrothal he had arranged for me. And I have to say, your mother was more than pleased to take me on."

A tinge of bitterness had crept into John's tone. Janna began speculating how relations had been between husband and wife over the years. Did Blanche know that she was second best right from the start? Or had she found out the hard way?

"But it seems as if, unknowingly, I have committed bigamy. Our marriage was illegal, and therefore you, my son, are illegitimate." John's glance strayed to Janna, and went back to his son.

"Illegitimate?" The boy's voice rose in an outraged squeak. "But...but I am your heir. You said so! You said I would inherit everything from you. My sisters won't get anything! And neither should *she*!"

Janna heard the satisfaction in his tone, and found that she was beginning to dislike her half-brother quite a lot.

"That's not how it'll be," John said. "I've made provision for your sisters as well as for you, Giles, no matter what you might choose to believe." He sighed again, and said more forcefully, "This news has come as much of a shock to me as it has to you. So we'll say no more about who inherits what until I have had time to get used to the idea that I may have another daughter." He cast a bemused glance at Janna.

"Just wait until my mother hears about this," the boy muttered.

"You will leave it to me to tell her the news," his father said quickly. "You are not to breathe a word of this, do you hear me?"

"My lord," Janna ventured, "I think she already knows." And she told her father then of her visit to his estate, and her conversation with his steward. "I wrote you a letter telling you about myself, and begging you to come to Winchestre to meet me."

After what had just transpired, Janna was certain that Blanche had never passed on her message, and her father's fist slamming onto the table confirmed it. "I never received your message. That whoreson steward of mine – "

"It's not the steward's fault, my lord." Janna hastened to set the truth before him. She had no love for the steward, but thought it more important to warn her father what he might face once he questioned his wife. "I spoke to the young messenger who told me of his voyage across to Normandy. He vowed that he'd handed over the message, and that he was told there was no reply. I had no reason to doubt his word. I only hoped that 'no reply' meant that you intended to come here in person to see me."

John was silent for a moment as he mulled over Janna's words. "To whom did the boy hand the message?"

"Your wife, my lord." Janna glanced at her half-brother, but looked away quickly as she read the hatred in his eyes.

"That explains why she insisted on coming here to England with me, and bringing our family," John mused. Janna wondered if he knew he was speaking his thoughts out loud and whether he intended her to hear them. "Johanna," he said then, but he did not reach out to touch her, even though Janna longed for some expression of affection from him. Did he still not believe that she was who she said she was? Surely she had said enough to convince him.

He shook himself, as if trying to come to terms with everything he had learned. Janna sat back, thinking to give him time. She became aware of a rising hubbub in the tavern; customers were shouting for attention. Some were even leaving, muttering and disgruntled. She sprang to her feet, ready to serve them. They had worked too hard to attract custom back to the tavern for her to jeopardize it now.

Her wrist was gripped by a strong hand. "You may or may not be my daughter, but if you are, I'll not have you working as a drudge in a tavern!" John insisted.

Janna glared at him, stung that he could still doubt her. "It's honest work, work I needed to support myself in your continuing absence, my lord." She couldn't resist the jibe. "Meanwhile, the taverner is – is indisposed and I must attend to our customers!"

She wrenched her arm from his grasp, picked up the pitcher, and splashed more ale into his mug. She set the pitcher down with a bang. "You recognize the taste of the ale because it's made to the recipe my mother taught me," she said more quietly. "No doubt you acquired a taste for it when she used to make it for you." And she hurried off, fighting tears of rage and humiliation, and a deep sorrow that what should have been a joyful reunion between father and daughter had gone so badly wrong.

Chapter 11

"I'm assuming that really was your father, Janna? Did all go well after I left you?"

"Ulf!" Janna was delighted to see him. After she'd finished serving all the disgruntled and impatient customers the previous day, she'd realized that Ulf had left the tavern, so she'd had no-one in whom to confide her dashed hopes over the grand reunion with her father. He and Giles had gone without speaking to her again, leaving Janna disappointed and resentful that not only had he made no effort to understand her situation, he hadn't given back her brooch either.

"Thank you for coming to my rescue," she told Ulf as she filled his mug. After a quick glance around to make sure the other customers had everything they needed, she sat down to tell him all that had transpired after he'd left them.

"I doubt I'll ever see my father again, or my brooch either," she concluded, and banged her fist on the table, caught between anger and tears.

"Don't take on so. Your father just needs time to get used to the idea of having a daughter," Ulf comforted her. "He loved your mother, so he'll be back, lass, you'll see. You'll have another chance to talk to him then." He leaned closer, dropping his voice so that only Janna could hear him. "Meanwhile, there's summat I have to tell you," he said seriously. "There's a rumor going around that the Bell and Bush is about to close. Do you know something I don't?"

"It's a lie! Who told you that?"

Ulf shrugged. "One of the regulars in Hell. I don't know his name, but I've seen him in conversation with Ebba several times. They seemed to be getting on very well, if you know what I mean."

Janna nodded. She understood perfectly.

"That merchant? Alan. Was he there too?" she asked, just to make sure.

"Nay, he weren't."

So the merchant had seen through pretty Ebba to the black heart within, and now drank at another tavern. And Ebba had found a replacement. "Is Ebba still slandering me? And Sybil and the tavern?"

"Aye. She's one of those saying the tavern's about to close. But why? Your customers have started to come back. You'll soon be as busy as ever." He looked about him. "Where is Sybil? I noticed you were in a right moither trying to serve everyone yesternoon. Why isn't she here to help you?"

Janna glanced about swiftly to make sure they could not be overheard. "Because she's lying upstairs on her bed, with the back of her head bashed in."

"*What?*"

"Shh! It's all right!" Janna hastened to reassure him. "She's not dead. But she does have a very sore head. She's not going to be up and doing for quite some time, I'm afraid. But you're not to say anything to anyone about it. Promise me?"

"Of course. But – what happened?"

"That's what I'd like to know." Was Mus responsible? Ulf didn't know that Mus had attacked Janna in much the same way that Sybil had been attacked. Ulf knew nothing about Mus. Really, Janna reasoned, it was up to her to follow that line of enquiry, if only she knew where to start. But Ulf could be useful to her in other ways. "I found Sybil lying in the brew house, senseless," she continued. "There was no sign of a weapon. Whoever is responsible knew what he was going to do and must have brought the weapon with him – or her – and taken it away again." Hoping to convince him as well as relieve her own conscience, Janna decided to test her thinking on Ulf. "I'm wondering if someone's out to destroy the tavern, Ulf. First, there was the tainted ale. Then the mouse pie, and now this attack on Sybil."

Ulf nodded slowly. "It seems too much of a coincidence, I agree. But who's behind it? And why?"

"Ebba?"

Ulf's mouth turned down. "Do you think a woman – a girl – would do something so wicked? Nay, lass! It seems unlikely." He shook his head.

"Why not? Ebba's the one with the grudge, she's the one saying that the tavern is going to close. It doesn't take much strength to knock someone down if you creep up behind them." Janna repeated what the taverner had told her. "Whoever it was took Sybil by surprise and got away without being seen."

"Why would Ebba be so vindictive?"

"Why not?" If forcing the tavern to close was the purpose behind their recent misfortune, then Ebba rather than Mus was a far more likely suspect.

"I'll keep my eyes and ears open," Ulf promised. "And I'll make a point of talking to Ebba, see what I can find out."

"Mind she doesn't set her cap at you," Janna teased.

Ulf snorted with mirth at the very idea. Looking at him, Janna wasn't so sure. He might look like a goblin and have questionable friends and practices, but his brown eyes were merry and his heart was a solid lump of gold. Ebba could do a lot worse for herself. It was unlikely that she would succeed in winning his love, but if she did, Ulf would prove far truer to her than Alan, who apparently dropped women as quickly as he picked them up. But someone was dressing Ebba in finery, someone was keeping her. So Ulf should be safe enough; nevertheless, Janna couldn't resist giving him a warning.

"Be careful, Ulf. If Ebba is responsible for the attack on Sybil, she's more dangerous than she looks."

"If? You're not sure, then?"

Janna wondered whether she should confide in Ulf after all. Half hoping that he would scoff at her fears, she said, "Sybil was hit from behind. I wondered if she was the intended victim, or if her attacker actually mistook her for someone else."

"Someone else like who?"

"Me."

"*You?*" Once again Ulf's voice cracked high in disbelief. "Why should anyone want to harm *you?* What aren't you telling me, Janna?"

"A man attacked me once, a long time ago. To silence me. But he made the mistake of trying to force himself on me first. I managed to fight him off and summon help." Janna grimaced at the memory. "Mus was caught, found guilty, and imprisoned for a while at Sarisberie, but his lord put up bail for him and so he was released. I was warned he would come after me again, and so he did. But Wat got the better of him on that occasion."

"Wat? This happened just recently? Why didn't you tell me?"

"It's in the past. I'm a lot more careful now." Janna made a dismissive gesture, partly to allay Ulf's fears but also to convince herself that all was well.

"But who is this man, Mus? You must point him out to me, Janna." Ulf hesitated. "If he's a threat to you, I know someone who could take care of him. If you know what I mean."

Janna did. But not for anything would she have Mus's death on her conscience. "No," she said. "Thank you, Ulf, but I don't want that. Believe me, I am being careful. Mus won't get another chance in a hurry."

"Except you believe he's now harmed Sybil by mistake?"

"I don't know. I just don't know. But whatever happens, I think we should keep quiet about the fact that anything's happened to her."

Ulf nodded slowly, but he didn't look happy. "I'll see what else I can find out," he said. "And you must also promise to be careful." He brightened. "But of course, you have your father to take care of you now. I'm sorry things went badly for you yesternoon, but you should go to him, lass, and talk to him again."

"No!" Not for anything would Janna relive the humiliation of her confrontation with her father.

Ulf frowned. "He has the brooch. He must believe you, surely?" He sat back, a half grin on his face. "I did wonder if you'd still be here when I came in. I thought your father would insist you come to live with him in his lodgings. You should go to him, Janna. That'd be the very safest place for you! And respectable. Much more fitting for the granddaughter of a king!"

"I have to keep the tavern going in Sybil's absence," Janna said. "Anyway, my father doesn't care where I live or what I do."

"Doesn't care?" Ulf's eyebrows rose high up to his cap. "After all you've said about him and your mother, how could he not care?"

"I'm not sure he believes me." Janna caught hold of Ulf's hands. "Thank you so much for finding the brooch," she said earnestly. "I really thought, when I gave it to him and quoted the letter he wrote to my mother, that he would greet me as his daughter. But I was wrong."

"Aye, lass. I can see you're heart-sluffened." Ulf put his arm around her.

Janna leaned against him, taking comfort from his presence and the knowledge of his concern for her. "I had hoped to win his love," she confessed. "Even more importantly, I'd hoped to win his support to avenge the death of my mother." It was the only reason Janna had set off to find her father, but now her quest seemed hopeless.

"Avenge your mother's death?" Ulf waited, obviously hoping for an explanation. But Janna was too cast down to give him one.

"It's no use," she said. "I know he loved my mother, but he has a wife and a family now – including a son who already hates me, and who will not willingly give up his inheritance. I can't do any more, so I might as well forget about him."

Ulf was silent for a few moments. "Your news must have fair stopped his heart in shock. Even worse that you spoke it in front of his son. Give him time to think about it, lass. I'm sure he'll come around."

"Or he may come round just to taste my mother's ale. He seems to like it!" Janna said bitterly.

"Time is on your side," Ulf reassured her. "At the moment his estate is only a pile of stone. It's going to take a while before he can move in. Where is he staying in the meantime?"

"I don't know."

"I'll see if I can find out," Ulf said, and slipped off his stool to set his promise in motion.

With a heavy heart, Janna began serving the other customers. Then, leaving Ossie in charge, she ran upstairs with a mug and a pitcher of ale.

She found Sybil struggling to get out of bed. "Lie still, mistress!" Janna ordered sharply. "You've got a nasty head wound. You mustn't try to move. Not yet, anyway."

"I have a tavern to look after." With a grunt, Sybil swung her legs to the floor and tried to stand. Janna saw her face contract with pain and hastily set the pitcher down to help Sybil in case she fell. The woman was trembling all over, swaying like an aspen in the wind.

"Lie down, Mistress Taverner," Janna said, more gently, and lent her support as Sybil sagged back onto the bed. "Stay there!" Not giving her any time to argue, Janna bent and picked up Sybil's legs and swung them up. With a sigh, Sybil stretched out and closed her eyes. "You're not to worry. I'm looking after everything for you."

"What are you doing up here, then?"

Janna grinned at Sybil's acerbic tone, reassured that the taverner sounded more like herself at last.

"Ossie's minding the customers." Janna poured a mug of ale and put it in Sybil's hand. "Can I get you something to eat?"

"No. Thank you. I'm not hungry." Sybil drank thirstily, and set the mug down for Janna to refill it.

"Now that you've had time to think about it, can you remember anything about the attack?" Janna was sorry to push her, but knew that they'd all be safer if the culprit could be identified. "Did you see anything? Hear anything? Smell anything?" She remembered, with a shudder, the acrid odor of Mus as he'd held her tight.

Sybil closed her eyes. When she didn't speak, Janna wondered if she'd gone back to sleep. But it seemed she was just thinking, for finally she said, "I heard a sound. Something familiar, something I've heard before. But I can't remember what it was!" She clicked her tongue in exasperation.

"Don't worry about it," Janna encouraged. "It'll come back to you." She waited a moment. "Anything else?"

Wearily, Sybil shook her head.

"I'll visit you later," Janna promised, and hurried downstairs once more.

As she moved among the customers, several queried when the tavern was going to close. Janna took comfort from the fact that they seemed pleased when she assured them that it wasn't. It might even have some curiosity value, she thought, if people came to see why the tavern was set to close and stayed to drink ale and order food instead.

Wat was busy clearing dirty mugs and trenchers from the table. She was about to send him back to the brew house to refill the empty pitchers with ale when she heard a query about the tavern's future.

She stayed silent, wanting to hear Wat's reply, for it was important that he reassure the customers that it was business as usual. The customer drained his mug and set it down with a bang, licking his lips to taste any stray drops. Janna smiled to herself, pleased that her brew was going down so well. That, more than anything, should entice customers back to the Bell and Bush. She noticed the other patrons sitting at the man's table had ceased their chatter. They too were anxious to find out the fate of the tavern.

"Who's to say how much longer we can keep open?" Wat hadn't seen Janna. She was about to intervene, to set the customer straight, but Wat leaned closer, obviously about to impart something important. Intrigued, Janna quietly shuffled closer. "Mistress Sybil's been attacked. She's half-dead now and a-lyin' upstairs." He pointed a dirty finger in the direction of Sybil's bedchamber.

Muttering curses under her breath, for she'd expressly instructed Ossie, Elfric and Wat to say nothing of the attack on Sybil, Janna swept forward. "Go and refill the pitchers, Wat," she said sweetly, and grabbed the half-full jug he was carrying. "Pay no attention to the scullion," she told them as she busily refilled the customers' mugs. "He knows nothing about anything. The taverner is indisposed, that's all, and this tavern will stay open as long as…as long as anyone has a thirst to quench!" She smiled around the table before hastening out to berate Wat for ignoring her instructions.

"They was askin' questions 'bout the taverner. I had to tell them somethin', didn't I?" he said, with a sideways glance that seemed to hold a hint of accusation.

"That's no reason to encourage tittle-tattle! I told you to say nothing of the attack on Sybil, or her injury. Just say she's not well if anyone asks. And the tavern is *not* about to close; make sure you tell them that."

Wat shrugged and bent to loosen the bung on the barrel, making a big show of refilling the jugs.

"It's your job that will go if the tavern closes!" Janna reminded him. "We've worked hard to bring customers back here after the destruction of the town and the hardship that followed it. Do you want to put our future here at risk?"

"It's not you lyin' up there with your head bashed in! Why're you makin' such a fuss about everythin'?"

Janna was about to shout at him for being so stupid, but checked herself, remembering how he'd come to her defense. But for Wat she might well be dead. And Sybil might have been safe. "Don't talk about Sybil or what happened, all right?" she said, squashing down her unease. "We want customers to have confidence in us, not think they might do better elsewhere."

"Mebbe they will." It was said so low that Janna wasn't sure at first if she'd heard right.

"What did you say?"

"Hell. Heaven. Paradise. They got a lot more customers than us." Wat kept his back to Janna so she couldn't see his face. But his backside, as he stooped low over the barrel, presented a tempting target. She itched to kick it.

"And that's why we have to work twice as hard as anyone else to tempt customers back to us again," she snapped. She couldn't believe Wat could be so stupid that he hadn't worked it out for himself. Not trusting herself to stay calm enough to deal with him, she snatched up a couple of brimming jugs and rushed back into the tavern.

A party of young men waylaid her. They'd obviously been drinking elsewhere and were somewhat the worse for it. As Janna passed, one of them grabbed hold of her sleeve and swung her around so that the brimming jugs slopped ale onto the rushes. Already annoyed with Wat, Janna had to press her lips together to stop herself from shouting at the oaf. She cast a glance of appeal in Ossie's direction, but he was busy talking to someone and had his back to her.

"Give us some of your best ale, sweetheart." The speaker kept a firm hold on her sleeve. He seemed to be the ringleader; he was red-faced and sweating; she could smell his foul breath as he dragged her closer to hear his order. His companions grinned inanely and thumped their fists on the table in encouragement.

Janna pulled away, her expression revealing her distaste. "I am not your sweetheart," she fumed. "And all our ale is of the best quality. In fact, it's the finest you'll get anywhere in Winchestre." She slapped some mugs onto the table and sloshed ale into them, keen to get away from the drunken sots as quickly as possible. They, however, had other ideas. As she pocketed their coins and began to walk away, the ringleader grabbed her once more.

"Don't be in such a hurry, sweetheart!" He spun her around and, before she could react, pushed her down onto his lap and put his arms around her. He reeked of ale and an acrid sweat that spoke of much labor out in the fields and not enough washing afterward. Janna felt her stomach churn in disgust.

She stamped down hard on his instep and, as he yowled in protest, she pushed herself free of his embrace and skipped out of his reach. "Behave yourself or drink elsewhere," she told him, pleased that Ossie had at last become aware of the disturbance and was coming her way. Arms folded across his massive chest, he took up a position next to the table and its occupants, daring them to twitch even a finger out of line.

Janna quickly made her escape. She was anxious to reassure the remaining customers that it was business as usual, to counteract anything Wat might have told them. As she moved between the tables, she became aware that she was being watched. She stopped abruptly. Her father. It took all her courage to approach him, thankful that at least he was alone today. She could hardly bear to look at him as she said, "Please take a seat, my lord, and I'll bring you some ale."

"I need to talk to you." His voice, his whole demeanor, was stiff with disapproval, and Janna knew he'd witnessed her humiliation. While she could try to explain it away, nothing would wipe the scene from his memory.

"I haven't got time to sit with you. I'm alone here, I have to serve the customers," she apologized.

"You call yourself my daughter, yet you're a drudge in a tavern and a magnet for any lackwit who cares to take advantage of you!"

"As I've already told you, I need to work to support myself," Janna snapped. If her father thought her rude, so be it. She didn't have to justify her actions to someone who, until a day ago, had not even been aware of her existence. She poured him a mug of ale and hurried away. If he had anything to say to her, he could do so after the customers had left and she had time for him.

She kept busy serving food and ale, and hovered over the tavern's patrons with reassuring words regarding the tavern's future, while her father remained, watching and waiting. Although she longed to go to him, hoping that in spite of everything he might welcome her into his family, pride kept her away until, finally, she ran out of chores and even the pretense of something to do. She walked over to his table and sat down, not waiting for an invitation. Although her heart was quaking in her breast, she faced him, assessing his features, so similar to her own. Even his mouth was familiar. Although half hidden by his mustache, she'd seen a feminine version in the empress and in herself, and its masculine counterpart in Robert of Gloucestre. If the earl was to be believed, they had all inherited most of their facial characteristics from the old king, Henry. She wondered if her father had at last recognized the resemblance. If so, then surely he could no longer deny her. She waited quietly for him to speak.

"You took me completely by surprise yesterday," he began awkwardly. "After all these years of thinking Emanuelle had died, and that an important part of my life was over and forgotten, I hardly knew what to say to you. Or to my son, when I had to give him an explanation of the past. But I do apologize if I offended you."

Somewhat mollified, Janna made a concession of her own. "I should have waited until you were on your own before speaking, sire," she admitted. "It was just that I was so..." Her voice faltered. She took a deep breath and plunged on. "I was so delighted to see you, to meet you at last, when I'd almost given up hope. I saw you in here before, you see, but had no chance to speak to you then. I didn't want to risk losing you again."

John chewed on his lip. Janna thought he was a man used to action, to making decisions, and that being at a loss was probably a new experience for him. She began to warm to him, to feel again the excitement of meeting him at last. But she should guard her heart, she reminded herself. She would not set herself up for more disappointment. So she stayed silent, giving him the chance to say what was on his mind.

"I've spoken to Blanche," he mumbled. "She denied it at first, but finally she admitted to receiving your letter. She said she thought it was a jest, someone chancing their luck, perhaps. She said she didn't want to worry me with it, and so she destroyed it."

"You were away at the time, sire." Even though she didn't believe the excuse, Janna was prepared to give Blanche the benefit of the doubt.

John nodded slowly. "Of course, your presence changes everything. Blanche knows that now. And she will not readily forgive me for what I have done." He sighed, and opened his purse. To Janna's great delight and relief, he withdrew the brooch and placed it into her upturned palm. At once she pinned it to her tunic, quickly, before he could change his mind.

"I accept you are my daughter, Johanna." A quick flash of humor momentarily lightened his face. "In fact, I only had to look at you to know that." Suddenly, unexpectedly, he caught hold of her hand and held it between his own. "I thought I'd lost your mother forever," he said brokenly. "I can't – I can't believe that we made a child together!"

Janna felt helpless in the face of his distress. What did he want from her? What did he expect would happen next? She wished she knew. But her hand lay within her father's clasp; she felt his warmth. The prickly barrier she'd raised against him began, slowly, to dissolve.

"Tell me about your mother," John implored, when he'd mastered himself once more. "Tell me about her life, your life together. And tell me also why you were so determined to find me when you had no idea who I was."

Out of the corner of her eye, Janna saw someone enter the tavern. It took her a moment to refocus, to recognize Hugh, but he noticed her at once and stepped her way. She watched him check as he saw her companion, and read the dawning realization on his face. He turned aside then, and sat down at an empty table. Janna was about to go to him, but saw that Ossie had picked up a jug of ale and was ready to serve Hugh himself. Nodding her thanks to him, she turned back to her father.

The brief pause had given her time to think, time to plan her strategy. She would tell him what he wanted to know, tell him about her life with Eadgyth. But she would not tell him how her mother's life had ended, not yet, not until she knew that she could trust him with the truth, and with her need to avenge her mother's death.

John listened intently to her reminiscences, occasionally asking questions or interrupting her with little anecdotes of his own. There seemed no doubt now that he had accepted her story. Janna began to relax, and even laughed occasionally, although the story of the hard life she'd shared with her mother stirred an aching misery that Eadgyth was no longer alive to be reunited with her one true love.

"You say your mother died from drinking tainted wine?" John still looked perplexed.

Janna hesitated. It was not yet time to tell him everything, lest he scoff at her suspicions and immediately ally himself with the lord of the manor. She needed to know that he trusted her judgment enough to act on it. "There was something wrong with the wine. By the time my mother realized, it was too late to counteract the harm," she explained, giving him something of the truth.

John was silent. Janna read the sadness on his face. But he seemed to accept her explanation, for he didn't question her any further. Instead, he drained his mug and set it down. "You must leave the tavern," he said. "Come away with me now, for I won't have you molested by any more drunken louts. Besides, I want you to meet my wife and my other daughters. They can't visit you here, it isn't seemly. Nor do I want them to know how you've been living and what you've been doing." He surveyed Janna with an anxious frown. "But I'll have to find you something else to wear before you can meet them," he muttered.

Almost speechless with embarrassment and anger, Janna struggled to find her voice. "I can't come with you, my lord," she said, as politely as she could. "I've already explained to you that I cannot leave the tavern while the taverner is – is indisposed. I've helped her build up a good business here, and I would not jeopardize that."

"But – "

"Nor will I leave her in the lurch." Janna spoke over him. "I owe her my loyalty for taking me in when I had nothing, and giving me work, food and somewhere to live." She was about to add, *Which is more than you've ever done*, but thought better of it.

Offended and displeased, her father glowered at her. "I will not have you disgrace my family by continuing to work here as a tavern drudge," he said stiffly, and rose to his feet.

Janna stared at him, then jumped up to face him directly. She gripped the table, needing its support in order to defy him.

"I am who I am," she said.

John glared at her. "And I am who *I* am," he said pointedly. "I am also your father, miss. You would do well to obey me."

"Just as you obeyed your father when you married my mother?"

John winced, but Janna felt little pleasure in wounding him. Nevertheless, she was sure she was doing the right thing in defying him now. "For all these years I have lived without a father," she said, "and I am who I am because of it. It's too late now to wish me different." It was as well for her father to know from the start that she was used to being independent and living as she chose. There could be little future for them together, unless he understood that.

"You have a choice, Johanna," he said. "You told me you've searched a long time to find me, and now you have. But my position comes with certain expectations and obligations. Unless and until you are prepared to accept them, I believe we have nothing further to discuss." He gave a brief bow and strode out of the tavern, leaving Janna with her mouth agape, stunned as a fish floundering on dry land. She had felt so sure of herself, so justified in her bid to repay Sybil's kindness. Yet it seemed that in trying to do the right thing by Sybil, she had put her quest for justice in jeopardy and, even worse, her own future along with it.

Chapter 12

As soon as he saw her father leave, Hugh rose and came over to her. "I'm so pleased that you've met up with your father at last, Johanna!" he enthused. "I came to tell you that he was in Winchestre, but it seems you already know that." As he studied Janna's expression more closely, his enthusiasm evaporated. "Is something wrong? Did the meeting go badly?"

"Yes." Janna felt wretched, yet she didn't know what she could have said or done differently. Surely she was in the right? And that meant her father was wrong. She shook her head, wishing she could make sense of what had just happened. Was this the end of her quest? Would her father decide not to upset the life he had with Blanche for someone so wayward and unyielding?

The answer seemed to be yes, at least while she continued to work in the tavern. But once Sybil was back on her feet, and if she could find someone else to take her place here, what then? Would her father welcome her into his life? Or, by refusing to bow to his will, had she poisoned their relationship forever? Janna's spirits plummeted further as she realized that, even if she knew how to mend things between them, it was too late. She didn't know where he resided so she had no way of contacting him.

Her panic began to subside, as she recalled what Hugh had just said. "Do you know where my father is staying, my lord, for I forgot to ask him?"

"He's staying with his cousin."

"His cousin?"

"Henry of Blois. The Bishop of Winchestre."

Janna's thoughts reeled as she digested the implications of what Hugh had just said. "Does that mean my father supports King Stephen?" she ventured at last.

"Everyone does nowadays. It's too dangerous to do otherwise."

Janna acknowledged the truth of Hugh's words. The tide had turned against the empress; there was no longer any future in supporting her against the king. Janna still held a secret hope that the empress might yet prevail in her bid to win the crown from her cousin, Stephen, but Hugh was right. It was not safe to say these things any longer.

"And where is the bishop living now?" she asked. The old palace in the center of the city had been destroyed and it was clear the bishop had no intention of rebuilding it. Likewise, the royal castle outside the West Gate had taken a battering. So far as anyone knew, it had stood deserted since the empress and her supporters had fled.

"The bishop's at his palace at Wolvesey, with his entourage. That includes your father." Hugh hesitated, looking suddenly awkward. "I should warn you that his family is with him," he said. "Do you know that your father has a wife, a son and two daughters?"

"Yes, I do. I haven't met his wife and daughters yet. Nor will I, if my father has anything to do with it." Janna stopped, feeling dangerously close to tears.

"Are things so bad between you?" Hugh's tone was gentle.

Janna nodded, and took a quick breath. "Have you met my – my father's family?" she asked, curious to know something about these rivals for her father's love.

Hugh shook his head. "I've only just arrived back here. I've been at Tuiforde with my – with Eleanor. I did ask around before I left, as I promised I would, but I got nowhere." He gave Janna a wry grin. "Then I heard Sire Geoffrey talking about a 'John fitz Henry' and I knew at once who that must be. So I suggested that he invite them to witness my...my marriage to his daughter, and so he has."

"May I come too, my lord?" The words were out before Janna had a chance to think through the consequences. She read Hugh's reaction in his startled glance at her tunic and spattered apron.

"My apologies, lord," she said quickly, feeling mortified. "I shouldn't have asked."

"Eleanor and I will make our vows in front of the priest," Hugh said doubtfully. "Anyone can come to witness that. But...but I'm sorry, Johanna, I cannot invite you to the celebration feast that follows, for how would I explain your presence to my...my betrothed? Or my future father-in-law?" The thought of his impending nuptials had cast a shadow across Hugh's face. "But for all that, I would like you to be there," he added wistfully. "Perhaps I could announce you as your father's daughter?"

"He won't thank you for that!" But Janna was aching with curiosity to see her father's family, as well as Hugh's betrothed. "No, my lord, I'm sorry I asked. I'll come to witness your vows, if I may, but I don't expect you to acknowledge me. I don't wish to embarrass either you or your bride. Or my father." It would give her the chance to see her new family without their realizing who she was. This thought was followed by another possibility, but Janna pushed it aside to think about later.

"In truth, I would like you to be there, Johanna." Hugh paused a moment, and cleared his throat. He took a deep breath. "Indeed, I wish with all my heart that it could be you by my side instead of Eleanor when I make my vows."

Janna heard the raw pain in his voice as he admitted his true feelings. But there was nothing she could say or do to make things right for him, and so she remained silent.

"It's too late for us, isn't it?" Hugh persevered, adding almost to himself, "I had my chance at happiness. I should have had the courage to take it." He reached out to touch her cheek in a tender caress. Janna caught her breath. If only this was Godric standing in front of her, if only…

She knew the regret on his face was mirrored on her own. "You will find happiness with your wife, my lord, if you come to the marriage with a loving and cheerful heart," she said firmly, hoping that her words would prove true.

"I shall certainly do my best," he said unhappily. "It seems that Eleanor is pleased enough to have me."

"And I wish you both all the joy in the world," Janna encouraged him. "When are you to be wed?"

"On Sunday at noon, a week after the fair closes."

The fair. Janna had planned toward it, but in light of the problems at the tavern and her father's arrival, she'd all but forgotten about it. Now, it was almost upon them. Already the town was becoming crowded with strangers, merchants eager to buy and sell and make up for their lost trade at the time of the siege. The guesthouses of the abbeys would also be filling rapidly. She did a quick calculation. If she could come up with a proper plan to convince her father to admit her into his family, there might be enough time for her to carry it through and also fulfil her obligation to Sybil. But first she needed to find out more.

"And where are you to be wed, my lord?"

"We'll take our vows at the door of the cathedral." Hugh sounded as gloomy as if he was speaking of his own execution. "Once our vows have been witnessed, there'll be a nuptial mass. After that, guests are invited to Tuiforde for a celebration feast at Sire Geoffrey's manor."

And after that, the marriage would be consummated. Janna's body, awakened by Hugh's soft caress, quivered at the thought of what it would mean to lie with a man. With Godric. She closed her eyes lest they betray her sudden hunger.

"Johanna," Hugh said, and his voice was husky with wanting as he stepped closer, close enough to kiss her. "Is it too late, even now, for us to make a life together?"

Johanna. Hugh had always called her that, just as her father did now. But in her heart she was still Janna, independent and free. All that would change if she became a daughter; more so if she became a wife. Or even Hugh's leman. This was not what she wanted: being told what to do, where to live, and how to behave for the rest of her life.

"No!" Janna put her fists against Hugh's chest and pushed him away. Everything she'd once thought she wanted had turned upside down. But there was one thing of which she was certain, and it must be said. "No," she said again. "If you break your betrothal now you'll bring shame on both of us, my lord. There's no future for us, none at all." And without giving him time to argue, she turned and fled.

She could feel her heart racing, pounding in her breast, but she knew she'd made the right decision. There was nothing to gain by leading Hugh on and fueling his desire. She had to get away from him, and stay away from him, preferably out of sight. And so she left instructions with Ossie to refill the pitchers of ale and keep on serving the customers.

After a quick look outside, and taking comfort from the fact that there were people to help her in case Mus should be lurking about, she fled to the brew house. But although she'd escaped from Hugh, she could not escape her own turbulent thoughts. There'd been a time when she'd dreamed of a life with Hugh, had desired it most desperately, but now that he was within her grasp, all she could think about was Godric – and his lord's plans for him and Cecily. She realized how lucky an escape she'd had in refusing Hugh. Being with him, either as wife or mistress, and having to confront Godric every day in his new life with Cecily would have made her own life a living hell.

A further thought intruded to unsettle Janna. Would Godric be with Hugh when he took his marriage vows? She feared it, while acknowledging that she longed to see him again, even if only for one last time. It was a risk she would have to take, because foremost in her mind was her need to fulfil the oath sworn to her mother. All being well, she would take the first step toward achieving that on the day that Hugh and Eleanor were wed. She began to prepare a new brew while thinking through the plan that she hoped might answer all her needs.

With Sybil out of the way, Janna had resolved to try a new recipe, this time using the sweetness of elderflowers to flavor the ale. Ulf's disparaging remarks about the ale at Paradise gave her the confidence to think that, barring any more accidents, she could continue to woo customers back to the Bell and Bush for the fine ales and the food they served. As she added barley malt to the hot water in the mash tun, she turned her thoughts to the more pressing matter in hand: what herbs she might use for the gruit, once the mix had fermented and been strained. Sweet flag, betony, or agrimony? Not wormwood; the bitterness would mask the sweetness of the elderflowers she would add right at the end, along with a pinch of Elfric's precious ginger, perhaps?

A flash of bright red caught her eye. Intrigued, she went to the door and peered outside. She saw a slight figure in a crimson gown. There was something furtive in her movements, in the way she glanced around as if making sure she was unobserved, that roused Janna's curiosity further. She stayed hidden in the shadowed doorway to watch, but saw nothing untoward, for the young woman stepped aside to make way for a patron leading his horse into the yard, then slipped through the gate and hurried away.

Janna frowned, wondering why she seemed familiar. Young women didn't often frequent the tavern on their own, unless their purpose was to leave with a man. But Sybil always did her best to discourage them, for she claimed that whores gave the tavern a bad name and attracted the wrong sorts of customers. It was clear that this girl hadn't come to pick up a likely prospect, for she had left alone – and unobserved, or so she hoped.

Janna looked about the yard, and saw Wat disappearing into the kitchen. Had he seen the woman in crimson? Did he know who she was? Janna followed him into the kitchen to find out.

"She's me sister." Wat blinked at Janna. "She just come to see how I'm doin', is all."

Fair enough, Janna thought, but why the secrecy? "Who is your sister?" she asked. "Has she been here before?"

Wat stared at her. "Why d' ya want to know?" he asked. "What's it to you?"

Janna shrugged. "Just curious," she admitted, wondering why he sounded so defensive. "I didn't realize you had any family living in Winchestre, Wat." As she said that, she remembered her introduction to the tavern so many moons ago. "*He's a lazy runt of a lad,*" Sybil had said, "*as bad as his sister.*"

Janna clapped her hand to her forehead as she made the connection. Ebba! But a very different Ebba from the humble drudge whom Sybil had once employed. No wonder Janna hadn't recognized her, dressed as she was in such finery. Her eyes narrowed in concentration as several possibilities occurred to her.

She became aware that Wat was still staring at her. "It's no matter to me that you have a sister, Wat," she said airily. "I was just showing a friendly interest, that's all. Do you see much of her?" She hoped Wat might speak more freely if he thought she hadn't recognized Ebba. But he scowled at her and left the kitchen without answering.

Janna looked after him, her mind spinning with questions. She couldn't believe that Ebba had come out of sisterly concern; the visit must have had another purpose behind it, and Janna very much feared she knew what it was. Why else would Wat be so reluctant to talk? On that thought, she hurried back to the brew house to test the ale.

To her relief, every barrel ran sweet. She came out again and saw that Wat was now busy scrubbing pots at the pump out in the yard. He glanced up briefly and went back to his task. Janna walked on to the kitchen, knowing that in Wat's absence she would be able to speak freely to Elfric.

"Did you see Ebba this afternoon?" she asked the cook.

"Yair." He lifted his shoulders in a noncommittal shrug.

"What did she want?" Janna's gaze circled the kitchen, seeking anything that looked out of place or untoward.

"She came to see Wat. Why, what of it?" Elfric took a pinch of mustard seeds from a small pot and stirred them into a cauldron of marrowbone stew hanging over the fire.

"Does she often visit her brother?"

Elfric paused to consider the question. "Haven't seen her before today, not since Sybil kicked her out."

It wasn't what Janna had expected to hear, and she frowned. But that didn't stop her fearing the worst. "Make sure you taste everything before it leaves the kitchen," she implored.

Elfric's eyebrows rose in an unspoken question.

"Mouse pie? Tainted ale?" Janna's gaze fell on the pot of small yellow seeds. She remembered the burning taste of the ale and quickly popped one into her mouth. She bit down on it, felt it hot and sharp against her tongue, and spat the seed into her hand.

"Mustard – and salt as an emetic." She nodded, pleased to have got to the bottom of the mystery. "Do you always have mustard seeds on hand, Elfric?"

"Yair." Elfric was starting to look at her strangely now. "I use them to flavor stews, especially vegetable pottage."

"Have you been using more than usual lately?"

Elfric sucked on his teeth as he thought about it. "No, not lately. But a while ago I had to send Wat out to buy some in the market place when I thought I already had a full pot here at hand." He shook his head in bemusement. "More salt too. Yet I could've sworn – "

"You didn't taste the tainted ale, but I did. The ale was hot as fire, and it made people vomit. Your mustard seeds – and salt – were added to the brew."

"Are you accusing me of poisoning the ale?" Elfric drew himself up, frowning ferociously.

"No!" Janna patted his arm to calm him down. "No, I'm just saying we need to be careful, that's all." She was thinking of Ebba. Or Wat? She wondered if Elfric had also made the connection. But he just grunted, and turned to give his full attention to prodding the marrowbones so that their rich contents spilled out, adding extra flavor to the stew.

She went back into the brew house, needing to give herself time to think, to come up with a plan. Once she'd given the mix a stir, she ventured back into the tavern. To her great relief, Hugh had left. Perhaps he too had sensed the danger of his proposal. She made herself a silent promise never to be alone with him in the future. She glanced about, hoping to see Ulf, but there was no sign of him either. Promising herself that she would talk to him the moment he came in, she went upstairs to Sybil.

The wound on the back of the taverner's head was starting to heal, Janna was pleased to note, as she unwound the bandage and carefully spread ointment over the affected part. Sybil winced, but bore her ministrations without complaint. "Thank you for your care of me, Janna," she said, when she was comfortably settled once more. "I really don't know how I would have managed without you."

Janna was pleased but tried not to show it. She knew that Sybil didn't like anyone to make a fuss. But she thought the words meant that Sybil had begun to trust her at last. The taverner was more alert now, and on her way to recovery. It was time to try to jog her memory once more. "Have you remembered anything at all about the attack on you?"

"No." Sybil shook her head in frustration, then winced at the pain of it. "Believe me, if I had I would tell you the moment I thought of it."

Janna decided to test her suspicions. She couldn't help hoping she was right, if only to soothe her own uneasy conscience about her silence over Mus. "Do you think you could have been attacked by a woman?"

"No!" The answer came without thought and Janna's hopes crumbled into disappointment. But it seemed that Sybil was reconsidering her reply. "At least, I don't think so," she amended. "Whoever it was came from behind. I didn't see anything."

"Or smell anything? Sweat, or – "

"No." To Janna's relief, Sybil sounded quite definite.

"But you heard something," Janna reminded her, thinking of the long crimson gown that Ebba wore. "The swish of a gown, perhaps, or the patter of a woman's shoes?"

"No." But Sybil sounded doubtful.

"Or the heavier tread of a man's boots?"

"No. I don't remember anything like that." Sybil grasped Janna's hand and pulled herself up to a sitting position. "I'm feeling quite well now," she said, swinging her legs to the floor to prove her point. "It's time I came downstairs."

Janna couldn't agree. "There's no need to come down yet," she soothed the taverner. "Business is picking up, we're doing a good trade again. You don't have to worry about anything, truly."

"Except that you could probably use another pair of hands if things are as busy as you say."

"We're managing quite well as we are," Janna contradicted. "And you don't want the customers to see you with your head all bound up. That would really give them something to tattle about!"

"What are they saying now?"

"I told them you're indisposed." No way was she going to pass on to Sybil the news that the tavern was about to close.

"I could become a local attraction if they knew what had really happened," Sybil said wryly. "People might come especially to see me."

"It's too much of a risk for you to come down and work in the tavern just yet. And I certainly can't take that bandage off either, it's too soon," Janna said firmly. "Besides, there's no need for you to be up and doing. Ossie is helping me serve the customers and Elfric is keeping Wat up to the mark." She hesitated, wondering if she could push things a little further, even at the risk of upsetting Sybil. "Ebba paid a visit to Wat this afternoon," she ventured.

Sybil's expression hardened. "Slut!" She thought for a moment, then shrugged. "But I can't stop her seeing her brother, I suppose."

"Has she visited him before?"

"Not Ebba!" Sybil gave a snort at the very idea.

"She was dressed very fine."

"Alan likes his drabs to be well dressed." Sybil's voice was sour as vinegar.

"But are they still together, do you know? Because I'm told that Ebba works at Hell now, but your – " Janna bit the words off just in time. "The merchant drinks at other taverns."

"If not Alan, she'll have someone else. That girl ever had an eye for a likely prospect."

"And Wat? Is he trustworthy, do you think?" Janna remembered how the young potboy had come to her rescue against Mus, and felt ashamed of her suspicions. But if Ebba wasn't responsible for the tainted food and drink, who else?

"He's a lazy son of Satan. I only took him on because Ebba begged me to give him employment. I suppose I could let him go now that she's gone. Who knows, I might find a more willing worker to take his place."

"No need for that!" Janna said quickly, anxious to salvage something of her conscience. Not for anything would she have Wat out of work because of her, not unless she could prove her suspicions. "He's doing well enough for the present." Should she mention the mustard seeds? Better not, she decided. Not yet, anyway.

"But it's time I came downstairs to see for myself what's going on." Sybil thrust herself upright and stood swaying, blinking against a sudden dizziness.

Janna grabbed her, her spirits spiraling downward at the realization that Sybil still didn't trust her. "You're not well enough," she said firmly.

Sybil took a breath. Her face had blanched pale as whey; she closed her eyes. "I think you have the truth of it," she said faintly, and sagged back down onto the bed.

"You'll just have to trust me." Janna couldn't keep the bitterness out of her tone.

"I do." Sybil reached up and caught hold of her hand. "Believe me, Janna, I do. But I'm used to being in charge, ordering things to my own satisfaction. I feel so...so *useless* lying here!"

Janna nodded, feeling slightly mollified. This, she could understand. "It won't be for too much longer," she promised, and whisked out of Sybil's room and down the stairs.

"I have another task for you," she said apologetically to Ulf, when she spied him later that evening.

"Let me guess. I'm going to Hell?"

Janna grinned. "More than that. I want you to make up to Ebba. Flatter her. Promise her whatever she asks. I want you to try to find out, if you can, who her protector is now."

"What if she doesn't have one?" Ulf looked thoroughly alarmed. "I'll look right daft if she takes me at my word."

"She won't." Janna told him of the girl's unexpected appearance in all her finery, and her relationship to Wat. "Ebba's got someone," she said, "and I want to know who."

"I doubt it's Alan. He's still playing the big man, but he's not looking quite so flash these days. Besides, he mostly seems to frequent Paradise, or Heaven."

"If not Alan, then it's someone else. I want to find out who's behind what's been going on around here. I want to know if she's working with someone, or if this is all her own idea." Janna went on to tell Ulf her suspicions about the tainted ale and the mouse pie. "She was snooping around here today, and I want to know why," she concluded.

"You could be reading far too much into all of this. Maybe Ebba just came to see her brother."

Janna needed to convince Ulf that she was right, but it would mean betraying a confidence. On the other hand, she was sending him into what could become a dangerous situation. That thought helped her make up her mind. She related to him what Elfric had told her about Sybil and Alan, and how their relationship had ended after they'd quarreled over ownership of the tavern. She told him too how the merchant hadn't hesitated to shame Sybil and taunt her in front of his friends.

"I might be wrong about Alan, but I'm almost sure Ebba and her protector are in this together. Her brother too. Please see what you can find out for me, Ulf. After all, our reputation is at stake here, as well as Sybil's safety."

The relic seller nodded and stood up. He hefted his pack onto his shoulders and walked out of the tavern. Janna watched him go. She felt restless, on edge. Something else was being planned, she felt sure of it. Unable to quieten her fears, she took off her apron and rushed to the kitchen to fetch her cloak. The tavern wasn't too busy at present. She would leave Ossie in charge while she was gone.

On her way out, she checked with him that he could manage. "I'll watch out for the customers," he assured her, and picked up a pitcher of ale to show he was willing.

"Get Wat to help with the food orders," Janna told him, thinking that her mission was more important that a few disgruntled customers if things did go wrong in her absence. But she knew that the ale was sweet, and Elfric was checking the food. And she wouldn't be gone for long. "I'll be back soon," she promised. Drawing her cloak around her, and taking care that her face was so shrouded as to be unrecognizable inside her hood, she stepped out into the night.

She wished now that she'd asked Ulf to stay and walk with her. Every shadow turned into Mus; every movement set her heart racing. Rats and cats disturbed rubbish, made scrabbling noises, turned into ghosts and assassins as she walked along the high street. There were plenty of people in the town, preparing for the fair. Merchants and traders alike were keen to make up for sales lost the previous year, and visitors were also flocking in, ready to pay their dues and stake their claim. With so many strangers about, Janna felt increasingly anxious. What if Mus had given up and gone back to Robert? What if Robert had set someone else after her instead, someone she didn't know, someone who could take her by surprise?

Thoroughly alarmed by this new thought, Janna scooted along as fast as if the devil was on her heels, desperately keen to reach the relative safety of the alehouses. She was shaking with fright by the time she came to Hell, and had to fight the temptation to go inside and ask Ulf to escort her to the next alehouse. But she forced herself onward, to Paradise. Ulf had told her that this was where he usually saw Alan. While Ulf was busy finding out what he could from Ebba, she would spy on Alan. And if he wasn't in Paradise, she would try Heaven instead.

Once inside, she looked around with interest, for she hadn't been into the alehouse before. It was busy enough; there were far more people drinking here than in the Bell and Bush, for it was near all the shops in the high street. Drawing the hood close and keeping her head down, Janna walked among the patrons. She assessed the crowd with quick sideways glances as she went, looking out for Mus as well as the merchant. While there was no sign of the former, Alan was there and surrounded by his usual hangers-on. Janna sidled closer, testing and discarding various strategies as she went.

"...no doubt in my mind that this is the finest alehouse in Winchestre." The merchant rose to his feet. Janna jerked back with alarm, not wanting to be seen.

"You don't have to leave so early," one of his companions pointed out. "You said yourself that your leman's busy elsewhere!"

"Busy doing what?" asked someone else, a smirk belying the seeming innocence of the remark. But the man quickly sobered as the merchant angrily swiped the mug out of his hand.

"Watch your mouth," he snarled, and spat into the rushes.

"Come on, Master Alan, she's friendly with everyone, you know that." Another man at the table laid his hand on the merchant's arm in a vain effort to keep the peace.

"You'll speak of her with respect or you'll answer to me!" The merchant jerked his arm free and strode off. Janna shrank behind a crowded table, analyzing what she'd just heard. That his companions sought to detain the merchant probably meant nothing other than they were hoping for free ale. But she'd found out part of the confirmation she'd sought: the merchant had a leman. If his mistress wasn't free to come to his bed just yet, it might mean that she was engaged elsewhere. In Hell? Or in some other man's bed? Judging from his appearance, the merchant appeared less prosperous than when she'd first encountered him. Was Ebba earning their keep now?

Janna stayed hidden, curious to find out what Alan would do next. She watched as he moved toward several men drinking steadily in the corner, watched as he beckoned to a passing serving maid.

"Another jug of your fine ale for me and my friends here," he said, his loud voice attracting the attention of the drinkers nearby. "I swear 'tis the best brew in all Winchestre, wouldn't you agree?" He looked about the table for confirmation. Several men nodded, but one or two looked somewhat dubious.

"They do a good brew at the Bell and Bush," one said, and slapped his mug down on the table. "Better than here, I reckon."

"The Bell and Bush?" Alan said incredulously. "The *Bell and Bush*?" He clapped his palm against his forehead in disbelief. "Why, I was there only last night. It's common talk the tavern's about to close. The taverner lies near death, 'tis said, and the brew tastes like slops because of it. No, you can forget about the Bell and Bush." He leaned on the table, pushing his face close to the one man who had dared to disagree with him. "Let me refill your mug, my friend. There's nothing to touch this brew, I tell you. Nothing." He seized the new jug as soon as it was brought to the table and made good his offer, sloshing its contents into all the mugs that were eagerly pushed toward him.

Seething, Janna had to make a huge effort to restrain herself from flying at the merchant's throat and choking him for his lying words. And yet she was glad to have heard them, for they confirmed her suspicions. Ebba was spreading poison in Hell on behalf of the merchant, while he busied himself likewise in the other two taverns. The two must be working together with Wat. It was the only explanation. The merchant had lied about being in the Bell and Bush, yet he knew all about the attack on Sybil and knew also that she was still alive.

Perhaps it was never meant to go this far. But when the tainted ale and the mouse pie hadn't succeeded in driving customers away, the attack had followed. With Sybil out of the way, they must have reasoned that the tavern would surely close, leaving the way open for Alan to claim it as he'd always wanted, while giving him a new and desirable source of income. His words indicated that Sybil had indeed been the intended target, not Janna. She felt the great weight of guilt lift from her heart.

But why had Ebba visited Wat? Janna felt a frisson of alarm run down her back as suspicion returned in full force. Now that the pair hadn't succeeded in removing Sybil, they would surely try again. And if so, what would they do next?

Chapter 13

Janna wasn't left long to wonder what had been planned, for on her return to the tavern she found the door closed tight against her. She could hear Ossie snoring inside. At once she hastened around to the back lane. The gate was still unlocked, and a faint light from the kitchen indicated there'd be someone awake to tell her what was going on. Once inside, she encountered a reproachful Elfric tidying up before going home.

"There's no ale to serve the customers. Why didn't you make sure the bungs were tight in the barrels?" he accused her, when she demanded to know why the tavern had closed so early.

"*What?*" Janna turned on her heel and rushed off to the brew house, closely followed by Elfric and also Wat, who'd been lurking about, cadging scraps. As she entered the brew house, her worst fears were confirmed. The hard-packed earth floor was now a pool of reeking mud. Horrified, she checked the barrels: all of them were empty.

"This is no accident, nor carelessness either. This has been done deliberately," she told Elfric as she tested the last barrel. "And I intend to find out who is responsible."

Distraught and angry, she straightened, just in time to catch a fleeting smirk cross Wat's face. The hot blood of anger pulsed through Janna's veins as she lunged at him, pushing Elfric out of the way to grab tight hold of his ear.

"You!" she shrieked, holding on and shaking him hard. "You sniveling toad! Your sister put you up to this, didn't she!"

"Did not." Wat struggled to break free. "You was the last person in the brew house. I saw you come out. Don't think to blame me, it's *your* fault."

"What are you suggesting, Janna?" Elfric put out a hand to save Wat from Janna's fury, but she gripped harder and gave the boy an extra shake. She was ready to rattle his brains, she was so angry.

"I'm suggesting that Wat was responsible for draining all this ale onto the floor, just as he once put mustard seeds and salt into the ale, and a mouse into your pie!" Janna spat out the words, hardly able to contain her fury.

"But...but why?" Elfric moved then to protect the cowering boy from Janna. "Why would he do such a thing?"

"Ask him!" Janna let go of Wat's ear. She stuck her hands on her hips and glared at him instead.

He stared back at her, sullen and silent. Janna felt a momentary qualm as she remembered how he'd rushed to her aid, his elation at having got the better of Mus, his assurance that she could call on him whenever she needed help. But things had gone too far now for sentiment to get in the way of the truth. Somehow, she had to get him to confess.

"If he won't answer, perhaps you should ask his sister and her lover!" she spat. "I know they're not responsible for this, because I've just seen them with my own eyes in the alehouses up the high street, spreading lies and slander about the Bell and Bush, how Sybil lies near death's door, how the ale tastes like slops and the tavern is about to close. They're trying to put us out of business, and you've been helping them all along, haven't you, Wat, with all your little tricks and games? You might have thought it was fun, but if Sybil had died I'd have seen you hang for it, Wat."

"I never done that, you know I never!"

"But you did the other things, didn't you?" Janna said softly. "Didn't you, Wat?"

"But…" Elfric looked from one to the other. "I don't understand."

"It's all down to that merchant, isn't it, Wat?" Janna hoped that by suggesting someone else was to blame, the boy might be encouraged to tell what he knew. "Alan. You know he wanted the tavern for himself, and this was his way of getting it, wasn't it? He persuaded you to make things go wrong, to drive the customers away. And when that didn't work, he told you to kill the taverner."

"No!" The potboy's eyes were wide with fright. "No, he didn't! I never! That was nothin' to do with me. You know that right well, Janna. It was meant to be you with your head bashed in, not Mistress Sybil."

"Me?" It hadn't occurred to Janna that Wat might also have misread the situation.

"Like what happened before, only this time that man attacked the wrong 'un!"

Janna was silenced, but not for long, for she was almost sure now that Sybil had indeed been the intended target. "No, Wat, he wasn't behind this," she said, hoping she might still get a confession out of him. "The attack was aimed at Mistress Sybil, you know that right enough. When your tricks to close the tavern didn't work, Alan had to find a way to remove the taverner instead. So who was responsible if not you, Wat? Think carefully, because trying to kill someone is a very serious offense. You don't want to be blamed for something you didn't do."

"It weren't me, I swear it!"

"Was it your sister, then? Or Alan?"

"I know nothin' 'bout the attack on Sybil. Nothin'! I swear it! I thought the man that was after you hit her by mistake." Wat looked frightened to death. It seemed he hadn't thought through the possible consequences of his actions until now. Janna wondered if he'd been threatened into silence by Alan. Now that the full extent of the plan to take over the tavern had been revealed, the boy seemed terrified. And no wonder, if he'd thought it was just about playing a few tricks.

"I'm quite sure Mistress Sybil was the intended victim," Janna stated, reading from Elfric's expression that he shared Wat's suspicions about the attack. "And I'll prove it to you," she added fiercely, even though she wasn't sure how to go about it. Wat's denial had shaken her belief that she'd read the situation right. For all their sakes, she needed to find out the truth as soon as possible.

"But I don't understand why you would play these tricks on us, Wat," Elfric said. "You've got a home here, and employment. Mistress Sybil looked after you through the siege when everyone else had closed their doors. She gave you food and shelter all through the hard winter when so many others were homeless and starving. Could you really wish to cause so much trouble for us?"

Wat sniffed, and wiped his nose on the back of his hand. "Ebba told me I had to," he admitted. "She told me Alan was gunna take over the Bell and Bush, and that she'd become the taverner here. She promised she'd take care of me. She said we'd live like kings." He sniffed again. "It was just fun, like with the mustard seeds and that. But they didn't hurt Mistress Sybil. You're wrong about that, Janna."

Janna wondered if she'd misread the situation after all. She really needed to prove it one way or the other – but at least Wat had admitted to his role in the plot to close the tavern. "So what do we do with you now, Wat?" she asked. She couldn't forgive him for what he'd done, nor did she want him at the tavern any longer. He'd betrayed them all. They couldn't trust him.

"I think you'd better go," she said. She looked at Elfric, and was encouraged when he nodded in agreement. "You can tell your sister and her lover that they won't get their hands on the Bell and Bush no matter what they try." She thought for a moment. "Maybe your sister can get you a job where she works? Hell's the best place for both of you."

She turned on her heel and walked out of the sodden brew house. She would have to start another brew just as soon as Ossie could bring fresh water, and she would have to double the quantity. It meant the tavern would again be without ale for a few days, but at least a new shipment of wine had come in. Hopefully enough wealthy merchants had come to town for the fair and would be willing to pay the price.

Angry and upset, she lay awake on her pallet beside the fireplace a long time that night. To her dismay, she found that she missed the presence of Wat in the alcove on the other side. He was company; he was also a measure of safety. But he'd packed up his few belongings under the stern eye of Elfric, who had then escorted him to the gate in the yard and made a big show of locking it behind them both before he left. And now Janna lay alone, mulling over what had happened and worrying how she might prove who was behind the attack on Sybil.

Ebba? It seemed less likely now. Wat would surely have known if his sister was responsible.

Mus? She shuddered, and edged closer to the banked-down fire.

The merchant? Sybil had told her that she'd heard something, a sound she recognized. Not footsteps. Not any sort of smell either – which must surely eliminate Mus. Janna turned her thoughts to Alan. He wanted to destroy the tavern's reputation and take it over – that much was obvious. So he had a motive; he was also well able to carry out the attack. She began to replay all she'd seen and heard that night, and an idea came into her mind. It was a very long chance indeed –

but there was nothing else she could think of that might prove her suspicions either way.

*

She rose early, for she wanted Sybil still to be asleep when she came into her room. It was a horrible trick to play on the taverner, but worth it if it produced the truth. She knocked softly on the tavern door, putting her fingers to her lips when Ossie opened it. She tiptoed quietly up the stairs and into Sybil's chamber, and hid out of sight behind a large chest while she waited for the taverner to awaken.

A heavy sigh and a creaking of the wooden bed frame as Sybil struggled to sit up warned Janna that it was time to put her idea to the test. She peered cautiously around the chest and was gratified to find that Sybil wasn't looking at her. The taverner had swung her feet to the floor, and was facing away from Janna. It seemed that she was going to try, once again, to rise from her bed. Although fearing that she would put the taverner's well-being at risk if her trick succeeded, Janna tiptoed out of hiding and cleared her throat. Hating the action, for she'd never done such a thing in her life before, she cleared her throat and spat on the floor.

Sybil screamed and whirled around to confront the sound. She launched herself at Janna, fists flailing in a desperate attempt to fight her off.

"No! No, mistress, no!" Horrified, Janna tried to protect herself. Through the sound of Sybil's shrieks she heard a heavy pounding as Ossie galloped upstairs.

"You...you..." Sybil lashed out, hardly able to speak for terror.

"Stop it! It's me. Janna. I'm not going to hurt you, I promise!"

Ossie burst through the door. He skidded to a halt and blinked as he tried to make sense of the scene. Then he launched himself at Sybil and dragged her off Janna. He wrapped his arms around the taverner and placed her on the bed, keeping a firm grip on her all the while. Sybil shrieked curses at Janna as she struggled to free herself.

"It wasn't me who attacked you!" Janna spoke slowly and clearly, trying to reach Sybil through her panic; trying to reassure her that she wasn't responsible for the assault, only for the sound that had triggered Sybil's memory. "It was Alan," she said. "He cleared his throat outside the brew house, and then he spat on the ground. He's always doing that. That was the noise you heard just before he hit you, wasn't it?"

Still quaking with fear, Sybil nodded dumbly. Janna was appalled that she'd caused such horror, yet she was triumphant too. "I'm so sorry," she apologized. "It was a guess, but I didn't know how else to test what I was thinking."

Sybil swallowed hard. "You could have just asked," she said in a hard voice. "You didn't have to go frightening me to death."

"It was your death Alan was after," Janna reminded her. "If I'd asked you, you might not have remembered. You might not have wanted to believe it, even if you did remember. But it seems to me there's no room to doubt it now."

Sybil tightened her lips, but gave a grudging nod.

"And there's something else you need to know about too," Janna said gently, hating to be the bearer of more bad news. It was hurtful enough that Sybil had found out the truth about a man she must have once loved and trusted. While she might not have had much love for Ebba and Wat, she had employed them and done right by them, and now she would have to find out how shamefully they had repaid her.

"You should hear this too, Ossie," she said, and nodded at the big man to stay. She began, then, to explain who was behind the recent problems at the tavern, and the reasoning behind their actions, finishing with the wasted ale from the night before. As she spoke, Sybil's face changed from the blanched white of fear to a deep flush of rage.

"I'll kill him!" she said fiercely, when Janna had finished setting out all the proof she and Ulf had gathered. "As for that wretched potboy and his slut of a sister – " She broke off, too choked with rage to continue.

"You can surely bear witness against them instead?" Janna thought there'd been far too much violence already. She remembered Ulf's offer to help her take care of Mus, and smothered a grin. No doubt that same faceless "someone" would be available to take care of Alan as well – but she wasn't about to mention it. "Wat might be persuaded to tell the truth, and I'll certainly tell all I know," she said instead. "And so will Ulf. You remember Ulf, with the big dog? He'll also tell what he knows, 'cause he helped me uncover what's really been going on here."

Sybil pulled a face. Her hands plucked restlessly at a loose thread in the woven bed covering as she thought through her options. "There's been precious little law and order around here since the troubles last year," she said bitterly. "The castellan's gone. He's also the shire reeve, but he's fled the castle along with the empress and her troops, so there's no-one who'll listen to my plea. Besides, why would anyone take a taverner's word against that of a merchant, and a man at that?"

"I would," Ossie said unexpectedly. "If you like, I c'n teach 'im a lesson 'e won't fergit in an 'urry."

Janna closed her eyes and groaned inwardly. Was Ossie the "someone" Ulf had in mind when he'd made his offer? She glanced at Sybil and saw that the taverner was watching him with a calculating gleam in her eyes.

"Just a warning. No rough stuff," she said. "Not yet anyway. Tell him I know what he's done, and he's to stay out of my way in future or there'll be a price to pay."

Ossie nodded.

"Tell him I also know about his leman and her brother. Tell him you'll be watching him closely. Any more trouble here, or if I hear even a whisper against me, or the Bell and Bush – "

"Or me," Janna put in quickly, still smarting after Ebba's calumny.

"Or any of us, I'll blacken his name from one end of Winchestre to the other and beyond. I know how he's cut corners, the shady deals he's done in the past. I can tell stories against him that will ensure no-one will trade with him by the time I've finished. I'll petition the king to have him put down. I'll go right to the top if I have to. Just you tell him that!"

Ossie nodded again. It seemed that the pair had a deal. Janna was content with the plan, for it seemed likely to have an effective outcome. What Sybil had said was true: there had been a general breakdown of law and order since the siege. The shire reeve of Hampshire and castellan of Winchestre Castle, William Pont de l'Arche, hadn't been seen since he'd supported the wrong side and earned the wrath of the king; there was no point appealing to him. But tavern talk claimed that lawlessness was everywhere, for the barons and lords who in the past would keep order and try criminals in their own manor courts were now far too busy seizing land and castles from each other to worry about justice within their own demesnes. Even the barons that the earl had left to protect the empress at Oxeneford were apparently deserting her to defend their own interests. None would concern himself with a petty squabble of this nature, not when there was so much else at stake.

Even Sybil's threat to go to the king, while a recognized route to justice, was unlikely to be carried through by the taverner. Although the king was always the last recourse in any dispute, Sybil would know that he'd have far more important things on his mind. But her threat to blacken the merchant's good name might be enough to keep Alan from trying any further tricks to get his hands on the tavern, especially with Ossie standing over him and uttering threats.

She smiled at Sybil, pleased to note the fresh color in her cheeks and the brightness of her eyes. "Do you feel well enough to get up this morn?" she asked.

"I do so," Sybil said grimly. "That hellspawn has fired my blood and put courage into me. He will not threaten my tavern ever again. Although…" She broke off and frowned. "Even if we brew enough new ale to float a ship, we'll be chasing after customers soon enough. It'll hardly be worth keeping our door open."

"But…why?" Janna couldn't believe it, not after what they'd all just been through. "The customers have started to come back to us now. Really, mistress, the tavern's doing quite well again."

Sybil gave an impatient sigh. "Easy to see you haven't been here while the fair's on," she said. "It's the rule that every business in Winchestre has to close – all except taverns and alehouses," she continued, as she noted Janna's puzzled expression. "All other trading takes place up St Giles Hill. So although we're allowed to stay open, that's where all our customers will be."

"Then why don't we set up a booth at the fair?" Janna suggested eagerly. 'It will show that we're still open for business.' All at once and with no effort on her part, it seemed that she might have the chance to put her plan to sell medicaments and lotions into action.

Sybil tipped her head on one side, considering her question. "We haven't in the past. I can't both brew and serve ale in the tavern and be up on the hill to sell it at the same time."

"But you could brew the ale and keep the tavern open, and Ossie could cart barrels of ale up the hill for me to sell at the fair," Janna suggested. "I don't mind keeping a booth up there, if you'd like me to." She crossed her fingers behind her back, hoping that Sybil would agree.

"I've never taken a stall at the fair before," Sybil said doubtfully. "I never trusted that Ebba enough to leave her here on her own."

"But you can trust me. You said so!" Janna greatly feared that Sybil would only agree if their roles could be reversed. When first devising her plan, she'd resigned herself to only being able to snatch stolen moments at the fair. Now she felt she couldn't bear to be stuck at the tavern while all of Winchestre and beyond were out enjoying themselves.

"True." Sybil's mouth curved up in an unwilling smile. "And you've worked hard to keep the tavern open while I've been upstairs. I owe you for that."

"We could take turns at the stall if you'd like to see the fair too?" Janna hoped her offer might tempt Sybil to agree with her.

Sybil gave a small huff of amusement. "I can see you won't rest until you've persuaded me to your way of thinking, miss. And if we call our stall the Bell and Bush it will bring the tavern to the notice of everyone up at the fair. Especially if we give them directions to the tavern while we serve them." She nodded thoughtfully. "Yes, I'm willing to trust you, Janna. This year we shall see if having a stall at the fair is worth our while."

"Thank you!" Janna could hardly restrain herself from dancing a little jig.

"Make sure you don't let me down!" But Sybil was smiling as she added, "I'll see about getting the permit then, shall I? And you, Ossie, you go and fetch water enough to keep all Winchestre afloat."

Chapter 14

Excited and happy, Janna glanced wide-eyed around the fairground. She had been to St Edith's fair at Wiltune in the past, but this was like nothing she'd ever seen before. There was almost a small village set up atop St Giles Hill, with Bishop Henry's pavilion dominating the surrounding stalls and lines of timber selds, long narrow buildings divided into separate booths, which were opening to trade.

Some merchants had set up their wares and organized their stalls in advance, those who had rented places large and secure enough to lock up overnight or with space enough for either themselves or a night watchman to be left on guard. Others had come in at dawn, carting their goods and produce on wagons pulled by horse or by oxen. They were now busy positioning trestles and benches in the most advantageous positions they could find, setting up canvas awnings to protect their goods from the weather, and arranging their displays to tempt passing fairgoers.

Packmen carried their wares on their backs, or pushed barrows or handcarts, or festooned their packs over donkey or carthorse. Those without sufficient coins to rent a stall or booth found an open space between to spread out their wares on a trestle covered with a woven cloth. A noisy quarrel had broken out between two traders over a position. Merchants shouted at journeymen and apprentices, and chivvied them along, while the clang of hammers rang through the air as last-minute adjustments were made. Animals and birds for sale or slaughter added their cries to the general cacophony, while their waste contributed to the pungent miasma that must only grow worse in the heat of the days ahead.

Like all the other traders at the fair, the group from the tavern had entered one of the two gates that gave access through the palisade that surrounded St Giles Hill. They had paid the toll on their barrels of ale as they passed through, along with the rent for the stall they would erect. Janna had come with Ossie and Sybil on the cart, which was laden with supplies that they hoped would be sufficient to quench the thirst of the fairgoers. Unknown to Sybil, Janna had secreted a box of her own on the cart. She'd made sure to stash it out of sight, for the taverner had insisted on locking the tavern doors and coming too. "Just to make sure our stall is in the best position, Janna, and to help you set up," she'd said.

Janna had made no demur, not wanting to deprive Sybil of experiencing the fair, so long as she was prepared to leave Janna in charge at the end of it and not send her back to the town to serve ale in her place. In fact, she was happy enough to have Sybil's company for now that she was here she found it quite overwhelming.

It seemed that everyone was making up for the lost profits of the canceled fair the year before. Every available space was taken, and brisk bartering and trading began as soon as the fair was declared open by the Bishop of Winchestre. The roads leading from the town to the fair were becoming increasingly clogged as townsfolk and visitors alike streamed along them, eager to find bargains or stock their households with those luxury goods that didn't often come their way. For the moment the Bell and Bush stall was quiet, as were other ale stalls in their designated area. People were far more interested in discovering what was on sale than in slaking their thirst.

Sybil nudged Janna, who stood lost in a dream of wonder as she gazed about. "Go on, then, go and have a quick look around. We're all set and ready now, so I'll stay up here and serve any customers that come. Just for a short while, mind. Ossie's taking the cart down and he'll open up the tavern for me. Make sure you're back soon."

"I won't be long," Janna promised, and left before Sybil thought better of her generous offer.

She hadn't been up St Giles Hill before, and she gazed at the town from its height, thinking that this must be how birds saw the buildings and the humans who inhabited them; small and unimportant as ants they looked, and yet the people had left their mark. The crooked high street ran down the center of the town, with the West Gate at the other end barely visible in the distance. Nearer to hand, on her left, were the high towers of the bishop's palace and the Hospital of St Cross. She could see the new building of St Mary's Nunnaminster rising from the ashes just inside the East Gate, and if she squinted her eyes, she thought she could even make out the Bell and Bush.

She turned her back on the town and began to roam up and down the lanes between the selds, keeping company with barons, lords and ladies, all dressed in the highest and brightest of fashion, but also rubbing shoulders with merchants, traders, whores, pickpockets, thieves and charlatans. No matter their status or how they were dressed, all wore the same expression of eager anticipation as they wandered about, looking at the goods on display. Janna was sure their expressions were mirrored on her own face, for she'd never seen such a vast and rich array in all her life.

Ulf had told her that merchants and craftsmen came together to sell their wares, and now she wandered past rows of stalls selling cheeses, vegetables and fruits, sweet candies and honey; her mouth watered as she eyed the confectionery. Fullers and dyers were there, displaying their brightly dyed and woven cloth. Wool merchants shouted out the merits of their produce: bales of greasy wool, and colorful dyed skeins of it, as well as fine woolen cloth of the highest quality. There were hay and corn merchants, and sellers of firewood and charcoal. Janna hastened quickly past them all, being more interested in the stalls of the craftsmen. There she lingered, admiring the fine jewelry and shining tableware of the gold and silversmiths and the goods produced by saddle, sword and shield makers. Potters displayed everything from common dishes to the finest tableware fit for a king. There were ribbons and laces, knives and candles, boots and shoes, belts and gloves, and fine parchment, but there were also serviceable goods: farming tools, cart wheels and kitchen implements. The smithy had a forge opened at the end of one lane to shoe horses, and to sharpen knives and weapons. But knife grinders also roamed about, offering their services to all they encountered.

She came to the rows of stalls frequented by foreign merchants and listened, fascinated, to a babble of voices in languages she could not fathom. She noted that a lot of the trading was done through pointing and pantomime, with finger counting to indicate prices and notched sticks to denote sales. She recognized the Norman tongue being spoken by vintners selling fine wines, but merchants from across the sea were also selling spices, soft furs and brilliantly colored silks, painted and lustrous pottery, items made of precious glass or finely carved ivory, and glowing tapestries depicting all manner of scenes, from biblical stories to beautiful meadows starred with flowers, birds and animals.

A shrill whistling and chattering attracted her attention; it came from several cages of bright birds splashed in colors of scarlet, green, blue and orange. Janna hurried over to inspect them. A dark man in a long cotton tunic materialized at her side, perhaps to make sure she didn't let the birds fly free. She smiled at him and slowly moved from cage to cage, admiring the shimmering colors of the birds' feathers. The merchant followed close to her elbow, and looked disappointed when she was tempted away by a cage of monkeys further down the track. There were falcons and hawks for sale, as well as ferrets. In a small clearing, a moth-eaten bear was being put through its paces by its trainer. They were surrounded by a ring of nudging, giggling children trying to pluck up the nerve to get close enough to poke the animal. Janna stopped for a while to watch, feeling pity for the captive.

She walked on, conscious of the small purse now hidden under her gown. She was greatly tempted to spend the wages Sybil had given her for her work in the tavern. But she desired everything she'd seen so far; how could she ever choose between what she might need and what she most coveted? One thought cheered her: by nightfall, God willing, her purse would be a great deal fatter than it was now.

She pulled a face as she noticed the pillory at the center of the fairground, unoccupied this early in the fair. Silently, Janna made a vow that she would never be one of the wretches displayed there, caught stealing or cheating. She couldn't stand the shame of it; it was an unhappy fate for the rogues, trapped as they were in the stocks and unable to defend themselves against the rotten produce and handfuls of mud hurled at them by irate customers, and also by children who were ever ready for fun and mischief. She cast a glance sideways, noticing how the bishop's guards prowled among the crowds looking out for wrongdoers. One of them looked straight at her, and Janna felt a guilty blush heat her cheeks, as she thought of her box of potions and creams. She must keep away from them just in case they picked her up for some misdemeanor – like selling wares for which she hadn't paid a toll.

She became aware of a stir among the crowd and a hushing of voices, although a few disgruntled murmurs were also to be heard. The bishop was making a progress through the fair, along with his entourage. Janna had seen the bishop from afar when he'd opened the fair, and she recognized him now. He was splendid in his miter and embroidered robes that shone brilliantly in the sunlight. As she swept a curtsy at his passing, she stole a quick look up at him, interested to see at close quarters this supposedly godly man who yet meddled freely in the worldly affairs of his brother the king; who had taken arms against the empress and burned his own town in his determination to drive her out; who had built the magnificent Wolvesey Palace for himself, but also the Hospital of St Cross to alleviate some of the poverty of his people.

The bishop was known for the wealth of the properties he owned throughout England and for the titles he bore, for he was Abbot of Glastingberie as well as the Bishop of Winchestre. He was also landlord of all the brothels on his estate of Southwark in London, so it was said. Yet it seemed his ambition ran greater than wealth and the title of bishop, for it was rumored that part of the falling-out he'd had with his brother the king, and his supposed alliance with the empress had come about because the king had nominated someone else as Archbishop of Canterberie, when that was the position the bishop most coveted.

Janna's impression was of a small man, too insignificant to carry such vast responsibility, for he was slightly built and somewhat paunchy. But perhaps that was an effect created by the magnificent heavy robes he wore. His face was of pale complexion; his eyes a faded gray, with heavy pouches beneath them that spoke of too little sleep and too much anxiety. Perhaps the anger of the townsfolk was partly to blame for keeping him awake at night. He must be aware that he was largely held responsible for the devastation that had befallen Winchestre, just as he would know that the townsfolk resented the fact that all rents and tolls for the fair would be paid to him, who didn't need them, rather than coming to the townsfolk for the rebuilding and repair of their property. Janna had heard that a delegation of merchants and craftsmen, some of them representing their guilds, had been to see the bishop on this very subject, and had been sent away empty-handed.

The bishop passed by, holding up his robes to avoid the worst of the animal excrement and other refuse littering the ground. Janna gazed with curiosity at those who followed him. One man she recognized only too well, and for one heart-stopping moment he paused to stare at her. Her hand lifted in an involuntary salute, but when she saw who accompanied her father she raised her hand further in pretense that she was merely shielding her eyes from the sunlight. Would her father offer public recognition, accompanied as he was by his wife and children, and in such exalted company? Seconds stretched to infinity, but there was no sign from him and the entourage moved slowly on. Janna knew she shouldn't be disappointed, yet she felt angry and hurt as she gazed after John fitz Henry. Now safe from scrutiny, she examined the small party that accompanied him. Giles she'd already met, but not the tall woman stalking beside him with her face fixed firmly forward, seemingly determined not to acknowledge those who bobbed their heads in respect at the bishop's passing. Her stepmother. Janna felt a flash of instant dislike, but told herself it was unfair to judge Blanche on such brief evidence. Yet Blanche's hands were like claws, gripping firmly the arms of the two young girls who accompanied her. For safety? Protection? Or control?

Janna gazed after her two half-sisters, but by now the whole party had moved on and all she could see was their backs, half hidden by the crowd. She waited several moments more until she judged it was safe before she resumed her own progress in the opposite direction. She found that she was coming close to the market area where beasts and birds were being traded. There seemed much interest in the horse yard as the animals were put through their paces, assessed for their strength if they were needed for agricultural purposes, for their fine breeding if prized for speed or prowess in battle, or for their looks and docility if intended for a lady. Cows, sheep and pigs moaned piteously from their respective pens, while hens, ducks and geese cackled and clucked and surveyed the fairgoers with bright and innocent eyes.

Janna sniffed, and sniffed again, conscious of a stench far greater than the dung of the animals. Closer inspection revealed she was close to the midden where butchers, fishmongers and the like spilled their waste. A woven wattle screen attracted her attention. Curious to know what it concealed, she stepped toward it, only realizing its purpose as a man emerged from behind the screen, still adjusting his clothing. She put her hand over her nose to block out the smell of the latrine and hurried away to some more enticing displays, all the while keeping a close eye on the passersby, conscious that even among a crowd she might be vulnerable to attack. But there was no sign of Mus. While that gave her relief, her ease of mind was tempered by the possibility that she might also bump into her father and his family, or Hugh and his betrothed. Although curious to see Eleanor, she dreaded an encounter. In her own mind, she had planned how to meet Hugh again, on her own terms and in a place of her choosing. But if they were here at the fair, and came to her stall to drink ale, she would have to greet them. She would have no choice in the matter.

Time was passing; she must get back to Sybil and start work, as she'd promised she would. She hurried along, deciding to take a shortcut down a lane to bypass some of the stalls, but became thoroughly confused in the process and had to retrace her steps several times before she finally found Sybil. At once, she launched into a breathless apology, but Sybil shushed her. "I've been enjoying myself," she admitted. "I'd also like to look around the fair before I go back to the tavern." She cast a critical eye at the crowds milling about, and sniffed. "There probably won't be any customers down in the town anyway!"

She gestured at the wooden sign so carefully lettered by Janna and hammered into place by Ossie, along with a fresh green bush attached to one side. "The sign's attracting customers," she said, "and we can ring the bell too." She picked up a tiny hand bell and shook it briskly, so that several people turned to inspect more closely the barrels stashed to one side, and the mugs displayed invitingly on the bench top. One fairgoer retraced his steps, and Janna poured him a cup of ale, relishing the first business to come her way.

But her conscience was biting. As Sybil continued to delay her departure, Janna began to wonder if her secret had been uncovered and if the taverner was waiting for an explanation. Under Sybil's watchful eye, she retrieved the wooden box she'd hidden and put it on the counter, thinking she had better confess. Sybil moved closer at once.

"Ossie thought this belonged to you," she said. "I wondered if you were going to tell me about it."

Janna reminded herself that the taverner missed nothing. "These are some creams and lotions I've made up," she said. "I wondered if I might sell them to the customers who come to buy our ale, and so earn some coins for myself?"

"What sorts of creams and lotions?"

"To smooth and perfume skin, to cleanse the body and lighten the hair – that sort of thing."

Sybil snorted. "You won't find much of a market here. I'll warrant that most of our customers will be men."

"And I also have medicaments to heal wounds and ulcers, soothe rashes, alleviate toothache, calm anxiety and aid sleep. There's also a noxious potion to sprinkle on clothes or on floor rushes to keep away moths and fleas and other biting insects."

"Where did you learn to make such things?"

"My mother was a *wortwyf*, a herb-wife and healer. And I also learned much from Sister Anne at Wiltune Abbey."

Sybil looked impressed. Taking her silence as permission, Janna hastily unpacked her box and began to display small pots and phials of liquid. But Sybil hadn't finished with her yet.

"You're not to take trade away from the tavern," she warned. "I expect you to take care of the customers' thirst before you start peddling your own wares."

"Oh, I will. Of course I will," Janna promised, hiding a smile of triumph that her plan could be put into practice with Sybil's blessing.

"And you can give me a pot of your cream as a trial, just so that I'll know you're not selling rubbish to customers who'll come here in good faith."

Now Janna couldn't prevent the grin from spreading across her face. "You may have this, and most welcome," she said sweetly, proffering a small pot of her most precious cream. It was scented with roses, and although she didn't think she should mention it to Sybil, her mother had always told customers that it was guaranteed to drive any man wild with desire!

Sybil opened the pot, took a sniff, then dabbed a small blob onto her hand and rubbed it into her skin. She held her hand up to her nose and sniffed again, then pocketed the cream. "Next time I'll pay you for a pot," she promised, and with a smile, she left Janna alone to take care of business.

*

Time went quickly, for Janna was kept busy as the day heated up and people became conscious of their dry and scratchy throats. She was sorry she didn't have food to serve to them, and made a mental note to suggest to Sybil that Elfric bake some pies to bring up to the booth. A mug of ale and a slice of pie would double the stall's attraction when fairgoers expressed hunger as well as thirst. To her joy, her medicaments proved popular. The fact that customers stood around while they drank their ale meant that Janna had a captive audience for her creams and potions, and her voice was soon hoarse from describing their benefits.

Once she looked up and thought she recognized Mus. Her heart dived into her boots; she steeled herself for the coming encounter. But when she looked again, the figure had vanished. Janna was left wondering if it was only her own fearful imagination that had conjured up the assassin. Nevertheless, it was a reminder to be careful. She was vulnerable, she knew, for the stall was open on all sides. While she faced customers at the front, ready to serve them, anyone could sneak up on her from behind and take her unawares. Mus had tried it before, and there was no reason to believe he'd not try it again. But surely not in front of crowds at a fair? Janna took some reassurance from the thought.

In the event, when an unwelcome customer did come her way there was nothing Janna could do to avoid him.

"Father!" The word was out before she could bite down to prevent it.

He looked at her and sighed heavily. "I'm sorry to find you here, still plying your trade," he said, looking thoroughly displeased with her and with the world. "My wife was determined to attend the fair, to see and sample its delights, and so I am here to escort her. But I want your promise that if she – if we – come here to your stall, you will not say a word to alert her as to your true identity."

"If you don't want me to say anything to her, don't bring her to my stall!" Janna cried, feeling outraged and deeply hurt at the same time.

"I won't if I can help it," he said, firing up with an anger to match. "But if she insists on stopping here, then you know what you must do."

Too angry to speak, Janna turned from him to pour a mug of ale for a merchant and his wife.

"And what is this?" the woman said, holding up a small phial for Janna's inspection.

"'Tis a rinse for your hair, mistress," said Janna. She shot a quick glance at her father. "My mother taught me how to make it up.

There's lemon and other herbs in it to cleanse your hair, to give it brightness and freshness."

"I'll take one." The merchant's wife looked mighty pleased with her purchase as she nudged her husband to open his purse. "And what's this?" She picked up a small pot.

Janna glanced at the rash on the merchant's cheek, small spots which he'd scratched so that they were red and angry, and full of pus. "'Tis a medicament to cleanse, soothe, and medicate afflictions of the skin," she said softly, transferring her attention to the merchant's wife.

"I'll take it," said the good wife, and gave her husband another sharp nudge.

"Do you serve ale too, or is it only here for show?" he asked sourly, obviously resenting his wife's extravagance.

Janna grinned at him. "We serve the best ale in town," she said proudly. Feeling generous after her successful transaction, she poured a mug for her father as well, but when she reached out to put it in front of him, she realized that he had gone.

Her next customer was more than welcome. "Ulf!" she cried. "Hello, Brutus." The huge dog wagged his feathery tail in greeting and licked his lips. Taking the hint, Janna poured some ale into a dish and set it in front of the dog, then pushed the unwanted mug of ale in front of the relic seller. "How's business?" she queried.

He shook his head in mild reproof. "I don't do business," he reminded her. "I only accept donations."

"Are many coming your way?"

Ulf grinned at her. "Quite a few." His smile faded as he continued. "Was that your father I saw with you?"

Janna nodded unhappily. "He's warned me to say nothing of my true identity if his wife comes to my booth. I hate him, Ulf. I wish I'd never met him!"

Ulf pursed his lips in a silent whistle as he thought about it. "Well, I can see that he's hurt your feelings, lass, but I can't say I blame him," he said eventually. And then, as Janna opened her mouth to protest, he continued, "Look at it from his point of view. He's already had to confess his disgrace to his wife, and – "

"Disgrace? He *married* my mother! He honored her, he did the right thing."

"That's probably not how his lady wife sees it. From her point of view, he broke their betrothal to marry a nobody, and now he's going to claim a nobody as his legal heir. Not only that, but she's just found out that her marriage was bigamous and her children are bastards. How would you feel about it, in her situation?" Not giving Janna time to respond, he continued, "If you were your father, wouldn't you want your daughter to make the best possible impression on a hostile wife?"

Janna was silent as she sifted Ulf's words and reluctantly acknowledged their truth. It was easy to see things from her own perspective, but she had to admit that what Ulf said also made sense. Perhaps she should do as her father asked, should the situation arise. Perhaps she should tread more cautiously around him in future, at least until she could carry out her plan to reintroduce herself to him and his family at a time of her choosing. She closed her eyes, fighting the anger her father's words had aroused in her. But there was something else at stake here, she reminded herself. Something much more important than her own wounded pride. If she wanted to avenge her mother's death and bring the culprit to justice, she would need her father's help. Better, then, to go along with what he had asked, to play the dutiful daughter in the hope and expectation that, when things were better between them, he would agree to what she asked of him.

But it was not time for that, not yet. The troubles at the alehouse were over, she felt sure of it, but she wouldn't make a move until Hugh's marriage after the fair. That would be the time to introduce herself to her father, and to his wife and family, and also to Hugh and Eleanor. That would be the time to meet them all on her own terms, and if things went as she hoped, she would get her own way with everything.

"You're right," she said, the admission as bitter as wormwood in her mouth. "But what will I do if they expect me to serve them?"

"Serve them as you would any other customer, with civility – unless your father indicates otherwise."

Janna bent down and gave Brutus's head a rub. "You have a very wise master," she told him.

"And a right thirsty one. I'll have another ale." Ulf produced a token. "And this time, I'll pay for it," he said firmly.

"Johanna!" Hugh's voice was as unwelcome as a crack of thunder on a sunny day. Reluctantly, Janna turned to face him.

"My lord," she said softly, and glanced at the woman standing beside Hugh. Her first impression was of a plump little figure wearing a silky soft dress of green. A thin gauzy veil covered her hair, which was dark and worn loose about her shoulders. The veil was secured by a jeweled band, which spoke of her father's wealth and her own social standing. Janna felt immediately awkward, and when she noticed Eleanor's white hands and soft skin, she quickly thrust her own chapped red hands behind her back. All the while she was conscious of Eleanor's close scrutiny, and knew that her action had been seen and understood.

"This is…er…this is Eleanor."

"Mistress." Janna lowered her gaze and bobbed a curtsy.

"And who are you?" Eleanor's voice was low and musical. Janna straightened to face her, noticing that while Eleanor was no beauty, her features were regular and her eyes quite striking, a deep greenish blue framed by lustrous dark lashes. But their glance was sharp and penetrating, and her mouth had thinned to a disapproving line as she waited for an answer.

"My name is Janna. Johanna, mistress," Janna said.

"And how do you come to be acquainted with my betrothed?" The scorn in her voice was unmistakable.

"I've...er...known Johanna for a long time. She was...that is..."

Janna realized that she would have to interrupt Hugh before Eleanor thought the worst of their relationship. "I was a laborer on my lord's manor farm before I came to Winchestre, mistress," she said, trying to hide her annoyance. "My mother taught me something of the art of healing, and I learned more from the infirmarian at Wiltune Abbey. After Sire Hugh was wounded at the Wiltune fair I helped to look after him while he recuperated at the abbey. And that's all," she added, answering Eleanor's unspoken accusation.

Eleanor nodded, but took Hugh's arm in a gesture of ownership that Janna noted with sour disapproval.

"May I serve you some ale?" she asked. Hugh nodded, but Eleanor pointed ahead to the stalls where the glovers displayed their wares. "I'd like to choose a new pair of gloves first," she said firmly, and dragged him away.

Janna watched them go. She felt a little sorry for Hugh, but thought that perhaps Eleanor might relax, be less possessive, once they were wed and she had him safely in her bed. From Hugh her thoughts moved on to Godric, and she gave herself a mental kick at an opportunity lost to hear news of him. Regret, sharp as a dagger, pierced her heart at the thought that he and Cecily might now be wed.

"Have I seen that man somewhere before, Janna? Who is he?" Ulf's voice dragged her back to the present.

"He's just someone I once knew." It seemed sad to think of Hugh in those terms, and yet Janna realized that her words were true. Whatever happened to her in the future, however her circumstances might change, she knew that Eleanor would make sure to keep Hugh away from her. But, whether Eleanor liked it or not, there'd be one more meeting between them all. Not for anything would she let her appearance today be Hugh's or his betrothed's lasting impression of her. Janna gave a wry smile as she recalled her plan, but she hugged the secret of it to herself. She was determined now to see it through, but she wouldn't tell Ulf, just in case he tried to talk her out of it. She wouldn't tell anyone.

*

The day wore on without further mishap. To Janna's relief, her father kept well away, as did Mus – if he was at the fair at all. By evening, she'd sold all of her potions and medicaments except for a phial of the bitter liquid she'd brewed to deter insects. Most fairgoers knew to pick tansy or fleabane out in the wild and were reluctant to spend good money on what they could find for free.

Most popular of all had been the ale, Janna's special brew, and the barrels ran dry. Many fairgoers had come back a second, third or fourth time to slake their thirst. Hugh and Eleanor, however, had not come back at all, and Janna was glad of it. She wished Eleanor joy of the marriage, but knew that Hugh's intended bride had divined more in their past acquaintance than she'd been told and instinct had prompted her to regard Janna as a threat. In the future, Eleanor would take care to ensure that she came first with Hugh in everything. And that was as it should be.

Many of the merchants spent the night either in their lock-ups or beside their booths at the fairground, sacrificing comfort for the security of knowing that their goods were watched and safe. But Sybil had arranged for Ossie to come up at the end of the day to fetch the empty barrels, which would be refilled and brought back to the fair early in the morning. Janna would return with him, there being nothing at the fairground for her to guard. But when Ossie arrived to fetch the barrels, the fair was only just starting to slow down and Janna was reluctant to leave so soon. "You go on," she told the big man. "I want to stay here a little while longer, and have another look around."

"Mistress Sybil said to tell you she needs you back at the tavern," Ossie said stolidly.

"I won't be long." Janna was wild to spend some of the coins now clinking in her pocket, the coins paid to her for her own medicaments. She'd kept them scrupulously apart from the payment she'd received for the ale, and these coins she now handed over to Ossie with the injunction to keep them safe. Sybil trusted the big man, and Janna knew that he was large and powerful enough to protect the coins from any roaming pickpocket or cutpurse he might encounter on his way back to the tavern. She felt a little guilty disobeying Sybil, but the call of the fair was a siren song in her ears and she could not resist it.

First, though, she would find something to eat. The scent of fresh bread and pies had tormented her all day, and she felt quite faint with hunger. Ale there'd been in plenty to slake her thirst, but she hadn't thought to bring anything for her dinner and so had gone without. Now her nose led her to a food stall and she stopped to inspect what there might be in the way of pies or any other delicacy to assuage her appetite. To her dismay, there was little left at all – others had gone through the fare like ravening locusts and a departing customer took with him the last pie. As Janna watched, he stuffed the meatiest part into his mouth and flung away the crust that surrounded it. The pieman barely acknowledged Janna; he was already tidying everything away, preparatory to vacating his stall. But there were still a couple of large pasties left over, looking somewhat mashed and leaking gravy through the pastry. They were past their prime, but Janna thought they'd make a tasty bite for want of anything better. She reached into her pocket, but hesitated as a furtive movement caught her eye. A grubby hand stole into view to snatch up the tossed piecrust. Janna blinked and looked again, but the hand had disappeared.

"How many do you want?" The pieman reached for the pasties; he was eager to be rid of them so that he could close for the night.

"Just a moment." The pieman rolled his eyes, impatient at the delay. But Janna didn't notice, for she'd already bounded around to the back of the stall in search of the owner of the hand. She was filled with pity, for she knew how it felt to be hungry. She forged on, pausing only when she found a young girl, pitiably thin, ragged and somewhat dirty, gnawing ravenously on the piecrust.

She shrank back in alarm at Janna's appearance, but Janna held up her hand to stop the girl running away. "Wait," she said. "Please." The girl continued to back away, surveying Janna with wary eyes as she stuffed piecrust into her mouth.

"Would you like a pasty?" Janna asked softly. "A whole pasty?"

The girl nodded, her mouth too full for speech.

"Come with me." Not wanting to waste time lest she find the cook stall locked and the pieman already gone, Janna strode off, not looking back to see if she was followed. But the girl was at her elbow as she asked the price of the two pasties and waited for the pieman's response. After buying and selling on her own behalf, she'd learned something of the art of bargaining.

"Too dear," she said, and looked down her nose at the two miserable specimens left on his board. "I might have paid a ha'penny at the beginning of the day when they were fresh and whole, but now…" She shrugged and turned her back, ready to walk away while beside her, the girl stiffened in alarm.

"You can have the two for a farthing," the pieman said hastily. Janna hid a smile, and handed over the quarter coin. She gave one of the pasties to her companion, and took a bite of her own. For a while the two didn't speak as they both stuffed their mouths full of pasty, enjoying the ease and comfort of a full belly at the end of it.

"What's your name?" Janna said, heaving a contented sigh as she brushed crumbs from her mouth.

"Mary." The girl looked up shyly. "Thank you, mistress. I never ate anything as good as that afore."

Janna smiled. "My name is Johanna. Janna." Her brain was working at a furious speed. Linked to her plan was a problem that had bothered her, but now it seemed that the solution might be within her grasp.

"Tell me, Mary," she began. "How is it that you're so hungry?" She looked more carefully at her companion, taking in the girl's ragged appearance and bare, dirty feet. "Do you have no home? No family?" she pressed, when the girl didn't answer her.

Mary shook her head.

"No place of employment?"

Mary's lower lip quivered. Mutely, she shook her head once more. Janna wondered if she was a runaway. Her imagination took flight as she visualized a miserable hovel with too many children to feed. Or a great lord's castle, perhaps, and she the lowest of the low, worked to death and beaten every day. Or perhaps the girl had been the object of an old man's lust?

"I know of somewhere that might employ you as a serving maid," Janna said, when it seemed clear that Mary wasn't prepared to share any details of her life. "You'd have your meals and somewhere to sleep. Your employer will treat you fairly as long as you are honest and work hard. Are you interested?" She watched the girl carefully, hoping she hadn't been mistaken in her. But Mary stared back without blinking.

"Yes," she said simply. "I'll work for anyone what treats me right. And I won't do wrong, neither. Not if it means being booted out on me backside. 'Tain't worth it."

Janna continued to survey her, hoping she hadn't been too hasty. The girl was a bit rough, certainly, but she could learn better ways. More, although she was scrawny, she would be comely enough after a good scrub and some clean clothes. Janna's hand went down to finger the rough weave of her homespun tunic. With a bit of luck, she wouldn't need it for too much longer.

"Do you know the Bell and Bush off the high street?" she asked Mary.

"Know of it, mistress, but I ain't bin in."

"You must come there after High Mass on Sunday of the week after the fair closes. Come and find me. The taverner is Mistress Sybil, and I will ask her if she'll employ you. I can't promise what she'll say – but I'll do my best to persuade her to take you on." Janna hesitated, wondering how best to word her request. "Wash your face and hands before you come," she said gently. "Make yourself as neat and clean as possible."

The girl scowled, wary as a wild cat. "Why?"

"The Bell and Bush has a good reputation. Wealthy merchants go there, even lords sometimes," she said, as she thought of her father. "Mistress Sybil won't take you on if you don't look respectable."

Mary gave a grudging nod. "I'll come," she promised.

"Good." Janna smiled and left her, impatient now to get on with her shopping. She could only hope that her impulse wasn't ill-judged and that, in finding the girl a safe haven, she had also solved a problem that had weighed heavily on her mind.

She idled along past the booths, tempted by everything that came into view. She drew a deep breath as a spicy aroma wafted her way, and began to follow its source, beguiled by the scent of cloves mingled with nutmeg, caraway and cinnamon, liquorice and aromatic galangal.

A chapman cornered her with a display of silver rings on a tray suspended by a leather thong around his neck. "Sterling silver, guaranteed," he insisted. "And a special price for you, pretty maiden." Smiling, Janna waved him away, sure that the rings would tarnish at the first sign of moisture.

The sound of singing caught her attention, and at once she thought of Master Thomas and the jongleurs she had traveled with on her way to Winchestre. She pushed through the crowd to greet them, but to her disappointment, this troupe were strangers to her. She recognized the song, however, and hummed the tune under her breath as she walked on.

A huge dog bounded over to lick her hand, and she stopped to pat him. "Where's your master, Brutus?" she asked softly, but he waved his feathery tail and bounded off once more. Janna watched him go, and saw Ulf deep in conversation with an expensively garbed merchant and his wife. Ulf's pack was open and all were looking at something displayed in his palm. Janna smothered a grin as her imagination supplied the missing details: some body part from a saint, perhaps; a fragment of clothing from the holy family or a splinter from Jesus's cradle. Ulf's pack always contained strange and wondrous articles, some with a very doubtful provenance indeed.

A rainbow of colored ribbons caught her eye and she stopped to choose one from the tray thrust at her by an old woman. She would wear the ribbon in her hair when she dressed up in her blue gown, she decided. She might also choose another color, so that she could change the ribbons about.

The woman stepped back toward one of the booths. "Blue or green, mistress?" she asked, in a high, quavering voice. "Maybe yellow?" She picked up a golden ribbon and dangled it in front of Janna, her rough hand crushing the delicate fabric. Janna marveled that the ribbons looked so unspoiled while being subjected to this sort of treatment.

"And a pretty lace collar for your gown?" the woman wheedled. Tempted, Janna looked about for a froth of lace such as she'd admired at other stalls. But there was no sign of any such thing. Puzzled, she stared at the crone. The woman's back was so bent, only the top of her head was visible, while her voluminous wimple covered the sides of her face. Janna felt a pang of pity for someone so old and infirm being condemned to such a chancy living. She determined to buy something to ease the woman's hardship.

"Come see all my goods, mistress." The woman indicated the booth behind her, stumbling over her long skirt as she turned. "I wager there's summat to tempt you inside."

Janna saw the tray of ribbons disappearing before she'd had time to choose one, and immediately followed after it. Although the stall appeared closed for the night, the ribbon seller unlatched the door and strode in, beckoning Janna to follow her.

Janna was over the threshold before she thought to question why the woman would have singled her out for a costly purchase of lace when she was dressed like a drudge. Her suspicions came together in a rush: the large, rough hand, the curiously pitched voice, the woman who walked like a man. But by then it was too late, for the door had slammed shut behind her.

The ribbon seller dropped the tray and whirled to confront Janna. It was dark inside the stall, but enough light leached through the ill-fitting roof and door for her to see the gleam of the knife pulled out from under the ribbons.

"At last," Mus said softly, as he straightened to his full height.

The thought flashed through Janna's mind that he'd tried to kill her twice before, and failed – he wouldn't fail this time; he wouldn't allow himself to fail. She stared at him, cursing the vanity that had caused her to drop her guard. Keep him talking, she thought. Anything to give herself time to think how to escape, even to draw breath just for a few moments longer. Life had never seemed so sweet, so precious. Fighting panic, she swiped her sweating hands down her apron, pausing momentarily as she came across the hard lump in her pocket.

"You certainly had me fooled, Mus." She was proud of how steady her voice sounded. "Have you sold many ribbons today?"

He growled deep in his throat. "There's not too many as gullible as you," he taunted her.

Janna faced him, holding his gaze so he would not notice her hand slipping in to her pocket to grip the small phial left over from her sales. "So at last you have me where you want me," she said, the tremble in her voice betraying her fear. Slowly, cautiously, she eased the stopper out of the phial. It was probably hopeless, but she knew it was the only chance she had.

Mus licked his lips as a cat licks cream. She could see how much he was enjoying himself. "Say your prayers, sweetheart." Savoring the moment, his mouth stretched in a wide grin, revealing teeth as crumbling and decayed as tombstones. He lunged toward her, his knife pointed straight at her heart. In one fluid movement, Janna flung the bitter contents of the phial at him, aiming for his eyes. The potion meant death for insects; she had no idea what it would do to humans, but it was the only weapon she possessed.

She threw herself sideways out of his path and raced for the door, hoping that he would be too blinded to stop her. She heard a howl of rage as she wrenched open the door and hurtled outside.

Almost at once she felt his hand fasten onto her arm. She screamed, desperate to attract attention, hoping that the noise would deter Mus from attacking her in front of witnesses. But he had gone too far to stop now. She struggled in his grip but he held her fast, clamped hard against him as he raised his knife to cut her throat. Janna closed her eyes so that she would not see her own death coming. But she continued to scream and to struggle; she would not make it easy for him – she would go down fighting.

A savage bark sounded over her cries, closely followed by a loud yell. The grip on her arm loosened and she risked opening her eyes to see what was happening. The realization that she was not dead, that her assailant no longer held her captive, gradually filtered through her panic. Just as she began to relax, an arm caught her and pulled her close. Quivering with terror, she wheeled to confront this new threat.

And recognized Ulf. She sagged into the safety of his arms. But where was Mus?

Alarmed, she scanned her surroundings, and saw that Brutus had Mus pinned to the ground. The huge hound was slavering over him in anticipation of being able to tear him to pieces. Silent and terrified, Mus had rolled himself into a ball to present the smallest target possible. Janna felt a great satisfaction as she noticed his red, streaming eyes. He lifted his head to glare at her. At the slight movement, Brutus growled and bared his teeth. Mus froze into stillness once more.

"No, Brutus!" Ulf commanded sharply. The dog looked up at him. "Just keep the old woman down on the ground. No biting!" Brutus must have understood the command, for he appeared somewhat disappointed. Janna knew how he felt. At the thought of how close she'd come to death, her body spasmed in a mighty shudder.

Ulf's face reflected his concern. "You're safe now, lass. There's nowt to worry about." He released her, and bent to pick up the knife Mus had dropped in the shock of the dog's attack. "Brutus will keep the woman captive until the bishop's guards get here." He turned a puzzled frown on Janna. "What business had you with the old crone anyway? Why did she come after you with a knife?"

"Look again," Janna advised. "That 'old crone,' as you call her, tempted me with a tray of ribbons. But his name is Mus. He's the one who attacked me at the tavern, but the potboy protected me then. This is the third time he's tried to kill me!"

Ulf drew a shocked breath. "Third and last," he said, and gestured urgently to the guards now moving in their direction, attracted by the cries of alarm and excited voices of the crowd gathering around Janna.

"That's the old hag who stole my tray of ribbons!" A young woman thrust herself to the front of the spectators. She looked down at Mus cowering under Brutus's guard and smiled with great satisfaction. "She thought to take my livelihood away from me, the old bitch. She deserves whatever's coming to her." She looked about, seeking the missing ribbons.

"They're in the booth back there." Janna inclined her head in its direction, and the ribbon seller darted off to fetch them.

"Tell your story to the guards," Ulf advised, as the girl reappeared, clutching her tray to her chest. He jerked his thumb toward Janna. "And Mistress Johanna will tell them how this devil spawn tried to kill her!"

A gasp of anticipation rippled through the crowd. They parted to make way for the approaching guards, then closed in tight once more, determined not to miss a single word of this exciting finale to what had already proved an action-packed and eventful day.

*

Sybil was horrified when Janna finally arrived back at the tavern and explained why she was so late.

"You should have come back with Ossie as I asked," she grumbled.

"If I had done, Mus would only have come after me some other time," Janna pointed out. She'd already explained to Sybil that Mus had tried to kill her on several occasions, and had given the taverner a small part of the explanation why. "But I'm safe now," she continued. "The bishop's justiciar has already spoken to witnesses about the incident. He knows about the dropped knife, and the stolen ribbons, and I've told him how Mus tried to kill me and how I managed to escape. He's assured me that Mus will be kept locked up until the end of the fair, and brought to trial after that."

Janna was determined that, when Mus came to answer the charge, he would also have to answer for the other times he'd attacked her with murder on his mind and fury in his heart. He would not escape on his master's bond quite so easily next time.

Chapter 15

The remaining days of the fair passed without incident. True to the justiciar's word, the Piepowder Court was convened at the bishop's pavilion to pass judgment on all those miscreants who had been charged with crimes during the course of the fair, though none was as serious as the charge against Mus. The bishop's agent and the jurors heard both pleas and complaints as the prisoners answered the charges against them and brought witnesses to testify to their good standing in the community. Evading tolls, selling shoddy or short-weight goods to customers, as well as picking pockets or more serious theft – all charges were heard and debated before sentences were passed.

And then it was Mus's turn. The reeve in charge of the bishop's guard told of Janna's accusation, and Ulf and other witnesses were summoned to give their version of the story. Janna was also called and related details of Mus's previous attacks to the fascinated court. She cited Wat as her witness, although she feared he might prove unhelpful after his banishment from the Bell and Bush. But although he was sulky at first, in the end the temptation to boast of his heroics proved too strong, and he painted a frightening picture of the attack on Janna and puffed up his own prowess, all of which was borne out by Ossie, who was called as the next witness. The case against Mus looked black indeed, and Janna waited in some trepidation for Robert of Babestoche to make an appearance, along with his henchmen, to bear testimony to Mus's impeccable character, as had happened once before. But no such witnesses appeared and the justiciar duly passed sentence.

Aggrieved, and still shouting his innocence, Mus was taken away in irons. Janna prayed with great devoutness that she would never have to face him again. She wondered at the absence of his master. Did Mus not have time to send for him? Or had Robert of Babestoche given up on his hired assassin, realizing that this time Mus had made too public an attempt to kill her and had thus gone too far to be saved?

*

With the fair over, the trial against Mus settled, and the time for Hugh and Eleanor to exchange their vows coming close, Janna had arrangements to make that must, inevitably, involve Sybil and her future.

She knew what she wanted to do and prayed for the outcome she desired, although she realized that she could only set events in motion – the rest of it was out of her hands. In the meantime, it was important to keep on side with Sybil, for if things went awry she would need to keep her position at the tavern.

It gave Janna satisfaction to note that, thanks to their stall at the fair and the chance for fairgoers to taste their ale, the tavern was once again as busy as it had ever been. It made her task both easier and harder, for there was more than enough work now to keep both her and Sybil rushed off their feet. But it meant that she had more than fulfilled her part of the bargain, and had justified Sybil's faith in taking her on in the first place. And she'd been duly rewarded by Sybil, with words and with payment.

"This for you, Janna," she'd said, pressing another silver coin into Janna's hand. "I'm so pleased I let you talk me into operating a stall up at the fair. I'll be doing so every year in the future."

Janna found she had a new sense of ease and freedom. With the removal of Mus, and the troubles of the tavern now settled, she was able to relax and enjoy what she was doing instead of startling at unexpected sounds and forever keeping a wary eye over her shoulder. Sybil had taken on a new potboy to help scrub the dishes; he seemed a pleasant enough lad and, unlike Wat, was willing to turn his hand to whatever task was set him. If extra help was needed when it came to serving customers, Janna thought that their new potboy might well fill the gap if her own plan didn't work out to her satisfaction. She had done what she could to prepare for the next step along her quest, and now she waited impatiently for Sunday.

Janna's thoughts kept her awake for much of the night before Hugh's marriage, for she knew there was far more at stake than merely witnessing the exchange of vows between him and Eleanor. Her whole future rested on the morrow, in more ways than one. As she lay wakeful in the darkness, she tried to prepare herself for the scene with Sybil. She could only trust that the taverner would understand; hope also that Sybil would take her back if her mission failed. Her father had said that he would accept her once she left Sybil's employment and Janna prayed that he would prove to be a man of his word.

What of his wife and children? She remembered the reaction of his son. Giles had openly shown his hatred. Would his other children be of the same mind? And Blanche? In her position, Janna thought she would resent any reminder that her husband had forsaken her to marry someone else, and that she was his second choice. Even more would she resent the fact that his previous marriage had rendered her own marriage invalid. No, she thought, she shouldn't expect to find any love or charity, or even acceptance, from Blanche. However pleasant the dame might show herself, Janna should stay on her guard.

She put aside her conjectures about her father and his family and turned her thoughts to the reason behind the gathering. Hugh was to be married. She remembered the first time she'd seen him, a dark figure against the bright sunlight, riding high upon his destrier. He had seemed like a god looking down on her, and so she had thought him, being so far above her in station as to be forever out of her reach. She remembered his unexpected kindness to her during the bitter sadness of her mother's death. She remembered also his dependence on her when, wounded and bleeding, he'd been brought into the abbey and she had tended him. She remembered the kisses they had shared, and how sweet and comforting they had been. She'd thought then that she would die if Hugh ever married someone else, but now that it was about to become a reality she found that she didn't mind at all.

An unsettling realization disturbed her musing. Hugh would take his vows in front of witnesses. Not only Eleanor's family would be there, but his family also: Dame Alice and her husband, Robert of Babestoche. If Janna intended to witness the exchange of vows, as indeed she did, she must take care that they did not notice her.

Finally, Janna came to what was uppermost in her mind: that this might be her only chance to talk to Godric; to make things right if he wished, and if it wasn't too late. Surely he would come to Hugh's wedding to witness the vows of his lord. But if Godric was there, then Cecily would be there too. What if they decided to exchange their own vows at the cathedral door after witnessing those of their liege lord? Hugh wouldn't put any obstacles in their path; after all, he desired the match, as did his aunt. Pain, sharp as an arrow, lanced Janna's heart at the thought.

The knowledge that it was her fault that things had come to this pass increased her anguish. A long time ago, Godric had told her that he loved her and he'd asked her to marry him. In her pride, and in her determination to seek her father without hindrance, she had refused him. Nor had she given him any reason to hope that she would change her mind. Small wonder, then, if he'd turned his attention elsewhere. It was her fault if he'd forsaken her, and she would have to live with that knowledge forever.

Godric. The thought of him and Cecily together was lacerating. Janna's sense of loss, acknowledged in this moment of truth, was overwhelming. She had never felt so lonely, so bereft; never felt so sure of her own heart as now. Because of her blindness she had lost the man she truly loved, the man she trusted above all others. Yes, she'd been dazzled and flattered by Hugh – and by Ralph – so awed by their status and demeanor that she'd been unable to see Godric's true worth. She hadn't valued him when she'd had the chance, but now that her eyes were truly open it was probably too late to tell him what was in her heart.

She forced herself to lie still on her pallet lest she disturb the new potboy, but she could not sleep for misery of what might already be. Nor, when she recalled the passion of the kiss she'd shared with Godric out in the tavern yard, could she subdue the wild hope that in spite of everything, he loved her still. Dry eyed, she kept vigil for the greater part of the night, and roused herself at dawn to face whatever the day might bring.

With Sybil's permission, she put the first part of her plan in motion, going up to rescue her blue gown from storage in the chest in the taverner's room. It was clean now, and if not looking quite as new as it once had done, it would give her the appearance of wealth and respectability. She took it into the brew house and gave herself a thorough wash in private before dressing. How she wished for a mirror so that she could see how she looked. She combed her wet hair with the dried teasel head she'd set aside for the purpose, wincing as the sharp hooks caught in the tangles. When she was satisfied that her hair was smooth and as clean and shiny as one of her precious rinses could make it, she brought out the gauzy linen veil that the nuns had given her to complete her ensemble. After a moment's thought, she set it aside and instead, braided part of her hair and tied it with the new blue ribbon she'd managed to purchase from the young ribbon seller at the fair. No need to wear a veil when she was not yet wed.

She shed her boots and put on the pretty blue shoes, which had been brushed and buffed to a semblance of respectability, even though they were still a little too small for comfort. She was determined to look her very best this day. For her father, she told herself firmly, while acknowledging that the show was also for Hugh's highborn wife and – she drew a quivering breath – for Godric. If he was there. And if he was not already betrothed or wed to Cecily.

As a last gesture, she extracted her purse from its hiding place under her shift, opened it, and pulled out the ring brooch. "This is for you," she told her mother, as she carefully pinned the brooch to the bodice of her gown. Would Eadgyth approve of her intentions this day? Janna thought she might. For her mother's sake, she prayed that at last she would be accepted by her father.

Out in the yard, she encountered the potboy. He gave her a startled glance, then set to industriously scrubbing the dishes once more. He was a far better worker than Wat, she acknowledged, as her gaze moved from him to the girl standing nearby. On meeting Janna's glance, she bobbed a curtsy. "Mistress," she said quietly.

It took Janna a few moments to recognize Mary, and she was delighted when she finally made the connection. The girl had taken some trouble over her appearance. Her hair was brushed and tidy, her face and hands were clean, her tunic washed, and the worst of the rips had been mended, if not very neatly then at least with good intent. Looking her over, Janna could see that Mary seemed a respectable girl. The fact that she'd gone to some lengths to do as Janna had asked spoke well of her determination to secure employment and, perhaps, to make sure she kept it. If she worked as industriously in the tavern as she'd done over her appearance, she could only prove an asset to Sybil.

"Wait for me to come and fetch you," she told the girl, and hurried on to the kitchen.

Elfric gave an admiring whistle as Janna poked her head around the door.

"Where's Sybil?" she asked.

"In the tavern – but she's not expecting any ladies to call so far as I know!"

Janna couldn't help smiling, in spite of her foreboding over how her plan might turn out. "Then this is my chance to turn her day into a celebration," she said, hoping that in fact it would be the other way around.

She walked into the tavern, and was relieved to find it relatively empty. Those patrons within sat contentedly nursing their mugs of ale. Taking advantage of the lull, she drew Sybil to one side and launched into the explanation she had prepared so carefully during her wakeful hours through the night.

"You're who? You're *what*?"

Janna winced at the disbelief in Sybil's tone. "I'm the legitimate daughter of an illegitimate son of the old king," she repeated steadily. "I grew up never knowing the true identity of my father, and I've come a long way to find it out. And yes, I've spoken to my father," she said quickly, anticipating Sybil's next question, "and yes, he accepts that I am who I say I am. But no, he won't introduce me to the rest of his family while I work here at the tavern." Despite her efforts to sound light-hearted – and more especially, not to offend Sybil – still Janna could not keep the bitterness from her voice as she repeated her father's warning.

Predictably, Sybil bristled. "It's good, honest work," she said, her annoyance showing in the angry flush tingeing her cheeks.

"Yes," Janna agreed. "It is, and so I told him. But – but he has a new family now, a wife and children, and I would like to go to them dressed respectably so that I can meet them as equals."

Sybil eyed her gown and gave a sniff. "You won't be needing the tunic I gave you, then," she said, and held out her hand. "Where is it?"

"It's in the brew house." Janna grabbed the taverner's hand. "I owe you so much," she said, "and I may yet need more from you, for there is no surety that my father will take me in to live with him. I may well have to beg you to take me back at the end of this day."

"And in the meantime you will walk away and leave me here to manage on my own. Today, and for all the days thereafter, unless things do not go well for you?" Sybil was still irate, feeling ill-used and ready to take it out on Janna.

"No," Janna contradicted her quickly. "I would not leave you on your own, not today, when people are always so thirsty after their devotions! Please, wait here a moment, mistress." Without giving Sybil a chance to argue, she slipped quickly outside to fetch the young girl patiently waiting for her in the yard.

"This is Mary," she said, as she ushered the girl into the tavern and presented her to the suspicious taverner. "Mary is willing to help you this day, Mistress Sybil, just to see how suited she is for the work."

"And if she's not?"

"I am sure you'll find her satisfactory." Janna cast a quick glance of appeal in Mary's direction.

"I warrant you will, Mistress Sybil," the girl said eagerly. "I ain't never worked in a tavern afore, but I'm willing to learn. I'll do whatever you tell me, I swear it."

"Humph." But Sybil's expression had softened slightly. She turned to Janna. "And what happens to Mary if your father won't have you, miss? Have you thought of that?"

Janna watched the glow fade from Mary's eager face. "We're so busy, there'll surely be work enough for the two of us," she said quickly.

"You test my goodwill more than anyone has ever done," Sybil warned her. She turned to her new serving maid. "You may work here this day, and you may wear Janna's tunic while you serve my customers. But I won't pay you for your labor, not today while I try you out. You may have your dinner and supper from the kitchen, but that's all."

"And may she break her fast here too?" Janna suggested, knowing that she was pushing her luck, but willing to wager that the girl had been scavenging for scraps ever since they'd eaten their pasties together.

She was rewarded by seeing Mary's face brighten at the prospect. Even the chance of three meals was enough to cheer the girl, but Janna was sure she'd also work hard enough to deserve Sybil's generosity. It seemed that Sybil agreed with her, for she gave a grunt of assent and directed Mary to the kitchen for bread and ale, with the injunction that she'd be out to find her and spell out her duties just as soon as she was done.

"My tunic's in the brew house," Janna called after her. Once Mary had disappeared, Sybil surveyed Janna quietly for some moments.

"You've worked well for me. Indeed, I could be dead and the tavern in the hands of Alan if not for you, so I will send you on your way with my blessing, Janna, and my hope that your father will prove worthy of your trust in him."

Janna stayed silent, struck by the sincerity of Sybil's good wishes. This was more than she'd hoped for, or expected. "Thank you, mistress," she said at last. "Thank you also for taking me in and giving me a chance, just as you're doing now for Mary."

"What do you know of her?" Sybil asked quickly.

"Nothing – except that she was hungry, and in need of honest work." Janna smiled at the taverner. "I'm sure she'll find a good home with you, mistress, and I expect that she will earn her keep."

"I hope so." Sybil returned Janna's smile. "Remember, you can always come back here if that father of yours lets you down." She leaned forward and gave Janna's cheek a farewell peck. "Go with God," she advised. "And good luck to you."

"And to you, mistress." Janna left the tavern with a light step. She'd dreaded having to face Sybil, but their parting had gone much better than she'd expected. She just hoped that she would survive the rest of the day so well. The sound of bells tolling from the cathedral hastened her steps. She didn't want to be too late to witness Hugh and Eleanor exchanging their vows. That wouldn't suit her purpose at all. As for Godric and Cecily...

She quickened her steps, trying to outpace her thoughts. Her shoes were beginning to pinch badly, but she ignored the pain, for she knew they looked well with her dress. As she neared the cathedral she found a far greater crush of witnesses than she'd expected. She raised her eyes above the crowds to the wedding party standing on the stairs beside the great door. Hugh, looking ill at ease in a new red tunic, with elaborate embroidery at neck, cuff and hem. His bride beside him, resplendent in gold cloth, looking happy and content. Janna sent the couple a silent wish for their health, long life and happiness together. Her gaze traveled on, seeking those whom she most hoped – or dreaded – to find.

Beside Hugh stood Dame Alice and her husband, Robert of Babestoche, ruddier of face and appearing more self-important than ever. At once Janna ducked her head, although she was fairly confident that she hadn't been seen. After all, there were other things of more immediate concern to the wedding party than a close scrutiny of all the witnesses. She risked another look and saw she'd guessed right. All attention was on the priest. Her gaze sharpened. They were not part of the wedding party, but they were here. Godric and Cecily, standing at the front of the crowd. Janna watched them closely, seeking signs. Cecily kept stealing glances at Godric, but he kept his face steadfastly forward, seemingly intent on the ceremony unfolding before them. Although they stood close together, Janna noticed they were not holding hands.

She was too far away to hear what the priest was saying, but she thought the bride and groom might now be exchanging their vows, particularly when Hugh took Eleanor's hand and slid a ring onto her finger.

There, she thought. It's done. She watched him kiss Eleanor on her cheek, heard Eleanor's delighted laughter ring out clear above the hum of the crowd. Janna smiled at her evident joy. Even Hugh looked cheerful as he began to shake hands with the well-wishers gathered around him. In trepidation, she waited for Godric and Cecily to take their place in front of the priest, but Godric walked over to Hugh while Cecily stood still, looking about her. Her gaze fell on Janna, moved on, and then came back again. She began to make her way through the crowd in Janna's direction. Realizing that she'd been recognized, Janna resigned herself to the meeting.

"Janna! It really is you. I didn't think I'd ever see you again." Cecily seemed nervous. Janna wondered why, until she remembered the young woman's secret – and her hopes for the future.

"Mistress Cecily. And I see Godric is here too. Are you...?" Janna's throat constricted. She could not continue.

Cecily shot her a worried glance. "Now that you're here I really need to talk to you," she said, and lowered her voice. "You may already know that it's Sire Hugh's wish that we should be wed, Godric and I, and that I should wait on his new wife. I want to ask you – beg you – not to tell anyone about what happened to me in the past, lest it endanger my future in Sire Hugh's household and my chance of happiness with Godric."

"But...Godric already knows about your past," Janna said faintly, feeling quite dizzy with relief that he and Cecily were still not betrothed.

"So he does, for I told him all about it," Cecily said firmly. "But while he does not hold it against me, I fear that Sire Hugh and Dame Eleanor might consider me unfit for employment in their household if they should hear about my downfall. Godric is Sire Hugh's steward and I would not jeopardize his position either. Please, Janna, I beg you, hold your peace – for Godric's sake, if not for mine."

"I've held my peace all these years, Cecily. I'm unlikely to break my silence now." Janna found she could not go so far as to wish them happiness. Although she dreaded Cecily's reply, she needed to find out the worst. "How long is it before you and Godric are wed?"

Cecily hesitated. "He has not asked me yet." She brightened. "But I am sure it is only a matter of time."

"Why the delay, if your liege lord is in favor of the match?" Janna was genuinely interested in the reason, while desperately hoping that she might not be too late after all.

The young woman scowled. "I fear you are still in his heart, Janna. He has not forgotten you, even though you turned your back on him all those years ago. You hurt him more than you can ever imagine when you turned your affection to Sire Hugh. By his courage, his wisdom and his strength, Godric has risen high in Sire Hugh's employ, while my love and kisses have coaxed him back to joy. Our future lies together now. Even though Sire Hugh was wed today and is now lost to you, Godric is not for you either."

"But I don't – " But Janna didn't get the chance to correct Cecily's misunderstanding.

"We've heard that you are related to our old king and that your fortunes have risen far beyond us," Cecily interrupted. "You'll be able to wed anyone you wish in the future. You have everything before you, while I will have nothing if Godric is lost to me." Betraying her agitation, she caught Janna's hand and pressed it tight. "Please," she begged, "please don't come back into our lives now. Please let us be."

It was impossible to ignore the heartfelt emotion behind Cecily's plea, even though Janna had the thought that it was not for Cecily to warn her off. She was chastened by the knowledge of how badly she'd hurt Godric, but surely it was for him to decide whether or not he could forgive her – or love her again. She couldn't give Cecily the assurance she wanted, but fortunately was saved from having to reply by a happy shout.

"There you are, Cecily! I've been looking for you." Hamo's intervention was doubly welcome, for Janna was delighted to see him again. She smiled at the lad as he bounced up to them. He blinked a moment before recognition came, and a smile split his face. "Janna!" His enthusiasm helped restore some of Janna's confidence, although she could only hope that his parents weren't watching him. "Are you here to see my cousin? Does he know you are here?"

"I've just come to see him wed, no more." Janna hoped that Cecily would understand the meaning behind her words.

"Stay away from us, Janna. Don't meddle where you're not wanted." It was said too low for Hamo to hear. Before she could respond, Cecily gave her a stiff nod and walked away. But Hamo stayed where he was.

"Why is Cecily looking so cross?" he asked.

Janna shook her head, thinking it too complicated to explain. She looked about for Godric. With a sinking heart, she realized that Cecily was heading in his direction with the intention, no doubt, of keeping him well away from her. Nevertheless, Janna was determined to speak to him, even if it was only for the last time. But she needed to see him on his own, to apologize and ask for his forgiveness and understanding. And then, if he loved her still, she could tell him how they might be able to choose a new path and be together.

In the meantime she needed to pursue the next part of her scheme. She turned to Hamo. "Tell me," she asked, "have you met John fitz Henry and his wife? Are they here today to witness your cousin's marriage?"

"I don't know them." Hamo shook his head. "But I'll help you look for them if you like," he said, brightening with self-importance as he took Janna's hand. Smothering a grin, Janna allowed herself to be towed around the crowd while she searched for her father, or even for his obnoxious son.

She found the family standing off to one side, waiting to offer their good wishes to Hugh and his bride. Her steps faltered as she saw the bishop standing beside them, conversing earnestly with her father. She hadn't expected to find him here. And yet, Hugh had told her that her father was staying at the bishop's Wolvesey Palace, so it was hardly surprising that they would also keep in company here.

"Is that him?" Hamo asked, following the direction of Janna's gaze. Without giving her a chance to reply, he tugged her forward.

Janna swallowed, her throat suddenly dry. Now that the moment she'd been waiting for was upon her, she felt unable to deal with it, or with the aftermath that must follow. "Hamo, wait!" But it was too late, for her father had seen her. He broke off his conversation with the bishop, and stared at her in disbelief.

Wanting desperately to run away, Janna was yet towed forward by the determined Hamo, who wanted only to make himself useful.

"Johanna," her father greeted her.

"My lord." She sank into a curtsy before him. She hadn't called him "father." It was up to him to recognize her or not. She would let him decide how their relationship would develop from here on.

He stretched out a hand, put it under her arm and pulled her up. Around him, the family had grown quiet. Even the bishop had ceased speaking. John looked at her, his searching gaze taking in everything from her apparel to her presence at the cathedral in the company of a young lord who was dressed in wedding finery equal to Hugh's own, and who obviously regarded her with affection.

"I am ready, sire, to be your dutiful daughter," said Janna, speaking so quietly that only her father could hear her words.

He cleared his throat. Beside him, Blanche stiffened. The two girls in the party looked at Janna with undisguised curiosity. Her glance flicked to Giles and, as quickly, flicked away. She was shocked by the hostility of his expression, understanding that the same hostility would be matched in Blanche's heart, even if it didn't show on her face.

"My dear, may I present my daughter, Johanna," John said formally, all the while retaining his hold on Janna's arm. It was both a comfort and a support to her as she bobbed a curtsy to acknowledge his family.

"My lady," she said.

Beside him, Blanche drew a deep breath. "Johanna. My husband has told us all about you."

Janna risked a look at Blanche, and flinched at the depths of hatred she could read in her eyes.

"My daughters," said her father. "This is Richildis." He indicated the older girl, who tossed her head and wouldn't meet Janna's eye. "And this is Rohesia, whom we call Rosy." His face softened into a smile as he pointed to the sturdy child standing beside her older sister. He nodded toward his son. "Giles you have already met."

"Giles," Janna murmured politely. Unsure how to greet them all, she held out her hand. Nobody took it. After an agonizing few moments, she withdrew her hand and tucked it behind her back. Her father let go of her arm, and she felt instantly abandoned. All her instincts urged her to flee. Only pride kept her standing still. She wished Hamo would drag her off somewhere else, anywhere, so she could make an excuse and leave them.

"I didn't know you had another daughter, John." The bishop's voice interrupted her panicked thoughts. He sounded kindly enough; more, he held out his hand to her. With great relief, Janna took it and heard Blanche's indrawn breath of disapproval. Was she meant to shake his hand or kiss his ring? Flustered, she snatched her hand away and looked to her father for guidance.

"It's an old story, and now is not the time for its telling," John said firmly. "I bid you, wife, make Johanna welcome. And you, my children, greet your half-sister." His sweeping gaze encompassed them all before moving on to the bishop. "With your permission, Henry, I'd like Johanna to stay with us at Wolvesey. She and I have a lot to talk about, for it is only recently that I have come to know of her existence."

"Of course!" But the bishop couldn't keep the surprise and curiosity from his face as he turned to Janna. "I bid you welcome, long-lost daughter of my cousin. I look forward to hearing all about you."

You'll only hear what I choose to tell! Janna didn't put her thoughts into words, but it was hard to keep her dismay from showing. She'd suddenly realized, now that it was too late, that she was about to go into the fortress of the enemy. True, Bishop Henry had seemed to support the empress's cause while his brother was imprisoned, but Janna knew, even if the present company did not, that he had always supported his brother and had worked actively to bring about the empress's downfall.

With a prick of alarm, Janna wondered if the bishop had heard of her own role in making sure his treachery was known to the empress. She must hope for the best, and be very careful indeed to hide her involvement with his agent. Nor must she let her thoughts show, never indicate by word or deed that she was at odds with the king and his brother, the bishop. So she pressed her lips tight shut and sank into another deep curtsy, thinking it safer than saying or doing anything else.

Apparently the bishop was pleased enough with her, for he helped her up, gave her a warmer smile than any other member of John's family had done, and then excused himself to talk to Eleanor's father, who had materialized at his elbow. Janna was left facing her new family.

"May I present Hamo, sire, cousin to Sire Hugh, whose marriage is being celebrated today," she said, hoping Hamo might ease the tension with his usual irrepressible high spirits.

"And how do you come to be on such familiar terms with a young lord?" Blanche demanded coldly, clearly having learned something of Johanna's upbringing.

"Janna rescued me!" Hamo said, not giving Janna a chance to reply as he continued, "Our reeve kidnapped me when I was staying with my cousin Hugh on his manor farm. Janna and Godric found me just in time. She's very brave. Hugh says she's also very clever."

Janna did her best not to smile, although she was delighted that Hamo had given her such a glowing testimonial. Perhaps it would help wipe away the sour expression on Blanche's face.

"Johanna has learned the art of healing from her mother," John added quickly, as if hoping to increase his daughter's standing in the eyes of his wife.

"She helped my cousin Hugh get better after he was stabbed at the fair in Wiltune," Hamo chimed in eagerly, happy to heap praise on someone he regarded as both a friend and an ally.

Janna was beginning to blush at all the unaccustomed attention she was receiving. "I have some knowledge of herbs and healing," she said modestly.

Blanche's mouth pulled down, apparently unwilling to think well of this cuckoo in their midst. Giles continued to scowl at her, but Janna hoped that she might be able to persuade the two girls into friendship. She smiled at them. "How old are you?" she asked, thinking to make them her allies, if she could.

"Richildis is the eldest of my children," Blanche answered quickly. "But you, of course, are some years older than she is." She looked Janna up and down with increasing disfavor. "At your age I'm surprised you are not wed."

"'Tis just as well she is not, for now it is in my power to find a suitable husband for her," John interposed.

Dismayed, Janna opened her mouth to protest, then quickly closed it again. It wouldn't do to antagonize her father right at the start. When she'd first pondered the consequences of finding him, and the price she might have to pay for being his daughter, she hadn't taken an arranged marriage into consideration. With a sinking heart, she wondered if she'd just made the biggest mistake of her life. She heard Hamo's joyful shout, and turned to see what had attracted his attention.

"Hugh!" He was jumping up and down and waving to his cousin. Janna watched Hugh's mouth open in shock as he recognized her. Feeling suddenly self-conscious, she smoothed her hands over the silky woolen fabric of her gown and flicked back her hair. For the first time ever, she would meet him as an equal. She savored her triumph as she watched Hugh hurry toward her, closely followed by his new wife.

Janna smiled at them both as they approached. She saw puzzlement give way to shock as Eleanor finally recognized her, and noticed the light die in her joyful face as she hurried to keep pace with her lord. It was enough to make Janna feel deeply uncomfortable. She had wanted to meet Hugh and Eleanor this last time just to show them who she truly was: not a drudge in a tavern but the granddaughter of a king. So focused had she been on her own ambition, she hadn't given any thought as to how her presence might spoil Eleanor's joy on this day of all days. But it was too late now to run, to pretend she hadn't seen them, so she kept her smile fixed firmly in place.

"My congratulations on your nuptials," her father said. His glance went from Hugh to Eleanor, who stood silent by Hugh's side. "I am John fitz Henry. Did you wish to speak to my daughter?"

"I..." There was such an expression of regret on Hugh's face that Janna turned away, lest she betray what she was thinking. She listened to his mumbled introduction, which seemed to meet with her father's approval, for he then introduced his own family in turn. There was a short silence, broken by Janna, who was desperate to do what she could to retrieve the situation.

"May I wish you both happiness and a long life together," she said, making a point of turning first to Eleanor before extending her good wishes to Hugh.

"But who...how...?" Eleanor seemed quite unable to equate the serving wench she'd met at the fair with this new, self-assured Janna in her pretty blue gown. She clutched Hugh's arm as if needing his support. Janna watched them both, her victory crumbling into bitter ashes. This was not what she'd wanted, not what she'd set out to achieve. Yes, she'd hoped to meet them as equals, but not at the price of Eleanor's happiness and peace of mind. For it was all too clear now that Hugh was an unwilling groom and she an anxious and needy bride.

At that moment, Janna heartily wished she could turn back time. If only she could be in the forest with Godric, listening to his declaration of love and the future he had planned for them. She should have stayed with him and loved him. She would have been happy. Yet Janna knew that, in truth, she would always have regretted it if she'd settled too soon, always have wondered about the world outside her home. And now she, and Godric as well, had journeyed too far and gone through too much ever to recapture that younger and more innocent time.

Nor could she regret going in search of her father, she thought, as she looked up at John. Even though she'd made mistakes along the journey; even though she'd let herself down, and others too, still she was proud she'd had the courage to do what her heart dictated. Briefly, she closed her eyes and wished with all her heart that it was not too late for her and Godric; that somehow she might still salvage her own happiness.

Conscious that a deepening and uneasy silence had fallen on the group, she roused herself. "Where shall you live, now that you are wed?" She addressed the question to Eleanor, making an effort to be friendly.

"On Hugh's manor farm, for the while." Eleanor's sideways glance at Janna answered much more than her question. It was clear she intended to take Hugh as far away from Janna as possible. "I'm looking forward to seeing my new home," she continued, letting Janna know also that she was to be mistress there, no matter what ideas Hugh might have to the contrary.

Janna sighed. It was going to be impossible to get around the prickles of the new bride, she could see that now. All she could do was wish them well, and she did so, and noticed the alacrity with which Eleanor tried to drag Hugh away as soon as it was polite to do so.

"Pray, come with me, Hamo." Hugh made the excuse to linger, putting his hand on the boy's arm to make his intention plain. "God go with you," he said quietly to Janna, then turned to his impatient bride. "Time for our nuptial mass," he said. He pulled her arm through his and walked to the door of the cathedral. Janna watched them go, and saw them reunited with their families, waiting there for them. She realized, with a shock, that their encounter had been noted by Hugh's aunt, Dame Alice, who regarded her with a puzzled air, as if wondering why she seemed so familiar. At once Janna turned her back on the dame, not waiting to see if her husband stood beside her. She could only hope, with all her heart, that Robert of Babestoche's attention had been engaged elsewhere.

She met the amused glance of her father, which told her he'd well understood the byplay between her and the newlyweds. "Fret not over the young lord," he whispered quietly. "He would have made a most unsuitable match for the granddaughter of the old king. There are many more worthy suitors for your hand, and I promise you that I shall give the matter my full attention just as soon as my affairs are settled here and we can go back to Normandy."

"We go to Normandy?" Janna wondered how many more shocks she would have to endure this day. Her heart contracted at the prospect of having to leave England before she could talk to Godric, and before she could fulfil her quest to bring her mother's killer to justice. The notion of her father taking control over who she would wed also filled her with alarm. She wished, now, that she'd given the matter a great deal more thought before she'd made her pledge of obedience.

"I have to stay to oversee the building of my new estate, but we'll leave as soon as my new steward is installed." John frowned, betraying his concern. "The delay will give you time to get to know my wife and family. But now is not the time to talk of such matters," he concluded hurriedly. "We must go inside to hear the mass."

"Yes, my lord," Janna said politely. The last thing she wished was to inflict her continuing presence on the bride and groom. She was desperate for a few moments alone to gather her thoughts and prepare herself for her new role. Her life had taken such an unexpected turn, and it was racing beyond her control. But, more than anything, she wanted to see Godric, to talk to him one last time.

She reached out and tugged her father's sleeve, for he'd already turned to escort his wife into the cathedral. "May I be excused, just for the moment, my lord? I have some things I need to attend to before I can come and...and make my life with you. I-I'll see you after the mass. I'll wait for you here."

Not giving her father any time to argue, she turned on her heel and pushed quickly through the crowd, hoping to find Godric on his own, but there was no sign of him. Janna finally concluded that he must already have gone into the cathedral with Cecily, for there was no sign of her either. However, she gave up looking for him only when the last straggler walked into the cathedral and the great doors closed.

Chapter 16

Unable to hide her tears any longer, Janna fled around the side of the cathedral, hoping to find a safe refuge among the gravestones. A sunny patch of grass caught her eye, and she sank down and gave herself up to weeping. In finding her father it seemed that she had lost her free will and all chance of happiness. Even if Godric chose to turn his back on Hugh and Cecily, it seemed her father would never permit the match on which she'd pinned her hopes. Cecily was right: if she persisted in her pursuit of Godric she would wreck everything.

An aching sense of loss, of desolation, filled Janna. Godric was lost to her; she would never see him again, never hear his voice, never have the chance to tell him how much he meant to her – how much she loved him. She would never feel the touch of his lips, the sweetness of his kiss –

"Janna?"

It seemed a dream that she could hear his voice through her distress. But his touch was real, as true as the sunlight warming her back and the cold ground beneath her. She raised her head to make sure of him.

"Do not weep for Hugh. You have so much to live for now." Godric sat down on the grass beside her. He made no further move to touch her, but his voice was like a caress, his concern for her as real as their kiss had been.

"Godric," she whispered. "What are you doing here?" In her mind she saw him still in the cathedral with Cecily, and lost to her.

"I wanted to see you, to talk to you one last time." His voice was formal as he continued carefully, "I witnessed your meeting with your father and his family. Sire Hugh told me that you'd found him at last, and of the good fortune of your noble birthright. I wanted to wish you well for the future, Janna." His tentative smile wrenched Janna's heart. "I suppose I should call you 'my lady,'" he said awkwardly.

"Never 'my lady,' Godric. I'll always be Janna to you." There was so much more she needed to say to him, she hardly knew where to start. "And please don't think I weep for Hugh. I realized a long time ago that I cannot care for him as I – "

"I've seen how he looks at you, how he touched you and kissed you – yes, even after he was betrothed!" Godric's tone was savage.

"You mistake what you saw, for that was his doing, not mine! But I kissed *you*, Godric, don't you remember that? And I thought our kiss meant as much to you as it did to me!"

"It did! Oh God, Janna, I – "

"But I know Sire Hugh wishes you to marry Cecily and I know also that your future lies with him at the manor – but only if that's what you truly want?" It almost killed Janna to say the words. She stared defiantly at Godric, but her bravado melted instantly as she noted the anguish on his face.

"What you say is true, but I would give anything – " Godric took her hand. "If my future seems certain, so is yours," he said. "Your father would never permit you to marry a lowborn serf like me."

Maybe I could change his mind! But the words stayed unsaid. Just as she'd been unwilling to jeopardize Hugh's future, Janna was unwilling to risk Godric's future either – unless he himself was prepared to turn his back on certainty and risk a future with her.

Godric still had hold of her hand. "I said once that I loved you, and I have never swerved from that, no matter what you may have heard from Sire Hugh."

Or Cecily, Janna thought.

"You should not have doubted me, Janna, for I have stayed true to you for all these years. And, now that I know your heart is not with Sire Hugh, I can tell you that I love you still."

"And I was ever a fool not to understand what love is, Godric. But I know full well how I feel about you now." Janna looked up at him, longing for him to take her in his arms. Yet he kept a careful distance from her as he continued.

"But love isn't enough, is it, Janna? Your noble father will make a match for you with someone of equal rank and wealth. That's the way of the world, although I wish with all my heart that things were different."

"They can be, if you're sure I'm who you want." Janna hesitated. "If my father won't permit the match we could run away, make a life together. I'm willing to take a chance if you are, Godric."

"No." Godric's face reflected his misery as he continued. "I love you too much to dishonor you, nor would I subject you to a life of hiding, living in penury. You deserve so much more than that. Besides, you know that your father would not rest until he found you. And I daresay my liege lord would not let me go either, not without a search. What you suggest is impossible, Janna."

"What if we just got married, then?" Janna thought of her father, who'd done exactly that. "If we exchanged our vows in front of witnesses, no-one could undo it."

"I cannot marry you, Janna, unless it's with the full blessing of your father. Besides, I'd also need permission to wed from my liege lord. Sire Hugh would not risk offending such a powerful baron unless your father approved the match. Which we both know he never will, for he will have his eyes on a much higher prize for you, someone who will reflect glory on his family."

Godric spoke only the truth, even if Janna hated to hear it. "I love you with all my heart, Janna," he continued steadily. "And I can tell you now, there'll never be anyone else in my life."

"Not even Cecily?"

Godric shook his head. "I will not marry to please my lord. I have already told him so. I will not marry someone I don't love."

A sweet joy swept through Janna as she understood what he was saying to her. Knowing that this was Godric's choice, and that it would remain unchanged despite Cecily's best efforts, gave her the freedom to open her heart to him.

"I was hoping to have this last chance to speak to you, because I couldn't bear to let you go to Cecily without telling you that at last I know the truth. I love you too, Godric. I always will. There'll never be anyone else for me either. Never. I want you to know that."

"My dearest Janna." Godric tried to smile, but could not hide his anguish.

"I'll talk to my father about you. He too married for love and may well understand that I need to follow my heart in this. If I can make him see things my way, he may buy your freedom from Dame Alice and Hugh so that we can be wed."

"He'll never agree to it. You know that, Janna, and so do I. But, like your father, I also want what's best for you, and I know that doesn't include a future with me. My dearest wish is that, in pleasing him, you'll come to find happiness with a husband of his choice."

The clamor of bells set the ravens flying and startled them. Mass was over. Janna knew that her father was expecting to find her waiting outside the cathedral. She must not delay.

Reluctantly, she rose to her feet, her hand held to Godric's heart as he stood with her. For a long moment he looked into her eyes, a searching look that scoured her mind, her heart and her soul. "I won't give up on us, Godric. Wait for me. Please."

"Forget about me, Janna. And may God be with you always," he said roughly, and kissed her cheek. Before Janna could respond, he released her hand and strode quickly away.

Stricken, she stared after him. She touched her cheek where his lips had been, and pressed her fingers to her mouth, already aching with loss. A scrap of parchment lying on the grass caught her eye, and she bent to pick it up. It must have slipped from Godric's scrip, but it was his and therefore precious. Curious, she unfolded it to read the words inscribed there. The page shook in her hand, betraying her emotion. She clutched the scrap of parchment tighter to keep it steady.

To Mistress Johanna, my greetings.

Mistress Johanna? This was a letter to her! Had Godric dropped it on purpose for her to find? But he'd never called her Johanna before! Why so formal? And no endearment either! She gazed unseeing at the green grass and the sheep grazing peacefully among the tombstones. "My dearest Janna," she spoke the words she wished were written on the page. She sighed, and kept reading, anxious to know what was on his mind.

Please forgive my presumption in writing to you.

Presumption? Godric? How could he say such a thing! This was not at all what she'd expected. Janna bent her head to the letter once more.

> *Lord Hugh has told me that you've had the good fortune to find your father at last, and has explained to me your father's relationship to our old King Henry, and the importance of your*

position in his household. I want you to know
that I feel honored to have known you, and that
I am at your service always.

The letter was signed simply, "*Godric.*"

Somewhat bemused, Janna reread the message. Why, after all that had just passed between them, had Godric left this for her to find? And then the truth came to her: he must have written this with the intention of sending it on if he didn't have the chance to talk to her himself.

Janna gave blessings to all the saints that they had met, for she knew how devastated she would have been to receive such a cold and formal message from him. Although the words did not reflect how they truly felt about each other, nevertheless she folded the parchment and slipped it into her purse. This was her last link with Godric and she would treasure it always. Now she could understand why her mother had kept the letter from her father, and how precious it must have seemed even though she thought he'd broken faith with her. This letter was valued above everything else that Janna owned.

She pulled her thoughts away from her grief to consider the path ahead. She knew it would not be easy, given her new family's antagonism toward her. Her spirits felt crushed already by that burden. She grimaced as she realized that at last she'd got what she wanted, but it was not what she'd expected. She was no longer sure that the prize was worth having, for in the gaining of it she had lost her freedom to go where she pleased, and do as she pleased. Nor could she marry as she pleased, and that was the very worst thing of all.

With heavy footsteps and a heavier heart, she began to make her way toward the door of the cathedral.

"Now then, Janna!"

She jumped at the sound of Ulf's voice. She'd been so sunk in misery she hadn't noticed him.

"I called in at the tavern to see you, lass. Sybil said you'd gone to meet your father and his family. She told me where to find you." Ulf's ready smile faded to a frown of puzzlement. "What's happened? You look as sick as a hen on a wet night."

Janna drew a quavering breath. "It's nothing." She forced a smile onto her face.

"Did it go badly between you, then?"

To avoid his penetrating gaze, Janna bent down to pat Brutus. "No, everything went well. I found my father. He's accepted me as his daughter. He even introduced me to his family."

"There, then! What did I tell you?" Ulf sketched a quick outline of Janna's shape with his finger. "That gown's a great improvement on that old tunic of Sybil's. It's brushed up right well. Any father would be proud to own you as his daughter."

"Yes, my father owns me now," Janna said bitterly, not responding to Ulf's flattery. "That's the truth of it. And his family hate me," she added, her voice sharp with resentment.

"Don't take on so, lass." Ulf patted her arm in an effort to cheer her up. "It all feels new and different now, having a family of your own. You'll get used to them and they'll get used to you. It'll all come right, you'll see."

Janna wished she shared Ulf's easy optimism. She straightened up from patting Brutus. "Did you want to see me about anything special?" she asked, remembering that he'd called in to the tavern looking for her.

Ulf gave her a long, considering look. "News of your father makes my news easier to tell, any road. I came to say that I'm leaving soon. I came to tell you goodbye."

"Goodbye?" Janna drew a long breath, fighting not to say aloud the words that clamored to be heard: *Don't go. Don't abandon me!* She clamped her teeth onto her tongue, and looked down at her shoes instead.

"It's time I moved on." Ulf sounded apologetic as he gave Janna his reasons. "The fair's over now. I've stayed as long as I can, but the townsfolk have had all they want from me. I can't earn enough for my keep any longer. I must move on to London for the winter."

Not able to say what she really wanted to, Janna fought back tears.

"I'll come back again in the spring, I promise." Ulf patted her arm again. "Will you still be here, or do you go to Normandy with your father?"

"I'll be here." On that point, at least, Janna was suddenly quite sure. "I'm going to stay here in England. I have things I still need to do."

Ulf nodded. "Then I'll look for you here. And if not here, then…?"

"Wiltune," Janna said quickly, thinking where her quest for justice might take her, if her father proved amenable. "Or I might be at Babestoche. Or a manor farm near Wicheford." Hugh's manor farm, where Godric was in service to his liege lord. Hugh's manor farm where she would *not* be made welcome by his wife. How could she go there?

How could she go anywhere if her father insisted she come to Normandy with the family? She would have no choice but to obey him if he did. Discouraged, she shook her head. "I don't know where I'll be," she confessed. On impulse, she threw her arms around Ulf and gave him a hug. "I shall miss you so much!"

"As I'll miss you, lass. But I'll find you again, come spring. I promise." Ulf's eyes were suspiciously moist. He gave a small sniff, then toed Brutus with his boot. "Come on, you lazy mutt," he said brusquely, and set off, waving a hand in farewell as he went.

Janna stared after him. What was supposed to have been a day of triumph had turned as bitter as gall. And the day was not yet over, for there was still so much more she had to face.

The bells had stopped ringing. Mindful of her father waiting for her at the cathedral, she picked up her skirts and began to run.

No matter that she was supposed to be a lady now, there was no-one to see her. She rounded the corner and glanced quickly about, and saw that those who had recently attended the mass were spilling out in search of refreshment and other diversions. No-one to see her whose opinion she valued, she amended. As she ran on toward her father, her words came back to her. *Wiltune. Babestoche. The manor farm near Wicheford.* Her thoughts began to spin with possibilities. She *must* persuade her father to see things her way. If she could only see Godric again, and introduce him to her father, what might happen then?

Her father was in sight now, and Janna abruptly slowed her flying footsteps to a sedate walk. They were all waiting for her, standing in a small, tight group that said they were a family and she was the outsider. Janna faltered; her hand went up to tidy her hair, and down to smooth the folds of her gown.

Her feet hurt in their tight shoes. Her heart was sore. She longed for a kindly word, an affectionate gesture. She tilted her chin, knowing that any hint of self-pity would bring another storm of tears. She would not show herself vulnerable to these people. *She would not.* So she walked steadily toward them with a smile fixed on her face, a smile that told them – told the world, and most especially her father – that she was a strong and independent young woman who knew exactly who she was, where she was going, and, most importantly of all, that she had the determination and courage to decide her own future.

Glossary

Aelfshot: A belief that illness or a sudden pain (such as rheumatism, arthritis or a "stitch" in the side) was caused by elves who shot humans or livestock with darts.

Alehouse: Ale was a common drink in the middle ages. Housewives brewed their own for domestic use, while alewives brewed the ale served in alehouses and taverns. A bush tied to a pole was the recognized symbol of an alehouse, at a time when most of the population could not read.

Amor vincit omnia: Love conquers all.

Baron: A noble of high rank, a tenant-in-chief who holds his lands from the king.

Breeches: Trousers held up by a cord running through the hem at the waist.

Canonical hours: The medieval day was governed by sunrise and sunset, divided into seven canonical hours. Times of prayer were marked by bells rung in abbeys and monasteries beginning with Matins at midnight, followed by Lauds, Prime, Terce, Sext and Nones through the day. Vespers was at sunset, followed by Compline before going to bed.

Chapman: Peddler.

Cresset: A primitive light made from a wick floating in a bowl of oil or animal fat.

Currency: While large sums of money could be reckoned in pounds or marks, the actual currency for trading was silver pennies. There were twelve to a shilling and twenty shillings to a pound. A penny could also be cut into half, called a "ha'penny," or a quarter, called a "farthing."

Dowry: A sum of money paid for a woman, either as a marriage settlement or to secure her place in an abbey.

Feretory: A shrine to hold the relics of saints or the area of the church where they are kept.

Feudal system: A political, social and economic system based on the relationship of lord to vassal, in which land was held on condition of homage and service. Following the Norman conquest, William I distributed land once owned by Saxon "ealdormen" (chief men) to his own barons, who in turn distributed land and manors to sub-tenants in return for fees, knight service and, in the case of the villeins, work in the fields.

Gambeson: A padded jacket worn under a hauberk for added protection.

Greaves: Leather or padded cloth (and later chain-mail) protection for the shins.

Hauberk: A knee-length chain-mail shirt worn by knights in battle.

Leman: Sweetheart, mistress.

Motte and bailey castle: Earth mound with wooden or stone keep (tower) on top, plus an enclosure or courtyard, all of it surrounded and protected by a ditch and palisade (fence).

Pentice: A shed, or a protected area, with a sloping roof projecting from a wall or side of a building.

Pottage: A vegetable soup or stew.

Scrip: A small bag.

Scriptorium: A room in a monastery (or abbey) where monks (or nuns) wrote, copied and illuminated manuscripts. In a private home it served as the office of the estate.

Solar: A private room where the lord could retire with his family or entertain his friends.

Steward: Appointed by a baron to manage an estate.

Tiring woman: A female attendant on a lady of high birth and importance.

Villein: Peasant or serf tied to a manor and to an overlord, and given land in return for labor and a fee – either money or produce.

Wort: The liquid that is left after barley malt is soaked in hot water and then strained (a process called "mashing," the first step in brewing ale.)

Wortwyf: A herb wife, a wise woman and healer.

Author's Note

The Janna Chronicles are set in the 1140s, at a turbulent time in England's history. After Henry I's son, William, drowned in the White Ship disaster, Henry was left with only one legitimate heir, his daughter Matilda (sometimes known as Maude). She was married at an early age to the German emperor, but for political reasons and despite Matilda's vehement protests, Henry brought her back to England after her husband died, and insisted that she marry Count Geoffrey of Anjou, a boy some ten years her junior. They married in 1128, and the first of their three sons, Henry (later to become Henry II of England) was born in 1133.

Henry I announced Matilda his heir and twice demanded that his barons, including her cousin, Stephen of Blois, all swear an oath of allegiance to her. This they did, but when Henry died, Stephen rushed to London and was crowned king. Furious at his treachery, Matilda gathered her own supporters, including her illegitimate half-brother, Robert of Gloucester, who became her commander in chief. In 1139 she landed at Arundel Castle in England, prepared to fight for her crown.

Civil war ravaged England for nineteen years, creating such hardship and misery that the *Peterborough Chronicle* reported: "Never before had there been greater wretchedness in the country...They said openly that Christ slept, and His saints." The civil war mostly comprised a series of battles and skirmishes as the principal players fought for supremacy, while the barons took advantage of the general lawlessness to go on the rampage and claim whatever land and castles they could, some of them changing sides several times in the hope of advantage.

The year 1141 marked a turning point in Matilda's fortunes. Two brothers, the Earl of Chester and William de Roumare, seized and occupied Lincoln Castle by first tricking the guards into admitting their wives. The Earl of Chester subsequently changed sides to support the Empress Matilda – a welcome move, as the Earl of Chester's daughter was married to the son of Matilda's chief supporter, Robert, Earl of Gloucester. After some negotiation, Stephen eventually mustered his troops and went to reclaim Lincoln on an ill-fated expedition. According to the chronicle of Henry of Huntingdon, when Stephen heard Mass and, following the custom, offered a candle to Bishop Alexander, it broke in his hands. Henry wrote: "This was a warning to the king that he would be crushed. In the bishop's presence, too, the pyx above the altar, which contained the Lord's Body, fell, its chain having snapped off. This was a sign of the king's downfall." And so it came to pass. The king was defeated and imprisoned in Bristol Castle. The empress met with the papal legate, Bishop Henry of Blois (Stephen's brother), who promised his support, along with several other bishops and archbishops. There was also a meeting between Matilda and Archbishop Theobald in Wiltune shortly before Easter, at which time the archbishop held off promising allegiance until he had spoken to the king and sought his permission to "act as the difficulties of the time required" (to which Stephen actually agreed!). Matilda then made her way to London for her coronation, supposedly with Bishop Henry's support. Shortly before her coronation, she was chased out of London by the queen's troops and the Londoners who had turned against her. She fled to Oxford, and spent July there, rallying forces and making promises to the barons, giving gifts of land and titles in return for their support. She had alienated many of them with her high-handed ways, including Bishop Henry, and when Robert of Gloucester visited Henry in Winchester in mid-July to settle their differences, he achieved little. He finally returned to Oxford to muster the empress's army.

A chronicle from the time, the *Gesta Stephani*, suggests that the bishop might well have been behind the London uprising. The same account also suggests that he may never have supported Matilda's bid for the throne at all. Other accounts date their falling-out from the time Matilda refused to honor her promise not to meddle in ecclesiastic affairs when she insisted on appointing William Cumin as the new bishop of Durham against Henry's wishes. But the real sticking point in her relationship with Bishop Henry was her refusal to confirm the Honor of Boulogne, held by the king, upon the king's son, Eustace. She may even have promised the title and lands to others.

I've kept to the place names listed in the Domesday Book compiled by William the Conqueror in 1086, but the contemporary names of some of the sites are: Barford St Martin (Berford), Baverstock (Babestoche), Salisbury (Sarisberie or Sarum), Amesbury (Ambresberie), Oxford (Oxeneford), Winchester (Winchestre), Ludgershall (Litlegarsele), Stockbridge (Stoche), Rochester (Roucestre), Reading (Radinges) and Bristol (Bristou). Wilton (Wiltune) was the ancient capital of Wessex, and the abbey was established in Saxon times.

Some of the most important accounts I have used while researching this series include *Gesta Stephani* (The Life of Stephen), William of Malmesbury's *Historia Novella*, *The Empress Matilda* by Marjorie Chibnall, *King Stephen* by R.H.C. Davis and *The Reign of King Stephen* by David Crouch. For those interested in learning more about the civil war between Stephen and Matilda, Sharon Penman's *When Christ and His Saints Slept* is an excellent "factional" account of that history. On a lighter note, I have also read, and much enjoyed, the Brother Cadfael Chronicles by Ellis Peters, which are set during this period. While Janna's loyalty lies in a different direction, her skill with herbs was inspired by these wonderful stories of the herbalist at Shrewsbury Abbey.

While writing medieval England from Australia is a difficult and hazardous enterprise, I have been fortunate in the support and encouragement I've received along the way. So many people have helped make this series possible, and in particular I'd like to thank the following: Nick and Wendy Combes of Burcombe Manor, for taking me into their family, giving me a home away from home and teaching me about life on a farm, both now and in medieval times. Author Sophie Masson, who provided the French translation of John's letter. Dr Gillian Polack, whose knowledge of medieval life helped shape the series and gave it veracity. Garrett Sherman, who explained the process of brewing ale in medieval time. Finally, my thanks to all at Momentum for their thought, care and expertise, and for enabling me to introduce The Janna Chronicles to a new audience.

www.ingramcontent.com/pod-product-compliance
Lightning Source LLC
Chambersburg PA
CBHW030957260626
47169CB00002B/588